D1625182

Millard Shuites
PO Box 93
Langston AL 35755-0093

DANGEROUS
GAMES

ALSO BY MICHAEL PRESCOTT

In Dark Places

Next Victim

Last Breath

The Shadow Hunter

Stealing Faces

Comes the Dark

Published by New American Library

DANGEROUS GAMES

Michael Prescott

AN ONYX BOOK

ONYX
Published by New American Library, a division of
Penguin Group (USA) Inc., 375 Hudson Street,
New York, New York 10014, USA
Penguin Group (Canada), 10 Alcorn Avenue, Toronto,
Ontario M4V 3B2, Canada (a division of Pearson Penguin Canada Inc.)
Penguin Books Ltd., 80 Strand, London WC2R 0RL, England
Penguin Ireland, 25 St. Stephen's Green, Dublin 2,
Ireland (a division of Penguin Books Ltd.)
Penguin Group (Australia), 250 Camberwell Road, Camberwell, Victoria 3124,
Australia (a division of Pearson Australia Group Pty Ltd.)
Penguin Books India Pvt. Ltd., 11 Community Centre, Panchsheel Park,
New Delhi - 110 017, India
Penguin Group (NZ), Cnr Airborne and Rosedale Roads, Albany,
Auckland 1310, New Zealand (a division of Pearson New Zealand Ltd.)
Penguin Books (South Africa) (Pty.) Ltd., 24 Sturdee Avenue,
Rosebank, Johannesburg 2196, South Africa

Penguin Books Ltd., Registered Offices: 80 Strand, London WC2R 0RL, England

First published by Onyx, an imprint of New American Library,
a division of Penguin Group (USA) Inc.

IN MEMORY OF
SAMUEL REESE COVINGTON
1989–2004

In those days there was no king in Israel: every man did that which was right in his own eyes.

—Judges 21:25

Prologue

Rain was in the air.

Kolb had never given much thought to the weather in Los Angeles. Most days were seventy-five degrees and sunny. But in January came drenching rains that flooded the streets, causing traffic snarls and fender benders and, sometimes, fatal accidents.

The rains could kill.

Kolb was counting on that.

He sat behind the wheel of his gray secondhand Oldsmobile. The car was parked in a public lot near downtown. He'd chosen the lot because it was used primarily by workers in the surrounding office complexes, which meant that at two thirty on a Wednesday afternoon it would be crowded with cars but nearly empty of people.

He had been waiting for a half hour. A pair of women had parked nearby, but he knew he couldn't handle two of them together. A solitary man had sauntered past, but Kolb wanted a female victim. A woman would be easier to control. There was a reason they were known as the weaker sex, even if that knowledge had been suppressed in today's dandified world, a world dedicated to expunging the masculine principle from society.

Besides, it would be more fun with a woman. A man ought to enjoy his work.

He checked his disguise in the rearview mirror. False mustache. Mirrored sunglasses, unnecessary on this overcast day, hiding his pale blue eyes. A baseball cap over his crew cut, which had been pure blond but now was littered with gray hairs, like a scattering of iron filings in straw. He shouldn't be graying so young—he was only thirty-one—but spending nearly a year in a state prison had a way of aging a man.

The key to a disguise was not to get too creative. Make just a few simple changes that added up to an easily readable story. Put a man in a neutral-toned jumpsuit, give him a toolbox and a cap, and he was a repairman. Give him a suit and a briefcase, and he was a businessman. People didn't see or remember someone who raised no questions in their minds.

Today, Kolb was a deliveryman. He wore a nylon windbreaker two sizes too big, helpful in concealing his wide-shouldered, prison-buffed physique. Hand-stitched to the back of the jacket was the name of a pizza chain. The cap matched the uniform's colors.

After he was finished, he would dispose of the jacket and cap. He wouldn't be needing them again. His plan was never to use the same ruse twice. Although he was no master of disguise, he would not make any obvious mistakes. He had known plenty of criminals, both on the street and in stir, and most of them were stupid. That was why they got caught.

Under the windbreaker he wore a navy blue pullover, matching his denim jeans. Night would have fallen by the time he left the tunnels, and deep blue fabric blended into the darkness better than jet black. If something went wrong and he had to run and hide, he was prepared.

But nothing would go wrong. He'd worked out all the angles. He wasn't even scared. He had thought he might be—opening-night jitters and all. But he was enjoying himself. He liked risk. He liked dancing on the edge.

And he liked what he saw coming toward him.

She was young and slender, a brunette in her twenties. No briefcase, only a handbag. Too young to be an executive. Somebody's secretary, probably. From a distance he couldn't tell if she was pretty. He hoped she was.

" 'Many an innocent flower,' " Kolb whispered.

She passed the row where he was parked. He got out, careful not to shut the door. Old cop trick—the slam of a car door would alert his prey.

A quick scan of the parking lot confirmed that he and the woman were alone amid the arrays of windshields and chrome. Anyone might be watching from the surrounding office buildings, but he would do nothing to attract attention.

He caught up with her as she reached her Toyota. She was unaware of his presence, and that made it easy for him to wait until she slipped into the car, then interpose himself between her and the door. She sucked in a shallow, strained breath.

"Don't scream." He had rehearsed the words. Everything would be ruined if she screamed.

She didn't scream. Didn't even exhale. Just stared at him, her glance flicking to the gun in his gloved hand, then to his face. "Oh, God."

"Stay calm."

"Oh, God." Her gaze returned to the gun.

He read her thoughts. "Yes," he said, "it's real and it's loaded, and I *will* use it if I have to." He didn't add that the gun was untraceable, the serial number filed off.

"Please," she whispered.

"Just cooperate and you'll get through this."

She nodded. She had wide brown eyes and smooth, pale skin.

"What do you want me to do?" she asked, her voice curling into a whine.

From his pocket he took out a writing pad and a pen. The pen was a felt-tip marker, chosen because it would be useless as a weapon. He handed both items to her. "Write what I say."

"Write?" She echoed the word as if it were in a foreign language.

"That's what I said. You can write, can't you?"

"Yes."

"Then here goes. First, write 'My name is . . .' and fill in the blank."

"Angie. I mean, Angela. Angela Morris."

"Don't *tell* me. Write it down."

She wrote slowly, her hand fisted over the marker. He dictated the message to her. She seemed to be focusing her full attention on putting it down on paper with a minimum of mistakes. She misspelled some words, anyway.

When she was finished, she stared at the message as if taking it in for the first time. "Oh, God," she said again.

He was tired of hearing her say that. "Give it back to me. Your wallet, too."

"I only got thirty dollars in there."

"Just give me the fucking wallet." She did. He glanced around the car and saw a small plastic box on the floorboard. "What's that?"

"Video. A rental. I was gonna return it today."

"What movie is it?"

"The one with Tom Cruise and, uh, that Hoffman guy. *Rain Man.*"

It was so perfect, it gave him an idea. "Take it with you."

"What?"

"Take it." He smiled behind his store-bought mustache. "You don't want to be charged a late fee, do you?"

She retrieved the video, holding it tight, her fingertips squeezed bloodless.

"Now, out."

"Where are we going?"

"My car."

"Let me go, okay? Just let me go."

He clamped a hand on her arm. "Shut the fuck up and get out of the goddamn car right now."

She obeyed.

This was the most dangerous part. If she squirmed free and took off running, he wouldn't be able to chase her without being noticed. He was betting he'd established sufficient control that she would engage in no heroics. That was why he'd made her write the message before moving her. He'd wanted to show her who had the power.

It worked. She made no effort to escape. She walked at his side, shaking all over and blinking back tears, the gun wedged under her armpit. To keep her distracted, he asked if she had any plans for the evening.

"Nothing, really. Order some takeout. Watch TV . . ."

"You play this smart, you'll be home in time for the ten-o'clock news. You can watch *yourself* on TV."

"Uh-huh."

"That'll be fun, right? You'll be a star. In this town everybody wants to be a star." He regretted the comment. It was trite, unworthy of him.

He led her to his Olds. Before coming here, he'd replaced the license plates with stolen tags. Later, he would toss the tags and reinstall his own.

He pushed Angela Morris into the car on the driver's side, then made her climb across to the passenger seat. He kept the gun on her as he got behind the wheel.

"I don't have money," she said. "My folks neither."

"I'm not interested in your money." He cranked the ignition. "Don't you remember? I said city revenues. City."

"Yeah, you did, you said that. City money. You want LA to cough it up."

"Damn straight."

"They won't pay money for me," she whispered.

"Sure they will." *Or if not you*, he added silently, *then the one who comes after you.*

"Why would they?"

"They'll have no choice. I'm going to squeeze it out of them. I'm going to bring this goddamn city to its knees."

She shrank low in her seat, staring at him. "Why?"

"Because they owe me." Kolb shifted into drive. "And payback is a bitch."

1

"She was found here," Crandall said. "On the embankment, just above the waterline."

Tess McCallum stared through the chain-link fence at the concrete channel of the Los Angeles River. A sullen trickle meandered down its center, past a shopping cart, a tire, broken beer bottles, and other debris. The smell of brackish water rose in the evening air.

"Who found her?" Tess asked.

"Couple of bicyclists riding along the riverbank."

To Tess, it seemed strange to call this gash in the landscape a river. A dry watercourse for most of the year, it filled with rainwater only during heavy storms. The river snaked south from the San Fernando Valley, through LA's East Side, and emptied into the sea at Long Beach. For most of its extent it was lined in concrete and flanked by high, inclined banks, fenced off, the occasional padlocked gates bearing signs that warned: TRESPASSING, LOITERING FORBIDDEN BY LAW.

A cool breeze gusted. Tess wrapped her trench coat tighter around herself.

"Have the bicyclists been ruled out?" she asked. It wasn't unusual for a killer to report the discovery of his victim's remains.

"They're clean. Alibied for the time of the abduction. Just a couple of kids, anyway. USC students." Agent Crandall hardly seemed older than a college student himself.

Tess looked toward the Olympic Boulevard overpass a few blocks north. "When did they find her?"

"A little after sunrise. LAPD took the call. Once they made the vic as Angela Morris, they brought in the Bureau."

"Autopsy results?"

"Pending. But it's pretty obvious she drowned. You don't have to be an ME to figure that out."

"You saw the body?"

"I saw it. Didn't they send you a pic?"

"Yeah, by e-mail." She remembered the angle of the corpse, the sprawl of limbs, the net of hair crosshatching a bloated face. Across the channel she saw a large rectangular aperture. "Is that where the water comes out?"

"Right. An outfall, it's called."

"Is it the one she came out of?"

"We don't know. Could have been any outfall upriver. There's no way to say how far the current carried her before she was thrown up on the bank."

"So she could've been held anywhere inside the sewers."

"Yes." Crandall cleared his throat. "Technically not sewers. Storm drains."

"What's the distinction?"

"Sewers carry waste from toilets. The storm system carries surface-street runoff."

"Then why does it smell like . . . ?"

"Like shit? Because there's shit in there. Dog droppings and other crap that gets washed into the catch basins. Not to mention pesticides, household chemicals, you name it. It's a toxic smorgasbord."

"Lovely. It's untreated?"

"Too expensive to treat it. It flows straight into the ocean. You see these big outfalls on the beach spewing out effluent. Kids play there."

"I used to read about the ancient Romans throwing their garbage into the streets, and I would feel superior." Tess looked away. "I wonder if that's what Angela was to him. Garbage."

She spent another minute staring down at the channel in the ebbing daylight. It was no one's idea of a resting place for the dead. Gray algae speckled the embankments, giving way above the waterline to intaglios of gang graffiti. The rumble of traffic from the overpass was the only noise. The flicker of newspapers blowing across the channel floor was the only movement.

"All right," Tess said. "I've seen enough."

Crandall seemed relieved. "Let's go, then. Don't want to be late."

"No, we wouldn't want to keep the ADIC waiting." Because of its size and prominence, the LA office was run by an unusually high-ranking agent, an assistant director in charge, or ADIC. The acronym was pronounced "A-Dick." In this case it seemed appropriate.

"Well," Crandall said, "it's not just the AD. Other people will be there."

"Like who?"

"The mayor, the chief of police . . ."

Tess frowned. When she'd been picked up at the airport, she'd assumed she was going straight to the field office in Westwood. Only after Crandall had taken the eastbound Santa Monica Freeway had she learned about the meeting downtown. If she'd known, she might have dressed in something nicer than her sensible shoes and gray business suit.

Still, she figured she looked all right. She was blessed with a smooth Highlands complexion that never needed makeup, and her reddish blond hair required no more than brisk brushing to straighten out its natural curls. In movies, female FBI agents always wore their hair short, either close-cropped or tied in a bun. Real life was more forgiving. Tess had grown her hair to shoulder length.

"Sounds like quite a get-together," she said.

"It's important I get you there on schedule. My instructions were explicit."

"This detour didn't cost us much time. And I wanted to see where she washed up."

"Why, exactly?"

Tess could have told him she'd spent the flight from Denver to LA reading the FBI report, written in dry Bureau-ese, learning only the bare facts. To make the case real, she'd needed to see the place where the first victim had washed up.

But she didn't think Crandall would understand, so she said only, "Curiosity," and let her shoulders rise and fall in a shrug.

Walking back along the embankment she passed a gate. On impulse she gave it a push. The gate swung open. Angela Morris's body had been removed only hours ago, and someone had forgotten to lock up.

"Hell," Crandall said, noticing. "That's sloppy. We'd better secure it before a civilian goes wandering down there."

"What do you say *we* go wandering?"

"Us? Now?"

"Just for a minute or two."

"With due respect, Agent McCallum, that's a bad idea."

"Probably. Let's do it anyway."

"I really don't think—"

She was already stepping through the gate. "Last one in is a rotten egg." She wondered why that turn of phrase had occurred to her. Something her mother used to say, probably.

The embankment was angled at forty-five degrees. Now she was glad she'd worn her sensible shoes. The rubber soles provided good traction on the smooth concrete. Toward the bottom, weeds and moss made the descent more treacherous. She was relieved when she reached the floor of the channel.

The smell was stronger here. A ground cover of wildflowers sprouted from cracks in the concrete, among fast-food wrappers and soda cans.

At an early stage of her career, she'd been assigned to Phoenix, another city traversed by canals. They were clean and landscaped, home to waterfowl, a pleasant place for a walk. The Los Angeles River, despite persistent attempts at cleanup and restoration, was a squalid, littered trench.

"Was she handcuffed?" Tess asked Crandall when he arrived at her side.

"Yeah, like Paula Weissman. The handcuffs held up during the first flood, but the second one, last night, must have snapped the chain. The cuff was still on her right wrist, which was badly abraded."

"Were the abrasions antemortem or post-?"

"Ante."

"She was conscious, then. Also like Paula."

Crandall nodded. "Pulling at the cuffs, trying to get free."

"Gagged?"

"Must have been. The duct tape on her mouth was gone, pulled away by the water, but you could see the sticky residue."

"Same MO as Paula," Tess said, "every detail." She imagined Angela's final moments—the terror and helplessness, the awful isolation.

"The chain breaking was lucky," Crandall said. "If she'd stayed where she was, we never would've found her."

"A search team would have discovered the body eventually."

"I doubt it. The storm-drain system is huge. We're talking hundreds of square miles, and she could've been anywhere. Unless a maintenance crew stumbled across her . . ."

Tess thought about the handcuffs. "I suppose you're looking into the S-and-M angle?"

"Sure. Doesn't narrow it down much. Lotta pervs in this town."

Her gaze traveled to the outfall on the far side of the channel, which had leaked a vomitus of dirty water down the concrete. "There's no grate over that opening," she said.

"A grate would get clogged with debris."

"How many openings are there like that?"

"Hundreds, thousands, along the length of the river."

"So our man can enter the system virtually anywhere."

"That's right. Although he probably uses one of the larger access points. We figure he drives the victim into the tunnels."

She nodded. The report had mentioned that some of the storm lines could accommodate a vehicle for maintenance purposes. This one couldn't. It was big enough for a person, though.

Tess stared at the outfall for a long moment. "You have a flashlight?" she asked.

"Why?"

"Do you?"

He patted his jacket pocket. "Penlight."

"So do I. Let's look inside." She pointed at the outfall.

Crandall looked stricken. "In there?"

"Why not?"

"There are approximately a million reasons I can think of."

"I need to get a feel for it. For what it's like in there. What it was like for her—and for him."

"I told you, we don't even know she came out of that outfall."

"I'm not looking for evidence. I just want to see what she saw. Walk in her shoes. One passageway is probably the same as another."

Crandall studied her. "You're not doing this to impress me, are you?"

"Why would I want to impress you?"

"Just asking."

She ascended the embankment, then lowered her head and stepped into the outfall. Sunlight reached only a few feet inside. The floor was slimy with moss, thick and velvety, a green carpet squishing under her shoes.

She took out her penlight and angled its beam down the passageway. A long, grim stretch of concrete faded into blackness. The tunnel was wide enough for a person and nearly tall enough to allow her and Crandall to stand upright.

"In the mood for some spelunking?" she asked as he stepped into the passage behind her.

"I hope that's a joke, Agent McCallum."

"Wherever she was kept, she certainly wasn't within sight of daylight. We need to go in deeper if we want to get a feel for her last hours."

"I'd be happy using my imagination."

"Neither of us has enough imagination for this. Come on."

"We're on a tight schedule, you know."

"Five minutes. Just to look around."

She pressed forward into the dark, led by the twin beams of her flashlight and his.

"If it starts raining," Crandall said, "we could get trapped in here."

"There's no rain in tonight's forecast. You ought to know that."

"I do. I was hoping you didn't."

A chill had settled in the tunnel, the permanent chill of a place where light could not reach. Tess found herself thinking of the catacombs haunted by the early Christians, of mausoleums and crypts. Places of hiding, places of the dead. Where she was now was a little of both.

"What kind of person are we up against?" she asked.

"I'm not a profiler."

"Me neither. But we can guess, can't we?"

"He's smart," Crandall ventured. "And careful."

"And very sure of himself. He wants to challenge both the municipal and federal authorities. He wants to run with the big dogs."

"That's our thinking, too. Delusions of grandeur, megalomania. Which narrows it down to only half the population of LA."

Tess smiled. "I'm starting to like you, Crandall."

"I'd like you better if you'd let us get the hell out of here, Agent McCallum."

"Just a little farther. I want to see what happens when we come to an intersecting pipe. What else do we know about our adversary?"

"He knows how to open foreign bank accounts. Could be a world traveler."

"Could be. But these days you don't need to go overseas to open a foreign account. It can be done by mail."

"One way or the other, he knows his way around the banking system."

"He—or they. Is it one man or a team?"

Crandall hesitated. "I'm guessing one guy."

"Easier to pull it off if you have an accomplice."

"Yes, but there's his megalomania. He doesn't think he needs help. That's my read on it, anyway. What do you think?"

"It's not my case. I have no opinion."

"That's a cop-out."

"Absolutely."

"You must have some opinion."

Tess acquiesced. "He's smart, as you said. He's got it all planned out. The way he's worked it, he hasn't given us even a glimpse of him. We haven't seen his handwriting or heard his voice. He's a ghost."

"He could be anyone," Crandall said.

"I'm afraid so."

"That's not very reassuring."

No, it wasn't, Tess reflected. But it was true.

She thought about the man they were after, the man who used these passages as his killing ground. He had played his game adroitly so far. No slipups yet.

The first note had been found on Wednesday afternoon, January 5, inside a videocassette box dropped through the return slot of a rental outlet. The note was written in felt marker on a sheet of notebook paper, a popular brand sold in thousands of stores. Paper-clipped to it were a driver's license issued to Angela Morris and an index card bearing a laser-printed bank account number.

The note's handwriting was large and clumsy, and there were several misspellings.

My name is Angela Morris. He is making me write this. He is kiddnaping me. He says my life is at steak.

He is going to put me under ground in the storm dranes. The storm dranes will flood tonite when it rains. You must transfer $1,000,000 in city revenus to the bank acount number on the card before it rains. When it rains it will be to late.

The money had never been transferred. Tess doubted that the kidnapper had expected it to be. Most likely he'd used Angela as a test case in order to familiarize the authorities with his method of operation—and to prove he was serious.

Because kidnapping was a federal crime, the Bureau had been brought in at once. The case was all over the media, of course. It had all the elements of TV drama, except a flashy moniker for the killer. For some reason the journalistic gimmick of nicknaming scrial offenders had become passé. To the Bureau he was the unsub—unknown subject—in the case code-named STORMKIL.

On Sunday, January 9, a second note was found, this time inside a Ford Taurus parked in a loading zone. A patrol cop traced the Ford to Paula L. Weissman of Reseda. He was writing Ms. Weissman a ticket when he saw the sheet of paper, the driver's license, and the index card on the dashboard. He had the presence of mind not to touch these items, but it made no difference; there were no prints on them but the victim's.

The handwriting of this note was more polished, but the message was nearly the same.

My name is Paula Weissman. I'm being held captive by a man who says he is responsible for the abduction of Angela Morris last week. He demands that $2,000,000 in municipal revenues be deposited in the bank account indicated on the attached card. He says you made a mistake last time, but he's sure you will cooperate now. He wants me to tell you he's very disappointed with you, and he doesn't want to be disappointed again. He says he doesn't handle disap-

pointment well. He says it's something he's working on. He says to remind you of the weather forecast.

That was all, except for a few scribbled, shaky words that trailed off at the end.

Please help me I don't want to die down there

This time the money, twice the kidnapper's initial demand, had been paid. Two million dollars was wire-transferred to a blind account in the Cayman Islands—a different account from the one specified in the first kidnapping, but equally untraceable. Authorities in the Caymans were cooperating, but by now the money had been moved elsewhere, vanishing in a maze of anonymous or pseudonymous accounts.

Fifteen minutes after the deposit, as the rain began to fall, the mayor's phone rang. Paula's recorded voice stated that she was handcuffed to a railing in a side passageway beneath the intersection of Wilshire and Vermont. The tunnels were flooding when the rescue team entered. They got close enough to see the victim before surging water forced them back. When the storm cleared, Paula's body was found, still manacled to the handrail.

And today—Monday, January 10—Angela's body had been found as well, washed out of the drainage lines by the same downpour. Perhaps out of the very passageway through which Tess was maneuvering now.

She arrived at the junction of two pipelines and beamed her light along the wider, intersecting passageway. Faintly she heard the rumble of traffic overhead. People were commuting home from work, listening to the car radio, talking on their cells, oblivious to the labyrinth below.

"It's a whole other world down here," she said.

She took a step forward, intending to explore the larger passageway. Crandall grabbed her arm.

"This *really* is not safe," he said.

"Afraid we'll run into the mutant mole people?"

"Who the fuck knows what we'll run into?"

"You're shaking." He didn't answer. "Crandall, are you claustrophobic?"

"Maybe a little."

"You should've said something."

"I was too busy panicking." He forced a nervous laugh.

"Retreat," Tess said.

"Look, I can handle it. I mean, it's not that bad."

She smiled. All of a sudden he was being brave. "I've seen enough," she said. "Anyway, we don't want to be late."

"Right. We definitely don't."

She was about to turn back when a prickling sense of dread stopped her. "Wait," she said, her voice dropping to a whisper.

She wasn't sure what had signaled her attention. Then she heard a faint, solitary splash in the darkness of the intersecting tunnel.

Instinctively she cupped her flashlight. Crandall covered his, as well.

They listened. Another splash. Closer.

Someone was in there, coming this way.

Crandall unholstered his gun. It seemed like a good idea. Tess reached into her coat pocket and drew her 9mm. Before terrorism had become a chronic worry, she would have stowed it in her checked baggage. These days federal agents were encouraged to carry their weapons while flying.

Another splash, closer than before.

She tried to estimate the odds that the stranger was somebody genuinely dangerous, somebody like the man they were after. On the one hand, Crandall had been right in saying that the drainage system was huge. There was little chance of encountering the killer by accident. On the other hand, serial offenders were known to return to the scene of the crime. Hearing that Angela Morris had been recovered nearby, the killer might have come here to retrace the route her body had taken.

Or it could be just a Department of Water and Power

maintenance man. But she didn't think so. A maintenance worker would have carried a flashlight. He wouldn't be sloshing around in the dark.

Tess raised her penlight, holding it away from herself and Crandall. If the beam drew fire, she wanted the shots to go wide.

"FBI!" she called out. "Identify yourself."

No answer. No further splashing. Silence.

"Identify yourself!" she shouted again, the command coming back to her in a flurry of echoes.

"I'm Manny," a voice said.

She and Crandall aimed their flashlights at the source of the voice. The two beams played like miniature searchlights over a small, lumpy figure in a shapeless black coat.

"Get your hands up. Up!"

Pale hands lifted toward the tunnel's low ceiling.

"Cover me," Tess told Crandall. She stepped into the larger passageway, her shoes sinking into a stream of filthy water. She approached the man, keeping her flashlight pinned on his upper body—his face, his hands. It was something they taught at the academy. The hands were critical because they could hurt you. The face was next in importance. Read his eyes and you could tell what he was thinking.

But these eyes told her nothing. They were smooth and white and pupilless, like eggshells. Cataracts, cloudy and thick.

Not the killer, then. Not anybody.

She pocketed her gun and patted him down out of habit, finding nothing inside the soiled coat except a thin, malnourished body that had gone unwashed for months or years.

"Okay," she said, "you can lower your hands."

He obeyed, blinking.

"What are you doing here, Manny?"

"Public property." He was defensive. "Can't stop me from living on public property."

"You *live* down here? What about when it rains?"

"Oh, you can't be here when it rains."

"No, you can't. It's dangerous. You could be caught in a flash flood."

He shook his head, his white eyes staring past her. "Won't get caught. Always know when there's rain coming. Can smell it."

"There are shelters. Places where people can help you."

"Not going to no shelter." He cringed. "You won't take Manny to no shelter, please. Don't want to go there."

She ought to take him. He wasn't competent to look after himself. But a shelter couldn't keep him against his will, and he was probably too lucid to be detained on a psychiatric hold.

"We're not taking you anyplace." An idea occurred to her. "Have you seen anyone else in these tunnels?"

Too late, she realized that *seen* was a poor choice of words. But Manny didn't notice. "There are worker guys, sometimes," he said.

"DWP. Anyone else?"

"No."

"Hear anything? Voices?"

He cringed again. "Don't hear no voices. Not no more."

Voices in his head, he must mean. He probably did still hear them, but he'd learned not to admit it.

"Not those voices," she said. "New ones. A woman, crying or shouting for help?" The victims' mouths had been duct-taped at some point, but they might have been able to cry out before they were gagged.

Manny gave it some thought. "You're a woman," he offered.

"Well, yes."

He smiled, showing black teeth. "You got a nice voice."

"Thank you." She wasn't going to make any progress here. It had been a long shot, at best. "You sure you'll be all right alone like this?"

"Always alone. Like it that way."

She removed some bills from her jacket pocket and thrust them into his hand. "Buy food. Hot food."

He stood there blinking, the money captured in a small, scabby fist. She hoped he understood.

Crandall had joined her sometime during the interrogation. His gun, she noticed, was still drawn. He seemed to have forgotten his claustrophobia.

"Let's go, Crandall," she said. "Manny can't be of any assistance to us at this time."

She retreated toward the smaller tunnel, following Crandall. Once, she looked back and saw Manny, a small, lost figure in the enfolding darkness.

A whole other world down here. A world she had never suspected, and one she wished she had never found.

2

She and Crandall didn't speak again until they had reached the daylight outside the tunnel. Crandall was obviously embarrassed by his admission of claustrophobia. Tess tried to take the edge off.

"Do I smell as bad as you do?" she asked as they climbed the embankment.

"No." He smiled. "You smell worse."

They walked back to Crandall's Crown Victoria. The sedan bore no FBI markings, but its color was the traditional Hoover blue of Bureau cars. Tess slipped into the passenger seat. Crandall keyed the ignition and drove back to Santa Fe Avenue, then accelerated toward the downtown skyline, bright against the dimming sky. It was only four thirty, but dusk came early on an overcast evening in January.

"No rain till tomorrow night," Crandall said. "Buys us a little time."

"Very little." Tess sighed. "Sunny California."

"It's a lot less sunny here than people realize."

"Yes," she said. "I know."

She stared out the window at the city blurring past in a smear of palm trees and stucco haciendas. There ought to be something exotic about LA's amalgam of desert and coastline, tropical verdure and urban grit, but to her there was no glamour here. LA was a city out of control, overcrowded, underfunded, its tax base eroding, its social services disappearing, the police outnumbered and outgunned, the citizens harassed by wandering mental patients and roving packs of gangbangers, the walls and fences and even the trees befouled by graffiti, and underneath it all, the ticking clock of the next earthquake, the one that might bring the steel-and-glass towers crashing down.

There were earthquakes in Colorado, she reminded herself. In many ways LA was similar to Denver—mountains, sprawl, traffic. But Denver felt solid, stable. LA was balanced on a knife edge.

She smelled aftershave wafted on the sedan's air-conditioning. Rick Crandall's scent. She took a closer look at him. His face was smooth and round, an innocent face. He did not look like a special agent of the FBI, though he was dressed for the part in his blue blazer and white, stiff-collared shirt. She studied his hands on the steering wheel and noticed cuff links. He might be the only agent under forty who wore French cuffs.

"You're quite the natty dresser, Crandall."

"Maybe I got a little extra dressed up."

"For an airport pickup?"

"Not just any pickup. You're something of a legend around here, Agent McCallum."

She didn't want to hear any praise. "I doubt your boss thinks of me that way."

"I don't know how he thinks of you." Crandall chose his words with care.

"Sure you don't."

She wondered how old Crandall was. Twenty-seven, she guessed—ten years her junior. Despite that remark about her status, he didn't appear to be intimidated, and she didn't think he was brown-nosing. He seemed very sure of himself. She wondered where his assurance came from.

"Been in the Bureau long?" she asked.

"All my life."

"That's somewhat cryptic."

"I'm a Bureau brat, you could say. My father . . ."

She understood. "Ralston Crandall?" she said, naming one of the top figures in the DC office.

"The one and only." He smiled self-consciously. "Hope you don't disapprove of a little harmless nepotism."

"Nepotism in the FBI? The Bureau is a meritocracy, Crandall. Didn't they tell you that in the academy?"

"They told me. Kept a straight face, too. Then they sent me straight to the LA office after graduation. Kind of a plum assignment for a new recruit, don't you think?"

"How long have you been here?"

"Six months. Still got my training wheels."

"What were you doing before this? Law school?" A lot of agents had legal training.

"Two years in business school and three years proving I couldn't run an actual business. My last start-up was a Web-based retail outfit."

"What did you sell?"

"Salmon. Flash-frozen, packed in dry ice and shipped to your door. The plan was to start with salmon, expand into other seafood, then beef and poultry, and before long we'd corner the market on Internet grocery shopping."

"How long did that last?"

"Eight months. After which, I surrendered to the inevitable and decided to follow in my father's footsteps."

"They're good footsteps."

"So he's been telling me since I was six years old. He used to call me his junior G-man." He winced. "Don't tell anybody I said that, okay?"

"My lips are sealed. I wouldn't knock having family connections. Take advantage of your . . . advantages. If being Ralston Crandall's son helps get you where the action is, so be it."

"I just want to earn it, you know? The way *you* did."

Pray you don't have to, Tess thought.

The car hooked onto Main Street, drawing close to downtown. Tess didn't like seeing the skyline. It reminded her of the last case that brought her to LA.

Back then, she had been simply Special Agent McCallum of the Denver office. Now she was Denver's special agent in charge, the head honcho. To be an SAC at the age of thirty-seven was an accomplishment for anyone—doubly so for a female agent. The Mobius case had gotten her there. Single-handedly stopping a serial killer who'd gotten hold of a canister of nerve gas would enhance anybody's résumé.

She had parlayed her celebrity status into the Denver ASAC job—assistant special agent in charge. Six months ago, when the Denver SAC was reassigned to Chicago, Tess had replaced him. She'd expected to be happy. The money was good, Denver was her favorite city, and there were no more than the usual ego clashes and prima-donna antics among her staff.

But she had discovered the truth in the platitude about being careful what you wish for. The top management job consisted mostly of politics and paperwork. She didn't like wasting her time on either. In her new position there was no fieldwork. Suddenly she had joined the rubber-gun squad, the desk jockeys she'd always despised.

Then the Greco case had come along, with its terrible resolution. And she had discovered that there was something worse than boredom. There was guilt.

Whenever she closed her eyes, she could see Danny Lopez. Whenever she tried to sleep . . .

All in all, things had been tough. The emotional rewards of her job were gone. She had only the drudgery of managerial responsibilities by day and the torment of bad dreams at night.

Until this morning, when she'd been called to LA to join the STORMKIL investigation. She had no idea why she was needed, whether there was an unannounced connection between this case and Mobius, or a lead to another of the two hundred cases she'd cleared during her career. It didn't matter. The call had pulled her back into the field, given her a chance to rediscover the purpose and meaning of her work.

And maybe something more. A chance at redemption—if that was possible.

Crandall glanced at the dashboard clock. "I really hope we're not late. I'll catch hell for it."

"You can say my flight was delayed. I'll back you up."

"Thanks, but they already know it landed on time. They're monitoring the airline's Web site."

"Really? Why?"

"Well . . . it's an important meeting."

"Is something going on here that I should know about?"

"Agent McCallum, I'm just doing my job. And my job is to get you downtown by five P.M."

She was sure he knew more than he was telling, but she didn't press the issue. "You get any music on this radio?" she asked.

He switched on an AM station. The song that emerged from the speakers surprised her. Sinatra, "All the Way."

Tess smiled. "I wouldn't have pegged you for a Rat Packer."

"Never used to be. I just got turned on to this stuff. Now I can't get enough."

"You're an old-fashioned guy."

"What can I say? I appreciate the classics."

He drove into the garage below City Hall East. When the Crown Vic was parked and Sinatra had been silenced, he led Tess to an elevator, which had taken her, last time, into the subterranean bunker used for coordinating the city's response to a terrorist attack. This time it lifted her and Crandall to the third floor.

A short walk down well-lit corridors brought them to the pedestrian bridge that linked City Hall East with the original City Hall. Night had dropped over the city, and the building's terra-cotta tower was lit up, bright white against the darkness. Tess looked skyward as she and Crandall crossed the bridge in the open air. There must be stars, but they were hidden by cloud cover. Beside her, Crandall whistled "All the Way."

She envied Crandall. He was young and enthusiastic. Maybe he even had a girlfriend. She hadn't had much of a personal life in recent years. One semiserious relationship that ended after a few months. Occasional dates that only left her feeling tired. Men outside law enforcement were intimidated by her—they made dumb jokes about her job, asked if she was carrying a gun, or maybe handcuffs, ha, ha—while the men she worked with in the Bureau were her subordinates, off-limits for intimacy. She was wary of the media people she encountered, and turned off by the community activists she'd met, most of whom knew nothing about law enforcement except what they saw on TV.

"They've booked you into a nice hotel," Crandall said. "The MiraMist in Santa Monica."

"I'm familiar with it." Her voice was flat.

"You've stayed there before?"

"No. Mobius killed a woman there. In room 1625, as I recall."

"Oh."

"I hope they didn't book me into that room."

Crandall was uncomfortable. "It *is* a nice hotel, though. The AD made the reservations personally."

Tess managed a smile. "I'm sure he did."

"He must have forgotten the connection to Mobius."

"He didn't forget."

Mind games. Bad enough that she had to deal with the twisted psychology of killers and kidnappers. Worse, she had to counter the stupid thrusts of her own colleagues.

Their FBI creds got them past the security checkpoint at the entrance to what was known as Old City Hall, built in 1928 and recently renovated. The third floor, home of various ceremonial chambers, was a maze of marble floors and walls, the ceilings decorated in murals of Malibu tile, the ornately carved doors sprouting bronze handles.

"Not a bad place to come to work," Crandall said as they proceeded down a glistening hallway.

"Where are we going?"

"Mayor's office. Just off the rotunda."

He led her through an anteroom, waving away a receptionist with a flash of his badge. Tess found herself joining a crowd in the spacious expanse of the mayor's office. A drone of conversation rose to the high, painted ceiling. Marble archways linked decorative columns. The place looked like a movie set—appropriate for LA.

Across the room she saw the AD, who was making an effort to draw as close to the mayor as possible. The room was large, and ordinarily she might not have recognized someone from a distance in a crush of people. But there was a reason the assistant director had acquired his nickname, and it helped him stand out in a crowd.

Resolutely Tess made her way toward ADIC Richard Michaelson, a.k.a. the Nose.

Michaelson had risen far in the three years since they'd worked together. She wondered how much higher he would climb. All the way to the top, possibly. He had the right combination of political canniness and narrow ambition. He was smart enough to get ahead, but not so smart as to threaten anybody. He was obsequious toward his superiors, contemptuous of those lower in rank—exactly the personality profile they looked for in Washington. And he'd never been much good as a field agent—another plus in the minds of those who did the promoting, most of whom had never been any good on the street, either.

She might be looking at a future director of the Bureau. Now, there was a thought calculated to keep her up at night.

Michaelson caught sight of her as she drew near. He left the mayor and intercepted her.

"Agent McCallum." His voice was more nasal than she'd remembered. His nose seemed longer, too, as if he'd been telling lies. No doubt he had. "You're almost late."

"If I'm *almost* late, then I must be on time," she said with a smile. She had promised herself she would not allow him to irritate her. Failing that, she would not allow him to see that he'd irritated her. "I'm not sure exactly what the occasion is, though."

"Crandall didn't tell you?"

"No."

"He was supposed to bring you up to speed."

Tess was sure this was untrue. Michaelson had probably instructed Crandall to give her no information whatsoever. That would be more his style.

"Up to speed about what?" Despite her promise, she was beginning to feel irritated already.

Michaelson shrugged, as if the answer were obvious. "The media event. It starts in"—he glanced at his watch— "four minutes." *Media event* was Michaelsonese for *news conference.*

"A news conference?"

"About the Rain Man, yes." He saw her look of confusion and added in a confidential tone, "That's what we're calling him. Because of the video."

Tess remembered the video from the FBI report. Efforts had been made to determine whether the kidnapper had known about the rental in advance, perhaps because he worked in the video store. Those angles hadn't panned out.

"Rain Man," she said. She disliked the name. It trivialized the suspect. "Who came up with that?"

"I did."

Naturally, she thought.

"Of course," Michaelson added, "that term is not for public consumption. Officially he's the unknown subject." He checked his watch again. "Almost zero hour."

"Why exactly are you holding a news briefing?"

"Well, it's a progress report, of sorts."

"I was under the impression we weren't making any progress."

"That's why there's been a change of organization. The Kidnapping Squad supervisor is no longer the case agent."

"Who is?"

"As of today, I am."

Tess had been afraid of that. "So that's the announcement—that you're taking over?"

"Not entirely." Michaelson's eyes shifted away. For someone with so much experience in prevarication, he was remarkably unskillful at it. "There *is* another purpose to the event."

"Which is?"

"Well . . . you." His face brightened in a poor imitation of a man delivering good news. "We need to announce that you're joining the investigation."

She let a moment pass. "Me?"

"I expect you to say a few words. I had my assistant write up some remarks, just to save you the trouble."

"This is all about me?"

"You're a big name in this town, Tess." He rarely addressed her informally. She knew he was pulling out all the stops to make nice. "A local hero. Some of the journalists call you Super Fed." His smile grew larger, but the muscles of his face were tight. "You saved the whole damn city."

"And now I'm on the job again."

"Exactly." He relaxed, pleased to think she'd bought into it. "If you could stop Mobius, you may be just the one to nab the Rain Man. Excuse me—the unknown subject."

"I see."

"Let me get you those notes, and we'll make our appearance. You'll be standing between the mayor and the chief of police. The whole thing is timed to lead off the five o'clock news, live. It'll be canned and recycled at six, ten, and eleven. Front-page coverage in the *Times* tomorrow. It's been orchestrated—"

"Forget it," Tess said.

Michaelson looked at her, at the expression on her face, and he knew the game was up.

"Agent McCallum . . ." No informality now.

"I'm not doing it."

"You have to."

"No, I don't. You hijacked me from Denver to put me on

display like a mannequin in a department store. It's not going to happen."

"Your attitude—"

"You knew all about my attitude. That's why you didn't let me know why I was brought here. You figured you'd trap me into being part of your public relations ploy."

"The Bureau's image in the eyes of the public is hardly—"

"You don't expect me to contribute a goddamn thing to this case. I'm a prop, that's all."

"Time," someone called out.

"We have to get out there," Michaelson said.

"*You* have to get out there."

"I'm ordering you—"

"All right." She shrugged. "Then I'll go."

That stopped him. "You will?"

"Certainly. If it's a direct order, I can't refuse, can I?"

"No," he said warily. "You can't."

"So it's settled, then." She waited for him to register a faint smile of triumph, then added, "But don't bother giving me that prepared statement. I'll make some extemporaneous remarks."

His smile was gone. "What sort of remarks?"

"Oh, how the LA office values image over substance, that sort of thing."

He stared at her, assessing her seriousness. "You really would," he said finally, "wouldn't you?"

"Sure." She doubted she would actually commit career suicide in front of a battery of TV cameras, but she was happy to let Michaelson think otherwise.

He gave in. "I'm not going to forget this, McCallum. You just screwed yourself, big-time." He stalked off, hustling after the mayor and the other dignitaries headed for the rotunda.

Tess released a slow breath. She should have known. Of course they hadn't wanted her for her expertise or insight. She was only a symbol, the heroine of the Mobius case returning to slay another dragon.

Sometimes she *hated* this job.

She recrossed the room and found Rick Crandall by the door. "Car keys," she said, palm out.

"What? Aren't you . . . ?"

"I'm not ready for my close-up. Car keys. Now."

"Technically the car wasn't assigned to you."

"I outrank you. My luggage is in that car. Keys, Crandall."

He surrendered the keys. "I hope you know what you're doing, Agent McCallum."

"I always know what I'm doing."

Tess left the room, thinking that Michaelson would have laughed if he'd heard that last declaration.

What was worse, he would have been right.

3

Tess didn't calm down even after she'd pulled out of the parking garage. As usual when she was in a state of serious rage, there was a part of her that seemed to stand back, observing her anger with slightly amused detachment. She knew enough about psychology to recall that this irritating presence was called the witness. Its purpose was to preserve some sense of perspective when the ego went haywire.

In this case the witness was wondering, in its quiet voice, exactly why she was so upset. From a public relations standpoint, Michaelson's arguments made sense. The Bureau had taken a black eye after the death of the second victim. Bringing in the woman who'd bagged Mobius was a way to restore public confidence. It was also a kind of tribute to her. If she'd played it smart, she could have used her importance as leverage for a position of authority in the investigation. She could have enhanced her status in the eyes of the honchos in DC. And, heck, she could have been on TV.

Instead she had stormed out, further alienated Michaelson, reinforced her reputation as a loose cannon, and damaged her career prospects. The witness wanted to know why.

"Because I won't be used," she said aloud. "I won't be put on display. . . ."

Like a department-store mannequin—yes, she'd sung that tune already. Not entirely convincing, was it? Truth was, she had allowed herself to be used at other times in her career.

Every agent did. No one in this business could escape from politics and bureaucratic games.

No, there was another reason, one that the witness, in its infinite smugness, already knew.

Danny Lopez.

That was why she'd recoiled from the prospect of the show Michaelson had arranged. That was why she hadn't been willing to face the cameras and accept the accolades.

She couldn't stand there preening, selling herself as Joan of Arc returning to do battle, when she slept every night with images of Danny Lopez crowding her dreams. She was no hero, and she wouldn't pass herself off as one.

But she couldn't have said that to Michaelson. He didn't know what had really happened in the Greco case, and even if he had known, he wouldn't have understood how she felt. Maybe no one understood. Certainly no one in Denver had seemed to grasp it or care. There had been the usual empty comments about how nobody could foresee every contingency, there were always risks, tragedies happened, and on and on until she thought she would start screaming just to keep herself from going insane.

She'd learned to accept the platitudes. She'd learned to sleep despite the dreams. But one thing she would not do was present herself to the world as . . . what had Michaelson said they called her? Super Fed.

She wasn't feeling very super these days.

The car glided west on Olympic Boulevard. She was scarcely conscious of where she was going. Her only impulse was to put distance between herself and the white tower of City Hall. She supposed she would head into Westwood and see what was happening in the field office—assuming her FBI credentials hadn't already been revoked.

One good thing had come out of the debacle at City Hall, anyway. She'd gotten the Nose seriously pissed off. The helpless frustration on his face had been almost worth the price of admission.

What she needed was to hear a friendly voice. She got out

her cell phone, which she'd turned off during the flight. There must be messages piling up in her voice mail—even a couple of hours incommunicado was enough to create an electronic logjam—but she would worry about them later.

She called the Denver office, connecting with ASAC Joshua Green, whom she'd left in charge. "Just checking in," she said.

"Good to hear from you. You'll be pleased to know the place hasn't degenerated into anarchy yet."

"I trust you to keep it running smoothly. Any headway in the Garrick case?"

"Lab came back with a blood-type match to the first crime scene."

"No surprise."

"Yeah, I didn't think there'd be two creeps running around with an MO that sick. Oh, the DA says Charlie Harris is copping a plea."

"What did they plead him down to?"

"Man one."

"Good deal for him."

"For us, too. He'll testify against Heinz. And he's walking us through the operation, spilling everything. They can't get him to shut up."

"That's good, I guess." She wasn't a fan of plea bargaining, and Harris had been guilty of much more than manslaughter.

"Try to contain your enthusiasm. So how is LA?"

"Violent and crazy."

"Your kind of town. Haven't you been pining for your glory days in Miami? The rampant crime, the drug cartels, the colorful hit men . . ."

"Miami was a long time ago. I think I'm getting too old for that stuff. Could I, uh, ask you a favor?"

"Is it sexual in nature?" He was always doing that in their private conversations—making inappropriate remarks. She should have found it objectionable. She didn't.

"It's botanical in nature," she countered. "I forgot to water the plants in my apartment. They'll be getting a little thirsty."

"Most plants can go a few days without water."

"I've been forgetting for a while. Sorry."

"No problem. I can swing by on my way home. How do I get in?"

"There's a spare key in the upper right drawer of my desk."

"While I'm in your place, maybe I'll snoop around a little."

"There's not much to see."

"I can check out the porn on your computer, the erotic toys under your bed."

"My computer is traveling with me. The only thing under my bed is dust bunnies."

"Well, at least I can say I've been in your bedroom."

"You've probably been saying that anyway."

"But now it'll be true. So how can I expect to be repaid for this favor?"

"I shouldn't have asked."

"I'm thinking a table for two at Tuscany. Sound good?"

Tuscany was one of Denver's better—and more romantic—restaurants. "Depends," she said. "Who are the two?"

"Don't be coy with me, Agent McCallum."

"Office romances—"

"Are the only kind workaholics like you and me ever get."

"You might have a point there."

"So, dinner for two? Is it a date?"

Dinner with Josh Green. Probably a bad idea. He worked with her every day. There was a large potential for embarrassing complications. Still, she did like the guy. Got along well with him. As a friend and colleague, anyway. But as a lover? She didn't think it would work. There was just something about him. He wasn't . . . wasn't . . .

He wasn't Paul.

Right. He could not replace Paul Voorhees. But no one

could, and it had been years, and what was she going to do, remain alone forever?

Dinner at Tuscany . . .

"Tess? You there?"

"I'm here."

"And your answer is . . . ?"

"It could be a problem, Josh. You're my subordinate. There are, you know, unwritten rules."

"Those are the ones that are easiest to break."

"I'll give it some thought. Really."

"Don't hesitate too long. I'm a hot prospect. Lots of nubile young things are just waiting to snap me up."

"You're delusional. Don't forget my houseplants."

"They'll be rejuvenated and refreshed. Just like you after a night with me."

"Good-bye, Josh."

"Don't go all Hollywood on us, Tess. We like you just the way you are."

This was so cornball and transparently manipulative that it was actually sweet. She ended the call, smiling.

Without Josh's voice, the car suddenly seemed too quiet. She turned on the radio, thinking that some of Crandall's Sinatra music might be good right now, but the station was doing a newsbreak. She heard a sound bite of Michaelson, his voice echoing in the rotunda.

"Although her arrival was unexpectedly delayed, we are happy to inform the city that one of our most experienced agents, Tess McCallum, has been brought into the investigation. Special Agent McCallum brings many sterling qualities—"

She snapped off the radio.

They were going to use her anyway. They were going to make her a hero, whether she wanted to play along or not.

She couldn't remember Michaelson's face any longer, or the expression she'd found so amusing a few minutes ago. All she saw was Danny Lopez huddled in a heap of trash, his small body sprawled crookedly among beer bottles and garbage bags.

She let anger at herself and anger at Michaelson fuse into a healthier, more useful emotion—hatred of the Rain Man. She would get him. She would break this case open. She had no idea how she would do it, or why she was any better qualified to find the killer than the other agents already assigned to the case. But she would find a way. She had to. She would stop this man, and then maybe things would balance out.

Except it never worked that way, did it? Some things couldn't be balanced. Some mistakes could never be fixed.

The Los Angeles offices of the Federal Bureau of Investigation were located in the Federal Building in Westwood, at 11000 Wilshire Boulevard. Tess left the Bureau sedan in the parking lot and entered the lobby, where she submitted to a brisk, professional search conducted by the guards. Her photo was taken and glued to a temporary ID badge, which she stuck in her pocket after boarding the elevator. On the seventeenth floor she announced herself and was buzzed through a security door, to be greeted by Special Agent Peter Larkin, lately promoted to Michaelson's deputy.

"Tess, it's good to see you, really good." He shook her hand, grinning. She almost expected him to clap her on the back and ask her to join him in a fine cigar.

It wasn't the greeting she would have predicted. Larkin had been cool to her throughout her previous sojourn in LA. But of course she hadn't been in charge of the Denver office then. If there was one skill Larkin possessed, it was the ability to kowtow to anybody who outranked him. He was an unapologetic sycophant. To call him a toady would have been an insult to amphibians everywhere.

"Really good," he said again as she extracted her hand from his grip and followed him into the reception area.

"Nice to see you too," she said with a twitch of her lips intended to convey a smile.

"Shame about the news conference. Your flight got delayed, I guess?"

"Something like that." He would hear the true story soon enough.

"Where's Crandall? Isn't he supposed to be chauffeuring you?"

"I prefer to chauffeur myself. Got a desk for me?"

"That we do. Hey, where's your visitor's badge?"

"In my pocket."

"Better wear it. It's the ADIC's policy. All visiting agents must be provided with a security pass, which must be worn on one's person at all times when in the office."

"How efficient."

Larkin key-carded a hallway door and led her inside. "Hey, with six hundred agents working here, we need all the efficiency we can get."

She might have been paranoid, but she took this as a reminder that the LA office was substantially larger than her Denver bailiwick.

"Want some coffee?" he asked as he escorted her down carpeted hallways, past conference rooms and interrogation rooms. "Surprisingly, it's now almost palatable."

Without waiting for a reply, he steered her into a small kitchen and poured coffee into a Styrofoam cup.

"It's good to have you aboard," he said. "I think you'll make a big difference."

"Why is that?"

"Come again?"

"Why will I make any difference to the investigation? What contribution can I make?"

"Well, I'm sure the ADIC—"

"The ADIC hijacked me as a publicity stunt." She sipped the coffee. It actually wasn't bad. "He feels I have some name-recognition value in this town."

"And you do."

"Name recognition won't help us clear this case."

"Well . . . maybe not." He gave her a sly, slightly disapproving glance. "Your plane wasn't late, was it?"

"No."

"You declined to participate in the news conference?"

"I walked out of the mayor's office."

Larkin made a *tsk-tsk* noise. "Tess, you just don't know how to play the game. How to get ahead."

"I've done all right for myself, Peter."

"Anybody else with Mobius under their belt would've been out of Denver by now."

"Maybe I don't want to be out of Denver."

"Why wouldn't you?"

"I like the scenery."

"Let me tell you something, Tess. This is just between you and me. It goes no further. You tell anyone we had this conversation, I'll deny it."

"Very dramatic."

"You're wasting your time in Colorado. You should be in Chicago or New York. Or here. You think Michaelson got this post on the basis of ability? He got it because he plays the game. You put your mind to it, you can outplay him without breaking a sweat."

"Why are you offering me this advice?"

"I hate to see ability going to waste. You've got it all. The résumé, the brains—hell, you're even a woman."

"Thanks for noticing."

"The Bureau would love to put you in a prominent post. But you need to show you're reliable. You need to—"

"Play the game. I got it."

"If you got it, you wouldn't be here with me right now. You'd be having dinner with the ADIC after wowing the local media at that news conference."

"I don't think the ADIC would have dinner with me, no matter how much wowing I did."

"He can be won over. Anybody can. You just have to approach them right. Give them what they want. Meet them halfway."

"Just out of curiosity," she asked, "what does all this have to do with apprehending the Rain Man?"

"Not a damn thing. We'll get him. Then another nut will come along, and the clock is reset to zero and it's a new ball game. In the meantime jerks like the Nose are getting ahead, and you're falling behind."

She thought about it for a moment. "You're not wrong, Peter," she conceded. "But I've never been any good at that part of the job."

"Only because you don't try to be."

"Exactly."

He gave up. "Remember, we never had this talk."

"I've forgotten it already."

He gave her a skeptical look, uncertain whether she was ribbing him. "It's your funeral." He was less personable than before. Evidently he'd decided she wasn't worth sucking up to, after all. "Let me show you to your workstation."

Down the hall was the C-1 squad area, home base of Criminal Squad One, a large room crowded with rows of workstations. Several were occupied by agents she didn't know, talking on the phone or studying the screens of laptop computers. A secretary, bending over a file cabinet, was the only other woman in the room.

Larkin led her to a workstation in the back row, where a stack of papers was waiting. "Here you go. Your homework assignment is all ready for you."

"Homework?"

"We set up a tip line on the Rain Man. We've got, let's see . . ." Each tip was numbered. He flipped to the bottom of the stack. "Two hundred thirteen call-ins here. We need someone with experience to go through the data and prioritize it."

"No one's done that already? How many bodies are working this case?"

"Over two hundred, and yes, someone has prioritized the earlier tips. These are just from the last twelve hours. The day crew turned them in a half hour ago."

"And I got elected to go through them because . . . ?"

"The ADIC specifically requested that you handle the assignment."

"He's a prince. Shouldn't the squad super be doing it? Or the case agent?"

"Sounds like you're trying to get out of a work detail."

"I'm just trying to understand the logic of putting me in charge of reviewing this information when all I've read so far is the report. I haven't even reviewed the full case file yet."

"Michaelson says we need a fresh pair of eyeballs. Namely, yours."

"And if my eyeballs miss anything, then I take the blame?"

Larkin shrugged. "I guess if you were running the show, you'd do things differently. But you aren't running the show—are you?"

"No." She let a sigh escape her. "I'm not."

He tapped the tall pile of printouts. "This needs to be done by tomorrow A.M., in time for the supervisors' meeting at oh nine hundred hours. Oh, and Michaelson wants a summary of the high-priority tips delivered to him before the meeting."

"So he can take the credit for any leads that might develop?"

"I'm sure it's just in the interest of efficiency."

Tess grunted. Suddenly the coffee was tasting sour in her mouth.

"Good luck, Tess." Larkin flashed a smile. "You might want to order a pizza. You'll probably be here pretty late."

He left the squad room. Tess sat at her desk and regarded the pile of paper with distaste.

When she looked up, she caught some of the other agents sneaking glances at her, either out of curiosity or in obedience to the bureaucrat's prime directive—defend your turf. No one made a move to approach her, and she lacked the energy to get up and endure a round of handshakes and smiles.

Instead she got to work on the tips, reminding herself that somewhere in this compilation of gossip and paranoia there might be a genuine lead to the identity of the Rain Man.

She worked for thirty minutes, sorting the tips into low-, medium-, and high-priority piles. Most were worthless. A few were sufficiently intriguing to justify a medium-priority rating. After combing through a quarter of the pile she'd found only two that counted as high-priority leads. It was a slow job. She had to read each tip several times to be sure she wasn't missing anything.

Many of the tips involved suspicious characters glimpsed in or near the LA River before one of the rainstorms. While any of these sightings could be significant, the simple fact was that the river extended for more than fifty miles, and along nearly all of its length it was frequented by shopping-cart people, soda-can scavengers, and other derelicts, not to mention joggers, bicyclists, and birdwatchers.

Potentially more valuable were reports of vehicles parked near major entry points to the storm-drain system. As Crandall had pointed out, the Rain Man had probably entered through an opening large enough to accommodate a vehicle. He had driven his victims deep into the tunnel system, then proceeded farther on foot.

The larger access points were used by maintenance crews from the Department of Water and Power. These entryways were locked, but a lock could be picked or shot off. So far no one had found a specific entrance that had been tampered with—a minor puzzle in itself. If an entrance used by the Rain Man could be found, some forensic evidence might be identified—tire tracks, shoe prints, fingerprints on the pad-lock—although, given the heavy rainfalls, most clues had probably been washed away.

She placed the vehicle sightings in the medium-priority pile. Locations and times would have to be checked against the known deployment of DWP personnel.

Much of the other material was useless. People called to speculate about the killer, to ask questions about the case, or to recommend an investigative technique that had worked on a TV show last week. It was possible that the Rain Man himself had called. Somewhere in the hundreds of tips there might be a sighting or suggestion planted by the killer, either to lead the investigators astray or simply to have some fun.

Tess knew from the case report that two persons had already called authorities, claiming to be the killer. In both instances the caller had been indiscreet enough to place the call from his easily traceable home phone. Both had been picked up. One was a twelve-year-old playing a prank. The other was a psychiatric patient who'd gone off his meds.

Across the room, two agents were holding a low conversation with occasional pointed looks in her direction. She ignored them until a new man drifted past her workstation on his way into the room.

"Just heard about that stunt you pulled at City Hall," he said as he passed her. "You're a real prick, aren't you?"

"Women don't have pricks," she said dryly.

"Fuck you." He walked on, joining the other men, who were glaring at her with equal hostility.

Oh, yeah, she'd screwed the pooch this time. Alienated not only Michaelson but every loyal foot soldier in his regiment.

Her desk phone rang. She picked it up, bracing for another salvo of antagonism. "McCallum," she said.

"Agent McCallum?" A clipped female voice, sounding a note of surprise. "Well, you're surprisingly easy to get hold of. The front desk connected me directly. Don't you have a secretary to take your calls?"

Yes, I do, Tess thought. *In Denver.* "Who am I speaking to, please?"

"I'm sorry. My name is Madeleine Grant."

"How can I help you, Ms. Grant?"

"I'm not sure you can. The fact is, I've already called the tip line, or hotline, that special phone number you people set up. No one got back to me. I assumed what I had to say just wasn't very useful, but when I heard you had been brought in on the case, I began to think I ought to try again."

"Why is that? What do I have to do with anything?"

"Well, it's Mobius, you see. That's the connection."

Tess wondered how long she would have to continue this conversation, which she had already dismissed as a waste of time. "I don't understand," she said patiently. "What connection?"

"The connection to my case. The stalking case."

"Stalking?"

"Haven't you people even reviewed the tips you've been given? What's the use of establishing a phone number—"

"I just got on board, Ms. Grant. I'm still not up to speed."

"Oh, I see. I suppose that's understandable, then." She sounded dubious. "Well, last year, someone was stalking me. He was arrested, sent to prison. Now he's out."

"He was sent to prison on a stalking conviction?"

"Yes, but it should have been kidnapping."

"Kidnapping?"

"He was planning to kidnap me. They found the evidence. I said all this in my first phone call."

"Can you remember when you made this call?"

"Of course I remember. It was just this morning, after I read the story in the *Times*. They quoted the text of that message he'd made the second woman write."

"And why did you call this morning?"

"Because the wording of that message was very similar to a message he sent me."

Tess was beginning to feel mildly intrigued. "You say this man was only recently released from prison?"

"That's right. Last December. He served less than a year. Can you imagine? Ten months for what he did. No wonder this city is falling apart, when they let animals like him—"

"You said there was a connection to Mobius?"

"This man was obsessed with Mobius. So when I heard you'd been brought in, right after I'd made my call, naturally I assumed there was something in this case connecting it with Mobius and that's why you were here."

"Ms. Grant, will you be home this evening?"

"Yes, I will."

"Would it be possible for me to come see you?"

"Absolutely. I can't believe that no one has followed up on my first call. It's been hours—and there's rain in tomorrow's forecast. What do you people *do* all day? The police, the FBI—we can't count on any of them anymore. . . ."

She went on this way until Tess had a chance to take down her address. She lived in Bel Air, conveniently close to Westwood. Tess promised to be there as soon as possible and hung up before the woman could begin another diatribe.

She rummaged through the tips until she found the one from Madeleine Grant. She knew she shouldn't run down the lead herself. That wasn't her job. She was supposed to pass it on to Michaelson. But if she passed it on, it might not be covered for days. And she had a feeling about this one. Or maybe she just wanted a little drama in her life.

She reviewed Madeleine's tip. Only the bare outline of her story had been taken down, and the details remained obscure. There was just one fact in the report that had not been included in their conversation—the name of the man who'd been sent to prison for stalking her, the man obsessed with Mobius.

His name was William Kolb.

4

Kolb lay on his futon, staring up at the dark ceiling. Behind the drawn window shade, night had fallen over Los Angeles. But even in darkness and solitude, he couldn't escape the events of the day.

"Live with your mama, don't ya, rent-a-cop?"

"You bet he does. He gives it to his mama every night."

"That true, man? You do it with your *madre*?"

Their voices snapped at him like small angry dogs. The kids passed him every day—young *pachucos*, gangbangers, or would-be gangbangers, anyway—and they always made comments as they went into and out of the store. They would laugh and make gestures and hand signals, and toss off jokes in Spanish that he couldn't understand, trying to impress their girls, the tattooed, nose-ringed, overly made-up girls who hung with them.

"Shit, man, don't ya even speak English?"

"You must be one sad dude, gettin' stuck with this job. Guys cleaning toilets got more dignity than you."

That had made their girls laugh, showing their white teeth. There had been two girls and three boys, none older than seventeen. Their faces were dark-skinned and broad, like Inca carvings.

"Don't you got an answer, jackoff?"

"Screw it, this guy's too dumb to say nothin'. Just stands there. He's a gork, man. Friggin' brain-dead."

"Bet he stands there when it's a hundred degrees."

"Shit, I bet he stands there even in the fuckin' rain."

They'd been wrong about that. He had better things to do in the rain.

Finally they'd left him, swaggering into the air-conditioned environs of Jonson's Food & Drug, a store that contracted him at $10.75 an hour to stand guard, unarmed, in a gray uniform and cap.

He knew that some of the other guards at Jonson's had tried to get friendly with the neighborhood kids, learn their names, make small talk. There was Thurber, for instance, the overweight guard who'd arrived this evening at four thirty-seven to relieve him and start the night shift.

"Hey, Bill," Thurber said with a smile.

He didn't like being called Bill. William was his name. "You're seven minutes late," Kolb said.

"What's seven minutes between friends?"

Thurber was not his friend. He had no friends. But he let it go.

"Any trouble today?" Thurber asked.

"Usual assholes. Smart-talking kids."

"You get to know some of these kids, they ain't so bad."

"Why would you want to get to know them?"

Thurber shrugged, as if the answer were obvious. "Can't just stand here all day."

"Sure you can. That's the job."

Kolb had nothing more to say to Thurber. Thurber was a fool. He wanted to make friends, wanted to be liked. This was a sign of weakness. Kolb was better than that. He never spoke a word to the kids. He showed no reaction to their taunts. He took the insults. He would not be provoked into any response. Nothing could touch him. He was forged of will and discipline. He was stone, he was steel, he was beyond all feeling.

But tonight his head sure hurt like a son of a bitch.

He'd been getting the headaches a lot recently. Bad headaches, the kind that pressed down hard between his eyes like someone's thumb grinding into the bridge of his nose.

The headaches annoyed him, less because of the pain than because of the betrayal they represented. He expected his body to function properly. It was a tool, which he kept in good working order, and he expected it to operate as required.

In the old days he never got headaches. He could tangle with gangbangers and street scum throughout an eight-hour shift, spend another few hours downing beers and telling lies in a cop hangout, get an hour's sleep, and return to work fresh and strong. He had never been sick.

But now the headaches would come and there was no way to fight them off, no way to deal with them except to lie down in the dark and make his mind blank and hope for sleep.

He'd never been any good at introspection, but vaguely he knew that the job had something to do with the headaches. At first he'd been happy to get the work. He'd been given a uniform and a badge, and it was almost like being a cop again.

Or so he'd told himself when he examined his reflection in the polished steel door of his locker. *I'm back*, he'd thought.

But it had been a lie. As a cop, he'd had power. He hadn't been obliged to take any abuse. The gangbangers and their whores wouldn't dare laugh at him. He'd enforced his authority, ruling the world defined by the parameters of his patrol. Wearing the blue suit, laden down with the Kevlar vest and the Sam Browne belt and the Beretta and the baton, he had been more than a man. He had been something mighty, something invincible, a lord of the earth, breathing power, inspiring fear.

Kids who went running and gunning after dark and expected to die before they turned eighteen, kids raised on legends of quick riches and quick deaths—those kids cast their eyes down to the pavement when he went by. No jokes, no mutterings in Spanish, no flashing teeth or indecipherable hand signals at his expense. He owned his turf.

All of that was lost to him now, and pulling guard duty at a grocery store was not enough to compensate.

But it didn't matter. The job was only a stopgap measure. When the security firm eventually ran a criminal background check, they would find he'd lied on his application when he checked the "no" box in response to the question: *Have you ever been convicted of a felony?* By all rights, they should have canned his ass already, but they were a slipshod outfit, in no hurry to discover that any of their employees needed replacing.

The job had served its purpose, brought in money when he needed it. Now he was free of such concerns. He could quit at any time. Only prudence kept him anchored to his daily routine. He had learned caution—learned it the hard way.

The phone rang. It rested only a foot from his head, on an end table, and its shrill cry drilled through his ear canals.

If he wanted to know who was calling, he would have to pick up. He had no message machine—didn't believe in putting things on tape.

He lifted the handset. The keypad glowed. He closed his eyes against the light.

"Yes," he said into the phone, without rising, without moving his head at all.

"She's here. They brought her in."

It took him a moment to process the words. "Who?" he asked, but he already knew.

"Who do you think?" The other man was cautious enough not to say any names over the phone.

Kolb frowned. "Why are you telling me this?"

"Because you'll find out anyway. It's been on the news."

"She's joining the investigation?"

"Yes."

"So she'll be in town awhile."

"For the duration."

"They must be putting her up at a hotel."

"I guess so."

"What hotel?"

"I'm not saying a word."

"Why not?"

"Because I don't want you getting distracted by a private agenda."

"I won't get distracted. I won't *do* anything."

"Then you don't need to know where she's staying."

"I'd like to get a look at her, that's all."

"You've seen her a million times."

"Not in the flesh."

"Maybe you've got a thing for her."

"Maybe I do. Love your enemy, right?"

"I didn't think that was your philosophy."

"Sure it is." Kolb stared into the dark. His voice was low and distant. "We love whatever gives our life meaning. Whatever brings us a sense of purpose. Our enemies do that for us. We'd be lost without them."

"Well, I'm glad to hear you're in such a charitable mood. Because we can't afford to get caught up in some kind of fucking vendetta."

"It's not an issue."

"Don't give me that crap. I know how bad you . . ." His voice trailed off momentarily as the call broke up. ". . . that woman."

Kolb lifted himself to a sitting position. "You on a cell?"

"Yeah."

"God damn it. You know cells aren't secure."

"Nobody's listening."

"How can you know?"

"There are ten million cell phones in this city. Okay? It's physically impossible to listen in on all of them."

"Fucking computers can scan ten million calls looking for hot-button words."

"Hot-button words? You mean like 'terrorist,' 'bomb,' 'assassination'—"

"Shut the fuck up, asshole." Kolb could imagine an array of supercomputers homing in on the conversation right now. Laughter on the other end of the line. "I'm just jerking your chain. Nobody's monitoring the damn call. Just chill."

"Chill? You're talking street now? You watch a Chris Rock special on HBO or something?"

"I'm in a good mood, that's all. Money in my pocket has a way of lifting my spirits."

"It's not in your pocket yet."

"Figure of speech."

"You haven't tapped into the account, have you?"

"Of course not."

"Because I don't want you spending it. That's a rookie mistake. Neither of us changes our routine. I keep my job, and you keep yours. And we both keep our heads down."

"I know the drill. I haven't touched it. Not one dime."

"Be sure you don't. We're not throwing it all away just because you get impatient."

"Don't worry about me. It's you I'm worried about. You and . . . her."

"I already told you, I won't try anything."

"I hope that's true. We've got more important things on our agenda. We can't go running around after some dumb bitch."

Kolb lay down again. "Now, now. Show the lady some respect."

"Love—and now respect? It's a whole new you."

He shut his eyes. "There's nothing wrong with respect. The Cherokee, you know, used to apologize to the spirits of the deer they hunted. They asked forgiveness for taking the animals' lives. That was a sign of respect."

"I doubt the deer saw it that way."

"You never see the big truths. You're too wrapped up in details."

"It's the details that can get us caught."

"And it's the truth that will set us free."

"Just leave her alone," the other man said. "I mean it."

A click, and the call was over.

Kolb replaced the handset, then folded his hands over his abdomen. He stared into the darkness, feeling the slow movement of his belly in time with the push and pull of his breath, and thought about Special Agent Tess McCallum of the FBI.

He hadn't lied. He did respect her, even love her, in his way.

He would like to tell her so, someday. And like the Cherokee, he would apologize before he slit her throat.

5

Larkin caught Tess leaving the office suite. "Done already?" he asked in obvious disbelief.

"Just stepping out for a while."

"Michaelson needs that report before nine A.M."

"He'll get it," Tess said, and disappeared through the door before Larkin could say anything further.

It occurred to her, as she drove out of the parking lot, that she should have been accompanied by another agent. FBI fieldwork was customarily done in pairs. She was alone—and heading for a rendezvous with a woman whose motives in contacting her were still not entirely clear.

She replayed the phone conversation in her mind. Something seemed wrong about it, but she needed a minute's thought to identify the anomaly. Madeleine had begun by calling the tip line and had followed up with a call to the Bureau. But why bother with either approach? Why not contact the LAPD detective who'd arrested Kolb?

A prickle of unease fingered her spine. Pieces of the story didn't fit.

She guided the Crown Vic out of Westwood. Bel Air sprawled to the north, in the foothills of the Santa Monica Mountains, which rose in folds and rifts to Mulholland Drive at the crest. She climbed twisting streets, following the map book she'd found in the glove compartment.

Rounding a switchback curve, she spotted a pair of bright

yellow eyes in the sweep of her headlights. They flashed away into the woods edging the road. She glimpsed lean gray legs and narrow hips—a coyote. They still roamed these hills, feeding out of garbage cans, prowling the carefully tended gardens. It was almost eerie to catch a hint of such wildness when the concrete clutter of the city lay only a mile away.

On another stretch of road she passed a security patrol unit gliding in the opposite direction, a sleek, dark vehicle, silent as a shark. Bel Air had its own private security to supplement the police force. She felt as if she'd left LA and entered a foreign territory, one with its own authorities and its own rules.

Madeleine Grant's home lay on a lushly landscaped cul-de-sac. The house was deeply secluded, nested inside a wrought-iron perimeter fence and layers of foliage. Posted on the fence was a sign warning that the property was protected by an alarm system. The fence itself was high and topped with sharp spikes. Trees that might have allowed an intruder to climb up and over had been trimmed back, their branches lopped to leave a zone of dead space around the fence. Ms. Grant took personal safety seriously.

Tess pulled up to the gate and lowered her window, announcing herself to the intercom. For a moment there was no answer. She had the curious sense of being watched. Then she saw a surveillance camera mounted over the gate, its lens gazing down at her.

Then a metallic voice rasped, "Come in," and the gate slid open on a metal track. She drove down a long circular driveway that looped around a lighted koi pond with a marble fountain, and parked alongside the front steps of the house. It was a two-story Tudor that looked disarmingly small but no doubt extended far back into the property. Lights were on, both inside and outside.

She got out, fingering the gun in her coat to reassure herself that it was there. She glanced around at the large property, taking in the thickets of eucalyptus trees, the beds of flowers artfully arranged.

A shimmer of movement attracted her eye. She turned, then relaxed when she saw that it was only the quick passage of a golden koi through the pond. Dozens of the fish streamed in the bright water like shooting stars in a clear sky.

She headed up the steps. Again she had the sense of being watched. Her gaze scanned the windows. She saw nobody, but when she reached the top of the steps, the door opened before she could ring the bell.

"Agent McCallum. Come in, please."

Madeleine Grant was not what Tess had expected. She'd pictured an older woman, harried and flighty, but Madeleine was no more than thirty-five and seemed perfectly composed. She wore a pantsuit that showed off her toned muscles. Tess guessed she spent a lot of time with a personal trainer.

"It's good of you to see me on such short notice," Tess said.

Madeleine waved off the remark. "I'm the one who should be grateful for your quick response."

With the practiced informality of a hostess, Madeleine led her through the paneled foyer. Tess noted a closed-circuit video monitor discreetly stationed in a corner, offering a view of the steps. That was how Madeleine had watched her.

They stepped into an elegant living room, meticulously appointed like a magazine photo spread. Tess contrasted it with the cramped living-dining area in her Denver apartment, afghans piled on the sofa and half-finished books scattered everywhere.

"You have a beautiful home," she said. "It must take a lot of work to keep it up."

"I have a small staff."

"Do you?"

Madeleine hesitated, as if regretting she'd spoken. "Yes . . . a live-in cook and housekeeper. This is their night off." Her glance flickered nervously to the dining room.

Tess followed her gaze. The dining table had been set for

one. The dishes had been only partially cleared, as if some-one had been interrupted while cleaning up. Not recently, though—the ice in the glass had melted.

Madeleine gestured toward the chairs and divan. "Have a seat. Would you care for anything to drink?"

"No, thank you." Tess settled into an armchair. Madeleine sat facing her.

Tess didn't want to begin the interview directly. It was better to establish a rapport. She asked a few questions and learned that Madeleine was unmarried and unemployed. Her father had been a film producer. "Reginald Grant, perhaps you've heard of him."

Tess hadn't.

"You never saw any of his films? Lucky you, they were all shit. Made money, though. That's all Daddy cared about. He was a moneymaking machine. Drove my mother to an early grave. Then he dropped dead of a heart attack at fifty-five." Her father had left her the house and enough money to be "comfortable," as she put it. "I know I sound like the quintessential rich-bitch Westside cliché, but I like to think I'm a little more complicated than that."

"Everybody is more complicated than that," Tess said.

"I never wanted to be one of those women who devote themselves to other people's charities because they have no interests of their own. Or one of those even less interesting women whose lives revolve around shopping, hostessing, and the beauty salon. Actually I've pursued three different careers in my life. At the moment I'm between things, but some friends and I are in discussions about a retail venture on Melrose. It would require hands-on participation. I'm willing, but I'm not sure they are."

"Well, good luck with that. Now—"

"My point is, I don't lounge around at poolside sipping drinks and chatting on the phone."

"Your personal life is really none of my business." Tess figured there had been enough small talk. "Now, Ms. Grant . . ." She paused, expecting to hear the words, *Call me*

Madeleine. She didn't. "I'm afraid I'm not entirely clear on what happened to you last year."

"I was being stalked."

Tess nodded. "By William Kolb."

"Kolb, yes." She spoke the name with distaste.

"And how did this start?"

"It started when he pulled me over. For running a red light, he said, though I still maintain it was amber."

"You're saying Kolb was a police officer?"

"LAPD, that's correct. He worked out of the West Los Angeles station. He was a patrolman. Six years' experience. He's thirty—no, thirty-one years old."

"So he wrote you a ticket. . . ."

"Which I paid, of course, though under protest, because as I said, the light was amber. It's the only ticket I've received in my life, by the way."

Tess waited.

"I thought, naturally, that the incident was behind me. Didn't think anything more about it. Didn't even connect it with the e-mails at first."

"The e-mails?"

"I started getting them three weeks later. Offensive, suggestive messages. Very personal. Not just junk mail—they were directed specifically at me. Descriptions of my appearance, my home, my car. Familiarity with my daily routine. And . . . sexual innuendo."

"They were anonymous?"

"Of course. I hired someone to trace them for me, and he said they had been sent through an anonymizer, which removed all the . . . What's the term?"

"Routing information."

"Yes. I suppose you have to know these things."

"Believe me, what I don't know about computers fills many books."

"At least you know *something.* The police"—her hands rose and fell in a gesture of futility—"were useless."

"When did you bring in the police?"

"Immediately after the messages started. It was obvious this person was spying on me, following me. He would say he'd seen me at a certain store or on a certain street."

"And the police . . . ?"

"Did nothing. Absolutely nothing. They said if the e-mails were untraceable, there was nothing they could do. I suggested having plainclothes officers place me under surveillance. They might catch sight of whoever was following me. They said they didn't have the resources to do that."

"It must have been frustrating. And frightening."

"No, I wasn't frightened. I was angry. I wanted to tell this person to come out of hiding and show himself. I would have, if I'd been able to reply to his messages, but of course that was impossible, since there was no return address."

"I don't think it would have been advisable, anyway."

"Now *you* sound like the police. Don't antagonize him. Don't provoke him. Just live in fear. I'm not so easily intimidated. I began going through my records to see if I could determine who might be harassing me. When I came to the notation in my checkbook about the traffic ticket, I thought of Officer Kolb."

"Why him, particularly?"

"He'd been rude to me. Hostile. Sarcastic and swaggering. A strutting martinet, all puffed up with authority. When I didn't grovel and cower, he became more offensive. He seemed to take it personally—that he couldn't make me back down."

"Even so, there was no direct link. . . ."

"It was a feeling, that's all. The e-mails began three weeks after the traffic stop. And he looked at my license and registration, so he knew where I lived."

"Not your e-mail address."

"Anybody can obtain that information over the Internet. You know that."

"You're right. But it would have been more direct for him to call you."

"Calls can be traced. Voices can be recognized. He was playing it safe. Or maybe he's just a goddamned coward."

"Did you tell the police your theory?"

"Oh, certainly. Tell the LAPD that one of their own is stalking me. No evidence, just a feeling. Woman's intuition. I'm certain they would have been all over the case. They might have brought in extra officers to assist in the investigation."

Sarcasm. Not Tess's favorite thing. "You could've tried. Police departments do investigate allegations of officer misconduct—"

"Whitewash them, you mean."

"Not always."

"I shouldn't argue with you. You work for the government, so of course you see it their way."

"It's not an us-against-them situation, Ms. Grant."

"Yes, it is," she snapped. She looked away, and Tess saw the swallowing movement of her throat. "In any event," she went on more quietly, "the point is moot. Officer Kolb was caught with incriminating evidence that connected him with me. He was charged with stalking. For some incomprehensible reason they allowed him to plea bargain for a minimal sentence. He was sent away for less than a year. Now he's out."

"Wait, I'm not following this. How was Kolb caught if no one was even looking at him as a suspect?"

"He was caught because of his own stupidity, which is hardly surprising. The man is little more than a shaved ape. Put a gorilla in a uniform, and he could write traffic tickets, too."

"How was he caught?"

"He left the stove on."

"What?"

"The stove, a gas stove. He left one of the burners on after fixing his scrambled eggs or whatever. He went to work, and the gas flame was still on. Typical of the bovine stupidity of his type."

"There was a fire?"

"A minor one. As I understand it, some dishtowels near the stove caught, and the kitchen wall started to smolder. It set off the smoke alarm. Someone heard it and called the fire department. By the time they got there, the whole place was full of smoke. They checked for damage and found . . ."

Tess waited.

"They found the things he was going to use on me. Not that I would've given him the chance."

"What things?"

"Handcuffs. Duct tape. There was a map of this neighborhood with my house circled. Of course, he could've gotten past the security system easily enough. The police around here know how to disarm these systems."

"The map led the police to contact you?" Tess asked.

"Not just the map. He had photos of me—digital photos, so he didn't need to have them developed. The quality wasn't great—it was a cheap camera—but he'd taken hundreds of shots. He'd been following me whenever he was off duty. In his van. That's what he intended to use for transportation after he . . ." She shook her head. "But it wouldn't have gotten that far. I never would've let him take me. In a situation like that, you don't submit. You fight."

"It's hard to fight an armed man," Tess said.

"Not if you're armed also."

"You're saying you own a firearm?"

"I do. I carry it at all times. And I know how to use it. Probably as well as you do, if not better."

Tess thought Madeleine was trying awfully hard to prove how tough she was. She seemed to need to prove herself in many ways. "Kolb pled to the stalking charge," she said. "So there was no trial?"

"No trial. Only a one-year sentence. With good behavior he got out in ten months."

"Did you ever think about relocating?"

"I'm not going to be driven out of my home."

"Have there been any problems since his release? E-mails? Sightings of him?"

"Nothing. And I've been vigilant, believe me."

"But now you think there may be a connection between Kolb and"—*the Rain Man*, she almost said—"the recent kidnappings. A similarity in the wording . . ."

"Of an e-mail he sent me, and the second ransom note. He made the victim write a message, and he left it in her car."

"Yes."

"The note was quoted in today's paper. It may have been made public earlier, I don't know, I haven't been following the news. But when I read it this morning . . . well, there was one part where he said he had trouble managing his disappointment, but he was working on it."

"I remember."

Madeleine got up and retrieved a manila envelope from the mantelpiece. It was filled with sheets of paper. She slipped out the top sheet and handed it to Tess.

"Here's one of the e-mail messages he sent me. The data all went to the police—my floppy disks, even my hard drive. But I kept printouts."

Tess read the message. The key text had been highlighted with a yellow marker: *I'm not so good at handling disappointment. Maybe I need to work on that.*

"I see." Tess glanced at the envelope. "Are those the rest of the e-mails?"

"Yes. You can have them, if you like. Of course, you can get the original data from the police or the district attorney—whoever has it now. Assuming they haven't thrown it all away."

"They should have returned it to you."

"I never wanted it back. Here, take this."

Tess accepted the envelope, slipping the first message inside. "Thank you. So you think Kolb may have gone beyond stalking to actual abductions?"

Madeleine sat down again. Tess noticed that she was perched on the edge of her chair. "He intended to abduct me. Maybe he still does. Who's to say he wasn't stalking those first two women? Now that they're dead, who's to say he won't focus on me next? But, of course, nobody will listen to the rantings of a pampered society woman."

"I'm listening right now."

"Yes. You are." She gave a short nod, as if taking note of this fact. "So were they?"

"Were they what?"

Madeleine spoke slowly, as if to a child. "Being stalked?"

There was nothing in the FBI report that suggested this scenario, but Tess couldn't say that. "I can't go into the details of the case."

"That sounds like a yes to me."

"You shouldn't interpret—"

A wave of her hand. "Never mind, I understand. It's confidential information, not to be shared with civilians. Although I think that where my own personal safety is involved, you might loosen up the rules a little."

"We haven't established that there's a threat to you, Ms. Grant."

"No," she said bitterly, "you'll have to wait until I'm dead to do that."

Tess ignored the remark. "On the phone you told me that Kolb was obsessed with Mobius. How do you know that? Did he mention Mobius in his e-mails?"

"No, never. But in his apartment the police found a scrapbook full of newspaper clippings about the Mobius case. And about you."

Tess felt a chill. "Me?"

"Well, you received a lot of press coverage, as well."

That was true. She'd used the PR to gain clout in the Bureau.

"I'm not saying he was focused on you," Madeleine went on. "Just that he was fascinated by everything pertaining to the case."

"Which is not a crime, obviously."

"No, it isn't. In fact, I think they even had to give back his scrapbook. He's probably still got it."

"Wonderful." Tess didn't like to think of articles about her in the hands of William Kolb. "Well, I think I have all I need from you, Ms. Grant. There's just one thing I'm wondering about. Why didn't you call the police with this information?"

"Why bother? They didn't pay any attention to me before."

"Things might be different now."

"We're still dealing with a cop. They protect their own."

"Kolb can't be a cop after a felony conviction."

"An ex-cop, then. It doesn't matter. Once you're part of the fraternity, you're in it forever."

This answer wasn't good enough. Tess decided to press the point. "Ms. Grant, what aren't you telling me?"

"What do you mean?"

"There's something you're avoiding."

"I'm sure I don't know what you're talking about."

"I'm sure you *do*."

"I called you because I'm trying to assist your investigation. I don't expect to be insulted and mistrusted for my efforts."

"Why did you call me at all? Or the tip line? No matter how you feel about the LAPD, the logical thing would have been to call the police detective who arrested Kolb."

"I did call—" She stopped.

"You called the detective?"

Reluctantly she nodded. "He was less than receptive to my suggestion."

"He didn't believe you?"

"The police never believe anyone. They'd rather give out traffic tickets than solve a serious crime. Do you know I have a neighbor whose home was burglarized while she was in Barbados—ten thousand dollars in losses—and the police wouldn't even dust for fingerprints? No time for that, they say. They're understaffed and underbudgeted, they say."

"So you're saying the detective ignored your tip?"

"He was quite rude about it."

"Why would he behave that way?"

"You'd have to ask him."

"Maybe I will."

"Even if you do, he'll only invent some face-saving excuse. It's what they do."

"And your staff? Where are they?"

"I told you, they have the night off. I didn't know the FBI was hiring people with attention deficit disorder. Or is it short-term memory loss?"

"They didn't have the night off. They made you dinner and were clearing the table a short time ago. When I told you that I was coming over, you hustled them out of the house. Why?"

"I made my own dinner and cleared my own table."

"So if I were to come back tomorrow and interview your servants, that's what they'd say?"

"That's what they'd say."

Tess rose from her chair. "I'm sorry, Ms. Grant. To be honest, I don't think I can help you."

Madeleine stood also, her face draining of color and expression. "What do you mean?"

"I don't feel you've been completely straightforward with me. And unless you're going to tell me the truth, I don't see how I can be of assistance." She handed back the manila envelope.

"You're returning this?" Madeleine said in astonishment.

"I won't need it."

"This is outrageous. You won't do anything?"

"I'm afraid I can't."

"It was a mistake to call you. You're as incompetent as the police—and as rude."

"I'm sorry you feel that way."

"This man could be coming after me. After *me*."

"If he is, you'll need to be more cooperative in order to enlist my assistance. I can't work in the dark."

"I'll speak to your superiors. I'll speak to whoever runs your office here in Los Angeles."

"That should be a pleasant chat." Tess smiled. "You and he may see eye to eye on a lot of things."

"What's that supposed to mean?"

"Good night, Ms. Grant."

"This is outrageous," Madeleine Grant said again as Tess headed for the foyer.

It was a calculated risk, walking away. Tess knew she could probably work through the LAPD if she had to, though it might be hard to get the e-mail messages from them without tipping off Michaelson. And, of course, there was the risk that Madeleine would follow through on her threat to report her to the Bureau. All in all, she would find it safer, easier, to work with Madeleine—but only if the woman stopped playing games.

Just past the threshold, Tess paused and dug a business card out of her coat. She handed it over. "If you decide to tell me everything, not just the sanitized version, let me know."

"Sanitized version? You're a disgrace to your profession."

"So they keep telling me."

Tess walked down the front steps, aware again of being stared at. But this time she had no doubt as to the source of the gaze.

6

Kolb cruised Hollywood Boulevard, surveying the crowds of moviegoers and club crawlers. The phone conversation had unsettled him. When he was restless, he often came here.

His headache was a cloud of pain drifting around his skull, a moving field that traveled with him. He steered his beat-up Oldsmobile through heavy traffic and exhaust fumes. The radio worked, but he never listened to it. He didn't need some talk-show jackass telling him what to think.

This part of the Boulevard was a dirty stretch of shotgun flats—cheap motels and week-by-week lodgings, liquor stores, and adult video shops, and all the social detritus they attracted. With the windows of his car rolled down, he could hear the competing squalls of boom boxes and car radios, the laughter of kids congregating on street corners, the blare of sirens. Although LA had funneled millions into giving the Boulevard a face-lift, much of it remained a festering garbage dump, a dark lump of scar tissue in the heart of the city, as the city itself remained a hungry tumor in the heart of the world. Los Angeles, the new Babylon, the breeding ground of the cancer eating away at civilization.

Above him was the perfect illustration of his point, a lighted billboard promoting the latest Hollywood product, a teen sex comedy. The gigantic image of a nearly naked girl floated against the dark sky. Kolb knew the kind of movie it would be, a joyless thrill ride laced with coarse language and empty titillation, a diversion for pampered children who wanted some meaningless fun in their meaningless lives. Another chunk of offal dumped by this city into the sewage canals of modern culture to pollute a dying nation.

He idled at a red light next to a boosted-up Jeep blaring rap music. Behind the wheel, a kid in sunglasses bopped to the pounding beat.

Who was it who'd said that civilizations were born to war anthems and decayed to waltzes and minuets? Hell, maybe nobody had said it. Maybe he'd made it up himself. Anyway, it wasn't exactly true. There were no waltzes anymore. America was rotting to the sound of ghetto slang rhymed and chanted at top volume.

Tenement noise for a nation of trash. Trash like the punks outside the Safeway and their tattooed whores. They came swarming into this country like termites infesting a half-dead tree, nesting in the dry wood and hastening the rot. He didn't hate them for their skin color, only for the culture they brought with them, the ugly music and stinking food and loud, undisciplined, street-smart attitude. They humped like stray dogs, too. It was as if they were in a constant state of arousal, perpetual heat. Maybe the baggy pants they wore gave their genitals too much room to float around. Or maybe some unconscious survival drive was prodding them to reproduce so prodigiously that they could complete their takeover of the country by sheer numbers.

Decadence. A society in decline. The signs were everywhere, but only a few men had the courage to see.

The attempted rehabilitation of the Boulevard had involved removing the most visible elements from public view. Those would be the hookers, of course. Arrests had been made, sweeps had been carried out, and the upshot was that the girls in microminis had moved a block south to Selma Avenue, where they gathered in the same numbers as always.

Kolb hooked onto Selma and watched the girls give him the bump and grind. Their squawks and howls sounded like the shrieks of beggars in some feculent Third World alley. They were the female principle in distilled form, raw and desperate, and like all women they bore the shadow of something enigmatic and prehuman, some lingering primitivism that found expression in menstrual blood and the damp, secret darkness of the womb.

The whores disgusted him. The thought of putting his cock between their legs, inserting it into a soup of disease . . . He might as well try screwing a test tube full of bacteria.

Even so, he found himself inexplicably slowing the car, easing up to the curb. He leaned toward the open window on the passenger side and smiled at the girl who drew near.

"Want some action, honey?" she asked in a bored voice.

"What'll it cost me?"

"You a cop?"

Not anymore, Kolb thought. "No way."

"For twenty-five I can give you a suction job you won't never forget. You want something more, or different, we can negotiate."

"You clean?"

"What, you mean, like, drug-free or some shit?"

"No, I mean, you have any fucking diseases you're going to give me?"

"You don't get no diseases from a lube job, honey."

That was bullshit. Any flesh-to-flesh contact posed a hazard. "You can get a disease from any goddamn thing."

"I ain't got no disease."

"Sure you don't."

He looked at her in the glow of a streetlight. She couldn't have hit thirty, but her face was already seamed with age. There were blisters on her lips, and her hair was thinning. The dim light and a layer of makeup could not conceal the film of sweat beading her skin. She repulsed him.

"You're a goddamned walking disease," he said, not raising his voice, "only you're too fucking stupid to know it."

She drew back. "Honey, I think we better call this thing off."

"It was never on. You think I would let you touch me, a piece of filth like you?" He felt his lips skin back, baring his teeth. "A piece of fucking *filth!*"

Another of the girls heard him and started yapping in melodramatic outrage, and suddenly the whole crowd of hookers had focused on his car, screeching imprecations, pointing and hip thrusting. Their fury emboldened the whore with the blistered lips.

"Who you think you are?" she yelled. "God's gift?"

Kolb smiled. "That's right, bitch. That's what I am. You have no fucking idea."

He hit the gas and left her and the other whores behind, proud to be feeling nothing, no arousal, no need—nothing but the ache in his forehead, harsher than before.

Kolb headed home, taking a back route to frustrate any possible surveillance. He knew his partner would laugh at him for thinking he might be followed, but hell, he'd been arrested once, hadn't he? Sometimes they really were out to get you.

As he drove, he looked around at the low-income residential streets lined with two-story apartment buildings, 1950s complexes with names like the Sunset Arms and the Hollywood Empress, buildings constructed around swimming pools and courtyards, on landscaped lots thick with date palms, buildings that had once been homes to middle-class families. Now they were hives where the filth of the city congregated, clustering together like roaches in a grease trap, playing their rap music and rutting like animals and breeding when they were fifteen, making more of their kind, crowding out men like him who had no place in the city they were populating. More and more of them every day, fording rivers, crossing deserts, riding into town concealed in the backs of delivery trucks, an ongoing invasion, a march of insects, like that movie he'd seen once, the one about the army of soldier ants that flowed forward in a flood tide, devouring everything in their path.

And no one would stop them. No one would criticize. No one would speak the truth, which was that the pattern of the world had been always that of masters and slaves—the elite to rule, the rest to be used as needed and disposed of when their value was exhausted. Past civilizations had crowned their warrior kings and left the rabble in shackles, but now it was the best of men who were penned up, made into milch cows and sacrificial animals, while the peasants ran free—

A blue van pulled out of a side street and cut him off.

He stomped on the brake and gave the other driver a long blast of his horn. The driver stuck his arm out the window and showed Kolb his middle finger.

Now, that just wasn't nice. Kolb sped up, tailgating the van, his fist working the horn.

The driver of the van decided to act smart. He hit his brakes, trying to force a collision. Kolb swerved to avoid him, and headlights sprayed his face as brakes squealed. Some bitch in a sedan, traveling in the other direction, had nearly hit him head-on when he cut into her lane.

He saw her mouth working behind the windshield, yammering at him for getting in her way.

The van pulled away, but Kolb didn't care. He had transferred his attention to the woman in the sedan.

He reversed down the street at high speed, then shifted into drive and shot forward, aiming his headlights at her car. Light flooded the sedan's interior, and in the sudden brightness he could see the bitch's expression change from hostility to panic. Everything slowed down, time congealing into a thick, clotted mass, and he was able to savor the fear on her face and the kick of adrenaline in his system. He saw her bending over the steering wheel, working the gear selector, finally punching the car into reverse and skidding partly out of his path just as his front end impacted hers.

There was a scream of shredding metal and a shower of

pinwheeling sparks, and for a moment the two vehicles were locked together like two dogs in a fight, his Oldsmobile snarling like a pit bull with its jaws fastened on a rottweiler's throat.

Then her car, still reversing, ripped free and fishtailed across the street, bumping up over a curb and spilling a line of trash cans onto the sidewalk. Her front fender had partially detached and was dragging on the street, her left headlight had gone dark, and it looked like one of the wheels was out of alignment because of some damage to the axle, but she got the car going and sped away.

He glimpsed her as she flashed past him, her head low, shoulders hunched, hands fisted on the steering wheel, a picture of terror, and he laid his palm on the horn and gave her a parting salute.

He thought about following her and maybe doing some more damage, maybe cornering her on a dead-end street and plowing into the car and smashing her against the dashboard and leaving her to bleed to death like roadkill.

No. It wouldn't be smart to do that. Probably hadn't been too smart to get involved in the altercation in the first place.

But what the hell, he'd needed to let off some steam.

And he could bet that some dumb bitch driving in this shitty neighborhood, probably without insurance, maybe without a license, wasn't going to report anything to the police. Even if she did, she hadn't had time to get his tag number or any kind of decent description.

Nobody was going to listen to her, anyway. This was the big city. Serious crimes took place here on a daily basis. Who cared about some bimbo who got her transmission banged up? He'd been a cop. If she'd come to him for help, he would have taken the report just to keep her quiet, and after she was gone, he would have chucked it in the trash. Some people didn't deserve police protection.

He drove away from the scene. The bitch's sedan had gotten the worst of the encounter, but his Olds had sustained some damage. Funny thing, when he'd been revved up in the heat of the moment, it hadn't occurred to him that his car could suffer in the collision. Now it was making a clunking noise, and there was a loose rattling sound coming from under the hood.

What pissed him off was that it wasn't even his fault. What the hell was he supposed to do when she'd dared to honk her horn at him, glare at him, make faces like an ape in a cage?

Of course, it was the scumbag in the van who'd started it by giving him the finger. Maybe if he'd stayed focused on the van driver, gone after him . . .

He shook his head. Wouldn't have made any difference. No matter what price either driver paid, it wouldn't have made him feel better.

They weren't the real problem.

It was McCallum. She was the reason he'd gone driving.

He'd been able to forget about her—almost forget—when she was in Denver, a thousand miles away. Now she was here in LA. She had come to his territory, almost as if she was meant for him. And because there wasn't a goddamn thing he could do about her, he'd lost his composure, and now he had a busted-up car to show for it.

Life sucked sometimes. And to top it all off, his headache was worse than before.

7

Tess was surprised that her hotel room was still available. Because she was checking in at eight fifteen, she'd expected her reservation to be lost, giving her an excuse to relocate. The desk clerk disappointed her with his reliability. The MiraMist had been told to expect a late arrival. At least the room waiting for her wasn't 1625, the crime scene in the Mobius case.

A bellhop escorted her to the seventh floor and reviewed the room's amenities, admitting only when asked that there was a daily eight-dollar charge for opening the minibar, whether or not its contents were consumed. The room was on Michaelson's tab. Tess made a mental note to open the minibar every day.

With the drapes parted to reveal a view of the moonlit ocean beyond the palisades, she unpacked her two carry-ons. One was filled with clothing and toiletries, while the other contained her laptop and various documents from Denver. She carried nothing more personal—no photos of loved ones, no mementoes of her private life. She hadn't had much of a private life in a long time.

She remembered when she'd been new at this, excited to be a genuine agent of the FBI. That was only twelve years ago, but felt longer. Now she was thirty-seven, unmarried. She had given all she had to the Bureau. She had given even the man she loved, Special Agent Paul Voorhees, killed by Mobius in a Denver suburb.

Had it been worth it? She couldn't say. Perhaps she didn't want to make that judgment because she knew what it would be.

Her cell phone rang. It had to be Michaelson, chiding her for walking out on his media spectacle.

Wrong again. The voice on the line was Madeleine Grant's. "Agent McCallum? I've been thinking about what you said."

Tess waited. It seemed unusual for a woman like Madeleine to change her mind so quickly.

"You were right," she went on. "I didn't give you all the information. There were certain matters I wasn't at liberty to discuss."

"At liberty?"

"It will all be explained. And you can have those e-mail messages I wanted to give you."

"All right. If you want me to come back to your place—"

"That won't be necessary. Where are you staying?"

"Santa Monica. Near the ocean."

"There's a coffee shop just a few blocks inland at Pico Boulevard and Tenth Street. The Boiler Room, it's called."

"The Boiler Room?" Tess repeated, certain she'd heard wrong. It hardly sounded like Madeleine's kind of place.

"Can you be there in fifteen minutes?"

Tess said yes and ended the call. Madeleine's sudden turnaround was intriguing, but something about it didn't feel right. And there was that odd phrase of hers—*certain matters I wasn't at liberty to discuss.* Madeleine Grant didn't seem like a person who would be restricted by anyone else's rules.

Tess left the hotel room, taking her cell phone and her gun.

A lighted sign spelling out THE BOILER ROOM in neon italics shone over a striped canopy and a small huddle of vagrants cadging change. Through the front windows, people could be seen sharing booths and sipping milk shakes. From what Tess could tell, nothing about the diner's décor had changed in at least forty years.

She stepped inside, taking a moment to adjust to the glare. The place was done up in white Formica counters, Naugahyde benches, and sleepy ceiling fans. The smell of hamburger hung in the air, reminding her that she'd had no dinner. She'd thought about ordering something from room service or scavenging in the minibar. Now she wouldn't have to.

About half the seats were occupied, a pretty good turnout on a Monday night at this hour. There were scattered couples catching a bite after a movie or a walk on the beach, a few solitary men who looked lonely, a slender kid in a baseball cap working hard on a pinball machine in the corner.

Madeleine Grant wasn't here. Tess wondered if the woman had changed her mind about showing up. Well, she would wait long enough to have a burger, anyway.

She took a seat in a booth away from the windows—an old precaution, not to be seen from the street. She positioned herself with a view of the entrance so Madeleine wouldn't surprise her if she walked in.

She flipped open the menu, skimming the items without interest, since she knew in advance what she was going to have.

A waitress arrived. Tess put down her menu to order. Only it wasn't a waitress, after all, but another customer, a woman Tess didn't know, who slipped into the bench seat opposite her own.

"Um, excuse me?" Tess said.

"You're excused."

Even by Left Coast standards this behavior was peculiar. "What I meant was, that seat is taken."

"Yeah, it is. By me."

"I'm waiting for someone."

"Right. You're waiting for me."

Tess got it. She wasn't meeting Madeleine, after all. Madeleine had sent an emissary.

She studied the woman. Early thirties, medium height. Pale face with high cheekbones and intense hazel eyes. Brown hair cut in a shoulder-length pageboy. She was trim and wiry, humming with fidgety energy, and she wore a bomber jacket, an open-collared denim shirt, and jeans. Her sneakers could be heard knocking together under the table.

Before Tess could break the silence between them, a waitress—a real one this time—appeared. "Soyburger, no fries," her new friend said without consulting the menu. "Ice water, and a side salad, no dressing." She had a low, rather throaty voice, edged with a huskiness that men no doubt found sexy.

Tess ordered automatically. "Hamburger, well-done. Coca-Cola."

"Well-done?" the brown-haired woman said when the waitress had walked away. "Yuck."

"I always order it well done."

"To each her own."

Tess leaned forward. "What's going on?"

"As you've probably gathered, I work for Madeleine. At least I did, a year ago."

"Doing what?"

"We'll get into that in a minute."

"Care to tell me your name?"

"It's no secret. Well, sometimes it is. I'm Abby Sinclair."

"Why didn't Madeleine say anything about you?"

"My clients are asked to keep me out of any conversations with officers of the law."

"Why? What do you do?"

"I'm a private security consultant."

"That's a fairly vague job description."

"Then let me get specific." Abby steepled her hands. "Madeleine was being stalked by a nut. The police didn't do anything. They're overworked, underpaid, yadda yadda. That's where I come in. I do the job the police can't do."

"What job?"

"I stalk the stalkers."

"Come again?"

"I identify them, infiltrate their personal lives, get to be their best friend, and assess their threat potential. If they're a nuisance, I scare them off. If they're something more, I take them down."

"Take them down," Tess echoed.

"I eliminate the threat."

"How?"

"By whatever means are available."

"Are you saying you're some sort of vigilante?"

"Vigilante is an ugly word. I would say that because I'm not part of any official law enforcement agency, I don't consider myself bound by all the restrictions and constraints that might tie the hands of, say, a police officer."

"Or an FBI agent."

"Yes."

"You do realize you're talking to an agent of the FBI?"

"Madeleine told me." Abby smiled. "Not that she had to. I could make you as a fed from a block away."

"How did you sneak up on me, anyhow? I was watching the entrance, and you weren't here when I came in."

"Sure I was. Over there."

Tess looked and saw the pinball machine in the corner. She remembered the kid in the baseball cap. When she glanced back at Abby, the cap was on her head, her hair bunched up underneath.

"The front of the machine is all glass," she said. "I could see the front door reflected in it." She pulled off the cap again, letting her hair fall back to her shoulders.

"Why the subterfuge?"

Abby shrugged. "Why did you choose a seat that lets you scope out the entrance? Habit, right? Well, I have my habits, too. I like to size up who I'm dealing with."

"How could you possibly size me up when all I did was come in and sit down?"

"You did a lot more than that. You panned and scanned

the room. You were edgy. Still are. Your hand keeps drifting toward the right side pocket of your coat, which is obviously where you're carrying your firearm."

"It's not supposed to print against the coat." The special pocket had been sewn in by her tailor and carefully rein-forced, with a matching, weighted pocket on the opposite side to counterbalance the gun.

"It doesn't print," Abby said. "But what else would you be reaching for?"

"I take it you're armed also."

"Snub-nosed Smith and Wesson thirty-eight. You're car-rying a SIG Sauer nine, I bet."

"How'd you know?"

"Standard Bureau issue. The two-two-six?"

"Two-two-eight."

"That's out of production now. Good gun, though."

"I'm glad you approve."

"What do you shoot, Federal Hydra-Shok JHPs?"

"Right."

"I like that ammo. Nice stopping power."

"How would you know? It's sold only to law enforcement agents."

"I have my sources. Guns are a vice of mine. They're sexy, don't you think?"

"I've never found firearms sexy."

"Not even when you're shooting a load of Hydra-Shoks?" Abby showed a lascivious smile. "We're talking rapid ex-pansion and deep, satisfying penetration. I mean, come *on.*"

"Where do you carry your Smith?" Tess asked, trying to change the conversation's focus.

Abby patted her purse. "Right here."

Tess felt a little bit superior. "I used to carry mine in a purse. But it takes longer to draw and fire."

"My purse has a special compartment that allows me to grab the gun without undoing the clasp."

"Even so, it's less secure. Someone could snatch the purse out of your hands."

"The strap's reinforced with wire to prevent a tearaway."
Now Tess was irritated. She could not seem to get the upper hand in this conversation. "It still will take you an extra second to get your finger on the trigger."

"True. But in my line, I can't afford to carry a piece in my coat. Some guy might give me a hug and feel a bulge where there shouldn't be a bulge."

"Do you get hugged often?"

"It could happen. Anyway, we weren't talking about me. We were talking about you. We've established that you checked out your environment, you're tense, you chose a seat with a view of the entrance so you wouldn't be taken by surprise."

"Lot of good it did me," Tess murmured.

"We also know you were expecting Madeleine, and you don't quite trust her."

"What makes you think I don't trust her?"

"Why would you be so edgy otherwise?"

"Maybe I'm just paranoid."

"No. I deal with a lot of paranoid people. Mostly stalkers, but sometimes the victims, too. Or alleged victims. Occasionally you get somebody who's not being stalked at all. They just think they are. They're the hardest ones to handle. They'll never believe they're safe. Anyway, you're not paranoid."

"How can you be sure? You don't know me."

"You're sitting there with your hands on the table. If you were defensive, your arms would be crossed. And you're looking right at me. A paranoid person would avert her gaze."

Tess was suddenly self-conscious. She felt the same way she had when a psycholinguistics consultant had started telling her where she'd grown up just from hearing traces of her Midwestern dialect. "You're big on body language, is that it?"

"It's a major part of what I do."

"I wouldn't want you doing threat assessment based on inferences like that. It's too subjective."

"Everything is subjective."

"The law isn't. And it sounds as if this work of yours is skirting the edges of it."

"In a good cause."

"Then you *are* a vigilante."

"I'm somebody people call when the authorities fail in their responsibility to protect the public."

"How exactly did you protect Madeleine Grant?"

The food came. They were silent until the waitress had departed.

"Chow down," Abby said. "The grub's good here. I wouldn't have ordered that burger well-done, though. Cooks all the juice out of it."

"You're eating a soyburger. What do you know?"

"I eat meat, too. Just not a lot of it. I'm not a fanatic, but you know, gotta watch your diet. Cholesterol, triglycerides, all that stuff."

"Given the nature of your occupation, I would think cholesterol rates pretty low on your list of risk factors." Not to mention, Tess added silently, the fact that Abby seemed to have less than 2 percent body fat on her lean frame.

"Point taken. The truth is, meat slows my reflexes. The effects are marginal, but why compromise my alertness at all? Sometimes it's the only thing that keeps me alive."

Tess wondered if this last remark were just bravado. She didn't think so. Abby didn't seem like the type to boast.

"How's the hamburg?" Abby asked.

"Very good," Tess admitted.

"Told ya."

"But what you haven't told me is exactly what went on with Madeleine Grant."

"Right, the sordid details. She gave you the lowdown on the e-mails, right? Speaking of which, I have them in my car. I'll give them to you when we leave."

"Why didn't you bring them in?"

"If you'd seen me carrying a package, you would've known I wasn't just some kid playing pinball, correct? Besides, I didn't want to get ketchup on 'em."

"All right. The answer to your question is, yes, I know about the e-mails."

"Madeleine suspected that Kolb was sending them. She knew the police wouldn't help, so she got hold of me."

"How?"

"Conventional way—telephone."

"Somehow I doubt you're listed in the Yellow Pages."

"It happens that I'd been of service to one of Madeleine's friends, who discreetly recommended me."

"So Madeleine hired you to . . . what, spy on Kolb?"

"She hired me to determine if Kolb was in fact her harasser, and if not, who was. But we never had to get to the 'if not' part because Kolb was the guy. Her instincts were right. They usually are."

"Madeleine's instincts?"

"Anybody's. That stuff'll kill you, by the way."

Tess realized Abby was referring to the Coca-Cola she was sipping. "Coke?"

"Caffeine. You may think it enhances your alertness, but all it really does is make you jittery."

"Look, you stick to your diet, and I'll stick to mine."

"Just trying to be helpful."

"I honestly don't need your help."

"If that were true, you would've already walked out of here. Anyway, instincts. People could learn a lot just by trusting their feelings. You have a bad vibe about going into a certain restaurant—don't go. Maybe that's the night the baked Alaska is going to set the place on fire. Or maybe you're going to choke on your roast duck."

"Or maybe you're just imagining things."

"Come on. You rely on instincts, too. You've got to."

Tess remembered the impression of being watched at Madeleine's house. The sense of another presence in the storm line, before she saw or heard the vagrant. "Some-times."

"You ever work undercover?"

"A long time ago."

"Heightens the senses, doesn't it?"

Tess couldn't deny it. "I always felt hyperalert."

"Welcome to my world." Abby grinned.

"We seem to keep getting offtrack."

"A conversation with me is a journey, not a destination."

"I'd like to make some progress toward the finish line."

"Fair enough." She surveyed Tess's plate with interest. "You gonna eat those fries?"

"No." Abby snatched a handful. Tess couldn't resist warning, "Careful. They could slow down your metabolism, make you vulnerable to predators at the water hole."

"Even with one or two fries in me, this gazelle can still outrun the lions." Abby popped a french fry in her mouth. "So where was I? Right, Kolb was the guy."

"How did you know?"

"Pillow talk. Guys tell you all kinds of stuff after sex."

Tess hesitated, unsure what to say, and Abby laughed.

"Gotcha. The look on your face—I wish I had a camera."

"Are you saying you did or didn't sleep with Kolb?"

"Bit of the mother superior in you, isn't there?"

"I just want an answer."

"I thought you Catholic girls were cool about sex. That's your rep, anyhow."

"I am cool about it. I mean, I . . ." She wondered how the hell Abby knew she was Catholic. A guess based on her last name, probably. "Did you sleep with Kolb or not?"

"No. That's almost never necessary." Tess noted the word *almost*. It didn't raise her estimation of Abby Sinclair. "Most of these guys are too inhibited for casual sex—at least with me. They might go to a prostitute, but that's business; it's impersonal, a transaction. Anything involving emotional intimacy is scary to them."

"Does that description fit Kolb?"

"To a T. Even the hookers. When I was working the case, I saw him check out the action south of Hollywood Boulevard. He stopped for a knob job—you know, a little lipstick on his dipstick."

"I understood the reference. You said you saw him?"

"Followed him. I'm good at tailing people."

Tess took another swallow of soda. "You seem to be good at everything you do."

"I'm still breathing, aren't I? Anyway, Kolb didn't have to tell me anything. He was careless enough to keep copies of all his e-mails to Madeleine on his computer."

"He allowed you to look in his computer?"

"The word 'allowed' might be overstating it. Let's say I became familiar with his daily routine, which made it possible for me to gain access to information of a private nature without his direct, written consent."

"You broke into his residence?"

"There's that mother superior again."

"Breaking and entering is a felony."

"So is stalking, and nobody was doing diddly-squat about that."

"The end justifies the means?"

"A minor transgression to stop a major injustice. That's what I call a pragmatic trade-off."

"And you get to decide which transgressions are acceptable and which aren't?"

"It goes with the territory."

"That particular territory is located pretty close to the county jail."

Abby arched an eyebrow. "You gonna arrest me, Sheriff? Look, Madeleine was in trouble, and I got her out of it."

Tess let a moment pass. "How exactly did you get her out of it?" she asked finally, already knowing the answer.

"Ah, the scales fall from your eyes. The truth is revealed."

"You set the fire, didn't you?"

"I prefer not to answer on the grounds that it would incriminate the hell out of me."

"You brought the fire department to Kolb's apartment."

Abby said nothing. The smile was gone from her face. She watched Tess as if assessing her reaction to this news.

"You could have burned down the whole building," Tess said after a pause, though they both knew this was not the point.

"Nope. The call to nine-one-one was made very promptly. Actually, before the fire even started. Someone must've had a premonition."

"Weren't you worried about a trace?"

"I believe the call was made from an untraceable cell phone."

"So you called from your cell, set the fire, and left. But before you did any of that, you put the evidence of the planned abduction in plain view where the firemen would see it."

"Maybe Kolb was stupid enough to leave all that stuff sitting around."

"Was he?"

Abby shook her head slowly. Her husky voice dropped to an even lower register. "He's not stupid. Very few of them are."

Tess mentally ran through the menu of felonies that had been committed for the purpose of jailing William Kolb. Breaking and entering, tampering with evidence, arson . . . "You took the law entirely into your own hands."

"I go by my own rules," Abby said.

"Sounds more like *no* rules."

"I got the job done."

"You put a man in prison for a year."

"And prevented him from putting a woman six feet under. He was going to kidnap her. The threat level was high. The risk was immediate. I had to take action."

"All you did was implement a stopgap measure."

"As it turned out, maybe. But there was no guarantee Kolb would survive his time in stir. Lots of times, a cop won't last long in a population of convicts."

"You were hoping he'd be killed?"

Abby shrugged. "It wouldn't have broken my heart."

Cold, Tess thought. This woman was cold.

"You're thinking I'm a cold customer," Abby said. The uncanny accuracy of this statement was unnerving. "Maybe I am. But I prefer to think of myself as practical. I do what has to be done. Anyhow, Kolb is still breathing."

"And he's out—which means Madeleine Grant is no better off than she was before."

"Not necessarily. A lot of times, these guys lose interest in a particular target. They move on to a new obsession."

"Or maybe they don't."

"Madeleine is aware of the risk. But she's not as helpless as she used to be. I taught her a few things."

"Self-defense measures?"

"Nothing fancy. Just enough to get her away from the bad guy—I hope."

"Is that the reason she carries a gun wherever she goes?"

"I may have suggested that."

"Well, there's the solution to all our civic problems. Let everybody be armed and dangerous."

"You're armed. I don't see you handing in your firearm."

"I'm a federal agent."

"That gives you more of a right to self-defense than the civilians who pay your salary?"

Tess looked away, rubbing her forehead. "Oh, my God, I'm not going to get into this." The last thing she needed was a gun-control debate.

"You see, from your point of view, only the licensed experts get to deal with crime. Everyone else should step back and get out of your way. Which would be fine—if you could handle the problem. But you can't. There's too much crime, and there aren't enough cops and *federales* to take more than a nibble out of it. So that opens the door for alternative measures—people like me."

"People like you only make the problem worse," Tess said through tight lips.

"I didn't make Madeleine's problem worse. The system failed her. I didn't."

Tess took a moment to calm down. She had decided she disliked and disapproved of Abby, but she couldn't let her personal feelings dictate the course of the conversation. "And why are you telling me all this?" she asked.

"After Madeleine talked to you, she called me and explained the situation. We agreed we'd better come clean. If Kolb is the Rain Man—"

Tess glanced at her. "How do you know that term?"

"I know some people."

"In the Bureau?"

"In the LAPD. On a personal basis, you understand. One or two of the rank-and-file types who are a little more open-minded about my contribution to crime prevention than their superiors. Word of the Bureau's nickname got around."

"What else do you know about the case?"

"That it's going nowhere fast. No leads, no ideas, and the clock is ticking."

A fair summary, Tess had to admit. "You wouldn't have met me and told me so much unless you had some intention of getting involved."

"That's true."

"What do you want to contribute? A debriefing?" Tess considered the idea. "You may know enough about Kolb to allow us to rule him in or out as a suspect."

"No, I don't. If I knew that much, I would've told you. My feeling is that Madeleine could be right, or she could be wrong. I have to know more. I have to get up close and personal—again."

"Renew your acquaintance with Kolb?"

"Why not? There are lots of ways for two old pals to bump into each other."

"Suppose he knows you helped send him away."

"He never made me as an undercover operative."

"You can't be sure how much he's figured out."

"I can never be sure of anything. It's all subjective, remember? I'm playing the percentages. Odds are, he hasn't got a clue."

"If you're wrong . . ."

"Then I'd better watch my back. But I would, anyway."

Tess looked down at the table. "I don't know. It might be arranged—if we had backup in place, and you were wired . . ."

"No, no, no." Abby had both hands in the air like a cop stopping traffic. "That's not my style. Backup, wires, all that stuff just gets in my way."

"Well, you can't go in solo. The Bureau would never allow it."

"I don't work for the Bureau. I don't work for anybody. I'm freelance. Emphasis on *free*."

"Then what exactly are you proposing?"

"That I reacquaint myself with Kolb, find out what I need to know, and report back to you. We keep it between the two of us, just us girls, our little secret."

"I'm not working with you in any unofficial capacity."

"Why not? It's my butt on the line. You only have to listen to whatever I say. I can find out if Kolb is or isn't your guy, and I can do it faster and more efficiently than anybody else."

"You're talking about a rogue operation."

"Rogue—I like the sound of that."

"This isn't funny," Tess snapped. "And it's not going to happen."

"Give me one good reason. I think we can work well together. I'm the ego; you're the superego. We'll be a team, like Cagney and Lacey, only without the overtones of sexual ambiguity."

"I can't agree to that."

"Okay, feel free to add the overtones, if that's what turns you on."

"You know what I meant."

"What I know is that you're passing up an opportunity to make some major progress. If there's any evidence linking

Kolb to the Rain Man, I'll sniff it out. I'm a regular blood-hound."

"Any evidence you found would be obtained illegally."

"I can arrange for you to find it all over again in whatever legally acceptable way you like."

"There are approximately a thousand things wrong with that answer."

"You're telling me you've never colored outside the lines, not even a little? Not even in the Mobius case?"

"My methods of operation aren't the issue here."

"No, the issue is nabbing a bad man who's killed two women and intends to kill more."

Tess didn't like where this was going. She leaned back in her seat, realizing too late that Abby would read her body language as a signal of discomfort. "What's your interest in this, anyway? Do you expect to be paid?"

"Well, I'm hoping you'll pick up the tab for my soy-burger." She grinned. "Joke."

Tess wasn't smiling. Abby didn't seem to care.

"I'm not in it for the money," she went on. "Kolb is unfinished business. I don't want to leave him that way."

"You could do this on your own, without my participation."

"But I'll have an advantage if I know what you know about the case. My sources in the LAPD can't tell me every-thing. Information is what I need to work this job."

"What kind of information?"

"I need to see the case file."

"You don't know what you're asking for. Even *I* haven't seen the case file yet."

"You haven't?"

For once, Tess had the advantage in the conversation. "The case file is every scrap of information collected by every agent working the investigation, collected in a binder the size of a phone book. Actually, several binders equaling several phone books. In a case like this, there could be five or six volumes by now."

"Not exactly the kind of thing you can smuggle out under your coat. Okay, so if you haven't seen the case file, what *have* you seen?"

"The FBI report," Tess said, then regretted the answer.

"That's the *Reader's Digest* version?"

"It's a summary of the evidence."

"And you've got a copy of this report."

"Yes . . ."

"Care to share?"

"No, I don't. It's a violation—"

"Of policy, procedure, protocol. I'm sure it is. But if I'm going to be effective, I need to see the data."

"I'm sorry. I just can't permit it."

"Sure you can. Once you take the first step down that slippery slope, the rest of the trip is easy." Abby waved off Tess's frown. "Just kidding."

Tess tried to reason her way out of a situation that made her increasingly uncomfortable. "What you're proposing isn't even necessary. With a warrant, the Bureau can toss Kolb's apartment and get any evidence that's in there."

"Who's to say Kolb has anything incriminating in his apartment? He may have learned his lesson from last time. He may have stashed it somewhere else."

"If he has, *you* won't find it, either."

"Oh, yes, I will. That's why they pay me the big bucks."

"You act as if you're better at this than we are."

"It ain't bragging if you can back it up."

Tess shut her eyes. "You're annoying, you know that?"

"Been called worse."

"I'm sure you have."

"The cat's got claws. So what do you say—is it a deal?"

A deal with the devil, Tess thought. "I don't know. I need to think about it."

"Fair enough. Here's my number for when you decide." Abby handed her a business card, blank except for a local phone number. "In the meantime, why don't I give you those e-mails? That is, after you pay for our meal."

"Didn't you tell me you were joking when you said I should cover the tab?"

"All humor has a basis in truth."

Tess put down enough bills to cover the meal and the tip. She left the Boiler Room with Abby, who led her to a red Mazda Miata parked down the street.

"My wheels," Abby said. "You've gotta have a convertible in southern Cal. It's a law, I think."

"Why would the law matter to you?"

"Touché." She retrieved a package from the car and handed it over. "Bedtime reading. Enjoy."

"I don't think I'll be able to work with you, Abby."

"Afraid of what the other sisters will say if word gets around the convent?"

Tess was really getting tired of the nun jokes. "I have principles," she said.

"So do I. Mine are just more elastic than yours." Abby turned serious. "Look, Tess—I appreciate the fact that this is unfamiliar territory for you. To be honest, it's unfamiliar to me, too. I don't go around having a hamburger with a federal agent every day of the week."

"You had a soyburger," Tess corrected.

"Yeah, well, it tasted like hamburger."

"Did it?"

"Not really. The point is, this is new for both of us. And there are risks—for both of us. But there's also a chance to cover a nice solid lead in a red-hot case. If Kolb's not guilty, then no one gets hurt and no one ever has to know about your walk on the wild side. If he's our guy . . . well, we can figure out some way to bring him to the attention of the authorities without getting ourselves in hot water. I've done it before."

"By setting fires."

"I'll come up with something more original this time."

Tess let a long silence pass while she weighed the envelope in her hand as if it represented the decision she'd been called on to make. "I can't give you an answer," she said. "Not yet."

Abby nodded. "Think about it, that's all." She walked around to the driver's side of the Miata. "But think fast. There's rain in the forecast."

Tess stood on the sidewalk and watched the red sports car speed away into the night.

8

It was ten fifteen when Tess got back to the hotel and found Michaelson waiting for her in the lobby by the piano bar.

"I was wondering when you'd show up," Michaelson said as he rose from his seat, abandoning his half-finished martini.

"Been waiting long?"

"Long enough. I came back from City Hall, expecting to find you at the FBI office, but Larkin said you'd left. Which surprised me, given that you have a lot of work to do on a tight deadline."

"I'm coming in early tomorrow. You'll have my report in plenty of time for the supervisors' meeting."

"Well, that's very reassuring. I shouldn't have doubted your work ethic. Then again, I wouldn't have thought it was necessary to doubt your loyalty to the Bureau, yet you managed to disappoint me with your behavior downtown. If you were trying to make me a look like a fool—"

"I wasn't."

He ignored her. "Since you'd already checked in, I assumed you would be in your room. Care to tell me where you went?"

"A diner. Had a burger. Want to smell my breath?"

He scowled at her. His gaze strayed to the manila envelope in her hand. "What's that?"

She could hardly tell him that it contained evidence pertaining to a secret STORMKIL lead. "Reading matter from Denver." She offered it to him. "We did this wiretap that picked up some extraneous—"

He brushed off the envelope. "Spare me."

It was surprising, really, how easy it was to lie to Michaelson. She thought she should do it more often. "Anyway, you wanted to see me?"

"Goddamned right I did."

"You could have called my cell."

"There are some conversations that need to take place face-to-face. I am not pleased with you, McCallum. You hung me out to dry, and if I hadn't been quick on my feet, I could've been humiliated in front of the entire Los Angeles media corps."

"Quick on your feet? You told them my plane was delayed. Not exactly a high-water mark of creative fiction."

"It was sufficient to salvage the situation, and to save the Bureau from embarrassment."

"To save yourself, you mean."

"Inasmuch as I represent the Bureau, I would say it's a distinction without a difference."

Tess shrugged. "That's one way to look at it."

"If you recall, I made it clear at the conclusion of the Mobius case that I never wanted to work with you again."

"If *you* recall, I made it equally clear that the feeling was mutual."

"And yet here you are. I would think you'd want to make the best of a bad situation."

"I would think you'd want to use me as something more than window dressing."

"You see, that's your problem, McCallum. You don't understand that there is a chain of command here, and I am at the top. You don't question me, you don't confront me, you don't disobey me. You do what you're told. You keep your head down and your mouth shut, and you play the game like a good little girl, and before long you get to go back to your little fiefdom in Colorado, which you can run any way you like. That's your turf. This is mine. Have you got that?"

"Like a good little girl?" Tess echoed. She hadn't made it past that part.

"I asked if you understand what I'm saying, or do I need to make myself still more explicit?"

She sighed. "Yes, Richard, I've got it. I hear you loud and clear."

"If I were you, I would lose the attitude."

"You don't like a little sass in your underlings?"

"I do not."

"Why am I not surprised?"

Michaelson started to walk away, then turned to face her again. "You know, it wasn't my call to bring you in. I argued against it. The decision was made in DC. They thought it would be a good idea, public relations–wise. I warned them you wouldn't play along. I told them you're not a team player, and you're overrated, to boot. That Mobius thing—anybody could've broken that case. You just happened to be in the right place at the right time."

"You were in the same place at the same time. How come you didn't clear the case?"

"Maybe I was too busy trying to clean up the messes you made along the way."

"Yes, that must've been it."

"I want that report on my desk by eight A.M. Not nine. Eight, and not a minute later, or your ass is on a plane back to Denver."

He stalked off, and she looked after him, wondering if that was supposed to be a threat, when all she wanted to do was get the hell out of this town.

But no, that wasn't true anymore. If she left, she wouldn't get to run down the lead provided by Madeleine Grant.

She took the elevator to the seventh floor. In her room, seated at a desk, she took out the e-mails. They were arranged in chronological order. Each one had a heading that read: *This message did not originate from the address above. It was remailed by an anonymous remailing service.* Below the heading was the text of the first message.

To Miss Madeleine Grant, Bel Air bitch—
What you need is to get fucked hard up the ass.
Tone down the attitude. Learn some respect.

Tess noted the reference to "attitude"—the same word Michaelson had used. The recognition sent a brief chill along her backbone.

Similar notes followed, several each day. After a week they became more specific.

Maddie,
Saw you on Rodeo today. Hope you bought yourself a nice pair of shoes. Shouldn't have stopped for that gelato. You don't want to start putting on the pounds.

So he'd been following her by then—and he'd wanted her to know it.

She flipped through the subsequent messages. By the third week, the threat was unambiguous.

M.G.,
Here's how it will happen. You're asleep in your bed when I zap you with a stun gun. I put you in my vehicle and we take a ride. You're cuffed and your mouth is taped shut and your ankles are taped together. I know a place in the hills where they'll never find your body.

Tess remembered Madeleine saying that handcuffs and tape had been found in Kolb's apartment. She hadn't mentioned a stun gun. Still, it seemed Kolb had been close to carrying out his plan.

The Rain Man cuffed his victims, too. And sealed their

mouths with duct tape, and transported them in his vehicle, and left them in a place where the bodies, under normal circumstances, might never be found.

The following e-mail was the one that had prompted Madeleine to call the tip line. Kolb's words weren't exactly those used in Angela Morris's note, but they were close.

Three more e-mails followed, all sent on the same day. Then the messages ended, without resolution. But of course there had been a resolution. Kolb had been arrested.

Arrested—thanks to Abby.

Tess didn't trust that woman. She didn't trust anybody who would put herself outside the law, make herself judge and jury.

It was true that she herself hadn't always played by the book. As a field agent, she'd sometimes arranged end runs around bureaucratic obstacles. She'd avoided filing some paperwork or having some decisions vetted. She'd gotten a reputation as a maverick.

But her rebellion, if that was what it was, had been within narrow parameters. She had always been conscious of carrying a badge and acting in an official capacity. And now that she had risen to the post of SAC, she would severely discipline any agent who got involved with a freelancer using vigilante methods.

Still, while Tess might not like Abby's approach, she had to admit she didn't like having Kolb running around loose, either. He'd been insanely fixated on a woman he'd known only as a driver in a traffic stop. He'd explained his plans to kidnap her, and acquired most of the necessary accessories for the job. If Abby hadn't stopped him, Madeleine Grant would be dead now.

"And if he is the Rain Man," she murmured, "and I don't follow up . . ."

She couldn't take the chance. She had to look into Kolb. And having burned her bridges with Michaelson, she had to do it through unofficial channels.

Well, it didn't get any more unofficial then Abby Sinclair.

She picked up her cell phone, not wanting to make the call from the hotel phone and leave a record for Michaelson. Already she was thinking like a lawbreaker. *Leave no paper trail, cover your tracks.*

She dialed the number on Abby's business card. The phone was answered on the second ring.

"Yo." Abby's voice.

"All right, we've got a deal."

"Of course we do."

"You were so sure I'd say yes?"

"I know how to read people. Anyway, it only makes sense. Now I need to see the report."

"You can see it, but you can't have it. I'm not letting it out of my possession."

"Fair enough. Where are you staying?"

"You're not coming here. I don't want to be seen with you."

"Like you're under surveillance or something?" Her tone was humorous.

"I'm not taking any chances." But of course she was—a big chance, just getting involved with Abby. "I can meet you at the Boiler Room again."

"You don't think it'll seem a little odd if we go there twice in one night?"

Tess realized she wasn't very good at this sort of thing—sneaking around, keeping to the shadows. "What do you suggest?"

"Santa Monica Pier. Twenty minutes. I'll meet you by the carousel. I'll wear a white carnation so you'll know it's me."

"That's funny. Really."

"Yeah, I'm a hoot."

"I'll be there in twenty."

"Okeydoke, artichoke." Click, and the call was over.

9

Tess parked on the Santa Monica Pier, finding a space without difficulty. It was nearly midnight, and the pier was occupied only by a strolling couple, a band of kids in absurdly loose-fitting pants, and the usual vagabonds. The rides were closed, the roller coaster and Ferris wheel looming in skeletal silhouette against a moon-streaked sky. A breeze gusted off the ocean, chilly and damp, making Tess glad she was wearing her trench coat.

Near the pier's entrance she found the carousel building, a turn-of-the-century pavilion in a faux Moorish-Byzantine style. High, mullioned windows looked in on the carved, gaily painted horses. The doors were locked, the lights out.

"Good place to meet, huh? No prying eyes."

Tess turned to face Abby, who'd somehow managed to come up behind her without a sound. "I wish you'd stop taking me by surprise."

"You'll get used to it." Abby noticed the folder in Tess's hand. "I assume that's the goods."

"Yes." Tess didn't hand over the folder just yet. "There's a question I forgot to ask before. Why wouldn't the police listen to Madeleine?"

"Like I told you, they're overworked, underpaid—"

"I don't mean last year. Madeleine said she called the police detective who put Kolb away and gave him the tip about the Rain Man. And the cop wasn't interested. Why not?"

Abby shrugged. "You got me."

"It doesn't make sense. It's a strong enough lead to be worth following up, but apparently they just gave her the brush-off."

"The LAPD works in mysterious ways. That's all I can tell you. Now, am I going to get my hands on those top-secret documents or not?"

With a last twinge of reluctance, Tess surrendered the report.

Abby hooked a penlight to the front pocket of her leather jacket, keeping both hands free to flip through the document. The pencil-thin beam wavered on the Xeroxed pages.

Tess turned away. She looked through the rippled glass of the pavilion windows and watched the pale blur of the horses. In the dimness they looked unreal—ghost horses, frozen phantoms on parade.

"This place looks familiar somehow," Tess said.

Abby glanced up from her reading. "It was in *The Sting*."

"I never saw *The Sting*. I think I saw the sequel."

"You never saw the original *Sting*, but you saw the sequel? The one with Mac Davis and Jackie Gleason?"

"I think so."

"That's like saying you've never seen *The Godfather*, but you've seen *Godfather Three*."

"I've never seen any of the *Godfather* films."

Abby stared at her. "Well, that's just bizarre."

"I don't like movies much."

"Then you're in the wrong town."

Tess sighed. "Don't I know it."

Abby went back to reading. "Hmmm. Carpet fibers found in Angela Morris's car. Short nap, burnt orange. They aren't hers, so they could be his. That's useful to know."

"Useful because you're going to check Kolb's carpet when you break into his residence?"

"That's the idea." Abby turned a page. "Interesting how he gets paid, isn't it?"

"How so?"

"Let's say you're going to kidnap someone for ransom. The obvious thing is to snatch a wealthy victim. No shortage of high earners in this town. You stake out a mansion in Beverly Hills, grab the hausfrau, then demand payment from her husband. But our guy doesn't do that."

"No. He doesn't."

"He snatches two relatively low-income victims. He doesn't care about their personal assets, if any. His ransom demands are submitted to the city. He wants the municipal government to pay."

Tess nodded. "It could be an antigovernment thing. We've been working that angle."

"With no results, I take it. What other angles are you looking at?"

"Links between the victims. Somebody who would have known them both."

"That'll never pan out. The guy we're after isn't settling scores with ex-girlfriends. He's playing a different game."

Tess was inclined to agree. "And he'll keep playing."

"Sure, why wouldn't he? He's already two million dollars ahead. Anyway, it'll be instructive to see if Kolb has turned antigovernment."

"He wasn't before?"

"Before, he *was* the government. A cop, an authority figure with a badge—like you. Now things might be different. He probably feels the government screwed him."

"Because they wouldn't let him kidnap and kill a woman?"

"I'm just telling you how he may see it. Getting inside his head a little. Now this is interesting."

Tess realized that Abby had kept reading throughout the conversation. "What is?"

"The bank accounts in the Cayman Islands."

"Does that matter?"

"It gives me something else to look for—records of Kolb traveling to the Caymans. Or, more likely, some correspondence between him and a bank there. That would be the easier way to set up the accounts. These days you can handle it all by mail. But no matter how you do it, it's not cheap. Two or three grand, minimum. That's the standard fee, and it's charged for each and every account you set up. If Kolb has multiple accounts, he spent some serious cash, and he did it before he'd gotten any ransom money."

"I take it Kolb isn't wealthy."

"No one gets wealthy on a cop's salary except crooked cops. And Kolb wasn't crooked. Besides, I'd bet he used all his liquid assets to pay for his legal counsel. So where'd he get the bucks to set up the accounts?"

Tess shrugged. "Maybe he didn't. Maybe he's not the one we're after."

"Or if he is, he could've pulled some small-time job to get his seed money. Knocked over a minimart or something. Or . . ."

"Yes?"

"Never mind. Passing thought." Abby flipped through the pages. "Here's another tidbit. The Rain Man left Paula Weissman's note on the dashboard of her illegally parked car. He took the plates off, too."

Tess saw what she was aiming at. "He knew that if the car had no tags, a cop writing a ticket would have to look at the vehicle identification number on the dash. That's how he could be sure the note would be seen. So the Rain Man might be a cop."

"Or an ex-cop. Like Mr. William Kolb. I assume you guys tumbled to that."

"I, uh, I think the inference was that he took off the plates just to call attention to the vehicle, make sure it would be ticketed."

"Oh."

Tess was feeling a little stupid all of a sudden. She tried

to rectify the situation. "He uses handcuffs to secure his victims in the storm lines—another possible cop link."

Abby was unimpressed. "Sure, that's obvious."

Miffed, Tess pursued the point. "Didn't Kolb have handcuffs in his apartment?"

"Yeah. And duct tape. And lookie here, the Rain Man's vics get their mouths sealed with duct tape. Kolb mentioned a stun gun in his e-mail. Any burn marks on the two women?"

"None on Paula Weissman. The autopsy results on Angela Morris haven't come in yet."

"Oh, yeah, here's Weissman's postmortem. No taunting wounds. No antemortem injuries except abrasions on her wrist from the handcuff . . ."

Tess wasn't ready to change the subject. "Why did you ask about the stun gun? You didn't find one in Kolb's apartment, as I recall."

"No, I didn't . . . but maybe Kolb just hadn't acquired that particular accessory yet. According to this, Weissman wasn't raped. I take it you don't know about Morris yet."

"There was no obvious evidence of it."

"If it's Kolb, I wouldn't expect him to commit rape. He's not the type."

"He was planning to rape Madeleine," Tess objected.

"No, he wasn't."

This time Tess was sure she'd caught Abby in a mistake. "In several of the e-mails he made specific references—"

"Sure, sure, I know. But that was all bluster. Remember when he laid out his game plan? He said Madeleine's ankles would be taped together. He even had the tape to do it. Pretty tough to rape a woman when you've trussed her legs shut."

"Unless we're talking about . . . anal abuse."

Abby chuckled. "Nice euphemism. I need to remember that one."

Tess simmered.

"Anyway," Abby went on, "there wouldn't have been any

abuse, anal or otherwise. It's not in character for him. He's a dick, but he doesn't *think* with his dick. Which actually puts him a cut above a lot of guys I know."

"You're a fairly cynical person, aren't you?"

"You noticed?"

"Have you always been so . . ."

"Delightfully insouciant? Nope. I was once all earnest and Girl Scoutish like you. Events have a way of changing a person."

"What events?"

Abby lifted her gaze from the report. "Betrayal. You know the saying: Keep your friends close and your enemies closer. But when your friends turn out to be your enemies, what are you supposed to do then?"

"You tell me."

"Keep everybody at a distance. Trust nobody. That's my solution."

"Doesn't sound like much of a solution to me."

"Well, it's kept me alive so far." Abby smiled, but there was sadness in it. "Our line of work isn't exactly conducive to trust. Haven't you ever been betrayed by someone you believed in?"

Tess couldn't deny her an honest answer. "Yes."

"Then you know the score."

"I guess I do. But maybe I've handled it better than you."

"Maybe you should run self-help seminars. There's big money in them." Abby returned her attention to the report.

So much for the heart-to-heart. Tess got back to business. "So Kolb talked rape, but didn't plan on doing it."

"Right."

"Why is that?"

"He's a control freak. Can't allow himself to be driven by lust or any physical need. Always has to be in control of his body."

"And the Rain Man . . ."

"Is a control freak too. He scripts the drama, stage-manages the situation. Plays with the authorities, yanks their chain, makes 'em dance." Abby shut the folder and handed it back. "All done."

Tess tucked it under her arm. "Speed-reader."

"Salutatorian at Sierra Canyon High."

"Not valedictorian?" As digs went, this one was pretty weak, but it was the best Tess could manage.

Abby shook her head. "Amy Malkovic beat me out by a tenth of a point on her GPA. Little snot. She never would've aced Trigonometry if she hadn't bribed the teacher with cupcakes. I just saw a story on her in the alumni newsletter. She's married to a chiropractor, drowning in rugrats, weighs more than a sumo wrestler. Revenge is sweet."

"You sure you don't envy her?"

Abby tilted her head quizzically. "What would I be envying, exactly?"

"Home, family, children. A normal life."

"I'd go crazy living that way. Wouldn't you?"

"I don't know."

"Ever been hitched?"

"No."

Abby watched her. "But you were close."

"How'd you know?"

"Saw it in your eyes. It ended badly."

"Yes."

"He cheated?"

"He died." Tess's voice was low.

Abby put a hand on Tess's arm. "Sorry. I didn't . . ."

"You didn't know?" Tess almost smiled. "I guess there are some secrets you can't read from body language. How about you?"

"How about me, what?"

"Have you ever been married?"

"Not even close."

"No serious relationships?"

"I don't necessarily make the best choices in that department. But who does?" She saw Tess's face and added, "Oh. You do. Or you did—with him."

"He was a good man."

An uncomfortable silence stretched between them. Abby broke it by clapping her hands in a businesslike fashion.

"Well, what we're interested in right now is a bad man— Mr. William Kolb. Thanks a mil for the sneak peek."

"Was it worth it? Did you learn anything helpful?"

"Bits and pieces. Some possible connections between Kolb and the Rain Man—duct tape on the victims' mouths, handcuffs, the way he covered the dashboard VIN with the ransom note. Then there's stuff for me to look for—the carpet fibers, a Caymans connection. None of that is the main thing, though."

"Then what is?"

"Nothing in here rules Kolb out. See, that was a possibility. There might be some detail that'd tell me I'm wasting my time looking at him."

"You don't think I would've caught a detail like that?"

"When you read the report, you weren't looking for it. Besides, you don't know Kolb. I do. Let's say the postmortem on Paula Weissman had turned up taunting wounds—you know, nonfatal knife sticks. That would eliminate Kolb right there."

"He's not a sadist?"

"No—or at least, not that way. He could lose his cool, beat the hell out of somebody in a state of rage, but he wouldn't go in for torture. It's not the way his mind works. Same with rape, as we discussed. Or if the Rain Man was sending private messages to the police or the Bureau, then I'd know Kolb's not our guy."

"Why not? He sent messages to Madeleine."

"You've answered your own question. He made that mistake before."

"Offenders frequently repeat their mistakes."

"Not Kolb."

"He's smart, then?"

"Street-smart. His IQ is probably nothing special—ten, maybe twenty points above average. But there are skills an IQ test can't measure. And there's one other thing that could've ruled him out. The Rain Man's attitude toward women."

"I'd say it's a pretty damn negative attitude."

"Obviously. But negative how? Anger—or contempt? See, anger is always based on fear. A guy is afraid of women, so he strikes out at them. That's not Kolb. And it's not the Rain Man, either. He doesn't brutalize his victims. He doesn't fixate on them."

"Kolb fixated on Madeleine."

"Madeleine pissed him off in a specific context—the traffic stop. That made it personal. Grabbing these women more or less at random—it's business. If Kolb's doing it, he's not exorcising any demons. He's just doing a job."

"Dumping them in the storm sewers . . ."

"Exactly. *Dumping* them—like garbage."

"Which is all they are to him." Tess remembered making the same point to Crandall at the river.

Abby nodded. "And you don't hate garbage. It's just something to be gotten rid of. That's how Kolb would see it. And it looks like that's how the Rain Man sees it, too."

"You're drawing a lot of inferences from a pretty slender database."

"I go with my gut. It hasn't failed me—at least not often."

"Okay . . . So when are you going to start?"

"First thing tomorrow."

"How?"

"A little meet-and-greet. I'll run into Kolb and renew old ties."

"Any idea how you'll accomplish that?"

"Don't worry about strategy and tactics. I can handle that end. I'm a pro."

"I don't want you taking any unnecessary risks."

"My whole job consists of unnecessary risks." Abby grinned. "That's what makes it fun."

"Take care, anyway."

"Always do. Night, Tess. And, hey—don't lose any sleep over this, okay? Whatever happens, your fingerprints won't be on it. You'll be clean. I guarantee it."

She walked away. Tess thought Abby might be right—but at the moment she didn't feel clean.

10

Abby caught five hours' sleep and woke to her alarm clock at five thirty A.M. She spent twenty minutes on tai chi exercises, then fixed a fruit smoothie in her blender. After showering, she donned a sensible ensemble of skirt and jacket, the sort of outfit an office worker would wear. An office worker—or Tess McCallum, maybe.

It had been a gamble, meeting Tess. But what the heck, everything in life was a gamble. She hadn't placed too many bad bets so far, and even her mistakes hadn't proven fatal.

Still, she was a little disappointed in Tess. She didn't know exactly what she'd hoped for. Or maybe she did, and just didn't want to admit it. Her job had plenty of perks, but it did get lonely sometimes, and it would be nice to find someone to shoot the breeze with, someone who understood. . . .

She shook her head, dismissing the thought. Tess McCallum was no soul mate. She was uptight in a major way, even more so than might be expected in a *federale*. The whole dance they'd gone through, with Tess taking time to think it over and make her decision, had been a big joke. There never had been any decision to make. Of course Tess was going to go along. Anybody would. Anybody with brains, and from what Abby knew of the Mobius case, Tess was smarter than the average Eliot Ness wannabe. She'd saved the elites of the city, and done it alone.

Abby ran through a mental checklist. Gun in her purse, fully loaded. Cell phone, fully charged. ID in her wallet in the name of Abby Hollister, one of her several false identities, and the one she'd used when she met Kolb last year.

She was ready. She felt the familiar excitement of knowing the scoreboard was at zero and the game was about to begin.

None of this was new to her. She'd been doing this job a long time.

For the first two years of her career, she'd worked as a consultant to assorted private security firms across the country. Then the Kris Barwood case had come along, changing her life and nearly ending it. Afterward, she'd broken off her connections with the security outfits and relied on word-of-mouth recommendations to acquire new jobs. Luckily for her, nearly all of her clients were happy with her work, and it was surprising how many of them had a friend, relative, or colleague who needed similar services.

If anything, her workload had increased. In a good year she might handle fifteen cases. Over the seven years of her career, she had worked more than eighty jobs. She used to keep count. She didn't anymore. It seemed like bad luck.

She made a good living, pulling in more money than she could spend. She had no complaints. Her only worry was what she would do when she got too old to do the work. Stalking stalkers was a young person's racket. Her reflexes and her sharpness would decline over time.

But she was thirty-three, and obsolescence was a long way off—at least a hundred more cases, she estimated. A hundred opportunities to get herself killed.

She locked the door of her one-bedroom condo and rode the elevator to the underground garage. Her building, in pricey Westwood, offered its residents impeccable taste and impenetrable security, a combination that more than justified her outrageous mortgage payments.

At the garage level she got off and walked right past her Miata, a car that was too flashy for undercover work. For years she'd used an ancient secondhand Dodge Colt until it finally broke down. Now she had an almost equally decrepit Honda Civic, a ten-year-old hatchback that had logged 110,000 miles, along the way acquiring a dent in the side panel, rips in the upholstery, and a broken latch on the glove box. She'd bought the car for twelve hundred bucks and then had the engine substantially rebuilt, ensuring that the Civic wouldn't fail her if she needed to make a quick getaway. Just because it looked like a piece of junk didn't mean it had to perform that way.

The Civic had an additional advantage over her Mazda. It was registered to Abby Hollister, not Abby Sinclair, at the address she used as a blind. If anyone ran the tags, it was the Hollister alias that would come back, while her real name and address would never show up. Her life was a set of Chinese boxes, and she didn't want anyone looking too deep inside.

She kept the Civic out of sight in a corner of the garage, paying an extra two hundred dollars a month for the space. The other residents, if they ever noticed the car, no doubt assumed that it belonged to a janitor on the building staff or to someone's private housekeeper.

Abby drove out of the garage as the sun was rising and hooked onto Wilshire Boulevard, eastbound. Her route took her through Beverly Hills, past Park La Brea and Hancock Park, and then into Koreatown, one of her favorite neighborhoods. Koreatown was nothing special during the day, but at night it was Disneyland, Vegas, and Rio all rolled into one. She often cruised the Asian clubs, frequently the only Caucasian in attendance, and it was like jetting off to the other side of the world. How many American cities offered this kind of ambience?

That was why she loved this town, the crazy energy of it, the mad mélange of different cultures and languages served up in a big tossed salad of ethnic neighborhoods. Some people, frowning, compared LA to a science-fiction dystopia. "It's turning into *Blade Runner* here," they'd say. Abby didn't care. She'd seen *Blade Runner* four times. She thought it was cool.

The streets of Koreatown were quiet now, in the pink dawn, and there was no fun to be had—only a rendezvous with William Kolb.

Kolb's previous address had been a rented two-bedroom in Mar Vista; he'd given up the apartment during his incarceration. Once released, he'd set up residence in a less-than-desirable area of the mid-Wilshire district, a fact she'd learned via an Internet service that provided unlisted addresses and other personal information for a fee.

The same service had informed her that Kolb owned a 1992 Oldsmobile Ciera, a used car he'd bought in November. When he'd been a cop, he'd driven a new Ford Crown Victoria, the kind of heavy, rear-wheel-drive vehicle that cops preferred, but he must have sold it to cover court costs.

She'd also learned his present employment—security guard at a supermarket. She knew this not from the Internet service, but from discreetly tailing Kolb two mornings in a row. That, of course, was a couple of days before she'd gotten the phone call from Madeleine Grant or met Tess McCallum.

It had been prudent to let them both think she'd been pulled back into the case last night. The truth was, she'd identified Kolb as a possible suspect on Saturday night, the night of Paula Weissman's kidnapping, when one of her cop contacts quoted her the text of Paula's ransom note. That night she'd obtained Kolb's address. On Sunday morning and again on Monday, she'd staked out his building. Each day he'd driven to the offices of the security firm and emerged wearing a guard's uniform, which he must keep in a locker on the premises. From there he drove to the supermarket, where his shift started at eight A.M. His working hours were probably eight to four thirty, assuming a half hour for lunch. She hadn't checked back to follow him after work on either day. There had been no rain in the forecast, and so she'd had no reason to worry about his after-hours activities.

Tonight there would be rain. If Kolb was the Rain Man, he would make his move.

Logically, if he'd already netted two mil from the Weissman case, he had no good reason to continue busting his hump on guard duty. But Abby figured he would hold on to the job simply to avoid any suspicious alteration of his routine. He was smart enough to think that way. Paranoid enough, too.

She was counting on his paranoia this morning. Paranoid people were acutely aware of their surroundings. That went double for paranoid cops—or ex-cops—whose street time left them hyperobservant. She wanted him to be looking around as he drove down Eighth Street, where, just after seven o'clock, she parked at the curb outside one of the area's countless *zapaterías*—shoe stores, to the uninitiated.

This particular section of Koreatown was less exotic than the main drag. Here were no cybercafés, no patio eateries, no hot nightspots, no high-priced acupuncture clinics. Instead she was surrounded by dollar discount stores, karaoke clubs, and massage parlors. Graffiti posted by the two competing local gangs, the Playboys and the Mara Salvatrucha, defaced walls and storefronts. A crowd of undocumented aliens gathered across the street hoping to be hired for a day's work.

Not a scenic neighborhood, but convenient for her purposes. The security firm was located at the corner of Eighth and Hoover. Although Kolb had varied his route both times she'd followed him, he'd always ended up on this stretch of road. If her timing was right, he would be here soon.

She killed the engine, got out of the car, and popped the hood. With a pair of pliers she disconnected one of the battery cables, letting it dangle. She hid the pliers in her purse and leaned over the engine, careful to keep her face in plain view while letting her body language communicate helplessness and frustration.

The next minute or so was the tricky part of the plan. Her worst fear was not that Kolb wouldn't stop to help her. It was that some other good Samaritan would stop first.

An unfounded fear. This was LA. Nobody stopped.

Then she spotted Kolb's Oldsmobile, coming this way.

The car, which had been in decent shape yesterday, clanked and sputtered now, with visible damage to the front end. She wondered if Kolb had caused the accident. Aggressive driving was consistent with his personality type.

She expected his attention to be drawn to the car with the open hood. And she expected him to recognize her. He would never offer assistance to a stranger, but to a woman he'd met, he might prove more gallant.

The Olds pulled past without slowing. She didn't dare follow it with her gaze. She began to think she'd overestimated either his chivalry or his perceptiveness.

Then she heard the car pull to a stop at the curb a few yards away.

Now it was all a matter of playing her part. She'd worked out the approach she intended to use. She only hoped he would go for it.

Her earlier relationship with Kolb had been extremely short-lived. She'd worked the case for only a few days, and had met Kolb exactly once. On a day when he was off-duty, she'd started a conversation with him at a produce market where he was stocking up on veggies. Like her, he was something of a health fanatic. This mutual interest had given them something to talk about. When he mentioned being a cop, she allowed him to think she was mightily impressed. She'd never known a cop, she said. It must be interesting work. And dangerous.

This, naturally, had prompted him to tell a couple of his favorite war stories from the field. By the time he finished recounting his adventures, they had left the market and were eating lunch at a Thai restaurant. When he got around to asking her about herself, she gave him a spiel about her boring job, which left no time for a social life. She hadn't been required to go into detail. He wasn't interested in her, except as a mirror reflecting his own self-image. He yakked about life on the streets, the perils of patrol work, the drug dealers and psychos, and she listened and nodded, oohed and aahed. Most likely this was the nature of his relationship with all women. Probably it explained why he was still single.

She learned enough from their initial encounter to make a preliminary assessment of the threat he posed, which she'd dictated into the microcassette recorder she carried in her purse. "Narcissistic, egocentric, arrested development, latent hostility, manipulative, needs to exercise power over others. Likely candidate for Madeleine Grant's stalker. But unable to confirm without physical evidence."

Physical evidence was obtained when she slipped into Kolb's apartment while he was at work. After their one meeting she'd given him her phone number—a number that, like her Civic, was registered in the name of Abby Hollister. He hadn't called, but he'd been a little busy, having been arrested and all.

Although he'd met her just once and hadn't seen her in a year, she'd been pretty sure he would remember her, partly because he probably didn't talk to a lot of women, and partly because she was just so darn memorable.

"Hello, stranger," Kolb said with a slow smile as he walked toward her car.

Up close, he was bigger than she remembered—more muscular, prison-buffed—and there was a tinge of gray in his crew-cut hair. He moved with an unconscious swagger, a type of body movement known as a broadside display because the side-to-side swing filled up an unusual amount of personal space. It was a combative, somewhat aggressive posture—body language not normally exhibited when a man was greeting a woman.

"Oh . . . hi." She gave a good imitation of someone who was both startled and a little nervous. The act was tricky. She had to pretend to show fear and also pretend to be hiding it.

"Engine trouble?" Kolb asked.

"It just conked out on me. I had to coast over to the curb." As she spoke, she let her gaze travel along his body, scanning him for weapons. She saw no telltale bulges, but his long-sleeved, loose-fitting shirt could conceal a knife strapped to his arm or a gun wedged into his waistband.

Kolb bent over the engine and smiled. "Yeah, well, a car won't run if the battery's not hooked up." He reattached the cable, hand-tightening the bolt. She noticed he didn't need pliers. His hands were strong. "Try it now."

She slipped behind the wheel and revved the engine, then got out of the car with a sheepish expression. "You're a miracle worker."

"As miracles go, that one was pretty bush-league." He lowered the hood with a bang. "So what've you been up to, uh . . . Abby?"

She smiled at the mention of her name. Some experts maintained that it was impossible to fake a true zygomatic smile, but she could do it. The trick was to let the corners of the lips curl upward, producing crow's-feet near the eyes.

"You remembered," she said. "I'm impressed."

"Still working at the paper mill?"

"It's a stationery wholesaler, actually. And yes, I'm still there."

He was taller than she was, which made it natural for her to lift her head when she faced him, thus exposing her suprasternal notch, the faint indentation above the collarbones. To bare her throat was a sign of submission.

Kolb seemed to pick up on the signal. He moved closer. "I think you promised me some personalized writing paper."

"You would've gotten it, if . . ." She let her voice trail off. It seemed right. It was how cautious Abby Hollister would respond in this situation.

"If I hadn't suddenly disappeared," Kolb said.

Averting her eyes. "Well, yes."

"Something came up."

She still wouldn't look at him. "I know."

"Do you?"

"It was in the paper. Not a lot of coverage, but, you know . . . when a cop gets arrested, it always makes the news."

"I guess it does. Hadn't really thought about it before. Maybe I should've saved the clippings."

"You didn't see the news stories?"

"I had a few other things to worry about at the time." His eyes were darting. He was uncomfortable, his body language more paranoid than before. "I guess it was kind of a surprise, seeing me in the *LA Times*?"

"They said you were stalking some woman. . . ."

"Yeah. That's what they said."

"Were you?" Instantly she brushed off the question with a flustered wave. "I shouldn't have asked you that. It's none of my business."

She expected Kolb, given an opening, to tell his version of the story, and he didn't disappoint her.

"There was this rich bitch in Bel Air," he said. "I pulled her over for a moving violation. She got it in her head that I was sending her anonymous e-mails. It was all a crock. I never sent any e-mails. I didn't even remember the traffic stop. Somebody else was hassling her, I guess—and I took the fall."

Abby barely registered the words. His behavior was more telling. He was massaging one arm, a common sign of deception. Of course, he might just have a rash on the arm—but he hadn't been rubbing it before.

She knew she couldn't accept his story at face value. No big-city gal would be that naive. He would expect skepticism.

"I read that you pled guilty," she said.

"It was a plea bargain. I had no choice. They had me by the private parts. I could plead guilty to something I didn't do, or take my chances with a jury. I don't trust juries. They're easily manipulated. I decided my best shot was to do the short time."

"How long?"

"Ten months in Chino."

"Doesn't sound so short."

"I survived. Not that it was easy. A cop in prison—you're a marked man."

"But they can't *do* anything to you, can they? I mean, you're protected by the guards."

He snorted. "Yeah, right. Fucking screws don't give a shit." He was loosening up now, using coarser language, a good sign. "And even the few who did care couldn't watch my back twenty-four hours a day."

"Were people actually out to . . . you know?"

"Snuff me? You bet. I figured I had one chance." He leaned against the Civic, settling into storytelling mode. "See, the prison population is divided into gangs—race gangs. The Asians hang together, the blacks, the whites. You've got your Black Muslim sector, your Aryan Brotherhood, and the crazy gooks who are still fighting the Vietnam War. My one shot was to join up with the white gang—if they'd let me. The white boys weren't crazy about cops either. Every one of them was put away by somebody wearing a badge. But I had two things working in my favor. Number one, I'm white, and number two, I have a German name. I was Aryan, see? Never thought of myself as Aryan, or even as a German. Shit, my partner and best friend on the force was a black guy, Wally Scrubs—used to invite me over to his house in Baldwin Hills for Sunday barbecue. But if playing the race card would keep me alive, I'd play it. So I pledged my loyalty to my Aryan brothers, and they let me join their club."

She noted a jerk of his Adam's apple, a sign of embarrassment. He didn't like admitting he'd signed up with the Nazis.

"You did what you had to do," she said. "Nobody can blame you."

"Some folks would. You want to see my initiation badge?

Take a look." He rolled up his left sleeve to reveal a prison tattoo—a jet-black swastika.

"Jeez," Abby whispered.

"Well, we all got our cross to bear." He rolled down the sleeve. "Sorry—bad joke. Anyhow, once word got around that I was protected, the predators switched to easier prey."

"At least now you're out. Can you . . . I mean . . . will they let you . . . ?"

"Be a cop again? No way. Convicted felons don't wear the uniform. Which is a joke, because there are plenty of guys on duty right now who've done worse stuff than I ever did."

"I thought you didn't do anything."

The comment caught him up short. He touched his mouth, another cue suggesting anxiety and, sometimes, deceit.

"I didn't," he said. "I was clean. And now I've got a prison record and a jailhouse tat. At least the tat can be erased. When I get the money, I'm having it lasered right off my arm." She didn't think he was serious about having the tattoo removed. His eyes were jumping all over the place. "I don't want anyone thinking I'm one of them. Bunch of ignorant skinheads, always jacking their jaws about how Hitler had the right idea."

"Were they all like that?"

"Dumb inbred yahoos? Yeah, pretty much. There was one guy, though—one guy with brains. This old, gray-bearded, motorcycle-leather guy, name of Hauser. He was as race-crazy as the rest of them, but at least he'd done some reading. He could talk philosophy—if anyone would listen."

"I'll bet you listened."

He shrugged. "Not much else to do in stir. When my cell-mate and Hauser's got paroled at the same time, me and Hauser ended up bunking together. There was plenty of time for conversation."

"What did you talk about?"

"Mostly the mongrelization of Western society." He smiled at her shocked expression. "That was his way of putting it, not mine. But some of what he said made sense."

She kept her tone neutral. "Did it?"

"Not the racial stuff. Other things . . . like how civilization's going downhill. Everybody kind of knows that. It's in the air, and we can smell it, sense it. But why? That's the question."

"What's the answer?"

"It's because we've got it all backward. Society's only as strong as its strongest members. But today everything's set up against the strong. It's all about protecting the weak." There was no deception now. There was honest anger. His jaw had tensed, and there was a canine growl at the back of his voice. "That's what decadence is. It's favoring weakness over strength. In any society there are a few natural leaders. The rest are followers. They're a herd. And like in any herd, there are some who are just too slow and weak. They get picked off, and the herd is strengthened. But if the leaders get picked off, the herd is doomed. That's what's happening today. We're picking off the best. Either we emasculate them with a lot of rules and regulations, or we send them off to . . ."

"To jail?" Abby prompted.

"To jail. Yeah." He was on a roll, punctuating his remarks with angry finger stabs. "What I'm talking about is heroes. The heroic man is the natural enemy of all the timid, needy types. They know it, and they resent him for it, so they make every effort to keep him down. They trim the tall trees and let the weeds run rampant. Weaklings and parasites—I used to see them every day when I was riding patrol. Welfare mothers, addicts, schizos roaming the streets, hookers spreading disease. They're what takes over when you give free rein to weakness."

There were a lot of ways to respond. Abby chose a middle ground between confrontation and agreement. "People can't help it if they're weak."

"A weed can't help being a weed, either, but that doesn't mean we let it grow and choke off the better plants. You know Hegel? The philosopher Hegel? He understood." Kolb spoke in the tone of a quotation. " 'So mighty a figure must trample down many an innocent flower.' "

"Innocent," Abby echoed. She signaled discomfort by shifting her stance, widening the distance between them.

He noticed. "I'm talking too much. Sorry."

She couldn't let him think he'd alienated her completely. She tried a smile. "The weeds didn't choke *you* off, did they?"

He smiled back. "They gave it their best shot, and I'm still here."

With a swastika on your arm, Abby thought. Prison had hardened him, radicalized him. She'd expected as much.

"Wow," she said, "you've got a pretty great attitude. I'd be pissed at the world. And especially that woman in Beverly Hills." She intentionally gave the wrong location because it might be suspicious if she knew her facts too well.

"Bel Air," he corrected. "You know, I got no hard feelings against her." The hell he didn't. His hands were fists. "She's just . . . I don't know . . . messed up. Paranoid or some damn thing." Projecting his own paranoia onto others. "This city, though . . ."

"Yeah?"

"They screwed me over. I mean, I was one of them. I wore the uniform. And they abandoned me. They abandoned one of their own."

"People in power don't care about the rest of us," she said. "We're just ants under their feet."

"Yeah." Kolb looked at her. "Well, sometimes ants can bite."

There was no anger in his voice, only calm determination. Abby found this more worrisome than any display of rage.

"Look," he added, "I'd better get going or I'll be late for work."

She let her gaze drop downward, a standard courtship cue. It worked.

"You, uh . . ." Kolb hesitated. "You want to get together sometime? Maybe have a meal, catch up a little more?"

It would be easy to say yes and assure herself of more time with him. But she knew better than to take the obvious path, especially with a man as paranoid as this one—and as shrewd.

"Oh, I don't know." She said it with a little shoulder shrug, a signal of uncertainty.

"We hit it off pretty good last time."

"We did, but . . ."

He filled in the blank. "But that was before I got arrested and spent three hundred days as a guest of the state."

"It's not that."

"Sure it is. I told you I was innocent. But hell, what else am I going to say?"

She let him think she was uncomfortable. "I didn't mean to offend you."

"Right. You didn't mean it." Angry again, his fist slapping his palm. "Even if I did what they said—and I didn't—I paid my dues. I put it behind me."

"I know."

"Yeah, you know." He averted his face, refusing to look at her. "You're still afraid, though. It's like I'm carrying the plague. The guys I worked with won't talk to me. All my old friends . . . oh, fuck it. It's not your problem." He started to walk away. "Glad I could help you out with the car."

"William."

This was the first time she'd said his name. He turned.

She spread her hands. "I'm sorry if I said the wrong thing."

"Sorry enough to give me another chance?"

She was silent.

"I didn't think so. Nice running into you, Abby."

He climbed back inside his car and pulled away into traffic. She stood watching him go.

All in all, a successful encounter.

She drove four blocks away and pulled into a mini-mall parking lot, then dictated into her microcassette recorder. A year ago Kolb had been an insecure, frustrated man. Now he was angrier than ever, but he'd learned to hide his insecurities behind a pseudo-philosophical smoke screen. The strong against the weak, the elite against the masses. Ordinary people were weeds. Was that what Angela Morris and Paula Weissman had been to him?

She was getting ahead of herself. There was no evidence that Kolb was implicated in those murders. Not yet.

Soon, maybe there would be. Once she had a look in his apartment to see what she could find.

11

At eight A.M. Tess handed in her report to Michaelson. "You're late," he said from behind his desk without looking up.

She glanced around at the office, crowded with plaques and photos advertising its occupant's career milestones. The standard term for such a display was an "I-love-me" wall. Here, the trophies covered two walls, implying a degree of narcissism rare even among the Bureau's elite.

"You told me to get it to you at eight," she said tonelessly, aware that he was needling her for no reason.

"It's eight-oh-two."

She didn't bother to check her wristwatch. "Your clock is fast."

He grunted, ostentatiously reviewing a file as if his attention were too precious to be wasted on her. "Any strong leads?"

"It's all there in the report."

"Any strong leads?" he asked again, still not raising his eyes. Over his shoulder was a posed shot of Michaelson shaking hands with the president of the United States. Michaelson looked awestruck and the president looked bored.

Tess sighed. "Half a dozen decent possibilities. A lot of maybes."

"There are always a lot of maybes. It was your job to weed out the maybes."

"It was my job to weed out the no-ways. I did. The maybes are another matter."

Another grunt. "Half dozen solids, you said?"

"Five, to be exact." She felt guilty because there should have been six. Madeleine Grant's tip had not been among the highlights of her report. It had been buried with the low-priority call-ins.

"That's five more than I expected. Usually these hotlines don't turn up a damn thing."

"I guess we're lucky, then." She turned to leave.

"How early did you come in this morning to finish this?" he asked.

"Five thirty."

"Would've been easier to work longer last night."

"I was kind of beat."

"Yeah, a ninety-minute plane ride will do that to you. Or maybe it was the strain of adjusting to a different time zone. We're a whole hour behind Denver here. It can throw off your entire metabolism."

"I got the job done. What more do you want?"

Finally he looked at her. "From you, Agent McCallum, I don't want anything at all."

She walked away, into the outer office where the ADIC's secretary worked. From behind, his voice trailed after her.

"Squad supervisors' meeting starts at nine hundred hours. *Not* nine-oh-one."

She had honestly forgotten how much she disliked Michaelson. It was all coming back to her now.

She retraced her route through the labyrinth of carpeted hallways and reached the C-1 squad room. At the door, she hesitated.

Rick Crandall stood at her workstation, going through the papers on her desk.

She stared at him for a long moment. No one else was in the room, and Crandall's back was turned. She could have watched him indefinitely, except that somehow he sensed her presence. Probably it was the same mysterious sense of being watched that she'd noticed last night outside Madeleine Grant's home.

He turned. "Oh. Hello, Agent McCallum."

She stepped into the room. "What the hell are you doing?"

"Just, uh—"

"Looking at my notes? My personal papers?"

"I was looking for your report. The AD wants it. It was supposed to be on his desk at eight."

"I just delivered it to him."

"Well, I guess you were a little late. He sent me to track it down."

"I don't want you or anyone else rummaging through my things, Crandall."

"I'm sorry. The director was very insistent—"

"I'll deal with Michaelson. He and I go way back. We have great rapport."

His eyebrows lifted. "You do?"

"We're old pals."

"I don't think the director is feeling very friendly toward you right now."

His voice was flat. She caught the tone and the hostility on his face. "I guess he's not the only one," she said.

"It was stupid, that stunt you pulled. Backing out of the media event. You could have stood there, accepted the accolades, helped out the Bureau."

"*You* could have told me about it."

"I was under instructions not to. I—" He stopped, looking flustered.

"And you were also under instructions not to admit that fact, weren't you?" She smiled at his discomfort. "Don't worry, I won't say anything to the Nose."

"The director, you mean."

"I think 'the Nose' suits him better."

"You ought to show some respect."

She was honestly baffled. "For Michaelson?"

"He's running this office. He's in charge—just like you

are, in Denver. Would you like it if one of your subordinates behaved the way you did yesterday?"

This jarred her. "No," she said quietly. "I wouldn't."

"We went to a lot of trouble to set up that event. We've been sucking heavy heat ever since Angela Morris was snatched. It's all over the news every day and night. Bringing you in was partly a show for the cameras—but it was necessary. We're trying to keep the pot from boiling over. And you didn't help. You went out of your way to make things harder for Michaelson"—he corrected himself—"for Director Michaelson. Made you feel good, didn't it? Kind of puts the 'special' in special agent? You're the rebel, the superstar. Well, it wasn't just the director you screwed over. You made it harder for the rest of us, too."

She took this in. "I'm not a rebel," she said. She didn't know why this denial mattered, in the face of everything else he'd said.

"You're not a team player, that's for sure." He moved to leave. She didn't stop him. But in the doorway he paused to look back at her. "You going to the supervisors' meeting?"

"Yes."

"He didn't have to let you attend, you know. He could have frozen you out. If I were in his place, that's what I'd do."

Crandall walked off. Tess wished she'd thought of something better to say in her defense. But there was nothing she could have said, because Crandall was right.

She'd let her personal dislike of the assistant director compromise her judgment. If anyone else had arranged a news conference for her, with or without her knowledge, she would have played along. She might have griped about it, but she would have done her duty. For teamwork. For the Bureau. But when it was Michaelson . . .

All she'd thought of was teaching him a lesson, making her foolish, futile little power play. She'd acted like a prima donna. And she'd let down her colleagues, who now disliked and distrusted her—even Crandall, who'd been her buddy up until five o'clock last night.

Now he was solidly against her, firmly siding with Michaelson.

She sat at her workstation. The printouts of the tip-line messages were stacked on her desk. She riffled through them and found her notes on the Madeleine Grant interview. If Crandall had seen them, he would know she was investigating a lead on her own. He might be sharing this news with Michaelson right now.

Or maybe she was just being unreasonably suspicious. This was what happened when you broke the rules. Everybody became a potential enemy. She didn't like it. She was beginning to wish she'd never met Abby Sinclair.

Too late for second thoughts. But if she was going to risk her job carrying out a clandestine operation, she was at least going to learn more about William Kolb.

As a cop, he'd worked out of LAPD's West Los Angeles station. She looked up the phone number and called from her cell phone, identifying herself as an FBI agent and asking to speak with the supervisor of detectives. A lieutenant named Collins came on the line. When she mentioned Kolb, he cut her off.

"It's Pacific Area you want. They handled the arrest."

"Why?"

"Because the investigation originated at Kolb's residence. He lived in Mar Vista at the time."

"Where's that?"

"I take it you're not from around here."

"I'm in from out of state, working a special."

"Mar Vista's a district of LA, south of the city of Santa Monica. You can find that, can't you?"

"I think I can track it down. You remember the name of the detective who arrested Kolb?"

"Goddard. He's still working out of that division."

Tess put in a call to Pacific. The duty officer said Detective Goddard was out on a case. He transferred Tess to Goddard's voice mail, and she left a brief, vague message, giving her cell phone number, but saying nothing about

Madeleine Grant. She still wanted to preserve some degree of deniability if Michaelson asked if she was handling a lead on the side.

She sat at the workstation for a while, rereading and re-sorting the tips. She thought about how badly she'd botched her first sixteen hours in LA. So far she'd humiliated Michaelson, alienated her colleagues, violated procedure, and hooked up with a vigilante who dated stalkers.

Still, she was committed. She was in it for keeps. All the way, like that Sinatra song said, the one Crandall had played in the car. It had sounded romantic when Frank sang it. It sounded ominous now.

When she checked her watch, she saw that it was nearly nine. Michaelson had been explicit about the virtue of punctuality. She preferred not to disappoint him again.

Before leaving, she hid her notepad underneath the stack of call-ins, placing both at the back of her desk drawer. If Crandall had filled Michaelson in, the assistant director would probably demand to see her notes. If she left them behind, at least it would buy her a little time.

She shook her head. Hiding things, skulking around—this wasn't what she signed up for. Or maybe it was. She'd made her deal with the devil, and she would have to live with it, if she could.

12

Kolb was still pissed off when he arrived at the security firm. He marched into the locker room, ignoring the other guards getting into their uniforms at shift change. He wasn't friendly with any of them. They were assholes and losers, willing to while their lives away playing rent-a-cop for starvation wages.

He opened his locker and stripped out of his civilian clothes. As always, he was careful not to let anyone see the swastika tattoo. With all the blacks and Mexicans around, he didn't think his skin art would go over too well.

Sure hadn't gone over with Abby Hollister. Weird, running into her like that. He'd met her only once before, but he'd thought about her a lot in stir. If he hadn't gotten pinched on the stalking charge, he was sure he could've nailed her. She'd been naively impressed that he was a cop. It wouldn't have taken much to get her into bed.

On many nights in his cell, he'd run through the scenario—the date at a nice restaurant, the stories he would tell to get her hot, then the drive back to her place, and the good-night kiss. Her throaty voice in his ear, asking if he wanted to come inside. After that, the fantasy took various turns, depending on what he was in the mood for. He liked to think she was up for anything and good at everything. He could picture her lithe, slender body folding into any imaginable pose. She would be as bendable as an action figure—and as durable.

Eventually he'd decided he was remembering her as hotter than she was, and if he ever met her again, he'd be in for a disappointment. He'd been wrong. This morning she'd looked damn good. Studying her lean legs and tight ass, he'd had yet another reason to regret being collared.

But she wasn't interested in him now—she'd made that clear. Besides, he wouldn't even be living in LA much longer. He had two or three more rounds of the game to play, two or three more bitches to put in the tunnels. Then he'd be cashing in his chips and leaving the casino. Couldn't push his luck too far. The house had a way of winning in the end.

"Hey, Kolb."

He looked up and saw another guard entering the locker room. Kolb didn't know his name. "Yeah?"

"Ran into Dicken in the hall. He wants to see you."

"What does he want?"

"Got no idea."

"I'm gonna be late."

"All I know is, he wants to see you. Now."

Kolb shook his head, irritated. If he was late replacing the night-shift guard at Jonson's, he would catch hell for it, and he wasn't in the mood for taking any shit.

He headed upstairs. He hadn't seen Dicken since the day he was hired, when he'd handed the application to the short, round man behind the desk, whose glance had ticked over it without interest. "Good enough," Dicken had said. "You start tomorrow. Be here at eight." Kolb had said, "Yes, sir," hating the *sir* but knowing that it was expected.

Since then he'd never had any reason to visit the boss's office. He would park out back, change in the locker room, then drive to the supermarket to pull his shift. Management was invisible, known to him only as a paycheck he picked up at the payroll office every Friday.

He went down the second-floor hallway and knocked on Dicken's door. The man had no secretary—he ran a no-frills operation.

"Come," Dicken barked.

Kolb stepped into the closet-sized office. Yellowish light spilled through grimy windows. The light made Dicken's pasty complexion look sallower than usual. He was reading the newspaper, his head lowered, the comb-over across his scalp embarrassingly obvious. He leaned back in his chair as Kolb approached.

"You wanted to see me," Kolb said, adding reluctantly, "sir?"

"You Kohl?"

"Kolb."

"Right. Kolb. You're fired."

"Excuse me?"

"You falsified your application. Said you had no criminal record. I just got the results of your background check. You did ten months in state prison on a felony. You're out of here."

There was no way to argue with this, and Kolb knew he shouldn't try. He didn't need the goddamn job, anyway. He had money in the bank, and more on the way.

"You can't, uh, pretend you never saw the background report?" he heard himself say.

"I run a legit operation here."

"Bullshit."

The man's bulldog face wrinkled into a frown. "What's that?"

"Half the guys on your payroll have a record. You know it. You just take your time about running the background checks to squeeze a few weeks' work out of us. We're all playing the game. We all know the rules."

"Well, if you know the rules, Kohl, then you know the penalty for getting caught."

"It's Kolb. Not Kohl."

"Whatever." He went back to his newspaper. "Get the fuck out."

Kolb took a step toward the door, then stopped. "I worked Sunday and Monday."

"So?"

"I need to get paid."

"You need to get out before I call your parole officer and let him know you been dicking around behind his back."

"I put in two shifts."

"I'm crying for you." The heavy-lidded eyes slid up to meet his gaze. "Background check says you used to be a cop."

Kolb's throat was tight. "Yeah."

"You must've fucked up real bad to go from being a cop to doing this shit."

Kolb wondered if Dicken kept a gun in his desk, and if so, how fast the man could reach it. Fast enough to defend himself if Kolb lunged across the space that separated them? Fast enough to stop Kolb from snapping his wattled neck?

"Turn in your uniform and go," Dicken said. He flipped to the next page of the newspaper.

Kolb drew a deep breath. He was calm. He was in control. He was always in control.

He went downstairs to the locker room. Someone asked him what the boss wanted. Kolb didn't answer.

He waited until the other guards had left, then stripped off his uniform. He was tempted to leave it balled up on the floor in a gesture of contempt, but instead he folded it neatly and hung it in the locker. A man could lose everything except his dignity. That was the one thing no one could take away.

He dressed in his pullover and shorts. He closed the locker for the last time.

Then, for no reason, he slammed his fist against the metal door, raising distant echoes from the corners of the room.

"Mother*fuck*," he whispered.

He didn't know why he was angry. The job meant nothing to him. He was glad to be rid of it. He ought to have thanked Dicken for letting him go.

But he'd wanted to leave on his own initiative, to be the

one calling the shots. Nobody liked being forced out—fired by some fat prick who didn't even know his name.

Still, it wasn't important. It didn't mean shit.

He left the building and got back into his car.

There was a whole day ahead of him, and he had nowhere to go except home.

13

Abby drove to Kolb's address and parked on a side street, then shrugged on a nylon jacket. The jacket was lined with hidden pockets crowded with lightweight tools.

The apartment building offered no security, just an open door to a deserted lobby. Kolb's unit was number six, on the ground floor of the two-story complex. She headed down a dim hallway. Near the stairwell she found his door.

She was assuming Kolb lived alone. A reverse-directory search had not turned up any other name listed at this address. Such searches weren't always reliable, but she thought Kolb was too much of a loner to have a roommate.

Even so, she gave the door a short, sharp rap. Nobody answered.

There was no one in the hall, no sound from the lobby on one side or the stairwell on the other. She could work unobserved. Reaching into her jacket, she took out a set of picklocks in a leather case. With a tension wrench inserted in the lock, she worked a pick in the keyway. The lock was the standard pin-tumbler type, not hard to defeat. In less than a minute she'd lined up the six pins, freeing the cylinder's plug. It turned, and she pushed the door open. She stepped inside and shut the door.

The apartment was a one-room hole, sparsely furnished, with a tiny kitchen and bath. There was no air-conditioning, not even a window unit. The place would be a sweatbox in the summer.

Kolb, it seemed, lived a Spartan life. Well, that wasn't exactly true. The Spartans had probably been tidy. Kolb was a slob.

His place last year had been different. Bigger, brighter, well furnished, and as clean as any bachelor pad was likely to be. Kolb had slid a long way down.

She pictured him alone in this dim, squalid room barely larger than his prison cell, a room not enlivened by color or beauty. He didn't have any audio equipment she could see; there would be no music in his life. There was no chance he did any entertaining, and it was doubtful he had a girlfriend—or any friends. He'd lost everything, and he wasn't trying to build himself back up. He seemed like a man who'd surrendered to failure.

And yet . . .

He was still trim and muscular—more powerfully built than he'd been last year. He hadn't taken up smoking—there were no cigarettes or ashtrays around. She doubted she would find liquor or drugs.

If he'd completely given up, he wouldn't care about maintaining his health and his strength. But he did. Which meant there was another way of looking at this apartment. Not as a home, but as a way station, a temporary place to crash.

In that case, he hadn't given up at all. He'd simply tightened his focus. He endured privation, knowing it wouldn't last.

The Rain Man might have an attitude like that. What would it matter if he suffered some transient inconvenience when he'd already scored a seven-figure payoff and was angling for more?

She needed facts, not theories. She pulled on a pair of cotton gloves and executed a search.

Normally her first move would be to pull down the window shades so as not to be seen from outside, but there was only one window here, and Kolb had left the shade down. Not a fan of sunlight, it seemed. She switched on the overhead light and went through a stack of papers on a wobbly end table beside the futon. Week-old newspapers, month-old magazines, coupons and other junk. She checked the wastebasket with a similar result.

Next, the closet, where a meager wardrobe was arrayed on wire hangers. There was a box on the floor, but it contained only photo albums and memorabilia from Kolb's police days—joke birthday cards from his pals on the force, pictures of him and his friends at a police picnic, a trophy his team had won in a basketball competition. His time as a police officer had been the best years of his life.

Reviewing his wardrobe again, she noted that he owned a pair of dark blue denim pants, a matching pullover, and watertight boots. A good outfit for moving through the storm tunnels. Still, there was nothing incriminating about owning dark clothes.

Trouble was, she wasn't quite sure what to look for. She had a wealth of experience nosing out clues to a potentially dangerous stalker personality, but she'd never gone after a serial killer. Even so, she knew something about the general mind-set.

First of all, there would be a fascination with media coverage of the case—newspaper clippings, videotapes of local news stories. An obsession with pornography was not uncommon, and while a stash of S-and-M mags or bondage gear wouldn't prove anything, it would tell her that not all was well in Kolb's noggin. Serial killers sometimes started out as Peeping Toms. A pair of binoculars or a camera with a telephoto lens might be lying around somewhere. A lot of these guys spent too much time alone with their thoughts. A diary would be the mother lode.

Then there were souvenirs. Stalkers generally didn't have an opportunity to acquire those items, but killers did—an article of the victim's clothing, a piece of her jewelry, a photo taken when she was in his custody. Perusing the FBI report last night, she'd noticed that one of Paula Weissman's shoes was missing—probably washed away, but it was possible the Rain Man had a shoe fetish. Angela Morris's autopsy hadn't been finished, so she didn't know if one of her shoes was missing, too.

Well, there was no ladies' footwear in the closet. Not a surprise. Kolb had never struck her as a fetishist.

Serial killers of the organized type were planners—she would expect to find a checklist, a timetable, a calendar with key dates noted, or surveillance pics of the victims. A map of the storm-drain system would constitute a solid hit.

There were other obvious things—handcuffs for the victims, a weapon to subdue them, the tape recorder used to record their voices for the phone calls. A big flashlight for prowling the tunnels, or possibly night-vision equipment, though she doubted Kolb could afford anything that pricey. Of course, if he was the Rain Man, he could afford it now, having obtained his first ransom. That was another avenue of investigation. Any record of a bank account in the Caymans or a large, recent purchase would clarify the situation in a hurry.

But she didn't expect to find anything like that. She figured if Kolb was into anything dirty, he wouldn't hide the evidence at his home. There was no telling when another kitchen fire might bring an engine company to the scene.

One thing stalkers and serial killers had in common was arrested emotional development. The serial killer was typically a sociopath, while the stalker was more of your basic inadequate personality type, but each had minimal grasp of his emotions, and minimal self-control. She might find evidence of violence—a hole punched in the wall, broken glass in the trash, hate-filled scrawls lining the pages of a notebook—something to suggest a personality that wasn't quite hanging together.

Then again, she'd already seen the bashed-in front end of Kolb's Olds.

Okay, she guessed she did have some idea of what to look for. Question was, would she find it?

Right away, videotapes of the news coverage were out—Kolb didn't own a VCR. He didn't have cable, either. He was pulling in signals off the roof antenna. The guy was living in the Dark Ages.

She searched the drawers of an old bureau that served as a TV stand. Socks, underpants, extension cords, hardware supplies. Nothing significant.

On homemade shelves constructed of cinder blocks and two-by-fours, there were a few books. She looked through Kolb's reading matter. Two paperbacks on the militia movement. A slim hardcover volume arguing that both the bombing of the Federal Building in Oklahoma City and the September 11 attacks had been engineered by the U.S. government as part of a master plan to repeal the Bill of Rights.

So he did have an antigovernment thing going on in his head. It could be relevant—the Rain Man seemed to be out to humiliate the municipal authorities.

There was one more book on the shelf, a compilation of nineteenth-century German philosophy—Nietzsche, Schopenhauer, Hegel. Most of the book was unmarked and probably unread, but the section on Hegel was copiously underlined. She remembered that Kolb was a Hegel fan. This fact didn't communicate a great deal to her. She barely recollected her Intro to Philosophy course in college. She had a feeling, though, that Hegel would tie in pretty well with the whole natural-elite, social-Darwinist, heroic-strongman tune Kolb had been riffing on.

A philosophical stalker. Maybe a philosophical kidnapper-killer.

"Cool," she said. It was stuff like this that kept her work interesting.

So far, her search was a big fat zero. No bondage gear, camera, binoculars. No souvenirs, photos, maps, calendars. No weapon, tape recorder, flashlight. She felt frustrated because Kolb wasn't giving her anything. She had a job to do, and he wasn't letting her do it. It seemed rude of him, but it also made him a challenge.

Ordinarily she didn't need a lot of raw data. She could tell a great deal from the artwork and knickknacks a person chose to display in his home. One charming fellow who'd set his sights on a fourteen-year-old girl had decorated his bedroom walls with prints of Munch's nightmarish painting, *The Scream*. He was still in prison, having been sent away for compiling a cache of child porn on his PC, which was discovered after a CD of the images had mysteriously found its way to the police, with the gentleman's name and address printed on the label.

Even if a guy's taste in art was subtler, there was much to be learned from almost any painting, figurine, or curio on display. Trouble was, Kolb had none of the above. His apartment was bare of decoration. She supposed the blank walls ought to be telling her something, but she wasn't sure what.

What else hadn't she found? An address book, for one thing. Maybe he didn't need one if he had no friends. A PC was also conspicuous by its absence. The computer he'd used when sending e-mails to Madeleine had been confiscated, and most likely he couldn't afford a new one.

The Rain Man had to have access to a computer. The FBI report had said that the bank account number for the ransom money had been computer-printed on an index card. And the electronic transaction itself must have been monitored over the Internet. But there was no computer here, no printer, and, as far as she could tell, not even any index cards.

She checked the bathroom. Sometimes items were concealed inside the toilet tank or taped behind the toilet itself. No luck. She examined the living room carpet to see if it had been taken up at the corners in order to slip something underneath. Again, nothing. And the carpet didn't match the fibers mentioned in the FBI report—it was a yucky gray-green, not burnt orange.

In the kitchen she found a poorly stocked minifridge and a pile of dishes in the sink. She beamed her penlight into the cabinets, moving pots and pans out of her way. The flash-light beam discovered only dust and dead bugs.

In one drawer she noticed a key half-hidden under a spat-ula. Funny place to keep a key. She picked it up. Round head, short stem. Looked like a padlock key.

From one of her hidden pockets she produced a key blank and an indelible marker. Carefully she traced the outline of the key on the blank. Then the key went back under the spat-ula, and the blank went into her pocket for later use.

Of course, the key would be no good to her unless she could find the padlock it fit. Most likely the padlock was used on a storage locker, a rental unit in one of the many self-service facilities throughout the city. If Kolb was rent-ing a locker, he ought to have some paperwork on it. She found a lidless apple crate stuffed with miscellaneous papers and flipped through them. Phone bills, utility bills, auto reg-istration documents, but nothing on any storage rental.

This was getting to be a little more of a challenge than she liked. She decided to switch to a more proactive mode.

Another of her pockets carried an infinity transmitter, a voice-activated bug that could be installed in any telephone. The bug worked off the microphone that was part of the phone's mouthpiece and would pick up both ends of any phone conversations, as well as discussions taking place in the apartment. Installing the bug did entail a small risk. If Kolb was sufficiently paranoid, he might take the phone apart to check for listening devices. But her search hadn't turned up a field-strength meter or any other surveillance-detection equipment. She was willing to chance it.

In less than two minutes she'd planted the transmitter. Its range was fifty feet. The receiver had to be stationed nearby, but preferably outside the apartment for easier retrieval.

She wasn't sure what she expected to pick up, since Kolb certainly would not use his home telephone to contact the authorities. Still, there was an idea that had occurred to her last night when she looked through the FBI report. It seemed unlikely that Kolb could have raised the cash or worked out the details necessary to open multiple secret bank accounts in the Cayman Islands. If he was good for the kidnappings, then he probably had help. A partner.

She'd almost raised the possibility with Tess, but the idea was too speculative and didn't fit what she knew of Kolb's paranoid, antisocial personality. Even so, she couldn't quite convince herself to drop the notion. She didn't see Kolb pulling off something this complicated all by himself.

If there was a partner in the picture, then bugging the phone could prove to be an investment that paid big dividends.

She took a moment to stand still and simply absorb the atmosphere of Kolb's home. Every residence had its own aura, not in any metaphysical sense, but simply as a result of the accumulated detritus of someone's life. The sparse furnishings and closed window shade and general air of neglect told her a lot about Kolb. They spoke to her of disappointment and frustration, of anger and desperate rationalizing. Though the apartment was bare, there was a lot of ego here. Kolb's ego, undeveloped past the stage of late adolescence, the stage when intelligent but alienated youths cultivated a liking for German philosophers and antisocial elitism.

Maturity, she'd learned, was a gradual process of discovering and then disowning the ego. An infant had no ego, no sense of self. By age two, the child had formulated a personal identity, but no empathy—hence, the "terrible twos," when most kids ran amok. Slowly this naked narcissism was suppressed by social conditioning, and the child was taught to think of other human beings. But egocentricity, still the dominant theme, persisted through the teenage years. For a teenager, every setback was a crisis, and every disappointment was a tragedy. The world orbited around the fragile, frightened self.

Most people outgrew that phase in their twenties or thirties, but arrested adolescents were narcissists for life. They never gained perspective on their problems. They continued to imagine themselves the center of the world, and when the world ignored or abused them, they would respond unpredictably. Some would retreat into solipsistic fantasies. Others would join cults. Others would seek power to avenge themselves against a universe that did not take them seriously. The ego—vain, defensive, covetous, angry, needy— would puff itself up into a monster, transvaluing its defects as virtues, its weakness as strength.

Kolb was one of the power seekers. Anger and ferocious self-absorption drove him. He nursed grudges and spun schemes for revenge. Possibly he was putting one of those schemes into practice. Possibly he meant to show the city, and by extension, the world, that he was not to be trifled with. Possibly he was the Rain Man. She couldn't prove it, not yet. But—

Outside, a noise.

The chug of a motor, a faint rattling sound.

Kolb's Oldsmobile. She recognized the clatter of the damaged front end.

She peeled back the window shade. The tenants' carport was directly outside. Kolb was pulling into his assigned space, number six.

He was back from work, much too soon.

She quickly left the apartment, locking the door behind her. The stairwell was only a few steps away. She started to push open the door, then froze with a thought.

In her stakeouts on Sunday and Monday, she'd watched the front entrance. But Kolb hadn't come out that way. Both times he'd gotten from his apartment to his car without using the lobby exit.

She hadn't seen any back door to the building, but a side door was possible—and it would open onto the stairwell.

She looked inside the stairwell, and yes, there it was, a door that must lead to the parking area. If Kolb had gone out that way, he would most likely reenter through the same door.

He would walk right into her.

She glanced up the stairs, thinking she could hide on the

landing. No good. The stairs were metal treads without risers, and the landing was a metal mesh. If Kolb looked up, he would see her. And she didn't think she had time to escape into the second-floor hallway.

She retreated from the stairwell. Make a run for the lobby? Two problems with that plan—number one, he might surprise her by returning that way, and number two, she didn't think she could make it there in time.

Directly across from Kolb's apartment there was a door with no number on it. Not an apartment. A storage room, janitor's supply closet, something like that. Unlike an apartment, a closet wasn't likely to have much of a lock on the door.

She whipped out a plastic shim, flat and flexible, and swiped it along the crack between the door and the jamb.

The latch popped. She opened the door, exposing a deep, narrow room crowded with slop buckets, brooms, mops, and bottles of cleaning solvent.

From the stairwell came the sound of the outside door squealing open.

She threw herself into the closet and quietly pulled the door shut, sealing the room in darkness.

Footsteps in the hall.

He must have entered through the hall door just as she'd shut herself in the closet. It was possible he'd seen her slip inside.

Carefully, working in the dark, she undid the clasp of her purse and found her gun, curling her finger over the trigger.

Then she heard a jangle of keys and a creak of hinges. The door to his apartment opened and shut.

"Close one," she breathed.

Now that it was over, she decided it had been kind of fun.

And it had delivered a fringe benefit. She'd found a place to conceal the receiver.

She tugged the pull chain that turned on the bare ceiling bulb. At the back of the closet, behind a row of paint cans overgrown with cobwebs and littered with insect carcasses, she cut away a section of the drywall with an X-Acto knife. She concealed the receiver inside and replaced the cutaway panel. The device would receive the infinity transmitter's intermittent signal and record a maximum of twenty hours of audio on a memory card. It had no moving parts and used little power. The fresh battery she'd installed this morning would keep it running until sometime tomorrow, eliminating the need for her to hardwire the device into the main current. When she returned tomorrow, she would do a diaper change—replace the card and the battery.

She left the closet and exited via the lobby, taking a long detour back to her car so she wouldn't pass in front of Kolb's window. Probably he kept the shade drawn, but she couldn't count on it—and she'd taken enough chances for one day.

14

The morning meeting was held in the ADIC's conference room, where a dozen squad supervisors gathered before nine o'clock to await Michaelson's arrival. No one spoke to Tess. She felt hostility radiating at her from every seat around the long conference table. She wondered if it was possible to spontaneously combust under the pressure of so many hot glares.

To distract herself, she fixed her gaze on a large pad mounted on an easel at the front of the room. Across the top sheet the word STORMKIL was written in black marker. The rest of the sheet was blank. It seemed like an appropriate metaphor for the case.

Michaelson entered on schedule, preceded by Larkin and by someone who apparently was with the media-relations office. Somehow it wasn't surprising that the AD would have his mind on the media even during a strategy session.

As he passed her, Tess searched Michaelson's face for any indication that Crandall had informed him of her unauthorized activities. She caught no sign of it.

Michaelson sat at the head of the table, the media rep at his side. Larkin positioned himself by the easel.

"Go," the AD said with a finger jab at the nearest supervisor.

The man delivered a weather forecast. Heavy rains were

expected to fall by ten P.M. The killer had snatched his first two victims roughly four hours before the storms broke. If he stuck to his previous pattern, they were looking at an abduction by six o'clock, an hour after sunset. That was nine hours from now.

Larkin leaned over the easel and wrote 1800 HRS: ABDUCT. The words seemed to shout at the room.

The next supervisor reported that all agents were working staggered shifts today—sixteen hours on duty, eight hours off.

The head of Communications said that the scrambler of every agent's Handie-Talkie unit had been reprogrammed, eliminating any possibility that the Rain Man could eavesdrop on FBI radio exchanges.

Someone else summarized a psycholinguistic analysis of phrase selections from the two ransom notes and Paula Weissman's tape recording. It was presumed that the wording of all three messages closely reflected the Rain Man's original text. The analysts believed the unsub was a Caucasian male with some college education, in his late twenties to early forties. Tess noted silently that, from what she knew, William Kolb fit the description.

Then there were the phones in the mayor's office, where the Rain Man was expected to call, if and when his latest ransom demand was met. A trap-and-trace had been installed on every line, allowing an instant trace if the killer called from a landline. If he used a cell, as he had last time, then a trace became more difficult.

"We're anticipating he'll have a new phone," the super said, "or at least a new number programmed into the existing phone." Working cell numbers could be snatched out of the air during cellular transmissions, or purchased at black-market Internet sites. "We need to identify the cell phone number, match it to the owner's account, then get the location of the cell tower at the point of origin. We've made arrangements with every major cellular provider in the area to have technicians on standby."

If the caller's location could be determined, LAPD SWAT units and FBI strike forces stationed throughout the metro area would be ready to move on him.

"And the money?" Michaelson asked.

For Angela Morris, the Rain Man had demanded one million dollars. For Paula Weissman, two million. The assumption was that he would again double the amount. Four million dollars in municipal revenues was available for electronic transfer.

The AD frowned. "There's no question the city will pay?"

"Officially they've announced no position. Privately they're committed to making the payoff. The mayor's already taken enough heat for hesitating on the Weissman ransom. People are saying if he'd paid sooner, she might have been saved."

Tess didn't think so. She was fairly certain the Rain Man didn't want his victims recovered alive. There was too great a risk that they could identify him.

"Suppose he goes higher than four million," Michaelson said.

"It starts to get a little tricky."

"Politically?"

"Yes—and also logistically. But I think they'll find a way to cough it up, no matter how much it is. I mean, as long as it's within reason."

Tess didn't think anything the Rain Man did was within reason. She said nothing.

"Assuming they pay," Michaelson said, "and he calls with the victim's location, what kind of response time are we looking at for the rescue effort?"

The supervisor handling the phone trace answered. "The same SWAT units and strike forces are ready to go underground anywhere in the city. The way they'll be deployed, we estimate that one of those teams can get to any point on the map in under twelve minutes."

"Twelve minutes is an eternity," Michaelson said. "Last

time, he didn't call in Weissman's location until the rain started falling. If he waits that long again . . ."

"Then we have to hope the response time is shorter. I said *under* twelve minutes. It could be a lot less."

"It had better be. Damn it, this son of a bitch is calling all the shots."

"Not for long," Larkin said out of habitual sycophancy.

Everyone ignored him.

As Tess expected, Michaelson took credit for sifting through the call-ins and identifying the few that seemed promising. These he doled out to the various squads, pointedly giving none to Tess. She was a nonperson, the invisible woman.

Michaelson wanted agents, police officers, and sheriff's deputies posted near as many storm-drain access points as possible. Coordinating this effort was the task of the C-1 squad supervisor, who had bad news.

"We've gone over this with DWP, and the simple fact is, there's no way we can cover more than a fraction of the entry points."

"Why the hell not?"

Before the super could answer, another voice cut in. "Let me field that one." Tess looked to the doorway, where a new man had joined the briefing. "Sorry I'm late," he added. "Traffic."

His gaze swept the room and briefly met hers. He was trim, wide-shouldered, his dark hair close-cropped. Unexpectedly he extended a hand across the table. A large hand with a powerful grip, though he wasn't much taller than she was.

"Ed Mason," he said. "Assistant chief engineer in DWP's Stormwater Management Division."

Tess got it. He could afford to annoy Michaelson because he wasn't a Bureau employee. She started to give her own name in reply, but Michaelson interrupted.

"So tell us—why can't we deploy our personnel at the entry points?"

"Because," Mason said as he took a seat, "the tunnel system is just too damn big. We're talking about sixty-four main lines and hundreds of smaller service tunnels. Fifteen hundred miles of underground pipe extending from Canoga Park to San Pedro. You can't post people at every ingress. It's physically impossible."

"There has to be some way to narrow it down," the AD insisted.

The C-1 super didn't think so. "His first two vics were taken in completely different parts of the city. It's not as if he just works one neighborhood. He could go anywhere."

"Then we seal off all the access points so he can't get in. We lock him out of the system."

There was a laugh, a deep, throaty sound.

Michaelson swiveled toward the source. "Something funny, Mr. Mason?"

Mason was still chuckling. "You want to seal off the entire drainage system of Los Angeles. That doesn't strike you as impractical?"

"Not the entire system. Just the access points big enough for a man to use."

"There are thousands of those."

"Then we seal off only the biggest ones. The ones that can accommodate a vehicle, say."

"It still won't work. Street runoff would cause major flooding."

"We'll use nets. Steel nets. Water gets through, but *he* can't."

"Nets would get clogged with debris in a matter of minutes."

Michaelson wouldn't be put off. "I've seen nets in place along the river channel."

"Sure you have. In the dry season, we use nets to filter out trash and debris. The last time we put up nets at the junction of the LA River and Ballona Creek, we caught a hundred thirty tons of waste. That was when the water wasn't moving fast."

Tess spoke for the first time. "Why would there be any water in the system during the dry season?"

"Because," Mason said, "there's always runoff from fire hydrants, construction projects, people watering their lawns or hosing down their cars. Or dumping chemicals—or taking a pee in a manhole. Even when there's no wet weather flow, the pipelines have plenty to carry. And tonight, in a big storm like they're predicting, we'll see twenty thousand times the dry season flow. Tens of billions of gallons. That's billion with a b."

"Christ," Michaelson said, appalled.

"Put up nets this time of year, and they'll be torn to pieces. And if they hold, you'll have logjams and citywide flooding. This system moves a lot of water, Chief."

Michaelson clearly didn't like being addressed as Chief, and Tess was pretty sure Mason knew it. "Personally," the AD said, chafing, "I wish you'd never built your goddamned system. Didn't it ever occur to anybody that installing the world's largest labyrinth right under your feet was an invitation to every psychopath within a thousand miles?"

"It's not the world's largest," Mason said, unfazed. "And it seems to have issued an invitation to only one psychopath. At least, he's the only one who's RSVP'd. Besides, if we didn't have the tunnels, where would all the water go?"

"I was stationed in Tucson once. That's a metro area of nearly one million, and they have no storm-drain system. They let the rain flow naturally into dry washes and percolate underground. You people could've done the same thing."

"That idea is only a little less impractical than those nets you tried to sell us, Chief." There was no doubt the nickname was a dig. Tess saw Mason's mischievous smile. "LA is basically one giant floodplain. Without proper drainage, you'd have water up to your armpits from East LA to the Westside. That's pretty near what happened back in the flood of 1938. Then the Army Corps of Engineers came in with three million barrels of concrete and paved the LA River. All it is, really, is an engineered flood-control channel."

Or a glorified ditch, Tess thought. She commented, "I'm surprised they even call it a river."

"It was a river once. Damn fine river jumping with steelhead trout. There were grizzlies on the banks, forests of willows and cottonwoods. That was in the 1760s, when the Spanish came here and found the Gabrielino Indian settlements. By the middle of the next century it was all gone—fish, bears, trees, and most of the Indians, too. Improvements had been made, you see. That's how the settlers thought of it, at any rate."

"Fascinating." Michaelson didn't hide his exasperation. "I'm sure we'd all benefit from your historical insights if we didn't have a murderer on the loose."

"Sorry. I get kind of caught up in my subject . . . Chief."

The meeting ended. Tess was gathering her papers when Michaelson called to her. "McCallum. One minute, please."

Maybe Crandall had squealed, after all.

She waited until Mason and the supervisors had departed and she was alone with the AD.

"You gave me all the strong leads, right?" Michaelson asked. "You're not holding anything back?"

"Of course not," she lied.

"Not keeping anything to yourself—you know, for a little freelance work?"

Crandall *must* have said something. She met Michaelson's gaze. "I don't operate that way."

"Yes, you do. You're always going off the reservation. That's how you played it during the Mobius case."

"It's a good thing I did," she said, then regretted the words.

Michaelson appraised her. "And maybe it would be a good thing if you did it again?"

"I'm just doing my job."

Michaelson dropped his gaze, losing interest. "Be sure that's all you do."

Tess relaxed. He'd been merely fishing. He didn't know anything.

She left the office. Either Crandall hadn't seen her notes, or he hadn't passed on the information to the AD. She'd gotten lucky. She wondered how long her luck would hold.

In the hall she bumped into Mason. He regarded her with an amused look. "Sounds like somebody got sent to the principal's office."

She smiled, a little warily. "Were you eavesdropping?"

"Just surmising. The chief didn't sound too happy with you."

"He's not happy being called Chief, either."

"Into each life, a little rain must fall." Mason's grin faded. "I guess, under the circumstances, that's a bad choice of words."

"I'm afraid I never properly introduced myself."

"Oh, I know who you are, Agent McCallum."

"My antisocial behavior is already that notorious?"

"I wouldn't call it antisocial. It's more like you don't play games. I'd call you a curmudgeon, but you're too young for that particular appellation. An iconoclast, maybe. Or hell, just a rebel."

"That's me. Rebel without a cause."

"What are you rebelling against?"

She lifted an eyebrow. "What've you got?"

He laughed, a rich, throaty sound. "I didn't think anyone under the age of forty remembered that one. James Dean was my hero when I was growing up."

She appraised him skeptically, estimating his age at early forties. "You're not old enough to have been a James Dean fan."

"Oh, he died before I was born, but I related to him anyhow. Must've been your typical teenage death wish. I even rode a motorcycle for a while. Nearly got myself killed on the damn thing more than once."

"I'm sorry you didn't get to finish your history lesson. I did find it interesting."

"It was for your benefit. You seemed to have an interest in the subject. Which made you unique in that crowd."

"Bureau employees aren't necessarily known for their patience. How long have you been consulting on the case?"

"Since right after it started. Since Angela Morris."

"It's been hard on you, I bet."

"Harder on the victims and their families and the case agents working their butts off to solve this thing. Me, I just sit in on some meetings and put my two cents in every now and then, and everybody ignores it, which is their privilege. They're federal agents, and I'm a lowly municipal bureaucrat. I don't expect them to listen to me."

"I'll listen," Tess said.

It was his turn to appraise her. He nodded. "Yes, I believe you will. If you'd like, I can finish the history lesson now. Maybe over a cup of coffee."

"You'd be fraternizing with the enemy."

"You're not my enemy. And I wouldn't be fraternizing."

She glanced at his left hand and noticed he didn't wear a wedding ring. "Are you, um, asking me out?"

"I guess so. Out for coffee, anyway. As first dates go, it's pretty low-stress."

She was flattered, even though she was sure things would never go anywhere between them. He wasn't her type, or something. He wasn't . . .

He wasn't Paul. Always she came back to that.

"Tess?" He simulated a polite rap on her noggin. "You still in there?"

"Sorry. Drifted away. Uh, I think I have to take a pass for now. Work, you know."

"Work. Yeah, there's always work to do."

"I . . . I'm not making excuses. . . ."

"Sure you are. But it's okay. Let's face it, the history of the LA River isn't all that mesmerizing a topic."

She'd hurt his feelings. "Ed, don't take it like that."

"Hey, it's okay." He squeezed her arm, an almost paternal gesture. "I took a shot. Didn't pan out. But if you change your mind, let me know. I'll be around."

"All day?"

"Mostly. On days like this, they need me here." He answered her unspoken question. "Days with rain in the forecast."

She checked her watch as she walked away. Nearly ten thirty. If the Rain Man planned to strike at six P.M., there were only seven and a half hours to go.

As she was heading back to the squad room, her cell phone buzzed. "McCallum," she said, taking the call.

"Agent McCallum—Detective Owen Goddard. You left a message on my voice mail."

"Thanks for getting back to me, Detective. I need to talk to you about an old case."

"I'm listening."

She didn't want to have this conversation in the field office. "It might be better if I could talk to you in person."

"I expect to be at my desk for the rest of the morning."

"Give me half an hour. I'll see you then."

She went to her workstation and opened the desk drawer to get out her notes. But something was wrong. The contents of the drawer had shifted slightly. Paper clips that had been resting in a plastic dish were scattered. Pens that had been lined up along one side of the drawer were in disarray.

Hastily she searched her notes and was relieved to find that the page of her notebook summarizing Madeleine Grant's interview was still there. Crandall hadn't taken it. But he could have seen it.

If he'd been looking. It was possible the contents had shifted when she shut the drawer earlier. She couldn't be sure. And she couldn't ask any of her squad mates if Crandall had been poking around her workstation. None of them would tell her a damn thing.

She didn't like not knowing. If Crandall had returned for a second look, then he was clearly suspicious of her. Maybe her anger at finding him at her desk had sparked his curiosity. Or maybe she was overreacting.

She hoped so.

15

Tess took the San Diego Freeway south to the Culver Boulevard exit and parked outside the LAPD's Pacific Area station. She found Goddard in the detectives' squad room, seated at one of many gray metal desks butted together to form common work areas.

The squad room did not compare favorably to the one at the field office. At the Bureau, the atmosphere was corporate, white-collar, while the Pacific station had a decidedly blue-collar feel. Cheap swivel chairs with squeaky casters rolled on the well-worn beige carpet. Potted plants that looked half-dead sat atop dented file cabinets. A copy machine idled in a corner, under a wall-mounted TV, volume off, tuned to CNN.

She took a seat at Goddard's desk, where a spread of documents lay on a green blotter in no apparent order. "You McCallum?" he asked. "You caught me on a good day. My partner's testifying in court, and I'm catching up on some paperwork. Now what did you want to see me about?"

"A case you handled last year, involving a police officer named William Kolb."

"I remember." Suddenly Goddard seemed uncomfortable. The ballpoint pen in his hand tapped the blotter in a nervous rhythm.

"You don't sound happy about it."

"It's never fun when you're dealing with a bad cop."

Tess thought there was more to his attitude than he was letting on, but she allowed it to pass. "Why don't you tell me about the case?"

"I assume you know the basics—the kitchen fire in Kolb's apartment, the stuff the fire department found. The engine company brought in a squad car, and the patrol guys called for an investigator. My partner and I were catching calls that day."

"Kolb lived in Mar Vista, as I understand. Good neighborhood?"

"Best he could afford. His apartment was no showplace, but I don't think he cared. He wasn't exactly known for hosting dinner parties."

"Antisocial?"

"Unsocial is more like it. You know how the neighbors always say the guy was quiet, kept to himself? In this case it was true."

"Did he have friends on the force?"

"A few. No enemies, far as I could tell."

"Did you know him?"

"He was patrol; he worked a different division—we might've crossed paths now and then, that's all."

"Did you know he was a cop when you went to his apartment?"

"All I knew was that the fire department had found some suspicious items in plain view."

"And when you found out he was a cop . . .?"

"Yeah?"

"It must have come as a surprise."

Goddard squinted at her. "I know what you're saying. You want to know if it affected the way we handled the case. The answer is, you bet it did. If he'd been a civilian, we would've taken twice as long to make the arrest. Everything was expedited once we found out he was LAPD."

"Why?"

"First, because we were afraid it would be taken away from us. High-profile cases get snatched up by Robbery-Homicide downtown. And second, there'd been criticism of the department for letting criminal complaints against police officers languish until the statute of limitations expired. We'd been getting some bad press, including an exposé in the *Times*. I saw Kolb as an opportunity to repair the damage."

"When you say the investigation was expedited . . ."

"My partner and I walked into the apartment at nine hundred hours, and we'd cleared the case to the DA's office by fifteen hundred hours the same day."

"Record time."

"I can't take too much credit. The case was open-and-shut. We didn't need a warrant for the evidence in plain sight, only for a search of Kolb's computer, and we found a judge who signed off telephonically. We brought in a tech from the computer crime squad, who found digital pictures of the woman Kolb was stalking."

"Madeleine Grant."

A nod. "And he found copies of e-mail messages Kolb sent her. There was no reason for Kolb to keep the stuff, except I guess he got off on it. A lot of these guys do."

"So you had him cold."

"Absolutely. We did all this while he was still on duty. At the end of his watch, we made the arrest."

"How did you handle it?"

"We waited for him outside the West LA station house. He went quietly."

"Did he make bail?"

"No, the judge set it high. All indications were that this would be a high-profile case. There was pretty strong media coverage in the first few days."

"I take it things didn't work out the way you expected."

Goddard didn't answer. The pen started tapping again. Tess began to think that this was more than a nervous habit. It seemed almost like a signal—as if he were sending her a message: *Read between the lines.*

She didn't pursue the question immediately. "Did Kolb show any remorse?"

"He didn't show a goddamn thing. He was giving us the thousand-yard stare. You'd get more information out of a prisoner of war."

"How about his record? Any problems in that area?"

"A few civilian complaints, nothing too serious. You work the streets, you're going to rub some people the wrong way. Professional Standards—what we used to call Internal Affairs—looked at him once or twice, gave him a couple of wrist slaps."

"I've heard he had an interest in Mobius."

"I was wondering if you would ask about that. He had a book of clippings about that case. It was all in there, everything the *Times* and the newsmagazines had to say. Including some stuff about you."

"Nice to know I have a fan. Did you ask him about Mobius?"

"We asked. He didn't tell us anything. Name, rank, and badge number—that's all we got out of him."

"What's the penalty for stalking in California?"

"Maximum is three years in state prison."

"Kolb got one year."

"That's right. With good behavior he served out his sentence in ten months."

"Pretty light sentence."

"I doubt he thought so."

"They didn't exactly throw the book at him, did they?"

No answer.

"I thought California was ahead of the curve as far as antistalking statutes are concerned," Tess said.

Goddard shrugged. "We are. But the whole area is dicey. Problem is, you're dealing essentially with a thought crime. You need to establish that the stalker's intent was to place his victim in a state of fear. So you're dealing with two states of mind, his intent and her fear. Both are subjective. What looks like stalking to one person might look like a prank to someone else."

"Kolb was planning more than a prank. He had the paraphernalia he needed to kidnap Madeleine Grant. That ought to show plenty of intent. The DA could have gone for the maximum. He didn't, though."

Tess let the statement hang in the air, an implied question. Goddard said nothing. He tapped a staccato code with his ballpoint.

She took a shot. "Was it political pressure? Going easy on a police officer to avoid giving the department another black eye?"

She thought he might give her a wink and a nod, but he surprised her.

"That's bullshit." Goddard took a breath, then added in a softer voice, "We police our own around here. This is still one of the cleanest departments in the country, I don't give a damn what anybody says. There were problems, but we cleaned house. We take all kinds of crap for the problems and get no credit for the cleanup."

Apparently she'd been misreading his signals. "I didn't mean to be confrontational. But if it wasn't to protect the department, why wouldn't they have gone harder on him?"

"You'd have to ask the DA's office about that."

"Why? Is it a secret?"

"It's out of my area. Once the case is handed to the DA, they're in charge."

"It's still your case."

"I'm not running the show. They are. Any decisions have to come from their office."

"Why do I get the sense that there's something funny going on here?"

Goddard looked at her. No, not *at* her. Through her. His voice was flat and firm. "The case was handled by Deputy District Attorney Richard Snelling. He's on the eighth floor of the Criminal Justice Center downtown."

"And if I see him, I'll get some answers?"

There was no expression on his face. "I can't say what you'll get."

"Then I'll have to find out for myself. One more thing,

Detective. Madeleine Grant tells me that she called the LAPD with some suspicions regarding Kolb's recent activities."

"She called me."

"She seems to feel the call wasn't taken seriously."

He still wasn't meeting her gaze. "I take every call seriously."

"So you're pursuing the lead?"

"I didn't say that."

"You're not saying much of anything all of a sudden. Why wouldn't you follow up on a tip like that?"

His voice was toneless. "You think Kolb has something to do with the kidnappings?"

"Not necessarily. I'm just curious why you'd be so cavalier about her call. She was right last year, wasn't she?"

"Sure she was."

"You don't sound entirely certain."

"I can't be responsible for what you read into my answers."

"No, you can't. Thanks for your help, Detective."

Tess left the squad room, thinking that Kolb wasn't the only one who knew about the thousand-yard stare.

16

Abby spent an hour in her condo, cutting notches in the key blank with a pair of Curtis clippers, then filing down the rough edges. She added the duplicate key to her already crowded key chain. Somehow she intended to find the padlock it fit. She had a feeling that when she did, she would learn a lot more of Kolb's secrets.

In the meantime she wanted to know why he'd returned home so early. She drove her Miata across town to the supermarket where he was normally stationed. She parked two blocks away and approached cautiously, ready to beat a hasty retreat if Kolb had shown up.

He wasn't there. A different guard was on duty. She put on her best ditzy persona and sashayed up to him. "Hey, where's the guy who's usually here?"

The guard looked her over. "Who wants to know?" he asked with what he apparently believed was a rakish smile.

"I'm Ginger," she said. It was the first name she could think of. Homage to *Gilligan's Island.* "I shop here a lot."

"How come I ain't seen you around? I think I'd remember you." The guy was doing his best to ooze charm, though as far as Abby could tell, the only thing oozing out of him was sweat.

"I just come here during the day. The other guy's always here. This is the first time I've seen *you.*" She put a provocative emphasis on the last word.

"Now you know what you been missing."

Smooth talker. Must be a devil with the ladies. "So what happened to him?" she asked. "He get moved to a different location?"

"What I heard, he got canned."

Abby set her face in a pout. "That's too bad. I liked him."

"Bet you could get to like me, if you give it a shot."

"You never know." She twirled her hair like an idiot, sending a signal of empty-headedness that was sure to mark her as easy sexual prey. "How come they let him go?"

"Probably the usual reason." Smiling conspiratorially, the guard stepped closer. "Some of these guys, they got prison records. They hide it for a few weeks, but sooner or later they get caught. Then they're out."

Abby feigned stupefaction. "You mean, he might've been in *jail?*"

"Kolb? Yeah, that's what I'd bet. He never said much, but he had that look about him. When you been in this business awhile, you get to know the signs."

"Well, I guess it's good he's gone, then. I wasn't interested in . . . I mean, if he's a convict, ex-convict, whatever . . ."

He bought her flustered-ingenue act. "Don't let it shake you up," he said in a fatherly tone, though clearly his intentions were fatherly only in the John Huston–*Chinatown* sense. "I can spot his type a mile away. But a little lady like you, well, there's no way you could know what you were in for."

"I guess not."

"Maybe I'll be seeing you, now that I'm working the day shift."

"Maybe you will." She showed him a parting smile, just enough to keep his hopes up—well, his hopes and anything else that might've been raised by the encounter.

She went into the supermarket and prowled the aisles, biding her time until a large Latino family was leaving. She blended in with them and exited, unnoticed by the guard, then doubled back to her Mazda.

So Kolb was out of work. If he was the Rain Man, he

didn't need the job anyway. But he'd kept it, which meant that for some reason he wanted it. She wondered how his premature termination would affect his emotional stability.

Her cell phone rang as she was slipping back into the convertible. The breathless voice on the other end of the line belonged to Madeleine Grant. "I think he's here. I think he's watching me."

Abby didn't have to ask who. "Where is he?"

"In the woods by my house."

"Inside or outside the perimeter fence?"

"Outside."

"Is your alarm system on?"

"Of course it is. I'm not a fool, for Christ's sake."

Abby pulled away from the curb. "Calm down; take it easy. Can you still see him?"

"No, I can't. The foliage is dense. I only got a glimpse. I'm not sure it was him. But who else could it be?"

"Which side of the house?"

"The north side. It's a jungle. A neighbor lost her dog in there once, and we all went looking. There are trees—he could climb a tree to get over the fence."

"You had all the trees trimmed back, remember?"

"You're right. I'm becoming hysterical, aren't I?"

"Not at all," Abby lied. "You're being observant and alert. Did you call the police?"

"Should I?"

Abby didn't want Madeleine taking any unnecessary risks, but with Kolb—or whoever it was—still outside the fence, and with the alarm system activated, there was probably no immediate danger.

"Why don't you hold off on calling nine-one-one? I'll be there ASAP. I'll park one street over and cut through the woods on foot, see if I can get the jump on him."

"What if he's armed?"

Abby patted her handbag. "So am I. Sit tight. You've still got *your* gun, right?"

"Of course."

"Keep it handy. But don't fire till you see the whites of his eyes."

"That isn't funny," Madeleine said, ending the call.

Abby parked on a cul-de-sac behind Madeleine Grant's house, then climbed a grassy hill that flattened out into thick woods. Trees swallowed the sun, leaving her in deep verdant shade.

She felt out of place here. She'd grown up on a ranch in the desert, and she was at home in the outdoors, where there was an open sky and a clear horizon. Having lived in the city for most of her adult life, she was equally comfortable amid skyscrapers and office towers.

But she had little experience with woods. She couldn't tell one tree from another or distinguish birdsong from cricket chirps. She didn't like the confusion of tree limbs and shadows, a meshwork of darkness that could conceal an enemy.

Madeleine's house stood tall enough to be visible above the trees. Abby moved toward it, using the roof as her polestar. As she drew closer, she saw a distant human figure framed in a gap in the foliage. A man, if she could judge by the figure's stance. He was standing by the fence, as Madeleine had said. She couldn't make out any details.

Abby watched him, wishing she'd brought binoculars. He seemed to have dark hair, but it might have been a cap. Her vision was good, but she was too far away to see anything useful.

She advanced, moving into a denser copse of trees, losing sight of her quarry. She wasn't worried about that. She would pick him up again once she'd left the deeper underbrush behind. For the moment, her attention was focused on the ground under her feet. She knew enough about the woods to avoid twigs, dry leaves, anything that would snap, crackle, and pop.

At some point her gun left her purse and wound up in her hand, leading her. She hadn't been aware of grabbing it.

Close now. The foliage thinning. Madeleine's house looming over the high wrought-iron fence.

The man ought to be in view again. She didn't see him.

It was possible he'd heard her approach and taken cover. She might be walking into an ambush. She hesitated, wondering if it was safer to stay put. Maybe not. He could be circling around to get a shot at her from behind.

Tricky situation. Lots of variables. No way to be sure what was going on.

She followed an old adage she'd just made up: When in doubt—charge.

With a burst of speed she tore out of the woods, running to the exact spot where the man had stood. She hit the dirt, rolled, and came up behind a tangle of scraggly ground cover, pointing the gun everywhere at once, daring him to take a shot and give away his position.

There was no shot. After thirty seconds, she began to suspect that the guy was gone. She also began to feel a tad foolish. She'd scuffed her knees, mussed up her skirt, and risked a sprained ankle with her little stuntwoman demo.

She made a quick circuit of the area and confirmed that no one was around. He'd left in a hurry, maybe because he sensed he wasn't alone. More likely it was just a coincidence. He might have gotten tired of the stakeout, or moved to another part of the fence, probing for weaknesses. She would have to check the entire perimeter.

Before she did, she took a closer look at the area where he'd been standing. She was no tracker, but there might be some kind of clue. In the movies, people were always leaving cigarette butts that somehow helped to identify them. Or a book of matches from a nightclub, or a monogrammed cigarette lighter. Fortunately for his health, but unfortunately for her purposes, this guy did not appear to be a smoker. Nor was he a litterbug. He'd left nothing.

She'd almost given up when she noticed a small depression in the ground where rainwater had collected during the last storm. The soil remained moist enough to have picked up the partial impression of a shoe.

She rummaged in her handbag for a measuring tape, then stretched it along the shoe print. Size nine or nine and a half. Not exactly Bigfoot. And not Kolb, either. His feet were larger than that.

"Coast is clear," Abby reported when she stepped into Madeleine Grant's foyer. "He amscrayed. And it wasn't Kolb."

"Then who was it?"

She shrugged. "Random prowler. Vagrant. Local kid sneaking off to smoke some dope."

"I don't believe that."

"Don't you? Funny. Neither do I."

"I wish you could be serious for once."

"I'm always serious, Madeleine. I just hide it behind a mask of insouciant bravado."

Abby moved into the living room. She noticed that Madeleine, in her agitation, had forgotten her normal social graces. There was no offer to be seated, no tendering of anything to drink. A born hostess like Madeleine Grant had to be seriously distressed to overlook such niceties.

Distressed—but not disheveled. She was dressed in a casual but elegant outfit that made Abby feel hopelessly déclassé in her faux-office-worker ensemble. She could learn a few things from Maddie's fashion sense.

"If you don't believe your own theories," Madeleine said, pacing, "then who *do* you think it was?"

"I'm beginning to think Kolb has a partner."

"A partner?"

"Gee, I knew this house was big, but I didn't expect an echo." Madeleine bristled. Abby held up a placating hand. "My point is, it's too big a coincidence—your meeting Tess McCallum yesterday, someone showing up here today."

"Kolb can't *know* I met Agent McCallum."

"Who knows what he knows? If he was watching the house and saw her arrive . . ."

Madeleine hugged herself. "Oh, God."

Abby tried to lighten the mood. "Hey, don't flip out on me. I'm engaging in pure speculation. For all I know, it really is a coincidence. But," she added truthfully, "I wouldn't bet the farm on it. I think it's more likely Kolb has an accomplice. He's found someone he trusts—or someone he needs."

"Needs?"

There was that echo again, but Abby prudently refrained from mentioning it. "If he *is* the Rain Man, it's a pretty complicated scheme for him to pull off all by his lonesome. Expensive, too. Maybe his partner ponied up the seed money for the secret bank accounts. Maybe his partner planned the whole thing, and Kolb is only the muscle. The partner handles the administrative chores, and Kolb does the wet work—no pun intended."

"If his partner is only an administrator, what was he doing here?"

"Keeping an eye on things, maybe. Watching to see if McCallum comes back for another powwow. Or . . ."

"What?"

"Nothing."

"What, Abby?"

She had to say it. "He might've been taking a look at your fence and your security system."

"To break in."

"To gather information."

"Information for Kolb, you mean? To tell *him* how to get in?"

Abby couldn't deny it. "Anything is possible. But I don't know why Kolb would come after you. If anything happened to you, he'd be the prime suspect."

"He might be saving me for last." Madeleine looked out the front window, as if expecting to see Kolb beyond the gate, waiting for her like an executioner on the gallows.

"When he's carried these kidnappings as far as they can go . . . when he's getting ready to leave town and live in luxury off his ransom money . . . then he might come for me. To finish things." She let a moment tick past in silence, then added, "I notice you're not disputing the point."

Abby bit her lip and tried to balance honesty with tact. "It's not impossible. *If* he's the Rain Man. That's a big if."

Madeleine was still looking toward the gate. "He hates me. He won't let go of me." Her voice dropped lower, edging into a whisper. "I gave a deposition, you know. In the pretrial phase. He was there. I had to sit in the same room with him and tell my story. He never said a word, just stared. Flat eyes. I've never seen a man look like that. He blames me for what happened. It's my fault. I put him in jail. He wants revenge."

Abby put a hand on Madeleine's arm. "He may want it. That doesn't mean he'll act on what he wants."

"He will."

"We don't know that. A lot of times, these guys never go near the original victim again. They develop a new obsession—or they stay clean. Scared straight. It happens."

Madeleine turned from the window and looked at her. "Has Kolb been scared straight, Abby?"

Those wide, unblinking eyes demanded a candid answer. "I don't think so," Abby said. "But even if your Peeping Tom was looking for a way in, he may not have found it. You've got good security here."

"Could you get past my system, if you had to?"

"Me, I'm just a cowgirl from Arizona."

"Abby . . ."

She surrendered. "I could get in. But I'm smarter than the guy who was here today."

"How do you know?"

"Because I'm smarter than everybody."

Madeleine had to smile at this. "At least you don't lack confidence." Then the smile fell away. "I want you to get him, Abby. I want you to put him in prison—like last time."

"I'm on the case. Just stay strong."

She and Madeleine returned to the foyer, where Abby noticed a framed movie poster, the image of a woman in silhouette against a moonlit sea.

"Hey, I've seen this movie," she said. "It really bites. Whatever possessed you to hang the poster?"

"It was one of Daddy's films."

"Did I say it bites? I meant, it's a biting social commentary. . . ."

Madeleine rescued her. "It's awful. But I like the poster. Quite good by the standards of commercial art, don't you think? The artist has captured something here—the woman's loneliness, her isolation . . . and her strength."

Abby took another long look at the poster. "I can relate," she said quietly.

Beside her, Madeleine nodded. "So can I."

17

Tess left the Pacific Area station but didn't head directly downtown. Instead, she returned to the MiraMist and asked the desk clerk if there was a package for her.

"FedEx SameDay, just arrived."

She accepted the package, a large and fairly heavy box that she didn't open until she was back in her car. Inside was a round metal device with a coiled, spring-loaded copper antenna on top and a magnet on its underside. Packed beside it were two carrying cases, which she left closed, and a small tool kit containing a putty knife, electrical tape, and work gloves.

She drove east, following directions she jotted down after consulting the map book in the glove compartment. The route took her to an unimpressive neighborhood in the mid-Wilshire district. She cruised past Kolb's apartment building and saw his Oldsmobile in the carport. He was home.

She knew his address and the make and model of his car because she'd run his name through the Department of Motor Vehicles database. The package she'd received via same-day delivery had been sent from the Denver office after she'd made a late-night phone call to the head of the Denver surveillance squad, waking him. She'd told him what she needed.

"They have those in LA, you know," he'd said sleepily.

"I want one of ours."

"Should I ask why?"

"No."

"Right. I'll send it out first thing tomorrow. You should have it by ten A.M."

If she'd obtained the items from the Los Angeles office, she would have had to sign for them. That would have required an explanation she didn't want to give. It also would have required a court order she had insufficient grounds to request. Getting what she needed from Denver had been a lot easier. Of course, it had also entailed breaking the rules. What she was about to do was even worse. It constituted breaking the law.

Her Bureau car was too conspicuous to be left anywhere near Kolb's address. Two blocks away she found a bank where she parked the sedan, hoping no one would boost it while she was gone. She removed the pair of carrying cases from the box and left them on the floor of the car, then wedged the box under her arm and walked to the apartment building.

There were significant risks in what she was about to do, and not just of the legal sort. Kolb knew who she was. He'd followed the Mobius case in detail. He'd kept a scrapbook about it. He would recognize her face. He was paranoid and potentially violent. If he glimpsed her in his neighborhood, there was no way to know how he would react.

Abby undoubtedly would not have been happy to know that Tess was here. She wanted to handle everything herself, unassisted, the Lone Ranger. But even the Lone Ranger had a sidekick—and although Tess didn't fancy herself in that role, she was going to help out, whether Abby liked it or not.

Abby's endgame, as she'd made clear, was to go on a date with Kolb. When she did, Tess intended to follow. But it wasn't easy for a single car to tail a suspect. Multiple vehicles could trade off in the command position to avoid being noticed. One car alone was easy to spot. And in city traffic, the tail car would have to stay close. Too close.

There was another way—electronic tracking. In her call

to the surveillance agent, she'd requested a vehicle-tracking transmitter, also known as a bumper beeper. Five inches in diameter, battery powered, it would transmit a pulsed RF signal with a line-of-sight range of five miles. Unfortunately, the signal would be blocked by tall buildings and other obstructions, which made its effective range much shorter within city limits.

She'd never planted one of these devices before, but she knew the procedure. Despite the gadget's nickname, it was rarely installed inside the bumper. A flat surface was preferable. The bottom of the gas tank was an obvious choice, but the metal there was too thin. The underside of the floor pans would provide better support.

The key was to make the plant quickly, before anyone noticed her fooling around with Kolb's Oldsmobile.

She entered the carport, checking to be sure that no one was in sight, and put the box on the ground. She opened the tool kit and pulled on the gloves.

The installation should take only a minute or two. As high-risk ops went, it didn't amount to much—as long as Kolb didn't need to use his car.

Kolb paced his apartment, his footsteps heavy enough to rattle the walls.

He'd grown progressively angrier since coming home. It wasn't losing the job that had turned him inside out. He didn't give a shit about the job. He didn't need to wear that crappy uniform or take abuse from goddamned loitering teenagers. And he certainly didn't need the money, not with two million in the bank and more on the way.

It was the way that fat fuck with the bad comb-over had talked to him. The bored insolence in his voice. The sleepy, contemptuous eyes . . .

He snatched his book of philosophy off the shelf and flipped through it, finding the chapter on Hegel, his gaze skipping from one underlined sentence to another, one great thought succeeded by the next.

There was the vision of Napoleon "stretching over the world and dominating it . . . one of the world-historical men, the clear-sighted ones . . . who tell their age what its will is."

They acted with zeal: "Nothing great in the world has been accomplished without passion."

They acted without regard for the rest of humankind: "The particular is of trifling value: individuals are to be sacrificed."

They acted with impunity: "So mighty a figure must trample down many an innocent flower—crush to pieces many an object in its path."

That line, above all, held him fascinated. He felt it had been written directly to him. His response, he knew, marked him as the heir to the philosopher's vision, one of the few who were worthy of it. He was the latest in a line of heroes from Caesar to Saladin to Napoleon, men who breathed power and disdained convention. He was a lord of the earth, soaring so much higher than his fellows as to be almost a new species.

"So mighty a figure . . . trample down . . . crush to pieces . . ."

This was greatness. This was progress. An inexorable march, a relentless advance. The weak things of the world had to perish, because they were weak and they were in the way.

In *his* way—like that dumb bitch last night.

He slapped the book shut.

He'd been wrong to let her off so easy. He saw that now. He should've stomped harder on her. Should've plowed into her sedan at even higher speed, blown her vertebrae out the back of her neck. Should've rammed her and rammed her until the bitch was dead . . .

The phone rang.

He whirled to it, startled by the noise.

It rang a second time. He watched it in almost superstitious fascination.

On the third ring he plucked the handset off the cradle. He held the phone to his ear but said nothing.

There was a beat of puzzled silence on the other end of the line. Then he heard a familiar voice, low and slightly muffled. "You there?"

His partner. That was who it was. For a second there, he'd almost thought . . .

Almost thought it was Tess McCallum. McCallum, calling him. Which was insane.

"I'm here," Kolb said.

"I thought you might be at work, but I don't know your hours—"

He didn't want to talk about work. "What do you want?"

"We need to have a conversation."

"We're having one."

"In person."

"Can't it wait?"

"No."

The man's tone worried Kolb, as did the fact that he'd muffled his voice. "There a problem?"

"Yes."

"What?"

"Aren't you the one who's always telling me not to say too much on the phone? We need to meet. Below, half hour. Can you be there?"

"Yeah, but—"

Dial tone. The asshole had hung up.

Kolb banged down the phone.

Now even his partner was treating him with disrespect. Giving him orders. That wasn't the way it was supposed to work. Yes, it was an equal partnership—in theory. And the money would be split equally. Kolb had no qualms about that. But it had always been tacitly understood who was in charge. Who was the boss, and who was the hired hand.

Maybe success was going to his friend's head. And maybe he would have to do something about that.

He wouldn't be screwed with; that was for certain. He was through being everybody's favorite fuck-me toy.

Kolb left the apartment, punctuating his departure with a slam of the door, and headed back to the carport.

Tess pushed the equipment under the car and slid in after it. From her pocket she produced a penlight, holding it in her mouth, aiming the beam upward.

The floor pan was slimed with grease and scum. She used the putty knife to scrape it clean, then pressed the transmitter into place, bottom side up. The magnet affixed it to the metal, but to assure that it wouldn't be jolted loose by a pothole, she secured it with the electrical tape. She taped it twice, then extended the antenna so it pointed straight down, clearing the metal surfaces that could produce interference. It would broadcast its signal for hours, operating on lithium batteries that had been newly installed before the package was sent.

She thought she should give the gadget a few more layers of electrical tape. Kolb's car was in bad shape, indicating that he was a reckless driver, and she didn't want—

Footsteps.

Someone coming this way, coming from the side door of the building, coming fast.

She knew it was Kolb, somehow just *knew*, the same way she'd known she was being watched at Madeleine Grant's house last night.

She switched off the penlight and stuck it in her pocket. Lying on her back under the car, she waited.

He entered the carport. She saw heavy, dark shoes. Shoes that approached the Oldsmobile and stopped by the driver's side.

It really was him. And it looked like he was going for a drive.

When he pulled out, he would see her in the space he'd vacated.

The sedan's door opened. The car creaked on its shocks.

Her best shot was to crawl under the adjacent car, parked

to the right of the Oldsmobile. If she moved fast, he was unlikely to see her through the passenger window.

She rolled sideways, trying to make it quick, but when she was halfway out, the sleeve of her jacket snagged on a bit of metal protruding from the sedan's underbelly.

Overhead, the engine coughed but didn't start.

When he got the car moving, he would back out, and right now she was trapped between the tires, certain to be run over.

She tugged at her sleeve.

The engine sputtered again—sputtered and coughed and came to life.

She heard the clunk of gears as the car shifted into reverse.

The sleeve ripped free.

She threw herself out from under the Olds, rolling beneath the other car.

Kolb's tires caught with a shriek of rubber, and he rocketed out of his space, fishtailing in the parking lot. He straightened out and tore off, and Tess lay on her side, trying to catch her breath.

The electrical tape and putty knife lay on the ground where the Oldsmobile had been parked, but Kolb hadn't noticed. She gathered them up and returned the items to the tool kit.

She was still shaking a little. *Tess's big adventure*, she thought.

It had been more dangerous than she'd expected. Still, it seemed trivial compared to the risks Abby took every day.

She wondered where that thought had come from. What difference did it make what Abby did? Abby had nothing to do with her. Abby was a freelance private investigator, more or less, and Tess . . .

What exactly was she, these days? It had been a long time since she'd done any hands-on investigating. A manager, then. A supervisor. A bureaucrat.

Maybe that was why she'd risked planting an unauthorized tracking device. She wanted to be *doing* something, wanted to be in the game. She'd spent too long on the sidelines, shuffling papers, handing out assignments, organizing schedules, running meetings. She didn't feel like a law-enforcement officer anymore. She didn't feel like one of the good guys.

So what was the solution? Cash out of her career and go freelance? Become a vigilante?

That couldn't be right. Yet she was edging closer to that precipice with every rule she broke.

18

Below Ground was, in its own way, a neighborhood bar, but not the kind of place where everybody knew your name.

On his first night here, Kolb had been flanked by a guy with a shaved head whose T-shirt read WIFE BEATER and by a goateed, ponytailed swish sipping from a wineglass. He'd gotten the message: *We take anyone's money and ask no questions.*

That policy suited Kolb fine. After his time in stir, he'd found himself unable to fit in at most drinking establishments. Naturally, his old cop haunts were off-limits. He would hardly be welcomed by his former buddies—his comrades in arms, who'd deserted him under fire. Nor could he waltz into bars where ex-cons hung out. Too many of them would remember him from his days in uniform. As for the yuppie bars, their patrons looked askance at a blue-collar guy with callused hands and a bodybuilder's physique.

Then he'd found this place. One of his aimless nocturnal drives had led him to this unprepossessing neighborhood near the intersection of Vermont and Olympic. He'd liked Below Ground immediately—a no-bullshit establishment, clean of pretensions, with just the right mix of civility and indifference, and an undertone of danger. It was a place that catered to people who wanted to be strangers, a place where he belonged.

In his nights here—he nearly always came at night—he'd seen the full variety of the bar's clientele. There was the meat-market crowd, whose quick sexual transactions were conducted in lavatories and stairwells. There were the tough guys who started brawls. The pool sharps, intent on the mechanics of their game. The guy in the cowboy hat who played "Ring of Fire" on the jukebox and made a toast to the memory of Johnny Cash. The rich Westside bitches who went slumming—"Dumpster-diving," one of them called it, the one who always left with a choice piece of trash. The cabbie who came here after his last fare and drank himself blind, murmuring obscure imprecations in some guttural foreign language. One or two guys who'd done time—Kolb could sniff them, and they'd caught his scent, as well. They circled each other, wary animals, keeping their distance.

And there were the voyeurs, the ones who stood back and watched the carnival. One of them was the bartender, a young, muscular guy who kept a Louisville Slugger behind the counter for use in crowd control. Another was Kolb himself.

The bar, true to its name, was a sunken cave. Kolb walked down a narrow staircase that descended from daylight into cool, subterranean gloom. By the time he reached bottom, the sun had been forgotten, along with any concept of time. One o'clock in the afternoon could have been one o'clock in the morning. There was no way to tell the difference, except that, from what he could see as his vision adjusted to the dimness, the daytime crowd was skewed toward a more professional class.

He didn't see his partner at first, but he knew the man was here. His song was playing on the jukebox.

Scanning the bar, he found his partner in a corner booth with an untouched mug of beer. Beer was what he always drank. Kolb distrusted that choice of beverage. A man should have a taste for hard liquor.

He slid into the booth. "What's so goddamn important?" he asked without preliminaries.

"There could be a problem."

"Could be? On the phone you told me there *was* a problem. Now it's 'could be'?"

"What, you're a semanticist now?" The man let out a soft, nervous chuckle. "You're parsing my grammar?"

"Don't laugh at me," Kolb said.

"I was just saying—"

"No, *I* was just saying. Don't you fucking laugh at me."

"Okay, okay."

"You laugh at me again, I'll kill you."

"All right, man. Chill."

"And quit talking like a goddamned homeboy."

He put his hands up. "No offense intended. I didn't mean to piss you off. I'm a little on edge, that's all."

"What've you got to be nervous about? I'm the one taking the risks. You don't even have to get your hands dirty."

"That's not quite true."

"Your manicured hands."

"I don't get manicures. And we're not here to discuss my grooming habits."

"Then why are we here?"

"Because of our problem." He hesitated. "We may have to call off tonight."

"I'm not postponing."

"I didn't say postpone. We may have to quit, cold turkey."

Kolb sucked in a harsh breath. "When they snipped your fingernails, did they snip your balls, too?"

"I haven't lost my nerve. There's a new element in the equation, that's all."

"What element?"

"McCallum."

The name hung between them like a threat.

"Are you saying she's on to you?" Kolb asked after a pause.

His partner shook his head. "No. She's on to *you*."

"That's impossible."

"She had a meeting with Madeleine Grant."

"You're bullshitting. What's the idea? You trying to scare me off the job because you got cold feet?"

The other man looked past his beer mug into Kolb's face. "I'm telling you the truth."

Kolb saw it in his eyes. No lie.

He banged the table. "Son of a *bitch*."

"Quiet down; keep cool."

Kolb didn't want to keep cool. He wanted to rage, smash things. That woman—that goddamned woman—she was fucking with him—fucking him over. . . . He didn't even know which woman he meant, Tess McCallum or Madeleine Grant—they were blending together in his mind.

Then he realized the other patrons were looking in his direction, their attention drawn by his outburst. With a fierce effort he calmed himself.

"When did this meeting happen?" he asked.

His partner took a sip of beer before answering. "Last night."

"McCallum just got into town last night."

"Apparently the lady works fast."

"How do you even know about it? Did she tell you?"

"She hasn't told anybody—at least not anybody connected with the investigation."

"Then how . . .?"

Another sip. "I'm your inside man, right? It's my job to know what's going on."

"What did Grant say to her?"

"I don't know, but I doubt they were talking about the weather. Well, then again, maybe they were."

Kolb looked away. He didn't want to see the man across the table puckering his lips as he tasted the beer's foam. "There's no way Grant could connect me with this," he said.

"Except she did. And now McCallum is working it. I don't know if she's made any progress, but I do know there's a good chance there'll be eyes on you from now on."

"What eyes? She hasn't told anybody, you said. She's working it alone."

"She may have brought in the LAPD."

Kolb knew that was bullshit. "The department's not going to help her unless they have clearance from her superiors. It's the way the bureaucracy works. *You* should know that. And she hasn't told her superiors, right?"

"Maybe she's planning to keep an eye on you herself."

He considered this prospect. "If it's just her, alone, I can handle it."

The other man put down the mug with a clunk. "She's a federal agent."

"She's a cunt with legs. Popping her is no harder than popping her cherry."

"You can't be serious."

"If she's watching me, she'll follow me tonight. I can spot a tail. I can lead her someplace where I have the advantage."

He saw apprehension on his partner's face. No surprise. The other victims had been strangers to the man, allowing him to pretend that Angela Morris and Paula Weissman weren't real. Easy enough, when they were only names in the news. But his partner had *met* McCallum. He knew her as a person, not as a game piece on a chessboard. Talking about the murder of nonentities was one thing. The murder of a real human being was something else.

Kolb had no illusions about the man he was paired with. He was little more than a wannabe, miles out of his league—like a guy at fantasy baseball camp who was suddenly tossed into the seventh game of the World Series. He enjoyed playacting as a badass, as long as things never got too serious. But in a tight spot, he was the type to lose his nerve.

It worried Kolb, having to depend on this man. Hell, having to depend on anybody.

"Say you do that," his partner said after a worried pause. "You . . . deal with her. Madeleine Grant will just tell somebody else whatever she told McCallum, and the Bureau will be all over your ass anyway. What have you gained?"

Kolb already knew the answer. He stared into the dim recesses of the bar. "Ten million dollars. That's what."

"Ten . . .?"

"Yeah. Ten."

His partner shifted in his seat. "I thought the plan—"

"The plan is being modified. I asked one mil for Morris, didn't get it. Asked two mil for Weissman, and the city came through. Tonight I ask ten million for whoever I put in the tunnels."

"They won't be expecting that large a demand."

"They'll cough it up."

The man picked up the mug and took his first healthy swallow. He was scared outright now. That was fine. Kolb liked being scary.

"It doesn't fix anything," his partner said. "McCallum will still be after you, and even if you can take her out, the rest of them will pick up the scent."

"That's why I'm going for the big bucks. I'd hoped we could up the ante more gradually, but circumstances are forcing our hand. So we go for the big score all at once."

"You mean this is it, then? This is the last time?" There was pitiful relief in the man's voice.

"It's the last. We leave town after tonight. I hope your bags are packed."

"I'll be ready. If you've got the papers."

"I've got them."

"Maybe I should take mine now."

"I don't think so."

"It's not like I'm going to run out on you."

"Then you won't be needing them, will you?"

No answer, just another nervous swallow of beer.

"It's a trade, jackoff," Kolb said. "I give you the ID, you give me the account number. And not that there's any mistrust involved, but I'll be using a laptop with a wireless modem to check that bank account before you go anywhere."

"Don't sweat it. Your half will be in there."

"Six million—that's my share. Not a penny less."

"That's if the city comes through with the ten mil tonight."

"They'll come through. I have those assholes by the balls." This wasn't bravado. Kolb knew they would pay. They had to pay.

"I really hate pressing our luck like this," the other man said softly, his gaze fixed on his beer.

"Since when did you start having opinions? And since when did I start to give a shit?"

"I'm your partner."

"My *silent* partner."

"I have a say. It's my ass on the line, too."

"Your ass. That's for sure. Your lily ass would last about five minutes in maximum security."

"That's why I don't intend to go there. If you get caught, we're both screwed."

"If I get caught," Kolb said, "there's always plan B."

There was a pause. "I know."

Kolb didn't like the uncertainty he heard. "Listen, I need to know I can count on you. If I get picked up, you have to come through for me. You don't, and I'll give you up in a minute. You hear me?"

"I hear you, God damn it. And I know what to do. Shit, I'm one step ahead of you. I already ran a recon mission."

"What the hell does that mean?"

"It means I went over to her house."

Kolb took a moment to figure this out. "Grant's house? That might not've been smart, if McCallum's been talking to her."

"She's still the one you want to use, though, isn't she? I mean, for plan B?"

"Yeah," Kolb said, tasting the words, "she's the one."

"Okay, then. I had to check out her security."

"What's the verdict?"

"It's a good system, but I can defeat it."

"Was this before or after you learned about McCallum?"

"After."

"Then you must've known I wasn't going to cancel tonight's operation."

"I didn't know what you were going to do. But I have the feeling that Grant is unfinished business with you. Even if we didn't go tonight, you'd still have a bug up your ass about her."

"Can you blame me?"

"I wouldn't dare."

"Wise policy." Kolb took the beer mug out of the other man's grasp and downed a long gulp, then made a face. "What the fuck is this, mule piss?"

"Light beer. Low-cal, low-carb."

"Jesus." Kolb gave back the mug. "You know, there's one advantage to McCallum meeting Grant. Now they've got a relationship. It gives us more leverage if you have to use her tonight."

"Which I pray to God I won't."

Kolb smiled. "I doubt God is listening to your prayers."

"Or yours."

"I don't pray. Prayer is for the weak. It's a crutch for them to lean on—and a stick to beat them with. Religion teaches the meek and humble to be even more meek and humble. That way they can be even more easily controlled. Turn people into sacrificial lambs, and they'll trip all over themselves marching to the abattoir."

"Right, right." His partner wasn't listening. He had no head for philosophy.

Kolb switched back to more practical matters. "There's no chance Grant saw you?"

"I was discreet."

"Well, maybe you're pulling your load, after all."

"Let's just hope we don't have to use her."

"Yeah. And let's also hope you remember how bad you'd look on TV doing the perp walk."

"You trying to scare me?"

"Just appealing to your self-interest. That's what'll motivate you to stick with me, not any concept of honor among thieves. I know you don't go for that. You're too well educated to really believe in anything."

His partner bristled. "Like you're so goddamn superior?"

"I *am* superior," Kolb said complacently.

"Right, I know, Nietzsche and the superman and all that crap. Nietzsche went insane, you know. He died in a mental hospital."

"It's Hegel I like, not Nietzsche."

"Same difference."

"If they put Nietzsche in the nuthouse, it wasn't because he was insane. It was because they have to lock up the superior man."

"I've heard this speech before."

"You haven't *heard* shit. If you'd heard, you would understand."

"We don't have time for this." His partner started to get up.

"Sure we do." Kolb grabbed his arm and forced him back into his seat. "Take a few extra minutes on your lunch break. Relax. *Chill.*" He pronounced the last word with a keen sarcastic edge. "You ever ask yourself why I'm doing this?"

"For the money."

"Go deeper."

"For revenge."

"Still not deep enough."

"I give up. Why?"

"Because," Kolb said, "this is how I teach the world a lesson. I show them who they've been dealing with. They thought they could break me? I'm fucking unbreakable. I'm more resilient than they ever guessed. I survived Chino and came back smarter and tougher than before. What doesn't kill me makes me stronger."

"*That's* Nietzsche."

"Yeah. And there's nothing crazy about it." He grabbed the mug again and took another swig. What the hell, low-cal or not, it was still beer. "They wanted me to bow down. But I'm making *them* bow to *me*. Making this whole city bow down. They have to recognize my will. They have to obey me. I intend to make them *see*."

"See . . . what?"

"Who I am. Their master. One of the elite."

His partner leaned forward, eyes narrowing. "You *want* them to identify you, don't you?"

Kolb didn't deny it. Nor did he give back the beer. "The great artist always signs his work. When this is over, people will be singing my song for a thousand years. Orpheus went down into the underworld and almost brought back his bride. Failed at the end, and lost her. But I'm going down into the underworld tonight, and coming up with ten million dollars. And the world will know my name and tremble. I'll be a fucking legend. All those asshole serial killers who got caught—they're nothing compared to me. They never held a city hostage."

"Mobius did."

Kolb paused with the mug halfway to his mouth. "Briefly."

"Is that why he's your hero?"

"He's not my hero. You've never understood about that. I don't admire failure. And I don't need heroes. I don't need anybody."

"No one's going to write any songs about you. They don't write songs about criminals."

Kolb finished the beer. "*The Iliad* is a song, and Achilles was a criminal. A pillager and a warlord and a straight maniac. *The Odyssey*—that's a song, too, and Ulysses was a thief and a pirate. You look at any great man, and you see a criminal. What was Caesar except a killer? But they put up statues to him."

"I hope you're not expecting any statues."

"Fuck, with my share of the money, I can buy my own. I'm on the verge of immortality. All I have to do is take care of one small problem. Which gives me an idea. You reprogram the phone for me?"

"Yeah." His partner extracted it from his jacket. "Here it is."

Kolb took it—an older cell phone, the same one he'd used to place the call to the mayor's office during the Paula Weissman job. Before each abduction, his partner programmed it with a new serial number and phone number, making it a clone of somebody's legitimate cell phone. Any calls made on it could not be traced to Kolb.

"I want you to call me on the cell whenever McCallum is coming or going," Kolb said.

"Coming or . . .?"

"Coming to the office, if she's out in the field. Or leaving the office, if she's already there. Give me as much of a heads-up as possible."

"I thought you were going to wait till tonight."

"I'm not much for procrastinating." He pushed the empty mug across the table. "If I can take her down now, I'll do it."

"I don't know, Kolb. . . ."

"Don't say my goddamn name."

"Sorry."

"And don't tell me you don't know. I've been to the Federal Building. Went there once or twice when I was a cop. Nice big parking lot, open to the public. Of course she might be using the underground garage—but I'm betting that as a visitor, she parks outside. If I see her there by herself, no one else around, I can blip her, easy."

"She probably knows what you look like."

"She'll never even see me."

His partner restlessly picked up the mug and transferred it from hand to hand. "This is not a good idea."

"It's the only idea. Look, either I do her this afternoon, or I do her tonight. Sooner beats later, right?" He didn't wait for a response. "You just give me a call when she's entering or leaving. With any luck, I can be in position to give her a little love tap."

"Killing a federal agent—"

"Is a crime? Every goddamn thing we've done is a crime."

"I was going to say, it'll put the whole city on high alert."

Kolb snorted. "Like they aren't on high alert already? Take a look at the weather forecast. Rain, rain, rain commencing by ten P.M." His voice hardened. "Just do it. No excuses."

"I'll do my best."

"That sounds a little too noncommittal." Kolb pushed himself forward, dominating the small table. "I need to know you're with me. Not just on this. On everything. Plan B and all the rest."

The other man was staring into the beer glass again. "Of course I'm with you."

"Look me in the eye and say it."

"That's kind of dramatic."

"Look at me—and tell me."

Finally his partner lifted his gaze and made eye contact. "I'm with you. In for a dime, in for a dollar. Or ten million dollars."

The statement seemed a little too humorous. "This isn't something you want to joke about," Kolb warned.

"It's no joke. I'm in it." The man raised his empty glass. "All the way."

19

Tess was driving east toward downtown LA and an unscheduled meeting with Deputy District Attorney Snelling when her cell phone rang.

"McCallum," she answered, and heard Josh Green's voice.

"Hello, Tess." He sounded curiously subdued.

"Checking up on me?"

"Not exactly."

"Did you water my plants?"

"Uh, yeah, I did. Look, I've got some news, and it's not good."

His tone finally registered with her. "What is it?"

He told her. She listened with the phone at her ear, driving the car without conscious thought.

"Okay," she said when he was through. "I see."

"I'm sorry, Tess."

"Right."

"It's not your . . . well, you know."

He'd been about to tell her it wasn't her fault. "I know," she said, though she didn't. "Thanks, Josh."

"How, uh, how's everything there?"

She couldn't have a conversation with him now. "Talk to you later," she said, ending the call.

She drove on, her vision narrowed by a fringe of dampness at the corners of her eyes.

Coming up on her right was the spire of a church. On impulse she swung the Crown Vic into the empty parking lot. She killed the engine and sat in the car, wondering why she'd stopped. There was no reason for her to be here. She hadn't been in a church in months—not since she'd looked into the trash bin behind the minimart and seen Danny Lopez. She wasn't sure why she'd stayed away. Maybe she hadn't felt worthy to go.

But that was the wrong attitude. It wasn't a question of worthiness. The most unworthy were the ones who were most welcome. The prodigal son and all that. Right?

"Right," she said.

She left the car and ascended the steps to the main doors. As she entered, she realized she was carrying her gun in her coat. Bringing a gun into church was probably a sin in itself. But she figured she could get away with it. Even in LA, there were no metal detectors in churches—not yet.

Out of habit she bowed at the knee just inside the narthex, then proceeded into the nave. The church was empty. Dim lighting from recessed lamps limned rows of straight-backed pews. Stained-glass windows let in faint daylight, illuminating scenes from the Way of the Cross. Behind the altar hung a small crucified Christ, frozen in his timeless suffering.

She took a seat near the back, reluctant to go forward, feeling like an intruder. She sat motionless, breathing gently in the great quiet.

There was a time when she'd been a stranger to her faith. That was after Paul Voorhees died—the only man she could honestly say she'd loved in the full sense of the word, not simply as a lover but as a partner in life. For him to have been taken from her was an assault on any meaning, any spiritual purpose in the world.

Slowly, by degrees, she'd allowed herself to rediscover what she'd lost. Other people could bear to exist in a universe leached of values, a random agglomeration of particles and planets held together by blind forces, proceeding only to oblivion. She could not.

Her belief wasn't what it had been in childhood, the naive acceptance of every tenet and doctrine. She had no particular commitment to theological niceties. She was willing to grant that a great deal of her religion was legend and symbol, ritual and tradition—myth, miracle, and authority, in the words of Dostoevsky's Grand Inquisitor. Even so, she loved some of the symbols and traditions—the musty smell of the missal, the flicker of candles, the great ethereal music of the mass.

But the surface trappings didn't really matter. It was odd how people could get so caught up in the rites and the sacred stories, which were no more than the vocabulary of faith, a language of symbols. The symbols varied from faith to faith, and most people accepted whichever ones they were born into, just as they accepted whatever language they were raised in. The particulars were arbitrary, but the underlying meaning was not. The imagery and symbolism were a way of reaching beyond the mundane world, into a transcendent awareness—to escape from pettiness, worry, jealousy, hatred, fear, if only for a few moments, and to lose oneself in something higher, something timeless and perfect. To defeat the ego and find the higher self.

That was the truth behind her faith and behind all faiths, a constant truth, however it had been mythologized and ceremonialized. It was a truth she couldn't phrase in words or defend with logic, but that was all right. She had enough of words and logic in her working life. She came to church to exercise another part of her being, a part that was neither analytical nor analyzable, but real. Maybe it was the realest part of all.

When she felt ready, she made her way down the aisle and knelt at the altar rail. Eyes shut, she prayed. She wasn't sure what she was praying for. Yes, she was. She wanted relief. Relief from the load of guilt and self-accusation, the dead weight on her shoulders, dragging her down.

"Come to me"—the Bible verse drifted through her

mind—"*all you who labor and are burdened, and I will give you rest.*"

She crossed herself and said, "Amen." But she didn't fool herself. She felt no different. Nothing had changed.

She wanted to leave but couldn't find the strength. She sank into a pew in the front row and wondered if she'd done something wrong, asked for the wrong thing, or if she really wasn't worthy, after all.

"Good morning."

She looked up and saw a young priest bending over her. "I'm all right," she said automatically, though she knew the tears on her cheeks gave the lie to her words.

The priest regarded her with sympathy. "Is there anything you'd like to tell me?"

"I'm afraid it's a long time since I've been to confession."

"My door is open," he said with a nod toward a corner of the room.

She had only painful memories of childhood visits to the confessional. And she had nothing to tell this earnest young man. He would never understand the problems she faced, the pressures, the choices, the compromises. He'd removed himself from the world, and she was part of the world, up to her elbows in it, and soiled by it, unclean. . . .

"I thought confession was taken on Saturday afternoon," she whispered.

"The schedule isn't carved in stone."

"I'm sure you've got other things to do. I don't want to waste your time."

He smiled. "This is what they pay me for."

She was sure she would say no, but she surprised herself. "Maybe it would help . . . just for a minute . . ."

"Drop in whenever you're ready."

She wasn't sure how long she sat in the pew, unwilling either to approach the confessional or to leave the church. Eventually she decided she was being a coward. Cowardice was hateful to her. She sometimes thought it was the only mortal sin.

She got up and entered the small, dark room. Some churches had done away with anonymous confessions, but this one was more traditional. There was the sliding grille, and the heavy darkness, and the strange, floating, disembodied sense of guilt that seemed to hover over the room.

She knelt, her heart beating fast.

The grille slid open, and the priest's silhouette, limned by dim light, appeared behind the screen. She remembered the ritual, but she wouldn't open with the traditional request for the father to forgive her sins. She couldn't say the words. She skipped ahead.

"It's been years since my last confession," she said. "Probably twenty years, at least."

She paused, hoping he would say something, but he was silent.

"I don't know why I've stayed away. Well, that's not true. I know why. I hate confession. I don't buy into it at all. I'm sorry, I just don't. I think it's a way for the church to exercise control, mind control. I don't mean to offend you, but that's the way it seems to me."

She was talking too much but unable to stop.

"You get people to come in here, and they tell you their secrets, and you forgive them, and that gives you power over them. I don't mean you personally. I mean that's the historical reason, the institutional reason for this sacrament. It's a way of maintaining control. And now people use it as therapy, but it's not therapy. It doesn't get to the root of the problem. It doesn't solve anything.

"So I know why stayed I've away. I just don't know why I'm here now. I guess I just need to talk to somebody, and I'm alone here in LA—no friends in this town, mostly enemies, in fact. Nobody I can really trust. Anyway, they wouldn't know what I was talking about, because it involves something that happened back in Denver, this case I was supervising—I work for the FBI, I should've mentioned that—and there was a case involving a pair of serial killers who were targeting young boys. We identified one of the killers."

He was Roland Greco, a tall man with hairy knuckles and acne scars, a man who owned two dogs and cleaned carpets for a living and preyed on kids. The plastic cover of the third victim's school notebook had yielded a thumbprint that matched Greco's print, on file from a prior conviction.

"We knew who he was. We knew he was our guy. We could have arrested him at any time. But then we might not have gotten his partner, because if the partner got wind of the arrest, he would run. So we had to make a decision—I had to make a decision; it was my call—a decision whether to make the arrest and risk losing the second killer or hold off and try to nab them both.

"I decided we would wait. I ordered a stakeout of the suspect's residence in the hope that he would go to his partner or his partner would come to him. But what happened . . . what happened is, the guy was so paranoid he eluded our surveillance. He didn't know he was being watched, but the next time he went to meet his partner, he took evasive measures out of habit, and he lost our people. And what he did was . . ."

She swallowed. It was difficult to speak.

"He got together with his partner, and the two of them killed another little boy, Danny Lopez, and they left his body in a trash bin."

She let a moment pass. She wasn't sure there was anything more to say, but then she knew she'd left unsaid the most important words of all.

"It sounds like an error of judgment, doesn't it? And I know an error of judgment is not a sin. To err is human—doesn't the Bible say that? Or was it Shakespeare? Anyway, I know we can't expect ourselves to be perfect. I understand that. But you see, I've gone over it a thousand times, and I'm not sure what my motive was in delaying the arrest. I just don't know. You could make a valid case for not arresting him until the partner was ID'd, but . . .

"I think, to some extent, I wanted to pull off a coup. Wanted a feather in my cap. I'd been in charge of the Denver office for only a few months, and this was a way to prove myself, score a major victory. If we nabbed both of them at once, it would be a classic bust, textbook. They would be teaching it at the academy.

"I think that's why I waited. At least that's part of the reason. I wasn't focused on the case. I was focused on myself. I wanted to look good. I wanted to show DC they'd made the right call putting me in charge. And then I looked into the trash bin.

"That little boy would be alive today if not for me. If not for my—I don't know what to call it—pride, selfishness, stupidity, whatever the word is. He would be alive.

"And even that isn't the worst thing. The worst thing is, we covered it up. We never let on that we'd had the suspect in our sights. We made the arrest as soon as Greco got back to his house, and got his partner a short time later—a woman, as it turned out."

A drug-addicted hooker named Wilma Brighton. Greco had given up her name almost at once, with no need for any pressure, and the partner hadn't tried to flee. The stakeout and the delay had never been necessary.

"Then we held a press conference congratulating ourselves on the job we'd done. And Danny's mother—she came up to me and thanked me, thanked me with tears in her eyes for apprehending the people who had killed her son, and I had to hug her and accept her gratitude and act like a hero, because the Bureau had decided it would be bad for our image if the truth got out.

"So I was a hero in her eyes and in the media stories. A hero.

"I didn't feel like a hero. I still don't.

"And then today I learned . . . Someone called me from Denver and told me Mrs. Lopez—a single mother, raising Danny all by herself, he was her only child—she killed herself. Took an overdose of pills. She couldn't go on without her boy.

"That's my confession. I don't know where in the Ten Commandments you find that particular sin. I don't know how many Hail Marys I have to say to atone for it. I'm sorry to lay all this on you. I guess I don't have anything more to say."

From behind the screen she heard the priest's quiet voice. "I'm not going to tell you to recite Hail Marys. But it's obvious to me you've suffered over this. You wanted to help your career; I understand that. But you also wanted to apprehend both criminals. You weren't content to get only one of them off the street. You wouldn't have felt your job had been done unless you could rid the city of them both. It sounds to me as if you had a mixture of motives. Most of us do, most of the time. I think you probably did the best you could."

"I didn't do enough," Tess murmured.

"None of us ever do enough. We only do what we can. If you hadn't caught those people, how many more children would they have killed? You did what you could. Probably you could've done better. You could've put all thoughts of your own advancement out of your mind. So here's the penance I prescribe for you. Keep doing your job, and do your best to think only of others, not of yourself. You'll find it's not easy. It may be impossible. But I want you to try. And spend some time thinking about the ones you've saved, not just the ones you lost."

Her voice was low. "Okay."

"And remember, you can only do your best. That's all anyone can ask."

She nodded, saying nothing.

"I absolve you of your sins in the name of the Father, the Son, and the Holy Spirit."

Tess made the sign of the cross.

"Go in peace," the priest said.

She couldn't remember what to say in response, so she simply told him, "Thank you."

She left the confessional and the church. She didn't know if she felt any better. She didn't know if she'd accomplished anything at all. But somehow she felt able to go on with her day. That was something, anyway.

Maybe it was a lot.

20

Kolb had lost it there for a minute. He'd started shouting in the bar. A mistake, unworthy of him. Unlike him, too. He was always in control. He couldn't let himself fall apart like that—especially not where he could be seen and noticed and, perhaps, remembered.

But once he was out of the bar, alone in his parked car, he let loose.

"Motherfuck!" He struck the dashboard with the flat of his hand, then with his fist, then with both fists, drumming on the cheap plastic until it cracked. *"Motherfuck!"*

A female pedestrian glanced at him. He gave her a furious stare, and she walked quickly away.

"Yeah, be afraid, bitch," he muttered, *"be afraid of me."*

Every woman in this city should fear him. Madeleine Grant should fear him. Tess McCallum—

He struck the dash again. Then he noticed that the knuckles of his right hand were bleeding.

He felt a twinge of fear. Screaming in his car, beating his fists bloody—what the hell was going on? It was like last night, when he'd given in to road rage. The same craziness, the same wild anger, the impulse to smash and kill without regard to consequences.

Losing control was not something he did—ever. He was always in control, in every situation. He never gave in to emotion. He was the superior man. He wasn't rocked and buffeted by feelings and circumstances. He was beyond all that. He could stand all day in front of the supermarket taking abuse from foulmouthed teenagers and feel nothing. He prided himself on self-discipline, self-mastery.

Now it was all going to shit, and he didn't understand how or why.

And it scared him.

With an effort he reasserted his composure. Whatever had come over him, it was temporary. Reaction to stress or some goddamned thing. He'd brought it out into the open, exorcised it, and now he was rid of it. There would be no more . . . episodes. He was himself again.

Nothing could touch him or wound him or move him. He would not allow it. He would be strong.

He sat unmoving until his breathing returned to normal and his pulse was low and steady. Aftershocks of rage shuddered through him. He let them pass. When they died away, he knew he was all right. He was calm. He felt fine. Better than fine. He felt nothing.

Except the beginnings of a headache, unwelcome and inexplicable.

But he could deal with that. Whatever happened, he could deal with it. Whatever McCallum was up to—

He shook aside that thought. Better not think of McCallum right now.

Anyway, he had things to do. Necessary things, practical things, which would take his mind off recent setbacks and refocus him on the job at hand.

The storage facility where he kept his equipment was only a couple of blocks from the bar, on a side street off Olympic Boulevard. He drove there and tapped his personalized entry code into the keypad at the gate.

Kolb had chosen this self-storage yard because all the lockers had outdoor access. Most of the facilities he'd investigated were indoors, with rows of lockers lining corridors. There were two problems with that setup. First, entry to the buildings was restricted to certain hours. Second, the entryways and halls were monitored by security cameras.

This facility had cameras also, but because they were outside, mounted high on the perimeter fence and the light poles, they would not record as clear an image. And his gate-access code allowed him entry at any time, day or night. There was a storage manager on duty, but Kolb had rarely seen him.

The rental fee was a strain on his budget, but he chalked it up to the cost of doing business. He couldn't risk leaving anything in his apartment. The tools of his trade were kept here, in a locker that could never be traced to him. He paid the monthly fee in cash, having filled in a phony name and address on the registration form. Even if he were arrested, no one could find his stash.

He cruised through the yard to the parking space outside his unit. He had two keys to the locker, one kept in his kitchen drawer, another worn on his person at all times. The keys were unlabeled and untraceable. He used one now to open the padlock, then lifted the roll-up metal door and stepped inside. There was a bare lightbulb in the ceiling, but he didn't turn it on. He didn't want any passersby getting a look at the interior.

The locker was the size of a large bathroom, customized with a few shelves and pallets. It held the few items of furniture he'd retained after he let go of his previous apartment and sold most of his possessions to cover legal fees. His current apartment had come already furnished, and since he'd known it was temporary, he hadn't redecorated.

Of more importance than the furniture were his newer acquisitions. A gun purchased from a black-market dealer whose acquaintance Kolb had made while he was a cop. A powerful flashlight to negotiate the storm-drain system. Sets of handcuffs to secure the victims, as well as a spray bottle of chloroform if they acted up. A laptop computer with a wireless modem. Sets of fake ID for him and his partner, paid for with his partner's money but obtained by Kolb, using his connections on the street.

He focused on the disguises he'd put together. Two had already been used and discarded. He took some time deciding which of the remaining three he would use for his swan song.

The simplest was a phony police shield that would allow him to pose as a plainclothes cop. Another choice was a business suit purchased at a thrift shop, along with a cheap briefcase, an ensemble that would allow him to blend into any commercial neighborhood. Then there was his repairman's outfit—a utility belt and rumpled jacket with matching cap. The cap had a decal bearing the name Steve, which he'd ironed onto the fabric. Steve, the friendly neighborhood repairman. That felt right.

He loaded the repairman's outfit into the trunk of his car, along with the other items he needed—except for the gun, which he wedged into his waistband behind his back, pulling down the long-sleeved pullover to cover it. An extra magazine of ammo went into his pocket.

He made a final check of the locker to be sure he'd overlooked nothing. His gaze fell on the scrapbook he'd assembled during the Mobius case. That had been three years ago, before his stretch in prison, before Madeleine Grant, before any of it. At the time he'd been working out of Newton Area, a bad neighborhood—"Shootin' Newton" in LAPD parlance. He spent his nights chasing down gangbangers—stupid punks hyped up on drugs or adrenaline, little better than animals scrapping over territory. To them, jail was no more of a hellhole than the shitty neighborhoods that had spawned them. They were shuttled back and forth between prison and the streets, learning nothing, going nowhere, dying young, and however many of them died, there were always more to take their place.

And then the Mobius story broke. Here was a guy who was smart, ambitious, ruthless, who terrorized the entire city over the course of Easter weekend, who'd had the LAPD and FBI working double shifts while politicians and department heads huddled in a bunker below City Hall.

Mobius wasn't some tattooed, body-pierced, street-trash, coke-snorting, drug-dealing product of the juvenile detention system. He didn't know any homeboys and didn't fuck around with two-bit back-alley deals for a gram of crack or a nickel bag. He was a *man*. He'd set his sights on something big.

Maybe it was Mobius who'd started Kolb thinking about what he could do outside the law. Or maybe he'd been thinking about it already. It was impossible to be a cop and not have ideas. He would see the dumb-ass mistakes the punks made, the truly dumb things they did that made arresting them almost too easy, and he would think, *I could do it better.* Cuffing a kid who'd shot a guy at an ATM, he would think, *I would've made sure the security camera never got a shot of my face.* Reading the Miranda warning to a junkie who'd broken into a pharmacy, he would think, *I would've deactivated the silent alarm.*

But he hadn't actually planned on doing those things. He hadn't been serious.

He wasn't sure if he'd been serious even with Madeleine Grant. She'd ticked him off, that was for damn sure, and he'd had a hard-on for her tight, aerobicized body, but whether he would have taken it all the way, he didn't know. Sometimes he'd thought he would. Other times it seemed more like a prank, a way to teach the woman a little humility, a little fear.

He'd been arrested before he'd learned what he would do. Ten months in prison had erased any qualms. He now knew he had to take care of Madeleine Grant. He'd intended to save her for last—the last one to die in the tunnels. She would be his signature affixed to the crime spree, his way of taking credit for his work.

Or, if things went sour before that, she would be taken in plan B.

He thought about the backup plan as he rolled down the locker door and resecured the padlock. He almost hoped it became necessary to grab Madeleine tonight. One way or the other he meant to finish her, even if he had to come back to LA six months from now and pay her a visit. She deserved it more than ever after setting McCallum on his tail.

Hell, maybe he would do her tonight, after the storm-drain job. Her and Abby Hollister, too. Sweet little Abby, too dainty and delicate to be seen with an ex-convict. She'd shied away from him like he was garbage, when all he'd done was stop to help her out with her piece-of-shit car. . . .

He frowned, pausing by the side of his Olds.

It was a hell of a coincidence—Tess McCallum talking to Madeleine Grant last night, then Abby showing up on his way to work this morning.

The last time he'd met Abby had been only a few days before his arrest. A few days before incriminating evidence had been found in his apartment by the fire crew.

First she'd shown up while he was e-mailing Madeleine. Now she'd shown up the day after Madeleine had talked to a fed.

It didn't smell right. She could be playing him somehow. Running a game.

She wasn't a fed, though. Couldn't be. Stalking Madeleine hadn't been a federal case. No FBI involvement.

He didn't think she was a cop, either. Not that he knew everything that went on inside the LAPD, but if there'd been an undercover op last year, he was pretty sure word would've gotten back to him after his arrest. Anyway, he had a feel for cops, and she wasn't one.

Maybe she was a PI. It was possible Madeleine had hired her for protection, and brought her back into his life after consulting with McCallum.

He wasn't sure, though. If Abby wanted to get close to him, she would have accepted his offer to go out. Instead she'd given him the brush-off. Why would she play it that way? Maybe to be less obvious, and to deflect any suspicions.

He knew what his partner would say about that: paranoid. Well, Kolb knew from experience that paranoia was sometimes simple realism. There were cases when the bastards really were out to get you. They'd gotten him, hadn't they?

And Abby Hollister—if that was her real name—might have been part of it. Figuring that her cover hadn't been blown last time, she was coming back for round two.

Or she might just be a horny, ditzy chick who'd had nothing to do with his arrest.

There could be a way to find out.

21

Abby was jazzed. It was always this way when she started work on a new job, any job, even a nonpaying assignment like this one. She could have squeezed Madeleine Grant for a little money, but she wouldn't have felt right asking for a fee when she was tying up loose ends. Her services didn't come with a lifetime guarantee, but she would follow up when circumstances required it.

Anyway, it wasn't money she was after right now. She wanted a way to work off her nervous tension and excitement. She wanted to kick back, have a little fun. Hell, she wanted to get laid. And she knew who to call.

He picked up on the third ring. She'd been pretty sure he was off duty during the daytime this week.

"Hey, Vic. It's you-know-who."

"Let me guess," Vic Wyatt said. "You want to pump me for information."

"Mmm . . . You got that half-right."

He needed a moment to get it. "Oh." The word rode a lilt of interest, though not quite the degree of interest she'd expected.

"Are you up for it?" she asked. "So to speak?"

There was a beat of hesitation. "Sure. Of course."

"Be at my place in twenty, or I start without you. *Ciao*."

She wondered why he'd sounded less than enthusiastic. The prospect of a roll in the sack with her was the sort of thing that ought to set off every Pavlovian response in the male repertoire. Was it possible Wyatt was getting bored with her?

She shook away that thought. Self-doubt was neither healthy nor helpful for someone who depended on herself to stay alive on a daily basis. Besides, she and Wyatt hadn't been together long enough for him to lose interest. It had been only . . . well, come to think of it, it had been almost four years.

The realization surprised her. She'd had no idea their little fling had lasted that long. There'd been nothing to mark the time, no anniversary celebrations, no nostalgic reminiscences. They just got together now and then—once or twice a week, or sometimes only once a month—and shared some quality time. It was always good, but never meaningful.

Wyatt was a sergeant in the LAPD and one of her few police sources. He'd been interested in her for quite some time before she'd succumbed to his persistence and her own curiosity. Right at the start she'd let him know that the relationship wouldn't go anywhere. She wasn't the type to get married and settle down. She needed her space. She felt easily smothered. Wyatt had said he understood. Maybe he had. But after four years of casual liaisons, he might be getting ready to move on to somebody who could offer him a more permanent commitment.

If that was the case, she couldn't blame him. He hadn't said anything, though. She might be reading too much into their brief conversation. Overinterpreting other people's behavior was an occupational hazard.

Precisely twenty minutes after her call, the front desk rang to say that Mr. Bryce was here. Bryce was Wyatt's alias. Using a phony name had been her idea. If the real nature of her work was ever exposed, Wyatt's career in law enforcement would hardly benefit from an association with her.

The doorbell buzzed. She opened the door and let Wyatt in. He was dressed in a T-shirt and nylon windbreaker, which he shrugged off, revealing his big biceps—not as big as Kolb's, but tighter and better toned. There was, she supposed, a slight resemblance between the two men. Wyatt, with his sandy hair and wide shoulders, could have been a younger version of Kolb. But he wasn't younger. He just hadn't spent a year in a maximum-security prison. That made the difference.

"Hey, Vic."

"Abby." His eyes passed over her and almost through her, as if she weren't quite there.

"You want anything to drink?" she asked a little uncertainly.

"You know what I want."

That was more like it. She'd gotten all frazzled over nothing. Funny how she could read stalkers and serial killers so much better than her own boyfriend.

He took her on the couch, fast and hard, not even undressing, simply opening his pants and guiding himself inside her. Sometimes there were preliminaries, but today he was in a feverish rush, as if driven less by desire than by pure need. She liked the feeling. There was something honest and uncomplicated about need. And she wasn't big on complications of any kind in her personal life.

"Damn, Abby," he whispered as he tunneled into her and she squeezed her thighs around his hips.

He released himself, and she held tight through the shuddering wave of his climax and hers.

They lay on the sofa, breathing hard. "Think you'll wanna go again?" she asked Wyatt after a long silence.

He didn't answer at first. "Abby, we need to talk."

"Isn't that the sort of thing a gentleman says *before* he beds the lady?"

"Well . . . yes. Sorry. I meant to . . . but, you know . . ."

She fingered his groin. "Something came up?"

"That's about right."

"Are you breaking up with me, Vic? And if so, does this mean I can't use you as a source anymore?"

He sat up, fastening his pants. "See, that's just it. That's what we need to talk about."

"I don't follow."

He stared across the room. "Abby, does this mean anything to you?"

"It means a lot," she said automatically.

"Does it? Because I have the impression . . . Let me put it this way. There was this bar I used to go to. They had a mechanical bull. You could ride it for a buck. One gal rode it every night. Once, when she was drunk, she told me it got her off. The damn bull gave her an orgasm every time."

"In the long run, the purchase of a vibrator would've been more economical," Abby observed.

Wyatt looked at her. "I get the feeling I'm like that bull to you. I'm just a way for you to get off."

"I believe the getting-off is mutual."

"But I want it to be more than that."

"Marriage, children, bungalow in the Valley, PTA meetings, Eagle Scouts? I'm not a den mother, Vic. You know that."

"I'm not talking about being married with children. I'm talking about being close." His face was pained. "Do you love me, Abby?"

A dozen glib remarks occurred to her, but now was not the time. "I care about you," she said slowly.

"That's not love."

"I wouldn't want to lose you."

"That's not love, either."

"Vic, you know me. I'm the cautious type. I need my—"

"Space. I got that. Elbow room, distance, freedom."

"I've always been that way."

"But you haven't always been . . ."

"Been what?"

"I should go."

"What is this, a cliffhanger? Am I supposed to tune in next week for the exciting conclusion? I haven't always been . . . what?"

He sighed. "Hard. You've turned hard, Abby."

"If you mean tough, I'll take it as a compliment."

"I mean hard. Hard like a shell. Like a wall. Like keeping people out. Out of your life, out of your thoughts, your feelings."

"But not out of my pants. That's something, anyway."

He turned away. "I figured you would joke about it."

"Sorry. Defense mechanism. I haven't changed, Vic."

"Yes, you have. Maybe you don't see it, but I do. It started after the Kris Barwood case. And it's gotten worse. You used to be an idealist."

"I still am."

"You're cynical."

"Am not. Delightfully irreverent, yes. But not cynical."

"I'm afraid there's a fine line between the two, and you've crossed it. You used to have a soft side. It's what I loved about you."

She noted the past tense. "Maybe," she said thoughtfully, "I've just gotten better at hiding my softer side."

"Or maybe it's so well hidden, even you can't find it."

"Vic, I can't afford to be soft. In my line of work—"

"Then quit your line of work."

"So I can be a barefoot hausfrau cooking you dinner?"

"There are lots of things you could do that aren't dangerous, aren't crazy, and don't require shutting down your emotions just to get through the day."

"I'm sure there are. But those other jobs aren't *me*. What I do is who I am."

"You're losing who you are."

"Don't give me that psychobabble crap. I'm the one with the psych degree. I can outanalyze you without breaking a sweat."

"I've been thinking about this for a long time, Abby."

"I say you've been watching too much Dr. Phil. Isn't it the woman who's supposed to complain that her partner isn't opening up? Traditionally the man doesn't give a damn about this touchy-feely stuff."

Wyatt shrugged. "Apparently I'm a sensitive guy."

"Hell." Abby puffed up her cheeks with a big inhalation, then blew out the breath. "Does this mean we're not going to see each other anymore?"

"I'm not exactly sure what it means. I ought to just break it off, but . . ."

"But the sex is so darn hot?"

Wyatt grimaced. "What kind of person does that make me?"

"A normal person. A good person. A better person than me, probably. At least you care about this emotional-intimacy thing."

"You don't?"

"I just don't think it's what I need in my life right now."

"There's such a thing as having too much space, Abby. Too much distance."

"Look, I may not have the perfect attitude, but at least it keeps me alive." That sounded defensive. "Staying alive," she added lamely, "that's the point, isn't it?"

"Living is the point."

"That's what I said."

"Not exactly."

"Oh, geez. You *have* been watching *Dr. Phil.*"

He got up. "I'll be in touch."

"This didn't go so well, huh?"

"Pretty much the way I anticipated."

She stood to face him. "You think I don't trust you, and that's why I won't open up. But you're wrong. It's not about my trusting you. It's about . . . well, I guess it's about my trusting *me.*"

"When do you think you'll start trusting yourself?"

"I don't know."

"And until you do, you're going to keep me at arm's length?"

"Don't take it personally. I keep the whole world at arm's length."

"I noticed." He started to go.

"I intend to keep inviting you over."

"I don't intend to accept those invitations. But . . . I probably will."

"Face it. I'm irresistible."

He kissed her. "I've always thought so."

Wyatt walked away down the hall, and Abby closed her door and looked around at her empty living room.

Hard, he'd said. She had grown hard.

It might be true. Probably was. He knew her better than anyone. Knew her better than she knew herself, in some ways.

Still, she was damned if she would give up her work. In the end, it was only the work that mattered. That was what Wyatt didn't understand. Feelings, commitments, relationships—all of that was secondary. Those were things that would come and go, unpredictable as the weather. No one could count on any of it.

But the work—the work was something she could count on, always. It was the work that kept her going. It was the work she lived for.

Everything else in her life was negotiable, expendable—except the work.

22

Last year, when he was still a cop, Kolb had run Abby Hollister's name and license plate number through the DMV, obtaining a West Hollywood address. He'd thought about going there and arranging to run into her by accident, maybe taking their relationship to the next level. Events had intervened—he'd been arrested. Thinking about it later, he'd figured it was just bad timing. Now he wondered.

He hadn't forgotten her address. 6548 West Lilac Street, apartment 22.

She could have moved during the past year. Not being a cop anymore, he couldn't check for updated information. But she might still be living there. It was worth a shot.

He cruised past the place on Lilac Street, an undistinguished three-story building from the 1950s, with palm trees bending in front of a glassed-in lobby. There would be a courtyard with a swimming pool, silent on weekdays and noisy with radios and splashing children on weekends. He had been in many such places when he was riding patrol.

He parked a block away and walked to the lobby door. It was locked, a security measure he easily circumvented by buzzing various units on the intercom until somebody answered, then identifying himself as United Parcel. The trusting tenant buzzed him in.

Mailboxes in the lobby were labeled with the residents'

names. Number 22 was listed as belonging to Hollister, A. So she was still here.

There were no elevators, only outdoor staircases rising to the second and third levels. Apartment 22 was on the second floor, its door opening onto the exterior hallway above the courtyard. Kolb was unhappy about the outside door. Someone could be watching him from one of the other units. If he broke in, he would have to do it fast.

He rapped on the door. If she answered, he wasn't sure what he would say. He supposed the truth would have to do, or part of the truth, at least. He would say he'd looked her up on the DMV database last year and remembered her address. Then he would give her some song and dance about why he'd come to see her in the middle of the day, and why he'd expected her to be home when she should have been at work.

Anyway, his explanations wouldn't be necessary. Nobody came to the door. He glanced through a gap in the curtains. The apartment was dark.

The door was flimsy and old, and he was pretty sure he could force it open with a kick to the side of the lock. But that would make noise, and if anyone heard it, the police would be called.

Unfortunately, he was no good at picking locks. This wasn't a skill taught at the police academy, nor one he'd picked up in Chino. He tested the window and found it was made of thin Plexiglas. With a pocketknife, he sliced out a triangular pane and let it drop inward, then reached through the gap and unlocked the door. The operation made no noise and took less than a minute.

He entered the apartment and shut the door. Probably he should've brought gloves to prevent leaving fingerprints, but it didn't matter. Break-ins were so common in Los Angeles, nobody bothered to dust for prints unless major valuables were stolen. He didn't plan to steal anything. He just wanted to look around.

At first sight, the apartment was perfectly ordinary. He

made a quick circuit of the living room, kitchenette, bathroom, and bedroom. The place was tidy enough, but with a few items strewn here and there, the sort of things that might be left lying around by a busy person—a magazine, a half-finished crossword puzzle, a book left open on a night table. Abby had the usual appliances—an old stove and a humming refrigerator, a microwave oven with an unpronounceable brand name, a thirteen-inch TV on a cheap stand, a boom box near a modest collection of CDs. There were clothes in her bedroom closet and silverware, plates, and pots and pans in her kitchen cabinets.

He began to wonder if he'd been unduly suspicious. Maybe Abby Hollister was who she said she was, after all. And he'd taken a considerable risk coming here. If he was caught inside her apartment, all his plans for the evening would be scotched. He would end up in a holding cell facing charges that would send him back to prison for parole violation. All because he'd gotten a bug up his ass about some woman he hardly knew, a stranger who didn't mean anything.

He decided he'd better get the hell out. He was retracing his steps through the living room when he glanced at the magazine tossed on the sofa. Something about it seemed wrong. He moved closer and took a better look. It was *People*, and the cover showed two celebrities whose recent marriage had already ended in divorce. But on the cover the stars were smiling over a caption that read, *Love At Last*.

He picked up the magazine and studied it in the trickle of light through the filmy curtains. The date was September of last year. He put it down and looked at the end tables flanking the sofa. For the first time he noticed a patina of dust on their surfaces. The apartment hadn't been cleaned in some time. He went into the kitchen and looked in the refrigerator. It seemed well stocked, but when he opened the carton of milk and sniffed, he discovered water inside—which was just as well, since the milk's expiration period had ended around the time that the *People* cover story had been new.

Water in the milk carton. Out-of-date magazine on the sofa. Dust everywhere, even coating the kitchen counters.

Abby didn't live here. Nobody did. This apartment was a sham, a shell. It was a dummy address, like the dummy corporations his partner had set up when establishing the overseas bank accounts. It could pass inspection if somebody came to visit, assuming the visitor didn't look too closely, but it wasn't meant to be used.

Now that he thought about it, the apartment was remarkable for what it did not contain. No computer equipment, even though most people of Abby's age were on the Internet nowadays. No live plants, only a couple of silk fakes. Nothing in the wastebaskets or the kitchen trash can.

He checked the phone and heard a dial tone. That made sense. She would have to keep the phone hooked up so she could give out this number.

He didn't expect to find anything that would point him toward her real identity. The place was obviously meant just for show. She would have files, records, but not here. He made a cursory inspection of the drawers and other hiding places, but found nothing.

Letting himself out, he returned to the lobby, where the postman was dropping off today's mail. On impulse he went up to the postman and smiled. "Wish I'd known you were here. I got somebody else's mail yesterday. Utility bill for Hollister in number twenty-two."

The guy frowned. "Twenty-two? That shouldn't have been delivered here at all. I've got a forwarding order on that address."

"Doesn't surprise me. I've knocked on her door a few times, and she's never there."

"Forwarding order's been in effect for months. If you give me the envelope, I'll have it sent on."

"Okay, next time I see you. Wouldn't want the lady to be late paying the electric company." With a cheerful nod, Kolb left the lobby and returned to his car.

She'd nearly fooled him.

But he was on to her now.

23

Tess found Deputy DA Snelling in his office in the Clara Shortridge Foltz Criminal Justice Center in downtown LA. He was eating a sandwich at his desk. His secretary had gone to lunch, allowing Tess to walk in unannounced.

"Mr. Snelling?"

"Who are you?" he asked through a mouthful of tuna fish. She told him. He swallowed what he was chewing and smiled. "The famous Agent McCallum. The woman who saved our fair city."

She hadn't gotten much of the hero treatment since her car ride with Crandall, and she found she almost enjoyed it now. It was a nice change of pace from her pariah status.

"Don't believe everything you read," she said glibly.

His smile vanished. "I don't." He took another bite of tuna fish. "It's all bullshit. Like that girl in the Iraq war."

"What?"

"You know, that girl soldier, the one who was a POW for a few days. She gets a parade, TV movie, book deal." He slugged down a huge gulp of soda from a Styrofoam cup. "Meanwhile there are guys coming home without body parts. No parade for them. No movies, no books."

She took a seat across from the desk. "And why is that?"

"Because the media wants its heroes young and pretty. John Wayne is old news. GI Jane is a fresh angle."

"So I'm GI Jane?"

He shrugged. "You were. For a couple weeks, anyway. I don't know what you are now."

I'm a pissed-off federal agent, Tess wanted to say, but didn't. "I need information."

"Fire away." He dabbed his mouth with a paper napkin.

"You arranged a plea bargain last year with a police officer named William Kolb. I've already spoken to Detective Goddard about it. I got the distinct impression there was something unusual about how the case was handled."

"Wasn't how it was handled that was unusual. It was the case itself."

"Meaning?"

He finished off his sandwich in two more bites, washing it down with soda. "Goddard didn't tell you, I gather."

"No, he didn't."

"Good. He's not supposed to."

"How about you? Are you going to give me the runaround, too?"

"Not me. I can talk. Goddard can't."

"Why all the secrecy? The case seemed straightforward to me."

"That's the problem." He wadded up his napkin and tossed it into a wastebasket. "It was too straightforward. Too neat and clean."

"Are you saying it was some kind of setup?"

"I don't want to use that particular term. Let's say there may have been some funny business going on."

"You don't think Kolb was harassing Madeleine Grant?"

"Oh, he was stalking her, all right. The e-mails and the digital pics we found on his PC were all the proof we needed. What made things a little tricky was the other evidence."

"The kidnapping gear?"

He nodded. "And how it was found. The fire in the apartment, and the stuff lying out in plain sight. Awfully convenient. Even so, we wouldn't have questioned it, if not for the lock on the door."

"What about the lock?"

"There were obvious signs of tampering. Scratch marks on the metal. Somebody picked the lock. And the forensic guys said it had been done recently."

Tess knew who had picked the lock. She said nothing.

"The lock is what got us thinking. Then we took a closer look at the phone call that reported the fire. Anonymous. Made from a cell phone. A phone we couldn't trace. Nobody in the building admitted making it. So who did? You see what I'm getting at?"

Tess saw exactly what Snelling was getting at. "I think so," she said cautiously.

"To cap it all off, there's the fact that the kidnapping equipment was just sitting out in the open, as if somebody wanted it to be found. Kolb, of course, denies he ever bought the stuff. That's to be expected. But what if he's telling the truth? What if somebody else bought all that crap and planted it?"

This possibility caught Tess's attention. "You don't think the kidnapping gear was really his?"

"Well . . . there are questions about that."

"What sort of questions?"

"We canvassed the apartment building. A maintenance man remembered seeing a woman get into the elevator on the morning of the fire. She was carrying a bag. A large, bulky bag full of stuff. Later the maintenance guy saw the same woman leave the building. She was still carrying the bag—but it was empty."

"When was this?"

"She left not long before the engine company arrived."

Tess kept her voice even. "Did you get a description of the woman?"

"Nothing helpful. She had on a cap—like a baseball cap—and sunglasses. That's about it."

Tess thought of the diner last night, Abby playing pinball with her hair tucked under a baseball cap. "She couldn't have been a tenant?"

"The maintenance guy knows all the tenants. This was

somebody else. So the question is, what was in the bag? The physical evidence? Evidence that ended up in Kolb's apartment?"

"Is that what you think?"

"Not necessarily. Kolb *was* stalking Madeleine Grant. He *had* threatened to kidnap her. He may have bought the gear himself. The mystery woman might be unrelated to the case. Frankly, I didn't know what the hell was going on. What I did know is that a defense attorney would have a field day with what we found. Juries—LA juries in particular—love conspiracy theories. I think the case of a certain ex-football player proved that."

Tess nodded.

"And make no mistake about it," Snelling added, "if the jury was convinced the kidnapping equipment had been planted, then the whole case goes out the window. There's no way we could convince them that the stuff on the computer was genuine if the other items were a plant. It would've been all or nothing. Under those circumstances, Kolb would've walked."

"So how did you handle it?"

"We kept quiet about the problems with the physical evidence. We let Kolb's attorney—somebody on retainer from the Police Protective League—believe we were going to use the kidnapping paraphernalia to push for the maximum on the stalking charge. In this state, a stalking case is usually a wobbler. It can be prosecuted as a felony or a misdemeanor at the DA's discretion. We indicated that the evidence of intent to kidnap made this case a felony. We used the kidnapping angle as leverage to force Kolb to plead guilty and accept a one-year sentence. Maximum sentence is three years, so it was a good deal for him—or so he thought."

"When actually, if he hadn't plea bargained . . ."

"We couldn't have used the kidnapping gear as evidence, and Kolb might've bargained down to a monetary fine and time served."

"Which is why you don't want anyone talking about the case to outsiders."

"It's a sensitive matter. The media would have a field day with it if the full story got out. So we're keeping it close to the vest. Can you blame us?"

She knew there was more involved than worries about the media. The DA's office should have shared its evidence and suspicions with Kolb's attorney. To withhold salient facts was ethically questionable, at the very least.

There was no point in mentioning any of this. All she said was, "No. I don't blame you."

Snelling nodded. "Now let me ask *you* a question. They brought you in to work on the storm-tunnel case. Am I supposed to think Kolb is looking good for that?"

"They've got me running down a lot of long shots," she said as casually as possible.

He studied her. "I'm not sure I buy that. You don't bring in a living legend, or whatever the hell you are, just to run down weak leads."

"You do if you brought in the living legend only as a publicity stunt in the first place."

His expression cleared. This made sense to him. It fit perfectly with his view of the world. What was worse, it was true—which meant that maybe his worldview wasn't as distant from reality as Tess liked to think.

"Right," he said. "I get it. That's smart thinking on somebody's part."

"Yeah, the Bureau is full of smart people."

"Well, anyway, Kolb's an asshole, and he deserves what he got, but I don't think he's the million-dollar man you folks are looking for. He hasn't got the sophistication to pull off a stunt like that. He's not dumb, but he's no criminal mastermind, either."

"Maybe the man we're looking for isn't a mastermind. Maybe he's just been planning this for a long time."

"Like, say, ten months in prison with nothing else to do?"

"You never know."

Snelling picked a piece of tuna fish off his desk and ate it. "You're right about that. In this business, you learn you can never really figure anybody out."

"I'm beginning to realize that," Tess said. But it wasn't Kolb she was thinking of. "One more thing, Mr. Snelling. On a gut level, do you think the stuff in Kolb's apartment *was* a plant?"

He seemed pleased by the question. Probably he wasn't asked about his gut feelings very often.

"Just between you, me, and the wallpaper," he said slowly, "I think it was. I think the mystery woman in the hat and sunglasses carried the kidnapping gear into the building. She picked the lock on Kolb's door and put the items in his apartment, then started the fire."

"Any idea who would do that?"

A shrug. "Madeleine Grant has money. Money buys a lot of things."

"Yes," Tess said, "it certainly does."

She left the office, thinking hard. Now she knew why Detective Goddard had disregarded Madeleine's tip. The police and the DA's office had already concluded that Madeleine had tried to incriminate Kolb last year. Any new suspicions she voiced would have been seen as part of her continuing campaign to put Kolb in jail.

That didn't mean Madeleine's tip deserved to be dismissed. It simply meant she had no credibility with the authorities in LA. She was seen as someone who'd gamed the system. She wouldn't be trusted again.

With a flicker of guilt Tess remembered her own fling with circumventing the rules—the bumper beeper she'd planted on Kolb's car. Yes, she'd avoided the paperwork, the bureaucracy, the red tape. But there was a reason for those things. A little reason, easily forgotten, called the Bill of Rights. Securing the tracker to the Oldsmobile had given her a thrill, but it was an illicit thrill, the shivery frisson of breaking the law. She had no court order, no authorization for what she'd done. She'd followed her own instincts, heedless of any social restraints. And she wasn't proud of it.

She probably seemed awfully stuffy to Abby Sinclair. And it was true that she cut a less than imposing figure, seated at her desk in Denver, reviewing forms and initialing documents. But the forms and documents weren't wastepaper. They were the government's way of upholding its end of the social contract. They were the leash that held the state's police power in check.

Men like Kolb were dangerous. But someone like Abby could be dangerous, too. And the worst part was, Abby didn't know it—or didn't care.

Tess waited until she was out of the building, then took out her cell phone and placed a call.

"Hello?" Abby's voice, cheerful as always.

"I need to talk to you."

"Like Ross Perot, I'm all ears."

"I meant, in person."

"You're in luck. My schedule for this afternoon is wide open. This evening is a different story. I'll be seeing our mutual friend then."

It took Tess a moment to realize the mutual friend was William Kolb. "You have a date with him?"

"Nothing that obvious—or that definite. But he'll be seeing more of me. He can count on that."

"In the meantime, we need to get together."

"The Boiler Room?" Abby asked.

Tess hesitated. "You don't think it'll seem . . . suspicious if we go there again today?"

"It wouldn't have seemed suspicious even if we'd shown up twice in one night."

"You said—"

"I was just messing with your head. You were so skittish about this whole undercover gig."

Tess set her jaw. "I'm glad you found it amusing."

"You feds are a hoot. You take yourselves so seriously."

She didn't trust herself to answer. "The Boiler Room at two P.M.?"

"Be there or be square."

Tess pocketed the phone. Abby could have her fun—for now.

She wouldn't be having fun much longer.

24

Tess found Abby in a corner booth at the Boiler Room. She took the seat across the table and nodded hello, wondering how to begin.

Abby was studying her behind a pair of sunglasses that hid her eyes. "You look a little uptight. More than usual, if that's possible. You need a humor transfusion, stat."

"I'm not in the mood for humor."

"That's just when you need it most. Okay, a rabbi, a priest, and a minister walk into a bar. The bartender looks at them and says, 'What is this, a joke?' "

Abby grinned. Tess gave her no response.

"Wow," Abby said, "tough room."

"I didn't come here for casual conversation."

"No, you came here for a progress report. And I do have some—progress, that is—to report. I think Kolb has a partner."

Tess didn't want to hear it. "Abby—"

"Hold on. This is too good to wait. I got a call from Madeleine. Somebody was scoping out her house from the bushes. Drove over there, but he was gone. But his shoe prints are the wrong size for Kolb, so I'm figuring he's Kolb's buddy—the one who handled the overseas bank transfers. Maybe the brains of the whole operation."

"Or maybe it was a vagrant camping out behind the house."

"I lean toward the accomplice theory, myself. I'm betting they found out you and Madeleine were talking. It spooked them."

"There's no way they could know that." Tess was irritated that the conversation had gone this far offtrack. "Besides, there's no evidence the Rain Man has an accomplice. The Behavioral Science profile indicates we're looking for a loner."

"Well, Kolb definitely fits that category. If he's hooked up with somebody, it's purely a marriage of convenience."

The waitress arrived. Tess waved her off, saying, "Give us a few minutes." She turned back to Abby. "I didn't say the Rain Man was Kolb."

"I know you didn't. But a lot of stuff is pointing in that direction. Kolb's got motive—he's royally pissed at the city for locking him up. Feels betrayed, abandoned. He's obviously got major issues with women. He was planning to kidnap a woman once before, and only got stopped because of some quick thinking and heroic action by yours truly—"

"Is that so?"

"Um, yeah, it's so. Haven't you been paying attention? Did you nod off during the third reel? I can give you a quick recap of the plot if you want."

"I think I've been able to figure out the plot pretty well on my own, thank you."

"Doesn't sound like it. Sounds like you went out to the lobby for popcorn and missed the whole thing. Though I guess I should stop using the movie metaphors. You're not a film buff, right?"

"Right. I'm a little too involved in the real world. I deal in facts."

"Just the facts, ma'am—it suits you. Change your name to Josephine Friday, you might get your own TV show."

"I met with the deputy district attorney today," Tess said.

Abby furrowed her brow. "You could have used a segue there. The transition was kind of abrupt."

"He told me some interesting things."

"Lay it on me, soul sister."

"There were tamper marks on the lock of Kolb's door. Evidence that someone picked the lock. That was sloppy, Abby."

"I'm only human."

"Kolb always insisted the evidence against him was bogus. Said he never purchased the items found in his apartment."

"What would you expect him to say?"

"You discovered the items in his place, right? Hidden away?"

"And put them out in plain sight, like I told you."

"So you didn't purchase the items yourself, bring them to the apartment, and leave them there?"

Abby pulled the sunglasses lower on her nose and peered over them. "You're saying I framed Kolb? I made up the whole thing?"

"Not the stuff on his computer. But the rest of it was your doing. Wasn't it, Abby?"

"That's the kind of question a girl could take personally."

"You wanted Kolb off the street for as long as possible. Intent to kidnap would give the stalking charge more weight, put him away for three years, the maximum sentence. You'd read the e-mail where he described how he would kidnap Madeleine. You bought the items he'd specified, brought them to his apartment, then called in the authorities. You even added a map of Bel Air with Madeleine's house circled, so the police would be sure to make the connection."

"Was this before or after I planted the second glove at Rockingham?"

"A maintenance man saw you enter and leave the building. You had a bag filled with items when you arrived, an empty bag when you left. What was in the bag?"

"There wasn't any bag." Abby took off the sunglasses and met Tess's stare. "Really."

"I don't believe you. I think you've let this vigilante

lifestyle go to your head. You've decided to act as judge, jury, and executioner."

"If I'd acted as executioner, Kolb would be dead."

"Protecting your client is one thing. Tampering with evidence is another."

"I told you last night I'd done a little tampering. I moved the stuff out of hiding."

"Moving the stuff would be bad enough. Putting it there in the first place—that's a whole lot worse, Abby."

"When you say my name that way, you sound just like my mother."

"This is the kind of thing people go to jail for."

Abby twirled the glasses by one temple. "I wouldn't do well in prison. I have a problem with authority figures. Think I'll have to pass."

"You may not have that option."

"Gonna send me up the river, Agent McCallum? Put me in the big house with the lesbian guards and the shower-stall rapists? I don't want my life turning into late-night viewing on Cinemax."

"As I said, you may not have a choice."

She put down the sunglasses and steepled her hands. "You're serious about this? Up on your high horse and out for blood?"

"I'm serious about the law."

"Wasn't it against the law to show me the FBI report?"

"I'm not proud of that."

"Yeah, I guess not." Abby nodded slowly. "Got the old guilt pangs pretty bad, don't you?"

"I have no idea what you're talking about."

"They're like gas pains, only harder to get rid of. Still, there is one time-tested way to find relief. It usually involves that handy convention of tribal folklore, the scapegoat."

Tess had no idea what the woman was talking about. "I think you've gone off the deep end," she said. "I mean that."

Abby paid no attention. "The scapegoat was just an ordinary goat, but the community pinned all their guilt on him.

Or her. Then they ran that poor goat right out of town. Ran her up the river into federal prison, for all I know. Once the goat was gone, so was all the guilt, and the people felt okay again." Her brown eyes narrowed. "You see what I'm saying, Tess?"

"No. And don't bother to explain it. I don't give a damn. I'm through working with you. And you are not to have anything further to do with this investigation. Do you understand?"

Abby shrugged. "I understand. I'm not saying I'll comply."

"Any further activity on your part relating to William Kolb will be carried out on your own personal initiative. I'm not sanctioning it in any way, shape, or form. I don't want to hear about it, and I won't help you with it."

"Like I need your help."

"You seemed to need it last night."

"I needed to see the report. There's nothing more you can do for me." Abby stood, donning the shades again. "Unless I need some expert advice on how to sit behind a desk. In that case, I'll be on the phone to you in a jiffy."

Tess knew that to remain seated put her at a psychological disadvantage, but she refused to rise. To rise would be to follow Abby's lead, and she'd done enough of that. "I would advise you," she said quietly, "to break off your involvement in this case."

Abby leaned on the table, staring down through the black lenses. "I would advise you to stick it where the sun don't shine."

"If this man Kolb is dangerous—"

"Oh, he is."

"Then by continuing to pursue this avenue of investigation, you may be endangering yourself."

"Well, duh."

"Is your own safety that unimportant to you?"

"Some of us have higher priorities than our own safety. The rest of us just like to think we do." Abby took a step away.

Tess wouldn't allow her the dramatic exit. "I'm not going

to let this drop. I think you framed a man by planting evidence. I intend to prove it."

"Do what you have to do. I've got a date with the Rain Man—even if he doesn't know it yet."

"He's not the Rain Man, and you know it. You've been stringing me along, looking for a way to put Kolb back in jail. You've been telling stories. Maybe that's all you're good at."

"If so, I'll have a hell of a story to tell tomorrow."

"You're on your own now," Tess warned. "No backup."

Abby shrugged. "So what else is new?"

She walked away, and Tess noticed that she didn't look back. It seemed she'd found a way to make a dramatic exit after all.

Slowly Tess sank back in her seat and released a breath. That had gone about as badly as expected. She decided she was a poor judge of character. She'd assessed Abby as honest and competent, a straight shooter by her own lights, even if she disregarded the rules that governed other people. As things turned out, Abby was neither competent nor honest. It had been sloppy to leave obvious tamper marks on the lock and to be spotted by the maintenance man. It had been inexcusable to falsify evidence that put a man in prison. What Abby had done—what she'd all but admitted to—had been wrong on every level.

And she would pay for it. Tess would see to that.

Her cell phone rang. She answered, "McCallum."

"This is Larkin. Where the hell are you?"

She had no ready reply. "Out," she said lamely.

"Yeah, I know you're out. That's why I'm calling. You've been out-of-pocket too long. The AD wants you back at the FO."

"ASAP?" she asked, just to use another acronym.

Larkin didn't get the joke. "That's right. The AD's starting to think you're working some angle on the side. He doesn't like it."

"I'm not working any angle." This was true—now.

"Tell it to him. How soon can you get back?"

The field office, or FO as Larkin put it, was only a couple of miles from the diner. "Ten minutes," she said.

"I hope you have an explanation for what you've been doing all day." Click, and the call was over.

"I do," Tess said into the dead phone.

If she was going to pursue an official investigation of Abby's activities, she would have to tell Michaelson about it. He wouldn't be happy with her, but the prospect of putting a vigilante behind bars, with the favorable publicity it would receive, might serve to mollify him.

Not that Tess cared. This wasn't about Michaelson, or even about Abby.

It was about doing what was right.

25

Kolb took a call on the reprogrammed cell phone as he was driving into Westwood. He answered, knowing it could be only one person.

"Okay," his partner said, "she's in the field and coming back to the office."

"You're sure?"

"Michaelson—that's the director—just had one of his flunkies call her. He wants to know where the hell she's been all day. She said she was coming in."

"ETA?"

"Ten minutes."

"Got it," Kolb said, snapping the phone shut.

There were two bitches on his trail. Soon there would be just one.

He cut over to Wilshire Boulevard and pulled into the parking lot of the Federal Building, maneuvering his Oldsmobile into a space strategically close to the building's rear door. He expected McCallum to go in that way.

Now it was just a matter of waiting. McCallum would park her Bureau car somewhere in the lot and walk toward the building's entrance. If no one was with her, he ought to have a clear shot.

He removed the pistol from his waistband and clicked off the safety. Had he remembered to wear gloves when he loaded the magazine? Yes, he would have known not to get fingerprints on the shell casings. Anyway, the ejected shell would fall inside his car. There wouldn't be any casing for the crime scene experts to collect—only the bullet in McCallum's body, and it would be mashed and pulped on impact.

He wasn't the world's greatest marksman, but he'd earned respectable scores at the police academy range. He could nail her from the car, then speed away before anyone knew what had happened. He kept the engine idling for a quick escape.

It wasn't exactly the way he would have wanted it. When he'd imagined this moment, he'd pictured something up close and personal, and preferably slow. There was a lot to be said for inflicting pain. He would have liked to make her beg, hear her scream. But life demanded certain compromises. He was practical. He could adjust.

A single round to the back of her head. She would never know what hit her. Which was too bad.

In a perfect world, she would have known.

Tess hit Wilshire Boulevard and headed east. Westwood, and the Federal Building, were less than five minutes away.

She tried to concentrate on what she would say to Michaelson, but other thoughts kept getting in the way—stories from Sunday school, stories of the dark days of the Hebrew judges, when the people, lawless, took justice into their own hands. Civilization had begun that way, in blood feuds and vigilante raids. Maybe it would end that way, as well. Maybe Abby was not an aberration but a harbinger.

No doubt Abby believed she was doing what was right. But there were some judgments she wasn't entitled to make.

She forced herself to focus on more practical matters. Her talk with Michaelson. How much could she reveal?

She would have to admit to holding back the Madeleine Grant call-in, but maybe she could play it to her advantage. She could say she'd never seriously intended to cooperate with Abby, but had been stringing her along to get more information on her methods. There was no way to disprove this unless someone found out about the transmitter she'd attached to Kolb's car. Even then, unless the Denver surveillance squad supervisor talked, nobody could link the bug to her. It would be assumed that Abby had planted it. Abby would deny it, but who would believe her? She was a habitual lawbreaker, after all.

That could work, Tess decided. Of course, she would have to get rid of the rest of the equipment she'd received from Denver—the receiver, the tools. Stop and dump them in a trash bin or . . .

She blinked. What the hell was she thinking of?

This was how she stood up for law and order—by lying to her superior, disposing of evidence, falsifying the record to make herself look good?

"She trusted me," she whispered.

It was true. Abby had risked everything by revealing herself to a federal agent. Behind her mask of insouciance, she had to know she was taking a terrible chance.

But if she'd framed Kolb . . .

Could you frame a guilty man? Yes, if you made him appear guiltier then he was.

The Federal Building rose on her right. She only had to pull into the parking lot, enter the building, and tell her story, and she would cost Abby her career and, quite possibly, her freedom.

But she wasn't ready to do that yet. She needed to know more. Needed to talk to Madeleine again. A real talk, this time—no artful evasions permitted.

And Michaelson would have to wait. To hell with him.

She sped past the Federal Building without stopping. Bel Air wasn't far. She would sit down with Madeleine and learn everything that had happened. And then she would decide what to do about Abby Sinclair.

*		*		*

Kolb had waited twenty minutes, and McCallum still hadn't shown. He was getting edgy when his cell phone rang.

"She hasn't come back," his partner said, voice hushed.

"Tell me something I don't know."

"Nobody knows where she is. She's not answering her phone. She must have decided to blow off the director."

"So she's not coming in?"

"Doesn't look like it."

"Fuck." Kolb ended the call and sat unmoving, the gun in his lap. There was a cartridge in the chamber that had been meant for McCallum's skull. Useless now. Damn, he'd been primed to whack that bitch.

Rage quivered in him. He raised his fist as if to strike out at the steering wheel, the dashboard, something, anything. Then he saw the bloody cuts on his knuckles. He remembered pounding the dash, savaging his hands. Not again. Not in the parking lot of the goddamned Federal Building, for Christ's sake.

With a shuddering effort he got himself under control and drove out of the lot.

Under other circumstances he might have waited longer, just in case she showed up. But waiting wasn't an option now. The sun was sinking over the western horizon, its orange glare lighting up the swollen bellies of storm clouds.

The rain was coming.

He had work to do.

26

Abby was pissed off about her meeting with Tess. She supposed she shouldn't be surprised. She'd known from the start that the woman had a yardstick up her ass. What Tess needed was a good lay. She'd gone without for way too long. Abby could tell. She had a sixth sense about these things.

And to be honest, she was more than just pissed. She was worried. There was no telling what Tess might do. If she decided to bare her soul to her fellow G-men and G-women, she could make some serious trouble. At the very least she would blow Abby's cover and make her unemployable in this town.

The threat of prison wasn't something she took seriously. She could always change her identity and relocate to another city. She was quicker on her feet than any posse on her trail. But to flee would mean leaving behind her condo and her contacts, her lifestyle, her few friends . . . and Wyatt. It would mean starting over from square one.

She was an idiot. Never should've met McCallum. Yeah, she'd wanted to see the FBI report, but it hadn't been important enough to justify placing her entire future in jeopardy. So why had she done it?

Well, she knew the answer to that one. She'd wanted to meet Tess McCallum. She'd thought . . .

Oh, hell, it didn't matter what she'd thought. It had been a mistake, that was all. A dumb, stupid, boneheaded mistake. She would pay for it, probably. There seemed to be some law of the universe that said you always paid for your mistakes. Personally, Abby would have liked to see that law repealed, but for now it was still on the books.

So she would deal with it. Later. Now she had more immediate priorities.

She was home, in the privacy and comfort of her condo, with the curtains shut and the lights off and soft instrumental music playing.

It was time to prepare for battle.

In a combat situation, which was how Abby viewed her upcoming encounter with William Kolb, she couldn't afford to be distracted or unfocused. The events of the day must be banished, their associated demons exorcised. She needed to direct her total attention toward her adversary—read his body language, assess his vocal intonations, watch every flicker of his facial expression. A second's slowness could be fatal.

So Tess had to go. The memory of her, anyway.

If her brain kept replaying the confrontation at the diner, then her body would continue to pump out chains of neuropeptides produced in response to anger, defensiveness, and fear, and those neuropeptides would continue to swarm throughout her system, into every branching blood vessel and vital organ, where they would crowd out other chemicals associated with serenity and detached alertness.

It helped her to visualize her body like this, as a network of pulsing fluids in which her emotions could be located anywhere—not only in the brain, but in the spleen, the kidneys, the heart, the gut. She saw no value in dividing her mind and mood from her flesh and blood. Those artificial barriers would keep her disconnected, when what she needed was unity, the absolute oneness of herself. She had to manifest a change of consciousness, rise above the mundane, transcend the world.

Other people went to church and prayed. This was *her* way.

Eyes closed, she reclined in an overstuffed armchair, her body limp and palms upraised, her breathing progressively slower and more regular. She descended toward sleep but resisted the final drop-off, holding herself suspended in a limbo between waking consciousness and dreams. Now her body was no longer even a meshwork of fluids, but a cloud of atoms, and each atom was nothing but a cloud itself, a field of energy extending through empty space. She sank into the emptiness and merged with it.

Thoughts came and went, but they were distant, like birds passing in the sky. She let them go, holding on to none of them, until there were no thoughts, only vague, disorderly images that flickered here and there. Then these, too, were gone, and there was only a humming stillness and an ever-expanding circle without a center.

She didn't know how long she remained in this state. Eventually, like a swimmer needing air, she surfaced. Her eyes opened, and her breathing, which had slowed nearly to the point of hibernation, began to normalize.

Tess wasn't there anymore. The incident at the diner had been forgotten, filed away, to be reviewed later if necessary, but of no importance now.

She felt refreshed, alert, ready.

She picked up her cell phone and called William Kolb.

27

The sun was setting when Kolb changed into navy blue denim jeans and a long-sleeved dark blue pullover, with a double layer of thick black socks to protect his feet from the dampness of the tunnels.

The repairman's utility belt, cap, and jacket were in the trunk of his car. He would put them on later. If he was seen dressed as a repairman when he left his apartment, his neighbors might wonder what was up.

He'd expected to go through this routine at least a couple more times. Tess McCallum had spoiled his plans. He didn't appreciate having to make adjustments because some goddamn FBI agent was sniffing his trail. And now it turned out Abby was screwing with him, too.

His partner kept telling him he was paranoid. But the fact was, he did have enemies everywhere. His instincts had been right. Tess, Abby, Madeleine Grant—three bitches, all out to get him.

He still couldn't figure out how Grant had connected him with the kidnappings. It worried him, because what he couldn't understand, he couldn't control.

There was a lot of stuff he couldn't control lately. Losing his job, for one thing. And that craziness last night on the road, and the way he'd lost it today in his parked car. It was like he couldn't stop himself, like things were spinning out of control.

He set his jaw. He was overreacting. This business with Tess and Abby had him worked up. Well, the odds were that one of them, maybe both, would show up tonight. He would be watching. He would—

The phone rang.

His partner, probably. Kolb picked up. "Yeah?"

"Hello . . . William?"

He took a long moment to respond. When he did, he was smiling. "Abby."

"Hi. I'm glad I got through to you."

I'll bet you are, he thought. He asked the obvious question, though he already knew the answer. "How did you get this number?"

"Information. You're the third William Kolb I've called."

Sure he was. She'd gotten his phone number and address off some database used by private detectives, he assumed. Probably his auto registration, too. She knew everything about him. Or she thought she did. There was one thing she didn't know—that he was on to her.

"I don't understand." He was playing dumb. "Why would you want to call me?"

"So I could apologize. For how I acted this morning. You were so nice, stopping to help me like that, and I was all standoffish and, well . . ."

"Scared."

"I've never known anyone who was in jail before."

He put concern in his voice. "Maybe you're better off not knowing anybody like that."

"Look, I don't know exactly what happened last year or who did what. It seems to me like you got involved in a personal situation that went haywire. . . ."

This irritated him. Bad enough she was lying. She could at least pretend to believe the lies he'd told her. "I said I was innocent."

"I think maybe there are degrees of innocence—and guilt. You know? Maybe you did something that was technically over the line—you got on this woman's case a little too hard.

It doesn't make you a bad person. It doesn't mean you're dangerous. You just showed some bad judgment."

He'd never showed bad judgment in his life, but he didn't make an issue of it. "Maybe I did."

"I showed some bad judgment, too—the way I treated you. I acted like you were a leper or something."

"Kind of felt that way." He felt like a sad sack, saying it, but he had to play along. He already knew where she was headed, and he only had to help her get there.

"Anyway, I just wanted to say . . . I'm sorry. Okay?"

"Okay."

"I'll try to be a little less judgmental. I guess that's all I wanted to tell you."

It would be funny to make her sweat on the line a little longer, but he decided to cut to the chase. She would be expecting him to think with his dick, anyway. "You got anything planned for tonight?" he asked.

"Not really."

Of course she didn't. Her evening was conveniently free. He'd assumed it would be.

"Maybe we could get a drink or some dinner or something."

Her hesitation lasted just long enough. "Well . . . sure."

She was a good actress. If he hadn't caught on to her, he would have bought her bullshit, no doubt about it.

He offered to pick her up at her place, but he wasn't surprised when she suggested dropping by his apartment instead. She probably wanted to get a look at where he lived. It was only fair. He'd already seen Abby Hollister's digs.

He gave his address. "That's right on my way home from work," she said with the right note of surprise. "I can be there in twenty minutes."

Another stroke of luck. He wondered where she was really calling from. Did she have an office somewhere, or did she work out of her home—her real home, wherever that was?

There were a lot of questions he meant to ask. He would have plenty of opportunities once he got her into the tunnels.

"Take your time," he said with a smile. "I don't want you running any red lights."

"Not me. Safety first, that's my motto."

He laughed at that. "See you soon, Abby." He ended the call.

Safety first. He didn't think so. She was a girl who liked taking chances, liked pushing her luck.

This time she'd pushed it too far.

28

Madeleine Grant wasn't at home. After some reluctance her housekeeper revealed that she'd gone to "the gun place." Further inquiries, aided by Tess's display of her FBI creds, yielded the information that the gun place was an indoor shooting range on Beverly Boulevard.

It was five fifteen and fully dark when Tess parked outside the gun club, under a sign that read FAMILY-ORIENTED SHOOTING. She was greeted at the entrance by an employee who wanted to see her membership ID. Again the FBI badge did the trick.

"Ms. Grant is shooting," she was told. "Stall six. If you're going out there, you'll need ear and eye protection. Club rules."

Tess donned shooting goggles and ear pads. She headed down the hallway, past the men's room and ladies' room, each said to be equipped with a baby-changing station. Family-oriented shooting, indeed.

There were sixteen lanes on the firing range. Even wearing the ear protectors, Tess could hear the pops of pistols and small-bore rifles. The sound always reminded her of microwave popcorn. Beneath the staccato gunfire thrummed the whir of the ventilation system, low-pitched and ominous.

She walked behind shooters aiming at bull's-eye and silhouette targets. One guy was using the automated retrieval system to pull up his target and check his score. He'd scored over 50 percent in the A-zone, a respectable tally.

Madeleine, in the sixth stall, was practicing with a .32. Tess hung back and observed as she ran through a double-tap drill with a silhouette target at seven yards. She started with her hands at shoulder height, drew the gun from her hip holster, took aim, expended two rounds, then reholstered the piece and repeated the procedure. Her technique was only fair. The draw was fast but shaky, and she seemed to be watching the target when she should have been focused on the front sight of her gun. Still, she was scoring kill shots often enough. Tess had no doubt who the silhouette target was intended to represent.

Madeleine emptied her gun and removed the magazine, checking the chamber to be sure there was no unexpended cartridge inside. Tess wondered if Abby had taught her the procedure. As Madeleine was picking up the brass casings on the stall floor, she saw Tess.

"Agent McCallum?" Her voice was raised to be heard over the gunfire from adjacent stalls. "To what do I owe the pleasure?"

"We need to talk." Tess gestured toward a side hallway. "Someplace quieter."

"One minute, please."

She collected the rest of the casings and put her unloaded weapon in its carrying case. "All right."

"Don't you want to check your score?"

"I would, actually." Madeleine brought up the target and surveyed the damage. She seemed satisfied. "Good enough, don't you think?"

"You would have stopped him. But you were more accurate with your first shot than your second. Recoil's throwing you off. Take an extra moment to steady yourself before the second trigger pull."

"I'll remember that. Thank you."

They proceeded far enough down the hall to put the worst of the range noise behind them, then took off the ear pads.

"Now we can have a civilized conversation," Madeleine said.

Tess wondered how civilized it was going to be. Madeleine wouldn't like hearing that Abby was in trouble. She decided to ease into the subject. "Brushing up on your shooting skills?"

"After what happened this afternoon, I felt it was a good idea."

"Abby told me."

"Did she? I've gotten rusty, I'm afraid. I became complacent. That was a mistake. You can't let down your guard, ever."

"The man you saw was probably just a vagrant."

"Of course *you* would say that." Madeleine rolled her eyes. "The voice of authority, forever offering faux reassurance."

"There's absolutely nothing to tie today's incident with Kolb."

"Then I'm just being irrational, aren't I?"

"You may be."

"Abby thought otherwise."

"Abby is the reason I'm here."

Madeleine gave Tess a shrewd look. "You don't get along with her, do you?"

"Actually, no."

"That's not a surprise. I was reluctant to bring the two of you together. Oil and water, as they say. But she insisted."

"Did she?"

"I called her after our meeting. You were right, of course—about my housekeeping staff. I'd dismissed them for the evening, right in the middle of dinner. I couldn't have you speaking to them. They knew about Abby. Not all the details, but enough to raise questions in your mind."

"And you didn't want me to know?"

"My agreement with her was to keep her name out of any official inquiries. But"—her voice turned hard—"since you were so suspicious and so very uncooperative, I phoned her to see what I should do. She allowed me to set up a meeting between you."

"That was big of her."

"It was, you know. She took a considerable risk revealing her activities."

"She wanted to see the official report on the investigation."

"No doubt. But she also wanted to work with you. She'd followed the Mobius case. She thought you were the type of law enforcement agent she could do business with."

This was unexpected. "What type is that?" Tess asked.

"Independent. A gunslinger, I believe she called you."

"If she took me for some sort of vigilante—"

"She took you for someone who didn't let bureaucratic rules and procedures get in the way of solving the case. She also said you had balls." Madeleine grinned. "She can be vulgar, can't she?"

"I don't see what this has to do with—"

"Of course, there's more to it than that." Madeleine's smile was gone. "She's lonely, you see. Much lonelier than she lets on. Lonelier than she knows."

"I'm sure she has plenty of friends."

"You're wrong. She doesn't. No one understands her. I certainly don't. And her line of work . . . well, it doesn't encourage a person to open up to others. Trust is a luxury she can't afford."

"It's the life she chose," Tess said, noting distantly how harsh the words sounded.

"Yes, well, we all make choices, don't we? Rarely do we see their full implications. Abby's closed herself off to other people. It suits her to live that way—but it also pains her, I think. So, at times, she reaches out."

"Are you saying she was . . . reaching out to me?"

"I think she was. She wanted a friend. Someone who would understand."

Tess didn't know what to say to this.

"I told her she was wrong," Madeleine added.

"Wrong?"

"After meeting you, I was convinced you and she would never get along. I told her that whatever sort of rule breaker you might have been during the Mobius episode, you'd changed. You were no different from the police officers who wouldn't help me when I was being victimized by Kolb's e-mails."

Tess wouldn't let herself be baited. "That's not quite fair," she said evenly.

"Isn't it? You're here to complain about Abby, aren't you? And she's the only one who's done anything to help me."

"That's the problem." Tess forced the discussion back into focus. "She may have done too much."

Behind the shooting glasses, Madeleine's eyes fixed on Tess in a hard stare. "What is that supposed to mean?"

"It means bending the rules is one thing. Trashing them is something else."

"Trashing . . .?"

"Framing a suspect with planted evidence."

Madeleine took a moment to absorb this. "Are you saying you think Kolb was innocent?"

Tess shook her head. "He *was* harassing you over the Internet. And he *was* following you and taking your picture."

"Well, then—"

"But I don't think he'd made serious plans to abduct you. That part of the case was trumped-up."

"The things in his apartment—"

"The things in his apartment were planted. By Abby. I'm afraid she was a little overzealous. And it's going to prove costly to her."

Madeleine turned away. Her mouth moved silently, whether in rage or in consternation Tess couldn't tell.

"Costly," Madeleine echoed after a moment. "How?"

"Planting evidence is a felony, Ms. Grant. I intend to see that Abby Sinclair pays the full legal penalty for her actions. I intend to have her prosecuted."

Madeleine spun to face her. "You *can't*."

"I'm afraid I can. And I'd like your help."

"*My* help?" She straightened her shoulders. "Go to hell."

"We can't have people running around planting evidence just to secure a conviction. It's wrong when the police do it, and it's equally wrong when a private citizen does it. We cannot have anarchy in this country."

"Oh, for God's sake. It's not a question of anarchy. The man was guilty. He was stalking me. He meant to do me harm."

"That still doesn't justify—"

"Doesn't justify what? Getting him off the streets? Putting him in a prison cell where he would be in no position to terrorize anyone?"

"He could have gone away on the e-mail evidence alone—"

"Bullshit." The word twisted her face into an angry mask. "He's a cop. They protect their own. If all they'd had against him were the e-mails, they would have charged him with a misdemeanor. As it was, he got only a one-year sentence."

"Because the DA knew the evidence was planted."

Madeleine blinked. She hadn't known the reason. But the information stymied her for only a second.

"The DA," she said, "also knew that Kolb was a rogue policeman following me, threatening me. And he let him off with a year in jail. Not even a year—ten months. Without the evidence that he was planning to abduct me, they wouldn't have gotten even that much. They wouldn't have put him away at all. They would have let him walk."

Tess studied her. "You've given this a lot of thought."

"Of course I have. It was my life at stake."

She decided to take a shot. "Is that why you let Abby plant the evidence?"

"You stupid bitch." Madeleine expelled a long, hissing breath. "Abby didn't plant anything. *I* did."

The words were clear, but at first Tess couldn't take them in. "You?"

"I told you I take care of myself."

It was impossible. A clumsy attempt to protect Abby. "You're lying," Tess said. "You couldn't have done it. You didn't even know Kolb's address."

Madeleine smiled, a mischievous, superior smile. "Not until Abby gave it to me in her initial report. She also reported Kolb's work schedule. He was working the day shift that week. She informed me that she would look inside his apartment the next morning while he was on patrol."

"You're saying you went to Kolb's apartment before Abby did?"

"Yes."

"What were you wearing?"

"How can that possibly be relevant?"

"There's a witness, a description. What were you wearing?"

"Sunglasses. And a baseball cap to hide my hair. And I carried a shopping bag with the items I'd brought, the items—"

"The items Kolb mentioned in his e-mail to you."

"That's right. I wanted him put away, you see—not slapped on the wrist."

Tess sighed. Things never were simple. She should have learned that lesson by now.

"How could you possibly get into his apartment?" she asked, though she had no doubt Madeleine could find a way.

"I'm not entirely helpless—or entirely inexperienced in that sort of thing. My parents were hardly ever around when I was growing up. Daddy was off making crappy movies. Mommy was always in the middle of a nervous breakdown or an affair—usually both. I had a great deal of unsupervised time on my hands. I got into an occasional spot of trouble."

"Breaking and entering? That kind of trouble?"

A shrug. "It was nothing serious. Pranks, you might say. Or perhaps it was a cry for help. The lock on an apartment door wasn't going to stop me from taking steps to protect myself."

"You picked the lock."

"It was easy."

"But you left tamper marks. Scratches."

"Did I? Well, I'm not a professional, you know."

"No, you aren't." But Abby was. She wouldn't have left signs of tampering. And she wouldn't have allowed herself to be seen by the maintenance man. She was too experienced, too capable, to make those mistakes.

"I broke in," Madeleine was saying, "hid the things I'd bought in the kitchen cabinet. Duct tape, handcuffs—it was rather embarrassing having to purchase those. And a map of my neighborhood with my address circled in red. I locked up when I left. Abby must have entered only a short time later. She found the evidence and arranged for it to come to the attention of the authorities."

"And she never knew it was planted?"

"Of course not. Why would she? *I* certainly didn't tell her."

"You *used* her."

"Everyone uses everyone else, all the time. When you grow up in this city, you figure that out pretty early."

"That's a lovely ethical precept to live by."

"If I'd wanted a theological discussion, Agent McCallum, I'd have gone to a priest."

Tess thought it might have done her some good. "You do realize I could have you prosecuted?"

"Go ahead. I have the money to fight it. And whom do you think the public will side with? The government, which refused to help me—or the victim, acting in her own defense?"

"You can't take the law into your own hands."

"I wouldn't have had to, if the system worked. Find a jury that will convict me. Find a jury that isn't as fed up as I am."

That was a tall order, and Tess knew it. "You never told Abby?" She'd asked the question already, but it seemed essential to hear the answer a second time.

"No, I didn't. As far as she knows, the things she found were Kolb's. All she did was move them out of the cabinet into plain sight."

"And start a fire to draw an engine company to the scene."

"Clever of her, don't you think? So are you going to have me arrested?"

Tess would have loved to snap the handcuffs on, if only to see the expression on Madeleine's face. For a moment she understood why this woman had gotten under Kolb's skin when he pulled her over for a traffic violation.

But she wasn't Kolb, and she wasn't interested in personal vendettas. And Madeleine was right. A jury would take her side.

"No," Tess said.

"Then do me a favor." The sudden sincerity in her tone was startling.

"A favor?"

"Don't tell Abby what I did. Please."

Tess was baffled. "Why not? What difference would it make?"

"It would needlessly upset her. You see, I know Abby better than you do. She has standards. She would be highly disturbed if she were to learn there was anything underhanded in a case in which she had participated."

"Underhanded? Everything she does is underhanded."

"That's not true and not fair. She plays by her own rules. They may not be your rules, but they're hers."

"Oh, for God's sake, she's a vigilante. She's the Lone Ranger."

"Some people might say the Lone Ranger is a hero."

"In the movies. Not in real life."

Madeleine smiled, a little sadly. "This is Los Angeles. The difference isn't always so clear-cut."

"That's very clever, but—"

"I'm not trying to be clever. You may not see it or agree, but Abby is doing what she thinks is right. She has integrity, Agent McCallum. Whatever you may think of her, she's on your side."

Tess didn't know about that. She wasn't sure whose side Abby was on.

But one thing was clear to her, as she gave back the goggles and ear protectors and left the gun club. Abby hadn't lied about her participation in the Kolb case. She'd told what happened, as best she knew it. And Tess had cut her off, refusing even to listen to her side of the story.

She punched Abby's number into her cell phone, but there was no answer. Either she'd turned off her cell or she wasn't picking up.

The time was six thirty-five. Probably she was with Kolb already—Kolb, who might be the Rain Man, on a night with rain in the forecast.

No support. No backup. Alone.

But maybe not for long.

29

Kolb wedged his gun into his waistband, then practiced reaching behind for the draw. When he was satisfied, he put on a leather jacket to conceal the weapon. In one pocket of the jacket he stowed a roll of duct tape and a spray bottle of chloroform. In the other, handcuffs and a powerful flashlight.

Abby would be wearing the tape and the cuffs soon. She was going into the storm drains. But first she would write the ransom note—he had paper and pen in his car. There would, however, be no need for her to record a message for the phone call to the mayor. There would be no phone call. Even after the city paid him the ten million, he wasn't giving them her location. He couldn't risk having her rescued. She had to drown.

His plan, like any improvised course of action, had certain weaknesses. If the authorities knew Abby was investigating him, then he would be tied to her kidnapping. As a precaution, he would not return to his apartment. He'd already loaded the few personal items that mattered into the trunk of his car. He would never see this place again.

Then there was the wild card—McCallum. She might be planning to follow him tonight. That would complicate things. He would have to either lose her or take care of her. The second option was preferable, but it would require subduing Abby first. The chloroform would knock her out, but he preferred to keep her conscious. He wanted her to know what was happening. And he had questions that deserved an answer.

If he could shake McCallum loose, he would. Then get Abby alone and make her talk. As a cop, he'd been good at getting suspects to open up, and he'd learned some new tricks in prison, tricks even a pro like Abby wouldn't know. He wondered how much pain it would take to break her. He looked forward to finding out.

There was a rap on his door.

He straightened the jacket, confirming that the gun was properly hidden. Then he opened the door and saw Abby standing there in her skirt and blouse, all eager innocence.

"Hi, William."

He smiled in reply. "Come in. I'd give you a guided tour, but this is pretty much all there is."

"It's not so bad."

"It sucks. But it's better than the last place I lived." He answered her questioning gaze. "Chino State Prison."

She hugged herself, a nice dramatic touch suggesting an ingenue's nervousness. "I'm glad you can joke about it. I don't think I could."

"If I couldn't keep a sense of humor, I'd have gone psycho by now." He shut the apartment door. It was better if his neighbors didn't see him with her.

Abby was looking around with polite curiosity. He wondered what sort of silent inspection she was conducting, what estimates of his personality she was drawing from the soiled futon and faded carpet.

"They say everything happens for a reason," she said. "Maybe what happened to you was meant to be."

New Age crap. He doubted she believed it, but she was playing a character who did. "Destiny? I don't buy that. I think you make your own destiny. You know that poem, the one that goes, 'I am the master of my fate, I am the captain of my soul'?"

"I think I've heard that one."

He was sure she had. It was the poem Timothy McVeigh had quoted before his execution for the bombing of the Oklahoma City federal building. He'd wanted to see her reaction to the quote, but she disappointed him, revealing nothing.

"Is that really the way you think of things?" she added as she poked at his small collection of books. "You think any of us has that much power?"

"We have as much power as we're willing to take. Most people are afraid to grab the brass ring. They live in fear." This was an honest answer.

She turned and met his gaze. "Not you, though."

"Not me."

She looked away. "I admire that. I'm a real weenie. Everything scares me."

He felt his face shift into a tight smile. "I have a feeling you're underestimating yourself."

"Nope. Here's how much of a scaredy-cat I am. On my way over, I kept thinking I might chicken out and not actually knock on your door. And I was afraid that if you saw my car parked on the street, you'd know I'd been here. So I parked two blocks away."

"Two blocks away?"

"See? I'm a wuss. All my friends say so."

"What did your friends say about your tracking down my phone number?"

"Oh, I didn't tell them. I didn't tell anybody."

"You never mentioned you might be coming to see me?"

"I never said anything about you at all. I was so ashamed of the way I'd acted this morning, I just didn't want to talk about it. It's one thing to be a weenie, and another to be rude."

She was good; he had to give her that. She'd succeeded in establishing that there was no way of connecting her with him. Her car wasn't parked near his building, and her supposed friends knew nothing about her encounter with him this morning. She was sending every possible signal that she was easy prey.

Obviously she hoped to goad him into taking action, with her friend McCallum acting as backup. The plan might have worked, if he hadn't tumbled to them both.

"I don't think you were rude," he said. "Just cautious, like a big-city girl should be. But now that you've spent some time with me, maybe you can see I don't bite."

She answered this with a little laugh, lowering her eyes daintily. He wondered how many men she'd had. He wondered if he could add himself to the total after he'd secured her in the tunnel.

"So," he said, "you want to get something to eat?"

"I'm starved. You have anything in mind?"

Kolb had lots of things in mind, and none of them involved dinner. "You like Mexican?"

"Can't be an Angeleno unless you like Mexican."

"Great." He picked up his key chain and opened the door. "I know a place. We'll take my car—it's parked closer."

"Yeah, rub it in."

They left the apartment. He took a last look at the dirty hole that had been his home since his release. Then he shut the door and locked it.

"Where is this restaurant, anyway?" Abby asked as they headed down the hall.

"Few miles away," he said vaguely. Near the river, but he didn't mention that detail.

She would find out soon enough.

30

The direction-finding gear was still in Tess's Bureau car. There were two carrying cases, one containing the antenna assembly and the other containing the companion receiver.

She opened the antenna case first. Inside were four antennas of a special low-profile design marketed exclusively to government agencies. The design reduced the antennas' visibility and simplified the job of covert tracking. She mounted the assembly on the sedan's roof, being careful to correctly orient the four antennas in a cross pattern—right, left, front, rear. No special attachments were required. The antennas were held in place by built-in magnets.

The system was of the switched-pattern type. When it was operational, the receiver would alternate among the antennas, picking up a signal from only one at a time. This procedure minimized multipath interference, the confusing ghost signals produced by reflections off buildings, bridges, and power lines.

But interference could never be completely eliminated in a cluttered environment like Los Angeles. She would have her work cut out for her just keeping up with Kolb—if she could find him.

She rolled down the passenger window and snaked the coaxial cable from the antenna to the second carrying case. The receiver inside was a single-channel, high-sensitivity, high-selectivity model equipped with microprocessors that analyzed the signals' phase shifts as additional protection against multipath noise.

There was a bracket for dashboard-mounting the receiver's remote-control head, but she didn't bother with it. She could see the displays and manipulate the controls on the receiver's front panel well enough with the carrying case lying open on the passenger seat.

This was supposed to be a turnkey system. All the pieces ought to work when the power came on. Tess hoped so.

The receiver was loaded with rechargeable gel-cell batteries, but she preferred to use the car's own power supply. She plugged the meter panel into the cigarette-lighter socket. When she pressed the power button, the displays lit up. The two that mattered most were the bearing indicator, consisting of sixteen LEDs in a full circle, which would indicate the signal's direction, and the signal strength meter, a twenty-segment bar graph that would show how close the target was.

Neither display showed anything at the moment; nor did the built-in speaker produce any beep tones. She dialed the system's sensitivity to maximum. Still nothing.

The transmitter in Kolb's car had a range of only five miles in flat, open terrain—less than that in the city. Wherever Kolb was, he wasn't within range.

If she was lucky, he hadn't left his apartment yet. She wasn't counting on it. And if he'd left with Abby . . .

It didn't seem likely that she could find them in the huge sprawl of LA. But she would try.

You can only do your best, the priest had said. She was beginning to see what he meant.

Abby was getting a funny vibe from Kolb, and she didn't like it. "What happened to your car?" she asked as they entered the carport. She didn't expect an honest answer, but it was a question he would expect.

"Somebody cut me off." Kolb unlocked the Oldsmobile.

She made a sympathetic noise. "There are lots of bad drivers in this city."

"Well, they'd better stay out of my way." He gave her an odd look. "People who get in my way sometimes get hurt."

Was she crazy to detect a double meaning in the words? She got into the car, not fastening her seat belt because she wanted to retain her mobility if she needed to react quickly.

Kolb backed out of the carport and headed down the street. She noticed that his gaze cut frequently to the rearview mirror. He was watching for pursuit. No surprise there. Paranoia was part of his usual style of driving.

She kept her purse on her lap, her right hand resting on the hidden compartment that contained her Smith .38, its muzzle conveniently pointing in Kolb's direction. If necessary, she wouldn't even need to draw the piece—just get her finger on the trigger and fire through the bag.

She'd never had to shoot one of her stalking suspects. Rarely had she allowed the situation to get so far out of control that defensive violence was necessary. In the few exceptional cases, she'd fought back without gunfire.

Tonight felt different. Tonight she might need her gun.

If Kolb was the Rain Man. She still couldn't be sure. To assess his intentions she needed to press his buttons, get him talking.

The car rattled over a pothole. It gave her an opening.

"This street's in pretty crummy shape," she said. "With all the taxes we pay, you'd think the city would keep the roads in good condition."

"The city doesn't give a damn about the roads or the people who drive on them." Kolb checked the rearview mirror again. "The politicians and bureaucrats only care about lining their own pockets. Goddamn civil servants are nothing but parasites."

Abby goaded him gently. "Not all of them."

"Yes, all of them. Every goddamn one. They're parasites leeching off the rest of us. Greasing the wheels of the sys-

tem with our sweat and blood. I'd shovel shit for a living before I'd work for them—or with them."

"The police, too?"

"The police more than anyone. And the FBI. And anyone
who works for them. Anyone who carries a badge."

She didn't like the way he'd said that—as if he were including her in his general condemnation.

"You used to be a cop," she said. "That's a government
job, last time I looked."

"I had a different perspective on things then. I was naive."

It was dangerous to keep pushing him, but she wanted to
see how far she could go. His police background was a sore
spot. She poked it. "Come on. You'd be a cop again if they'd
let you."

A shake of his head. "No way would I ever wear the uniform. I see through it now."

"You see through the uniform?" she teased. "You've got,
like, X-ray vision?"

He didn't crack a smile. "I see through the bullshit. I'm
not buying the party line anymore. I'm not so easily fooled."

His glance fell on her as he spoke the last words. For a
moment she was sure he *did* have X-ray vision, and he could
see the gun in her purse and read the thoughts in her mind.

Nutty idea, but it had come from somewhere. It was a way
for her subconscious to send a warning.

Kolb could be on to her. She had no definite reason to
think so, only a feeling. But she trusted her feelings.

It was how she'd stayed alive.

Tess found Kolb's apartment building and cruised past.
His Oldsmobile wasn't in the carport. He was gone, and there
was a good chance Abby was with him.

He could be anywhere. But she hadn't picked up a signal
between West LA and his mid-Wilshire address, so the odds
were fair that he'd headed east. Of course, he could have
gone north into the San Fernando Valley or south to Long
Beach, but she couldn't cover the entire city. She was al-

ready traveling east, and she continued in that direction. Maybe she would get lucky.

Her cell phone rang. Caller ID said it was the field office. She didn't want to have that conversation. She turned off the phone and kept driving.

Questions nagged her, questions about Abby. More precisely, about her own feelings with regard to Abby. Her reactions—or overreaction, as the case might be.

She tried to reconstruct her thought processes of a few hours ago. Yes, she'd been concerned that Abby had gone off the reservation completely. But there'd been more to it than that. Something had made her leap to the conclusion that Abby was guilty and cling to that opinion with fierce righteousness.

Righteousness, she'd found, was invariably a cover-up for some unattractive and unadmitted motive. Criminals were often righteous. The more obviously guilty they were, the more righteous they acted. It was a defense mechanism, a way of directing blame away from oneself and onto others. A way of finding a fall guy . . . a scapegoat.

That was the term Abby had used.

It was always safe to blame the scapegoat, because the scapegoat was entirely separate from the self. Tess had worked hard to convince herself she and Abby had nothing in common. She hadn't wanted to believe there could be any part of herself in Abby or any part of Abby in her.

Yet there was, of course. She'd planted the bumper beeper, hadn't she? She'd shown Abby the confidential report. She'd been willing to break the rules, just like Abby. They both spent part of their time in shadow. Abby might be more comfortable there, but Tess was no stranger to the darkness, either. She hadn't wanted to admit it, that was all—so she'd disowned that part of herself, and Abby along with it. She'd wanted to prosecute Abby, lock her in a cell, because that way she could exorcise the shadow side of herself.

And what was worse, Abby knew it. In the coffee shop

she'd told Tess exactly what was going on and why. Well, why wouldn't Abby have known? She was a psychologist. Her job was to read people and intuit their motives. She was good at it. She was very damn good.

An LED on the meter panel blinked on. The diode at 135 degrees—southeast.

The signal-strength meter flickered feebly, showing two bars on the twenty-increment graph. There was no audible tone from the speaker. That meant the signal was so far away as to be barely within range.

Still, she had a bead on it.

She'd found Kolb.

31

"I don't think most cops would feel that way about their work," Abby said as the car glided along dark streets.

Kolb looked at her, his face unreadable. "You're awfully protective of the police. You got someone in the family who's a cop?"

"No."

"You ever know any cops other than me?"

"Well, no."

"So you don't know shit about it, do you?"

"I just think—"

"I know what you think. You think it's good guys versus bad guys." He made angry stabbing motions with his forefinger. "There are evil people out there on the street, and the boys in blue have to put them away."

"Something like that."

"It's a load of crap." Kolb cut south on Western Avenue, driving too fast, the tires squealing as he made the turn. "Let me tell you what really goes down. The typical cop would feel right at home with those neo-Nazi cellmates of mine."

An interesting criticism, since Kolb was the one with the swastika tattoo. "Why would police officers get along with a bunch of thugs?"

"Because the police officers *are* a bunch of thugs." Kolb thrust his chin out, a threat display. "You know who becomes a cop? The bully from your local playground. The kid who wasn't as smart as the other kids, but he could beat the snot out of them. Then that kid is all grown-up, and he can't go around pounding on people anymore. Until he finds out there's a job for him. A job where he gets to carry a club and handcuffs and pepper spray and a big honking gun. A job where nobody can question him or even look at him cross-eyed without putting themselves in a world of hurt."

"You're saying cops are just dysfunctional kids who never grew up?"

"Dysfunctional—I like that. Yeah, they're dysfunctional, all right. They want to strut. They admire Mafia guys and high-rolling pimps and crack addicts. They all want to prove they've got the swingingest dick on the block."

"So it's a macho thing."

"Not macho. Not in the true sense. A real man doesn't need to prove himself. He can take any amount of abuse, and it runs off him like water off a duck. He can stand there and take the insults without flinching, no matter what those spic assholes say. . . ." He had detoured into some private memory. She saw him shake himself back into focus. "My former colleagues aren't strong enough, centered enough, for that kind of discipline. They don't rise above their environment. They lower themselves to it. You know what the LAPD is? A gang. A street gang."

"I think that's a little extreme."

"What else would you call a bunch of guys who roam bad neighborhoods at night and smack down anybody who pisses them off?"

There was some truth in this, Abby knew, but there were plenty of good cops, too, like Wyatt. Anyway, her personal feelings didn't matter. She had to keep working on Kolb. "The police aren't outlaws," she said. "They *are* the law."

"That only makes them more dangerous." At the Santa Monica Freeway he took the on-ramp, racing east in the fast lane. "Except I shouldn't say *them*. I should say *us*. I was one of them. Every night it was our gang against theirs, our colors against their colors. Their colors were black, brown, and yellow. The blacks, the Hispanics, the Asians."

"I thought you didn't care about skin color."

"I don't. None of us did. It wasn't racism. We didn't hate them. We went up against them, *mano a mano.*"

Abruptly he veered across three lanes and shot down the Vermont Avenue off-ramp. He'd been on the freeway less than a minute.

"What was that about?" she asked.

"Changed my mind," he said curtly. "Decided to take the surface streets."

Abby knew his real reason. The maneuver was a standard technique of evasive driving. Anyone on their tail would have been lost during the quick exit.

She saw Kolb glance again at the rearview mirror. He nodded, satisfied.

"But race does matter?" she pressed.

"Only as a signal. It tells you who to look out for. You know about that, I'm sure. Picking up signals. Reading people."

She phrased her response cautiously. "Why would I know anything about that?"

"You live in this city, don't you? You couldn't survive here for a week if you didn't know how to size up a threat."

This was innocuous enough, but she still wondered what had made him raise the issue in the first place. "It sounds like everyone who's poor and nonwhite is a threat."

"I told you, we didn't hate them. Tell you the truth, we probably respected them more than most of the law-abiding citizens we met. At least the guys we tangled with had *cojones.*"

"If you didn't hate them, why tangle with them at all?"

"Because they weren't us. The battle lines were drawn. We were on one side, and they were on the other."

"They were civilians, you mean?"

"They were combatants."

"How about someone like me? Am I a combatant?"

He looked at her, his face lit by the glow of the dashboard. "I don't know, Abby. Are you?"

She didn't care for that question or for the intensity with which he asked it. "What's that supposed to mean?"

He laughed, evading an answer. "Just trying to give you an education in the real world. Giving you the benefit of my new perspective, now that I've broken free from the group-think of my police fraternity."

"Maybe your new perspective isn't any more valid than your old one."

"Oh, no. I'm seeing clearly now. You can't believe how clearly I see . . . everything."

He took Hoover Boulevard north, shooting under the free-way overpass, then hooked up with Washington Boulevard as it headed southeast. The towers of downtown were visible to the north. Ahead there was nothing but increasingly run-down neighborhoods—and the river.

There was a confrontation coming up. Abby could feel it. And it could be dicey.

She had some things going for her. She had the advantage of experience—she'd been in comparable situations many times. She had a gun, and she'd mastered the street-fighting skill of Krav Maga, a no-holds-barred form of combat imported to the U.S. from Israel. Her reflexes were quick, her nerves steady.

But Kolb was no pushover. He was an ex-cop and an ex-con. He'd stayed fit. His arms were huge, his body packed with muscle. He'd been in street fights himself. And there was a good chance he was armed. His gun, if he had one, was concealed under his leather jacket, maybe tucked into the waistband of his jeans. He could get it into his hand as fast as she could find the Smith's trigger.

So they were evenly matched, more or less. She gave herself a slight edge—but then, she always did.

Never bet against your own team. That was her motto.

Kolb sped along Washington Boulevard. A block north, the freeway ran parallel to the surface street. Through gaps in the buildings Abby could see the rush of traffic on the elevated roadway.

The car hit another pothole, rattling fiercely, and Abby tightened her grip on her handbag. "Nowadays," she said, "you must identify with the people you used to arrest."

"I don't identify with anybody. I'm beyond that."

"Beyond what?"

"Trying to fit myself in with some group, like a piece in a jigsaw puzzle. Pledging allegiance to my Aryan brothers came easy to me. I'd already pledged allegiance to my brothers in blue. In both cases, all I had to do was let someone else do my thinking for me."

"Now, I take it, you're thinking for yourself."

"Damn straight. That's why I'm thinking clearly at last."

At the next corner Tess headed east, watching the meter panel as the lighted position switched to forty-five degrees.

If she could judge by the signs in Asian characters all around her, she was in Koreatown. Downtown LA lay straight ahead.

Still no tone from the speaker, but there were three bars showing on the graph. The signal was weak, vanishing for as long as a minute before reappearing. The lights of the bearing indicator blinked on and off, sometimes at forty-five degrees, sometimes at ninety. The target's bearing wasn't actually shifting that much––she was picking up multipath reflections. As long as she stayed in motion, the false bearings would average out.

At Lafayette Park, Wilshire Boulevard curved southeast, and the signal drifted close to zero degrees. The signal-strength meter showed ten increments on the bar graph. And from the speaker came low but audible beep tones. She was getting closer, but there was still significant interference. She adjusted the variable attenuator to cut down on weaker signals, which were almost certainly reflections.

As she cut through the intersection of Wilshire and Union Avenue, the signal abruptly swung to the northwest

side of the dial. Could be an artifact. She ignored it for another couple of blocks, but the signal grew stronger, and
she had to follow it. She steered northwest on Lucas Avenue, skirting the downtown area and the flow of traffic on
the Harbor Freeway, which hemmed in the city center like
a moat.

The signal was still strong, but she was sure she was on
the wrong track. The tones from the speaker were no longer
pure. They'd developed the raspy quality caused when multiple reflections hit the antenna almost simultaneously, dis-
torting the audio. She was following a ghost signal. The
clutter of downtown and the surrounding freeways had sent
her on the trail of a reflection.

She pulled a U-turn and retraced her route, exceeding the
speed limit. The ghost signal faded, but she didn't pick up
anything else. She dialed up the receiver's sensitivity. Still
nothing. She passed Wilshire and continued south, hooking
onto a series of side streets that led her to the Harbor Freeway. She sped onto the southbound lanes. The freeway
raised her up high over the surface streets. Height was what
she needed. It was easier to pull in a signal from a high
point.

There. No beep tone yet, but one of the diodes on the
meter panel was flickering. She'd reacquired the target.

The signal came from the southeast. At the freeway in-
terchange, she connected with I-10, heading in that direction, while the signal strengthened and loud beeps came
through the speaker, clear and undistorted. A true signal
this time.

The bearing indicator shifted from forty-five degrees to
ninety, then to 135. She'd overshot the mark. Kolb was traveling on a surface street, moving slower than the freeway
traffic. She took the next exit, at San Pedro Street, and
turned west on Washington Boulevard. The transmission
was strong now, the signal-strength meter maxing out, the
bearing indicator's LEDs flickering with false readings. She
adjusted the attenuator until only one signal remained, cen-

tered at zero degrees, dead ahead, and getting stronger. Kolb was on this street and headed right for her.

And he shot past. She caught a glimpse of him behind the wheel of his Olds, Abby in the passenger seat. Tess didn't think he'd noticed the antenna array on her roof.

Then the car was gone, speeding east, while the signal lessened and the bearing indicator shifted to 180 degrees.

She swung onto a side street, executed a K-turn, and peeled onto Washington, cutting off traffic as she veered into the eastbound lane. Kolb wasn't far ahead, and as long as she remained locked on the transmitter's signal, she couldn't lose him.

If Kolb was the Rain Man, he would be taking Abby to the storm drains. He would have to stop the car at some point, either to take her into the tunnel system on foot or to gain access to a vehicle entry point. When he stopped, Tess would have a chance to take him out.

She ought to call for backup. She was reaching for her cell phone when the signal strength abruptly increased.

He must have stopped already. That was a surprise. She hadn't expected him to stop on a crowded thoroughfare like Washington Boulevard.

She cut her speed but continued. There was no sign of Kolb's Oldsmobile, though the speaker was screaming at her, the bar graph showing signal strength at 100 percent, the bearing indicator fixed on zero.

And then the signal was coming from behind her. She'd passed the target without seeing it.

Impossible. It didn't make any sense. It was as if she'd driven right over his car.

No. Not his car. Only the transmitter.

Tess braked the sedan on the shoulder of the road and got out, leaving the engine running. She ran a few yards back down the road, and yes, there was the transmitter, lying on the pavement, some of the electrical tape still in place. As she watched, vehicles drove over it, and one of them mashed it under its tires.

The mounting hadn't held. She remembered she hadn't had time to finish securing it with tape. Kolb had hit a pothole, and the impact had jarred the device loose.

Now she had no signal to follow.

She ran back to the sedan and pulled the antenna array off the roof, dumping it on the roadside. She didn't want Kolb seeing the antennas if she got close enough to make visual contact.

Then she was behind the wheel, driving fast. Kolb couldn't have gotten far. As long as he stayed on Washington, she had a good chance of catching up.

"So I guess," Abby said slowly, "you must regret the time you spent on the police force."

"Oh, I don't know. There was a good side to the job. There were the perks."

"What perks?"

He smiled, a man gathering fond memories. "The best thing was the head rush. Pulling over some jagoff in a BMW who was exceeding the speed limit. Making the guy sweat behind the wheel before you get out of the car and come up to his side door. That guy might pull in more money in a year than you'll make in your life, he might have a supermodel girlfriend and a condo in Aspen and a free ride on a corporate jet—but at that moment, you've got him by the short hairs. You tell him to bend over and kiss his own ass, and he'll give himself a hernia trying to do it."

"So you had power," Abby said.

"I sure as hell did."

"And now you don't."

"Well, now, I never said that."

She stayed silent, hoping he would expand on this remark.

He did. "Maybe I do have power. Maybe I have more power than I ever had before. Maybe I have enough power to make more important people than some jerk in a BMW jump through hoops."

This was getting close to a confession. "Which people?"

"That's my little secret."

At Alameda Street, Washington Boulevard and the freeway diverged, with the freeway sweeping northeast and the street continuing in a straight line. Kolb kept going. Toward the river.

"A secret's no fun," Abby said, "unless you can share it with somebody."

"I don't think you'd want to know."

"Try me."

"Sorry."

The river wasn't far now. If that was where he was taking her, then he must be the Rain Man. And if he was, he would have items in the trunk of his car, incriminating items.

She didn't have to wait any longer. She didn't have to let him make the first move.

Unless she was wrong. Then, by taking preemptive action, she would blow everything.

"You're awfully quiet, Abby." They passed Santa Fe Avenue. "I'd offer a penny for your thoughts, but a penny doesn't buy much anymore."

She forced a smile. "In this case you'd get your money's worth."

Washington Boulevard curved right, then left.

"Oh, I don't know about that. I have a feeling there's a lot of interesting stuff going on in that pretty little head."

He was toying with her. She had to act.

She slid her hand deeper into the purse, reaching for the trigger of her .38.

And Kolb slammed the Oldsmobile sideways, careening onto a side street, and there was a scream of tires and a blur of the world beyond the windows as he jammed the brake pedal to the floor.

The car slammed to a stop. Abby was flung forward

against the dashboard, and her handbag flew out of her lap into the darkness at her feet.

She'd lost the gun. She was disarmed.

She lunged for the purse. Kolb shoved her back in her seat. She saw his face, and the gun in his hand, coming up fast, the muzzle pressed to her temple.

She had time for one thought: *This is it.*

32

But he didn't fire. His hand was shaking, the gun's muzzle drilling into her cheek, but so far he hadn't pulled the trigger.

"Who the fuck are you?" he growled.

"Just calm down, William."

"Fuck you, bitch. You don't tell me to calm down. You answer my questions. Got it?"

"I got it." She stared straight ahead, through the windshield. The car had come to a stop on a narrow dead-end street wedged between rows of high windowless buildings—warehouses or deserted industrial plants. A single purplish streetlight cast a dismal glow over the street.

"You ready to answer my questions?"

"Fire away." She swallowed. "Poor choice of words."

"I want to know who you are."

If he wanted to know who she was, then he couldn't have found out much. She might be able to snow him.

"I already told you—" she began.

"Don't give me any bullshit about how you work for a company that makes stationery. I know that's a load of crap."

"What makes you think so?"

"Because I went to your apartment. Your phony apartment, the one you never visit."

He'd been to her Abby Hollister address. That was bad, but not necessarily fatal.

"I haven't been to my apartment in a few weeks, that's

true. I've been staying with a friend." She allowed an edge to creep into her voice. "So what? Why does that matter?"

"You're not staying with any friend. You keep the apartment as a blind. What are you, a private detective?"

"Private detective? William, I don't know where you got this idea, but the reason I haven't been at home is, my best friend just went through a bad divorce and she needs somebody to stay with her, hold her hand. I've been sleeping on her couch. That's all."

"You're full of shit. Am I supposed to think it's a coincidence, you showing up now? Coming back into my life after a year, and it just happens to be right now?"

"What's so special about right now?"

"You goddamn know. You're *lying* to me."

Careful now. He was on the verge of losing control. "William, I'm not telling any lies. And you're really, really scaring me with that gun. I wish you'd put it away so we could talk and work everything out."

"Yeah, because you're so easily scared, right? Think I bought that bullshit about how you're a wimp and a fraidy-cat? I see right through you, bitch. I see what angle you're playing. Setting yourself up as the perfect victim. Using yourself as bait."

"I don't want to be bait. I don't want to be a victim. I don't know what you're talking about."

"Okay, you want to play that way? I'll get the truth out of you. By the time I'm done, you'll tell me everything. I'm going to learn all your secrets."

"I don't have any secrets."

"I know how to make you talk. And when you're done, you get to go into the storm drains. You like that plan, Abby? You up for it?"

So that was it, then. Madeleine had been right. Kolb was the Rain Man.

She put bewilderment in her voice. "Storm drains . . .?"

"Yeah, that's a big surprise, isn't it? Sure it is. You know who I am. You knew, or suspected, all along. I kidnap women, and I put them down in the tunnels when it rains. I make good money at it. I'm going to make a fortune on you."

Everyone in the city had followed the case. She could no longer feign incomprehension. "You're . . . *him?*" she whispered, striking what she hoped was the correct note of fear and astonishment.

"That's right, Abby. I'm him."

"Oh, God . . ."

"Right, act like it's a news flash. You're giving a hell of a performance, I'll give you that. Performance of a lifetime, I guess you'd say."

"I'm not acting, William."

He wouldn't listen. "Hell, maybe I'll up the ante to twenty mil. If you've been working with the feds, you're worth it. They'll try their damnedest to get you back."

"I haven't been working with anybody. I don't know what you're talking about."

"You've been working with McCallum. Probably counting on her to back you up if things got hot."

He even knew about Tess. Where he'd gotten hold of that information, she couldn't imagine. "I don't know anyone named McCallum."

He ignored her. "Guess what, Abby. McCallum's not here. If she was tailing me, I lost her."

"I said, I don't know anyone named McCallum!"

"Yeah, and you don't know Madeleine Grant, either. You don't know anything. You're just a babe in the woods, aren't you?"

He leaned closer. She could smell his sweat, feel the mist of spittle from his mouth when he formed sibilant sounds.

"Listen to me, Abby. It's just you and me now. You're all alone, not a friend in the world, and your lies aren't cutting it. You're not buying yourself anything but pain. Now I'm going to ask you straight-out, and if I don't hear some facts coming out of you, I am going to be royally pissed. You understand me?"

She took a breath. "I understand."

"Good. I'm glad to hear it. Now, who are you? I want an answer. You lie to me again, and it's going to go hard on you, Abby. Who are you?"

She tried to calculate the best response. If she continued stonewalling, he might pull the trigger in sheer frustration. But if she told the truth, any part of the truth, he could become enraged and shoot her in a spasm of anger. There were no good options. And she was running out of time.

Kolb shifted in his seat, crowding her, the gun pressing even harder against her skull. "Tell me, Abby."

She was out of answers. Lies had failed her, and the truth would get her killed.

"Who are you?"

She heard the mounting violence in his voice.

"God damn it"—he was almost screaming the words—"*who are you?!*"

The car exploded.

For an instant Abby was sure the gun had gone off. The explosion was the blast of the bullet in her brain.

Then she fell against the dashboard as the car lurched forward, rocking on its shocks. They'd been hit from behind, struck by another vehicle. Kolb was off balance, taken by surprise, the gun swinging down.

She pivoted in her seat and delivered a sideward fist hammer blow, aiming for his neck, but missing and chopping only his shoulder. The blow momentarily delayed him from realigning his weapon. She seized his gun hand, fully extending her arm to lock her elbow for maximum leverage, and held the gun away from her as she threw a backfist to his face, hoping to catch him in the nose—a broken nose was a painful and disorienting injury—but again he dodged the attack, taking the hit on the cheek.

Limited room to maneuver. Kicks, knee smashes—they were out. She followed up the backfist with a foreknuckle fist strike to his throat, a potentially lethal assault that could crush the Adam's apple and induce asphyxiation. He warded off the blow with his left arm. She grabbed his sleeve and yanked down the arm, exposing his face, then executed a knife-hand strike to his neck, connecting this time.

He groaned. She'd hurt him. She tried for another strike to the face, but he brushed aside the attack and launched a punch at her head, which she evaded by inches, his fist sinking into the headrest. But the movement cost her control of Kolb's gun hand. He tore free, and now the gun was circling toward her. She ducked under his right arm, squeezing close, making it hard for him to shoot without the risk of hitting himself, and grabbed his right wrist, using her thumb to apply painful pressure to the scaphoid bone. His grip on the gun loosened, but he didn't let it go.

He would be expecting her to go for his face or neck again, so she changed her tactics and went low, driving an elbow strike into his ribs with enough force to make him jerk forward with a release of breath. His head briefly dipped, and she took the opportunity it presented, springing up to land a chopping blow to the back of his neck.

There was another groan, and an expulsion of watery puke from his mouth. She seized the gun and twisted it out of his grasp, his lax fingers no longer resisting. She held the gun on him while he sat blinking, his face a pale mask.

And Tess was there on the driver's side, her SIG Sauer pointing at Kolb. "FBI, don't move!"

Abby, breathing hard, managed a smile. "He can't move. He's only half-conscious. Anyway, I've got him covered."

Tess's gun didn't waver. "We both do."

Carefully, Tess opened the door on the driver's side and secured Kolb's hands behind his back with plastic handcuffs, then patted him down, finding some items in his jacket pockets that she tossed to Abby.

Flashlight, duct tape, handcuffs, chloroform. He'd had plans for her, all right.

"Out of the car," Tess ordered.

Kolb, still groggy, let his head fall back against the headrest.

"I said, out!"

"Let me help you with that," Abby offered. She retrieved her purse, then went around to the driver's side. Together she and Tess hauled Kolb out of his seat and pushed him down to his knees, then forced him to lie alongside the Oldsmobile.

"Stay there," Tess said, cuffing him. "Don't move."

She took the keys from the Olds so Kolb wouldn't get any ideas about attempting an escape. Then she motioned for Abby to step away from the car.

By this time Abby had noticed Tess's Bureau car, bumper-locked with the Olds. "You rammed us," Abby said. "Headlights off so he wouldn't see you coming. Pretty slick."

"You don't seem surprised to see me."

"I'm in a mild state of shock after nearly getting a bullet in my noggin. Come to think of it, what *are* you doing here?"

Tess kept her voice low, obviously worried Kolb would overhear. "I put a tracker on his car. It led me to you."

"That much I figured out on my own."

"You did?"

"The evasive maneuvers he performed would have thrown you off if you'd been tailing him visually. The bumper beeper was unauthorized, I presume."

"Yes."

"Agent McCallum breaks the rules. I'll turn you to the dark side yet."

"I'm not proud of it."

"You should be. You saved"—*my life*, Abby wanted to say, but she wasn't very good at thank-yous—"the situation. But you'd better get rid of the tracker before your colleagues examine the vehicle."

"Not necessary. The damn thing fell off about a mile west of here. That's why I was almost too late. I made visual contact with the car just as it pulled off Washington."

"Your timing was perfect. Of course, I seem to remember you saying I'd be on my own tonight."

"I changed my mind about that. Had a talk with Madeleine. She persuaded me you didn't plant the evidence last year."

"How'd she pull off that miracle?"

Tess hesitated. "It doesn't matter. Let's just say I owe you an apology."

"And I owe you"—she still couldn't say it—"a cheeseburger. On me, this time."

"Before we make any dinner arrangements, we need to decide how to handle this. How much does Kolb know?"

"A surprising amount, actually. He knew or guessed I was some kind of private operative, and he knew I'd been working with you."

Tess bit her lip. "That's bad. He'll repeat all those claims when he's interrogated."

"So what? Nobody'll believe him. He's a paranoid wackjob, always seeing conspiracies. And he doesn't know my real name or anything about the real me. To him, I'm Abby Hollister. That's who I'll be to the feds, too, when they talk to me."

"You're going to stick around to deal with them? With us, I mean?"

"Got to. It'll look suspicious if I walk away."

"You'll be interviewed."

"No problem. But you'd better take my gun till I'm done with the interview. I might have trouble explaining why I was carrying a concealed weapon."

Tess took the gun and stuck it into the pocket of her trench coat. "I think you're underestimating the degree of your involvement."

"Wait and see," Abby said with a smile. "The real question is, how do you explain showing up here? We need a story. Something too simple to be disproved."

Tess considered it. "We're near the river, aren't we?"

"Couple blocks away."

"Okay, then. I was cruising the area on the chance that the Rain Man might use an entrance near the river. I happened to see this car parked on a side street and I noticed a struggle going on inside."

Abby ran the scenario through her mind and saw the plot holes. "No good. Kolb's connection with Madeleine will come out as soon as they run a background check. She'll be called in, and she'll have to admit she met you."

"You're right." Tess looked chagrined. "Why didn't I think of that?"

"You don't have enough practice at this sort of thing. Now here's the story. You admit you interviewed Madeleine. You were running down a lead on the side. You followed Kolb tonight because you thought he might be the Rain Man."

"Followed him visually," Tess said. "I can't admit to using the tracker."

"Sure, that'll work."

"I don't know." Tess looked away. "Michaelson will suspect there's something more going on."

"He's the director, right?" Abby shrugged. "So let him suspect. Suspicions don't matter as long as there's no proof. Anyway, you're forgetting the most important thing. You got him. You got the Rain Man."

"We got a man who assaulted you in his car. Whether or not he's the Rain Man remains to be seen."

"You saw what he had in his pockets."

"Duct tape, handcuffs—it's good, but not enough. He could just be a regular nutcase."

"Could be, but isn't. He's our guy. He told me so himself."

"He did?"

"In plain English. Said I was going into the storm drains like the other two."

Tess took this in, and her face cleared. "Then it's over," she said quietly. "It's really over."

Abby frowned. "Well, there's still his partner to worry about."

"I'm not convinced there is a partner."

"He said I was working with you. Someone had to give him that information."

"Nobody could have. Nobody knows. He was bluffing, Abby. He was working alone."

Abby let it go. The partner angle was something she could pursue on her own. "Whatever. Anyway, we got the guy we wanted. We ended the crime wave. Saved the day, in the best tradition of Mighty Mouse."

Tess stared at Kolb, prone on the pavement.

"We did, didn't we?" she said. "We really did."

Abby smiled. "I told you we'd make a good team."

33

An outsider would have assumed that bagging the Rain Man would merit an enthusiastic reception from the staff of the LA field office. Tess knew better. When she arrived with Abby, she was met with uncomfortable silence from Larkin, Crandall, and the others. No one seemed to know what to say—except Mason of the DWP, who clapped her on the shoulder and boomed, "Great work, you *got* him!"

"See?" Abby said in a low voice when they'd moved on. "You have some friends among your fellow *federales*."

"He's not a fed. He's our liaison with DWP."

"Oh."

"Thanks for trying to cheer me up, though."

"That's me, always looking on the bright side."

After that, they'd been separated. Abby was to be interviewed. Tess was called to the AD's office.

As she'd predicted, Michaelson was unhappy with her on a variety of levels. The fact that she'd apprehended the city's most wanted killer hardly compensated for her flagrant disregard of his orders. She'd pursued the Madeleine Grant tip without authorization. She'd kept secrets from her superior. She'd failed to return to the field office or to accept Larkin's subsequent phone calls.

"And I'm still not convinced you're telling me all you know," Michaelson ended ominously. "I think you're hiding something, Tess. That's a mistake. You've practiced enough skullduggery as it is."

She just gave him the same thousand-yard stare that Detective Goddard had used on her earlier in the day.

The stare unnerved Michaelson. He looked away. "We'll talk about this later," he said.

"I look forward to it." Sure she did. She was a masochist.

"For the time being, you're off this case. Restricted to your desk."

"It may be difficult to explain to the media why the person who cracked the case is no longer involved in it."

"The media have not yet been alerted to this arrest. We are keeping this story under wraps until we know exactly what we've got."

"They'll find out eventually. Then they'll come to me for comments."

"Which you are not permitted to give."

"Which will only heighten their curiosity."

Michaelson surrendered. "All right, you can continue to participate, but in an observational capacity only. You take no action. You just watch. I'll do all the heavy lifting."

"That should be interesting to see."

Together they went to the observation room, where a bank of closed-circuit television monitors displayed the image of Kolb, next door. He sat unmoving at a long table, his wrist chained to a steel eyelet embedded in the wood. Tess thought of Angela Morris and Paula Weissman, both of whom had died with one wrist shackled. She wondered how Kolb liked it.

For the moment he was alone in the interrogation room. Tess assumed Michaelson would send in one of the squad supervisors and a profiler. He surprised her, announcing to the small crowd of agents in the observation room that he was going in alone.

"I took over this investigation," he said, "and I'm responsible for handling the suspect."

In other words, having had nothing to do with the Rain

Man's capture, he could at least finagle a way to take credit for his confession.

Tess watched the monitors. On the far end of the table where Kolb sat, a few items had been placed out of his reach. The duct tape and flashlight from his pockets. The notepad and marker found in the trunk of his car. The cell phone in his glove compartment. The idea was to unnerve him, obviously—to show him there was no way out.

He didn't look unnerved. He looked oddly serene, almost smug. But of course serial offenders were often sociopaths, incapable of emotion.

As she watched, Michaelson appeared on the sweep of TV screens, pulling up a chair at the table. Standard procedure would have been to crowd Kolb, get in his face, but Michaelson hung back, keeping a safe distance between them. It would be nice to think he had some clever psychological strategy in mind, but Tess figured he was just scared.

"Mr. Kolb"—the AD's voice, crisp and loud, came over the speakers—"I'm the assistant director in charge, Richard Michaelson. I have some questions for you."

"I don't have any answers."

"You're in serious trouble, Mr. Kolb."

"Am I?"

Michaelson gestured toward the evidence on display. "You can see some of the things found on your person and in your vehicle. The notepad matches the one used in the abductions of Angela Morris and Paula Weissman. We found an index card with a bank account number on it. Our people are tracking down that account right now."

"Good for them."

"There's a tape recorder, which I assume was used to record your victims' statements. And of course there are the handcuffs you intended to put on your victim, and the duct tape to seal her mouth, and the cell phone you would have used to call the mayor's office. In addition, you were carrying a firearm, with the serial number filed off. Possession of a gun is illegal for an ex-convict, and a gun without a serial number—well, that's illegal for anyone."

"Maybe I believe in the right to bear arms."

"Our evidence technicians are continuing to go over your vehicle, and of course they've been dispatched to your residence as well. They've already found a number of items directly connecting you with the kidnappings and murders in the storm-drain system. Obviously there's more to come. Now, you were a police officer, and you know you're not going to walk away from this. We have you. Your only chance for any leniency is to cooperate fully and unreservedly. The game is up, Mr. Kolb."

Kolb just sat and stared at Michaelson for a long, disconcerting moment. "So," he said finally, "you running this play on your own?"

"I'm not sure what you mean."

"I have a little experience with the interrogation process. Normally it's played two-on-one, good-cop, bad-cop. So are you the good cop or the bad one?"

"I'm just trying to talk straight with you, man-to-man."

Kolb snorted. "Yeah." He leaned forward and took a closer look at his adversary. "You're not the good cop or the bad one. You're not a cop at all, are you?"

"I'm a federal agent."

"That's not what I meant. I meant you're not a street hump. You ride a desk, push paper."

"I do a lot of things, none of which are relevant to this conversation."

Kolb looked away. "McCallum—she's a cop."

"Agent McCallum is an agent of the FBI, just like me."

"No, I don't think so. Not just like you." He turned toward the ceiling, searching for the hidden cameras. "You watching this, Tess? You going to let this empty suit steal your righteous bust?"

His gaze fell on a corner of the ceiling that concealed one of the camera lenses. Tess stared into the monitor and saw Kolb staring back.

"Mr. Kolb," Michaelson was saying, "this case is in my hands now. It's me you want to talk to."

"It is, huh? What was your name again?"

"Richard Michaelson."

"Okay, Mike. Here's the thing. I don't *want* to talk to you. And I'm not *going* to talk to you. I'm not *ever* going to talk to you."

"And why is that?"

"Because you're a dickwad."

Michaelson stiffened. "That kind of talk is not helpful, Mr. Kolb."

"Fuck you, Mike. How about that? Is that helpful?"

The AD rose from the table with ostentatious dignity. "I hope you enjoy sitting around in custody. With this attitude, you may be here a long time."

He was halfway to the door when Kolb said, "Send McCallum in."

Michaelson turned. "What was that?"

"I'll talk to McCallum."

"I don't believe Agent McCallum is in the building."

"Cut the bullshit. She's here. I can smell her. She's in the next room, watching me on a TV monitor, and wishing she was asking the questions because she knows she can handle me a lot better than you can. Isn't that right, Tess? Hey, Tess, tell your boss he's an asshole. Tell him it's time to let one of the grown-ups have a turn."

He was looking into the same camera lens. It was as if he were seeing her through the glass screen of the monitor.

"You're only making things worse for yourself," Michaelson said.

"Give me McCallum. I'll have a conversation with her. I may not tell her what she wants to hear—but I'll talk."

Michaelson returned to the observation room, looking flustered and uncomfortably aware that his status was at stake. Tess didn't say anything. She knew that if she made any comment or suggestion, it would boomerang on her.

Whatever was decided had to be Michaelson's idea. He had to save face.

Finally he said, "Tess, he seems to feel he has some kind of connection with you, Christ knows why. Maybe you'd better take a crack at him."

He spoke loudly so everyone could hear, as if it were something he'd just thought of, a brainstorm, an executive decision.

"Yes, sir," Tess said quietly, willing to give him the pretense of dignity he needed.

She was about to step out the door when his voice stopped her. "Agent McCallum. You're not wearing your ID badge."

She'd forgotten to clip it to her lapel. "I had a few other things on my mind."

"The rules matter. Put it on."

As power plays went, this was rather sad. Still, she couldn't suppress her irritation as she dug the laminated badge out of her pocket and clipped it in place.

He was right, though. The rules did matter. It was a lesson she wouldn't let herself forget.

34

Tess walked into the interrogation room and saw Kolb smile. He felt he'd won this round. Tess was determined to give him no more victories.

She sat at the table. "I don't know why you're being uncooperative," she said without preliminaries. "You can only hurt yourself at this point. We have more than enough evidence to put you away."

"Do it, then." His eyes glittered with uncanny assurance. "Lock me back in a cage. You'll feel safer that way."

"Why would you say that?"

"Because you're scared of me."

"Am I?"

"Damn straight. You're terrified—because you know what I am."

"And what is that?"

"A man."

"Are you saying I'm afraid of men?"

He shrugged. "I don't know. Maybe you are. Maybe that's why you're a frigid bitch. But that's not what I'm talking about. I'm saying I'm a man. Not just a male. A *man*. And in your world, that's the one thing that isn't allowed."

"I'm not following you, Mr. Kolb."

"Sure you are. It's like I'm looking right inside your head, reading all your secrets, isn't it?"

"Not really."

"You won't admit it, but you know it's true. What scares you is that I'm better than you. I'm stronger, smarter, tougher. I'm in control."

"You're wearing handcuffs. Does that sound like you're in control?"

"This is how you want me. Manacled, caged. That way I'm no threat. You can't allow me to be on the loose. Your whole fragile social order is based on denying that men like me exist. When you find one of us, you throw us in a dungeon, keep us out of sight, so this fantasy you've constructed can continue uninterrupted."

Tess was surprised by Kolb. He saw himself as a big man, a figure inspiring terror and awe, when in fact he was only an inflated ego, a puffed-up narcissist. He was big only in his own eyes. "I'm not the one dealing in fantasy," she said mildly.

Her dismissive tone seemed to rattle him. He raised his voice, squared his shoulders. "You can't face the reality of what you are and what I am. You don't dare to even look at me—you'll be blinded by the light."

She fixed him with a steady gaze. "I'm looking at you right now."

"You can't allow yourself to see. You can't allow yourself to know you're in the presence of what you fear most."

"Meaning?"

"The life force. The will to power."

This answer must have sounded audacious to him. She saw his chest swell.

"You enforce laws meant to tie up men like me, but all you're doing is destroying yourself. A society without leaders has no future. A nation of eunuchs can't survive. You emasculate the strong, then wonder why nobody has the balls to get the job done."

"That's a nice speech. I particularly liked the part about castration. Colorful metaphor."

"You know it's true—every word."

He really did think his warmed-over master-race rant was

some kind of philosophical breakthrough. In a way she almost pitied him. He was an arrogant child thumping his breast.

"Let's say I agree with you," she said. "Let's say the world is divided between the weak and the strong. What exactly qualifies you as one of the strong? From everything I've seen, you're a weak man, Mr. Kolb."

The sudden heave of his abdomen with an intake of breath told her she'd hit him in a vulnerable spot. "You wouldn't say that," he whispered, "if I didn't have these cuffs on."

"Why? Because you'd beat me up? Is that what makes you so strong?"

"It's not physical strength that matters. It's strength of will."

"I don't see that kind of strength in you. I see a man who can't control his own anger. I see a bully and a psychopath."

His Adam's apple was jerking in his throat. The glitter of malicious enjoyment was gone from his eyes.

"And you know what I see when I look at *you?*" he said. "An Affirmative Action hire. A token gash. Arm candy for the Bureau. A pussy with legs." He growled the words, a feral animal. "I see two pairs of lips that are always open—your mouth and your cunt. How many times did you lie back and spread 'em for every promotion? You're a hooker with a badge. In a world that made sense, you'd be walking the Boulevard, selling suction jobs for twenty-five bucks a blow."

She was bored with this. "Mr. Kolb—"

"You're a sheep. I'm the lion. You have to pretend I don't exist. How else could you sleep at night—you and all the other sheep?"

"Was Angela Morris one of the sheep? Or Paula Weissman?"

He almost said yes, which would be as good as a confession, but some residual shrewdness stopped him. "Trying to bait me—that's a waste of time. You're no match for me." He sat back, breathing fast.

She decided to try a different approach. "I was a match for Mobius, wasn't I?"

He flicked off this question with a wave of his hand. "Mobius was nothing. Mobius was a failure."

"Then why'd you put together a scrapbook about him? You wanted to be the next Mobius, didn't you?"

"Why would I? He got caught. He fucked up."

"That's no way to talk about your hero."

"He wasn't my hero."

"You're the one who'll be getting the newspaper coverage now. Maybe somebody will make a scrapbook about you. Or maybe not—since after all, *you* failed, too."

He was silent for a moment, stewing, his eyes burning into her. "Okay, Tess. You want to know about that scrapbook? Here's a little secret. The scrapbook was never about Mobius. It was about *you*."

"Was it?"

"I got a little bit obsessed with you. Don't take it the wrong way. It wasn't any kind of sexual thing. It was the way the media built you up into a superstar."

"Why would that bother you?"

"Why?" He chuckled at her stupidity. "Maybe because I was an ordinary cop, a blue-collar guy busting my hump on the streets every goddamn day and getting no thanks, no commendations, no keys to the city or any of that crap. All I get is civilian complaints, black marks on my record. I'm out there doing the job, and nobody gives a shit. And there you are—you clear one case, you bag one bad guy—and you're soaking up the spotlight. It got under my skin."

She remembered the deputy DA complaining about *that girl soldier*, the POW who'd gotten book and movie deals. "Would it have bothered you so much," she asked, "if it had been a man getting the same attention?"

She thought he might be angry, but he seemed to appreciate the point. He liked talking about these things, she realized. He fancied himself a deep thinker, and he was eager to show off his insights.

"Fair question," he said amiably. "Answer is, no, it wouldn't have bothered me so much."

"You seem to have a problem with women."

"It's women who have the problem. Women are bitches, all of you." He pronounced this verdict without ire, as a statement of fact. "You want to know why?"

"I gather you have a theory about it."

He actually smiled. "How'd you know?"

"You seem to have a theory about everything."

"I know how the world works, that's all. Women are bitches because you resent your own weakness. You overcompensate by becoming manipulative, controlling, emasculating. You're impotent, so you want men to be impotent like you. You want an impotent world. That's the only kind of world where you can compete."

"Interesting perspective."

"Go ahead, deny it. I know the truth."

"The truth couldn't possibly be that you feel threatened by women?"

Another expansion of his chest. "I don't feel threatened by anybody."

"So you didn't feel threatened by Madeleine Grant when you pulled her over for speeding and she didn't allow herself to be intimidated?"

"She was a bitch playing mind games. Just like you. I'm used to it."

"I think she got under your skin—the same way I did."

Kolb had settled back into eerie complacency. "Then what happened to her was her fault. If she'd handled things right, she never would've gotten any e-mails. The whole thing escalated because of her."

"Because she stood up to you?"

"Because," he said softly, "she didn't bow down."

"Is that what she was supposed to do?"

"Yes."

"What does it mean, exactly—to bow down?"

"It means she was supposed to acknowledge me. Acknowledge who I am, what I am. She was supposed to show fear."

"And I am, too?"

"Yes."

"The whole city? The whole world?"

"*Yes.*"

She smiled. "Well, I have news for you, Mr. Kolb. No one is bowing down to you now."

Tess rose to leave. Kolb's voice stopped her. "What's the deal with that other bitch?"

She hesitated, not wanting to deal with the issue, but knowing it had to be faced. Slowly she took her seat again. "What do you mean?"

"Abby Hollister, or whatever her real name is. What is she, a PI? Did Grant hire her?"

"I have no idea what you're talking about."

"Yes, you do. You were working with her."

"I think your paranoia is getting the better of you. Abby Hollister is just an ordinary woman, like the first two you kidnapped."

"Ordinary? I don't think so. That bitch tussles like a streetfighter."

"Lots of women in LA have taken courses in self-defense."

"This was more than a few tae kwon do moves you learn at the health spa after yoga class. She knows how to take care of herself. She's a pro."

"Maybe you just can't deal with the fact that an ordinary woman could stand up to you."

"You're covering for her. It's not coincidence she showed up in my life just before I got arrested, both times. Her apartment—"

The interview was heading in a dangerous direction. Tess cut him off. "I'm not interested in hearing more of your theories." She put a derisive emphasis on the last word. "You need to concentrate on your own future. Trying to divert our attention with made-up stories will only make things worse for you."

Kolb wasn't listening. "Tell your boss to look into Abby, find out what she was up to. Check her residence, her document trail. I'm betting he finds she's a ghost. The two of you were working me—together. What kind of game are you running with her, anyway? She your girlfriend? Maybe the two of you take turns being on top. Is that the deal?"

In Kolb's world, any efficacious woman was either frigid or a lesbian. He really was an arrested adolescent, perpetually sneering at the girls who ignored him.

"You don't get to ask the questions," Tess said. "In fact, you don't get to do anything. It may come as a shock to you, since you're so interested in power, but you have no power now. And you never will again."

Kolb stared at her, his face hard and unrevealing. "Don't be so sure."

At the far end of the table, the cell phone rang.

The noise startled Tess. She turned to the items of evidence displayed for Kolb's consideration, among them the confiscated phone, its touch pad glowing. It rang again.

"You might want to answer that," Kolb said.

She looked at him and saw something in his eyes that, for the first time, frightened her. Amusement, and an utter lack of surprise.

Slowly she got up and approached the phone as it rang again. On the fourth ring, she answered. "Hello?"

There was an odd moment of silence, then a female voice, slightly muffled—but instantly familiar. "This is Madeleine Grant."

A chill rode Tess's shoulders, and the room around her twisted out of proper perspective, the floor and walls curiously skewed.

Madeleine continued talking, her voice strangely hollow. A tape recording, Tess realized—like the others. "I've been . . . taken captive by an associate of William Kolb. I'm being held—oh, God . . ."

Paper rustled. Madeleine had been forced to read this message.

"I'm being held in the storm drains. My location will be revealed only in exchange for the release of William Kolb. If Kolb is not released by the time the rain falls, it . . . it will be too late. It's his freedom for my life. Kolb's freedom for my life . . ."

Her control broke, the last word catching on a sob.

Then silence. The tape was over. With a click, the call ended.

Tess put down the phone and became aware of things again—the fluorescent lights overhead, the hidden cameras recording this scene, Kolb watching her with narrowed, alert eyes.

"Who's got the power now, Tess?" he asked.

She didn't answer. She left the room, followed by his laughter.

35

Tess found Abby in the kitchenette, pouring a cup of coffee. She wasn't supposed to be in there unsupervised, but as Tess knew only too well, she had a penchant for breaking the rules.

Things were happening fast. Michaelson had been informed of the recorded message. An LAPD unit had immediately been dispatched to Madeleine Grant's home. She was gone. It hadn't even been necessary for Kolb's partner to defeat the security system. He'd simply ambushed Madeleine in her car as she rolled up to the front gate. The car had been left there, unnoticed by the household staff. Madeleine's purse was found on the street, along with the carrying case for her .32, with the gun still inside—the gun she'd counted on for protection. She'd never even unzipped the case.

There was no blood at the scene, no sign of violence. Probably she'd been forced into her abductor's vehicle at gunpoint. Tess remembered her saying she would fight rather than submit. Brave words, but not always so easy to put into practice.

Michaelson had been sufficiently distracted by Madeleine's kidnapping that he hadn't raised the issue of Kolb's allegations about Abby. At some point he would remember. Tess wanted Abby out of the field office before then—and before

Abby heard about the abduction. If she found out Madeleine was in danger, she would insist on remaining involved.

For this reason Tess put on a conspiratorial smile as she walked into the kitchenette. She was glad the two of them were alone. "Give your statement yet?" she asked, hoping she sounded casual.

Abby nodded. "Talked to Agent Crandall. Isn't he a little young to be carrying a firearm?"

"They get younger every year." Tess lowered her voice. "Any problems?"

"With Crandall? Spinning him wasn't exactly a challenge."

"What did you tell him?"

"The truth." Abby raised her hand with a smile. "Spare me the freak-out. When I say the truth, I mean the truth as I see it. Which means the truth as I wanted him to see it."

"Which means a lie."

"Well, yeah. More precisely, it entails the omission of certain possibly relevant facts. I told him all about how Kolb and I got together by accident this morning, and then I showed up at his apartment and he asked me out, and he went all Mr. Hyde on me in the car. And how he said I was going into the tunnels like the other two. All of which is true—except for the part about our meeting by accident. It wasn't an accident. But it could have been."

"Crandall believed you?"

"Of course."

"Even so, when this goes to trial, the defense will pick that story to pieces."

"When this goes to trial, Abby Hollister will have disappeared off the face of the earth."

"You're not going to testify?"

"What am I, an idiot?" She took a sip from her cup. "My identity as Abby Hollister is only one of several alter egos I've constructed. It's going straight into the dumper. There's a furnished apartment I've been renting in her name—it's history. The car I've been using on the job, which is registered to Miss Hollister—it's going to be abandoned in a really bad neighborhood. Shame, too. The car's a piece of junk, but the engine's been rebuilt. Had a lot more miles left in it. *C'est la vie.*"

"You've done this before, I take it."

"Spoken French?"

"Disappeared."

"Once or twice. I try not to make a habit of it. It takes a lot of time and effort to put together one of these aliases. Phony paper, a credit history, the whole shebang."

"I'm not sure I want to know the details."

"Because it's all so highly illegal? Come on, that's what makes it fun. You buy a dead person's Social Security number, use it to get a credit card, establish a history, maybe vote in an election or two—"

"You voted under an assumed name?"

"Last election, I voted under *four* assumed names. How's that for public-spiritedness? I was a one-woman political machine. And you know what? My candidates *still* lost. But what are you gonna do?"

"I know what *you're* going to do, Abby."

"Not sure I'm liking the ominous tone."

"You're going to go home, and start doing all the things necessary to cover your tracks. Now—before somebody else decides to interview you. Somebody more thorough than Crandall."

"Are you kicking me out?"

"I'm kicking you *loose*. You did a great job. You got the Rain Man for us. And I'm sorry I doubted you. But we can take it from here."

"Sounds almost like I'm not wanted."

"You've done all you can. And I want to thank you for it. Really." She was already easing Abby toward the door.

Abby frowned. "Don't get all choked up. These overt displays of emotion can be so embarrassing."

Tess realized she was pressing too hard. "Abby . . ."

The attempted apology was waved off with a smile. "I'm

just ragging on you, Special Agent. I know when the manager's taking me out of the ball game. I just hope the closer doesn't blow my lead."

"Don't worry. Everything is under control." Tess only wished this were true.

"Okay, but I need my Smith."

"Right. It's in my coat." Tess had left the coat at her workstation. "Wait here."

She hurried down the hall to the C-1 squad room, which was empty, all the agents either conferring with Michaelson or working the scene of the kidnapping. She found Abby's gun in her coat pocket and took it out. When she turned, Abby was right behind her.

"I asked you to wait," Tess said, irritated.

"I'm no good at following orders. Haven't you picked up on that by now?" Abby took the gun and put it into her purse. "Much better. You know, I felt naked without it."

Tess wanted to say that carrying a gun hadn't helped Madeleine Grant. Instead she forced a smile. "Let yourself out. No one will stop you."

"Just let 'em try. So . . . this is it, I guess. End of the road for Cagney and Lacey."

All Tess wanted to do was get back to working the abduction. "I'm afraid so. Good-bye, Abby."

"Hey, why so formal?" Unexpectedly, Abby stepped up and gave Tess a quick, jarring hug. "It's been good to know you, Special Agent."

Madeleine's voice came back to Tess: *She's lonely, you see. Much lonelier than she lets on. Lonelier than she knows.*

She'd found it hard to believe. But maybe it was true. She didn't know what to say as Abby pulled back.

"I'm just an old softy," Abby said with a slightly embarrassed grin. "Besides, it's not every day somebody saves my butt. Hey, I still owe you that cheeseburger."

"Another time," Tess managed.

"Sure. Count on it."

Abby saluted Tess with a brisk wave, and then she was gone, heading down the hall in the direction of the reception area, and Tess relaxed. One problem had been solved, at least.

Abby Sinclair was off the case.

36

Abby left the Federal Building and crossed Wilshire, smiling. It had been a hoot to see the expression on Tess's face when she received that spontaneous gesture of affection. Abby hadn't given her a hug for laughs, though. Nor had she wanted to share the love. What she'd wanted to share was the ID tag clipped to Tess's lapel.

What the heck, Tess didn't need it. She had other FBI creds, and Abby had none at all. It didn't seem fair. Fortunately the unequal distribution of resources had been rectified. Abby had the small, laminated clip-on tag now. She figured it would come in handy when she visited Kolb's apartment building. Tess might not be interested in Kolb's partner, but Abby was, and she thought the bug in his phone might give her a lead.

Having left her Honda in his neighborhood, she would have to catch a cab in Westwood. There was usually one outside the Westwood Marquis hotel. She hiked into Westwood Village, weaving her way through the usual crowd of college kids, fending off an occasional drunken advance. At the Marquis she was pleased to see a cab in the taxi lane.

She told the driver Kolb's address, and he grunted an affirmative. As the cab rolled east on Wilshire, she inserted the ID tag into her wallet so Tess's photo showed through the plastic window, then spent the rest of the ride studying the photo blowup of the driver's cab license and trying to figure out how to pronounce his last name.

When they reached Kolb's block, she saw police cars around the building, but no media yet. The arrest had been kept out of the news. "Drop me at the corner," she said.

She walked back to the apartment building, where patrol officers guarded the front and side entrances. She wished she were dressed a little more upscale, but regardless of her ensemble, she could pass for a fed. It was all about attitude. Feds had this strut, this cock-of-the-walk thing going on. She picked up her pace and made sure she wasn't smiling. Feds never smiled at cops, and vice versa. There was too much territorialism in their relationship to allow for such niceties.

As she hiked up her skirt and stepped over the crime-scene ribbon, one of the patrol cops approached. "I'm afraid you can't go in there right now, ma'am."

Her wallet was already in her hand. She flipped it open and flashed the ID tag. "FBI."

She knew there were other feds present. They would never yield control of Kolb's apartment to the locals. The cop wouldn't be surprised to see another special agent swing by.

"Okay, no problem," he said, stepping back.

She barely acknowledged him as she strode into the building's lobby.

Easy as one-two-three. Now came the hard part. She had to get into the janitor's supply closet, almost directly opposite Kolb's door. Trouble was, there would be FBI agents—real ones, not cheap imitations like her—in and around Kolb's digs. It would be tricky. Still, everything was relative. Compared with having Kolb's gun to her head, breaking into a closet was no sweat.

She headed down the hallway and was glad there were no police in view. But the door to Kolb's unit was open, and from inside she could hear voices and the drone of a hand-held vacuum cleaner. The crime-scene guys were sucking up hairs and fibers.

Obviously she couldn't afford to seen by the criminalists, who worked for the Bureau and would know she was an impostor. She'd been hoping they would keep Kolb's door shut. No such luck. And Kolb's apartment was a studio. No back rooms for the trace-evidence experts to vanish into. What she needed was a ploy to divert their attention from the doorway to the hall.

She took two items out of her purse—a membership card bearing the name of a local athletic club, and her cell phone. Kolb's home number was the last one she'd called. She pressed redial and heard his phone start to ring.

Predictably the crime-scene team paused in what they were doing to look at the phone. The vacuum cleaner was switched off. A male voice asked, "He got a message machine?"

"No," someone else said.

"Shit. I'd like to know who's calling this joker."

Abby slipped the membership card into the crack of the supply closet's door. The card was fake, its only purpose to serve as a shim. It was thin and highly flexible, but tough enough to force open a spring latch.

The door unlocked. She eased it a couple of feet ajar and ducked inside. It took her only a few seconds to find the hidden receiver, still in place behind the cutaway section of drywall. She removed the unit and pocketed it. When she slipped out of the closet, Kolb's phone was still ringing. She stepped away from his apartment, toward the stairwell, and ended the call.

"Thirteen rings," one of the criminalists said. "Must have been an important message."

"Star-sixty-nine it," his partner said.

Abby had expected them to do that. It didn't matter. Her cell phone was set up to block a standard phone-company trace. The FBI might be able to get the number some other way, but not for a while. By the time they did, she would have ditched the phone, which was registered to Abby Hollister, the woman who was soon to be a ghost.

She had no intention of retrieving the infinity transmitter in Kolb's phone. It would stay there forever unless the techs found it. She doubted they would—why look for a bug in his phone? They knew law enforcement hadn't bugged him. Even if they did find it, the item couldn't be traced to her. Everything was going smoothly. No problems.

"Think the call could've had anything to with the kidnapping?" the first tech said.

Abby paused by the door to the stairwell.

"Doubt it. Whoever snatched Grant knows Kolb's in FBI custody. Why call him here?"

The vacuum cleaner came on again. Abby barely heard it. She stood motionless, taking in the words.

Whoever snatched Grant . . .

Kolb's partner had Madeleine. And must have called the FBI to let them know.

It was a trade. Had to be. Kolb's release for Madeleine's life.

And Tess . . .

Had she known? Was that why she'd been in such a hurry to say good-bye?

Of course she'd known. There had been something stiff and false about her smile, her banter. A snow job all the way. She hadn't wanted her pal Abby to interfere any further, even though it was Abby's own client who was in danger.

"Well, I got news for you, sister," she whispered. "I'm not so easy to get rid of."

Another cop was guarding the side door. Abby put the cell phone to her ear and went through the stairwell and outside. As the cop looked up, she spoke into the phone.

"Tell Michaelson they're still collecting evidence," she said. "It may take a while."

Michaelson, she remembered, was the head man at the LA field office. She figured a little name-dropping would make her sound more official.

Apparently it worked. The cop let her pass without a word.

As she walked away, she noted uneasily that the stars were invisible behind thick clouds, and a few drops of rain were falling now and then, not enough to matter, simply a warning of what would come.

Abby thought of Madeleine alone in the storm drains, tugging at the handcuffs. She had maybe an hour before the tunnels flooded.

The feds would never release Kolb. That was obvious. If Madeleine wasn't found in some other way, she was dead.

Truth be told, Abby had never especially liked Madeleine Grant—too prickly, too haughty, too much the pampered prima donna—but it was her job to keep the woman alive. And she would.

Somehow she would.

37

Michaelson snapped his head up to look at Tess as she stepped into the observation room. "Where the hell have you been? Never mind. You need to go in there again, talk to Kolb."

"I'm not sure he'll tell me anything."

"Maybe not, but you're the only one he's willing to have a conversation with. Seems you and he have some sort of rapport."

"Not that I noticed."

"Just get in there. Pump him. Find out who he's working with."

Tess had a feeling this was easier said than done. She left the observation room and took a breath, trying to clear her mind of unwanted thoughts. Thoughts of the Lopez case— again.

She had the sick sense that history was repeating itself. Another pair of killers, another unforeseen victim taken after the danger should have passed.

And another error of judgment on her part? She hadn't believed Abby's theory about Kolb's partner, hadn't listened to her when she reported seeing someone outside Madeleine's house. If she'd been more alert, would she have dispatched agents to Bel Air as soon as Kolb was in custody? Or was that merely the perfect clarity of hindsight?

You can only do your best, the priest had said. She tried to convince herself of that, but images of Danny Lopez's small body in a trash bin kept getting in the way.

Straightening her shoulders, she returned to the interrogation room, her face set in a stern mask. "Apparently, Mr. Kolb, you haven't been working alone."

He showed her a blasé smile. "Whatever gave you that idea?"

"It seems your partner has taken matters into his own hands." She sat at the table, forcing herself to face him. "He's abducted a woman. He's demanding your release in exchange for her whereabouts."

"That's enterprising of him."

"You have to know there's no way we can release you."

"Then I guess there's no way this woman can survive."

"You were a cop. You know the rules. With the evidence we've got against you, you're never going to walk out of here. It's not an option. You have to know that."

"Do I?"

"Yes, I think you do. And you're smart enough to know there's no percentage for you in allowing another victim to die. It'll only make things worse for you at trial."

"Worse." He chuckled. "Yeah, I guess the judge might let me get away with two kidnappings and two murders. But a third one would be the last straw."

"I admit your situation is bad. But that's all the more reason for you not to pass up any opportunity to do yourself a favor. Cooperation at this point might mean the difference between life in prison and capital punishment."

"Maybe I'd rather die. Maybe I want to go out as a martyr."

"You won't be a martyr. You'll just be a criminal. You can be a dead criminal or a live one."

He was silent for a moment. "I wonder if you could put that in writing," he said quietly.

"What?"

"The business about the death penalty. You've got pull, don't you? I'll bet you could get the DA to commit to life imprisonment—no lethal injection."

"I don't know about that."

"Then I don't know about cooperating."

"It takes time to work out a written agreement. Time we don't have."

"Grease the wheels. You can get it done if you have to."

"I can't promise anything. I'll have to check with the assistant director in charge of this field office, see what's possible."

"So why don't you go do that?"

"First I want to know what I'm bargaining for. What can you give us?"

"Information."

"Your partner's name?"

"No can do. I don't know his name."

"Don't bullshit me, William."

"Calling me by my first name now, are you? That seems a little forward, doesn't it . . . Tess?"

"Quit playing games. It's your life at stake, remember?"

"And somebody else's life, too. Who is she, anyway? Who got snatched this time?"

"Don't you know?"

"I couldn't hear that end of the phone call. I knew somebody was taken. But who?"

"It doesn't make any difference."

"If it really didn't make any difference, you'd tell me. You'd give me that piece of information to establish trust and begin the bargaining process. See, I know about negotiating, interrogating. The fact that you're not telling me who she is suggests that her name means something."

She gave in. "It's Madeleine Grant."

His eyebrows lifted. "You don't say. The bitch of Bel Air herself."

"If you want any leniency, you're going to have to tell me

your partner's name. It's the only thing you've got to offer. It's your only bargaining chip."

"Wrong, Tess. Wrong on both counts. I don't have to tell you his name. And that's a good thing, because I don't know his name. Never did. But I've got something better to trade."

"What's that?"

"I know where he took her."

"You're saying you know where she is right now? Her location in the drainage system?"

"You got it."

"How could you possibly know that?"

"We rehearsed the first four jobs. Did a dry run for every one. Chose our points of entry and the locations where the victims would be secured. Tonight was intended to be number three. Now that it's gone to shit, my partner must have jumped ahead to number four."

"You can't be sure. He might have taken Madeleine anywhere."

"I don't think so. He's like me in one respect—he doesn't do a lot of improvising. He sticks to the plan. I'm betting he used the last location we scouted, and that's where Madeleine is holed up."

"And if we can arrange the deal, you'll show us on a map?"

Kolb shook his head. "Can't find it on a map. I know where to go in, but I don't know every twist and turn along the way. Not unless I'm down there."

Down there. Tess needed a second to understand. "In the tunnel system?"

"It's the only way. We left marks on the walls. If I can find them, I'll lead you straight to your damsel in distress."

"Just tell us what to look for, and we'll find her."

"You'll never spot these marks. They're not obvious. You have to know where to look."

"You're saying you can lead us through the tunnels to Madeleine?"

"That's the long and short of it."

She thought about it. "I doubt we can get the DA to commit to dropping the death penalty on such a shaky basis."

"Then make it conditional. If I find Madeleine for you, I get life. If I don't find her, you can put the needle in my arm yourself."

"If we find Madeleine—*and* if she's still alive."

"Hey, you take too long to process the paperwork, and she'll drown. That's not my fault."

"I'm saying it is. We get her alive or you get nothing, no special consideration."

"What the hell. It's probably the best deal I'm going to get."

"I'm not even sure you'll get that one. I have to talk it over with the people here."

"Talk fast. Madeleine's waiting."

Tess left the room and met Michaelson in the hallway outside the observation room. The AD's face was set.

"We're not dealing with him," Michaelson said.

"We don't have any choice."

"No way. Besides, it's all bullshit, anyway. He's stringing you along. He doesn't have a clue where she is."

"Then we have nothing to lose."

"Forget it, Tess. It's not going to happen."

"Fine. We won't negotiate. Now, who's going to open the press conference?"

"I didn't think you were exactly a fan of media events."

"In this case, I intend to be there. I want to make a statement about how Kolb offered to lead us to the victim, but we wouldn't agree to his terms. That should go over well with the public, don't you think?"

Michaelson studied her as if she were a particularly vile species of insect. "I'm getting more than a little tired of your veiled threats, Agent McCallum."

"I wasn't aware that it was veiled."

"You're bluffing. You're not going to sink your career with that kind of stupid, treacherous move."

"Just like I wasn't going to walk out on your press conference yesterday? The thing about you, Richard, is that you don't know me at all. You don't know what I'm capable of. And you don't want to find out."

He backed down, as she knew he would. "If we do this," he said slowly, "it's your show. You want to accompany that psychopath underground, you do it at your own risk. Count me out."

She was amused that he thought she would want his company. "I'm sure I can find a couple of street agents to go with me," she said, stressing the term *street agents* to indicate that it didn't include him. "You can stay aboveground and do what you do best—cover your ass."

Michaelson swallowed whatever retort might have occurred to him. "I'll call the DA and set things in motion, just in case we go ahead. But before I make a final decision, we're going to have a more extended discussion with Kolb. I want to know what the hell we're getting into."

He started to leave, then turned back. "What the hell happened to the Hollister woman, anyway?"

"What do you mean?"

"She's gone. She walked out of here."

"Without giving an interview?" she asked innocently.

"She gave her goddamn interview to Crandall, but I didn't give permission for her to leave."

"Well," Tess said, "I guess you'll have to track her down at home."

"I'll do that." Michaelson was staring right through her, broadcasting waves of hostility. "I haven't forgotten what Kolb had to say about you and her."

"Kolb is a paranoid lunatic."

"For your sake, I hope that's all he is. I intend to look into this, Tess. I intend to ask a lot of questions. It's bad enough you were handling a lead behind my back. If I find out you were in bed with some private detective, compromising the integrity of our investigation . . ." He let the threat trail away unfinished.

"I think we need to stay focused on Madeleine right now," Tess said evenly.

"Of course we do. I have a lot of questions for her, too."

He stalked off, leaving Tess alone in the hall.

38

Abby hadn't lied to Kolb about one thing. She really had parked two blocks away. She hadn't wanted him to see her car near his building, or he might have had second thoughts about using her as his victim. Of course, she hadn't known he was already on to her.

He'd been to her apartment, he had said. The fake apartment, the one in the Hollister name. What had prompted him to go there? What had raised his suspicions? It had to be more than general paranoia. With everything he'd had on his plate tonight, he wouldn't have spent time investigating her unless he'd already had a reason to distrust her.

She must have slipped up somewhere. The thought bothered her, because if she'd made a mistake once, she could do it again. And next time she wouldn't have Tess around to save her bacon.

Retrieving her car, she drove out of the area, just in case any of the cops happened to cruise past and wonder what an FBI agent was doing in a beat-up Civic. She found a parking spot at an all-night pharmacy and rummaged in her glove compartment for a set of earphones and a PDA.

The receiver recorded the infinity transmitter's signal on a memory card. She inserted the card into the PDA and put on the earphones, then used the PDA's media player to play back the recording. She wasn't expecting to hear much. Since the bug was voice activated, there was a good chance it hadn't picked up anything other than her own phone conversation with Kolb, their chat when she stopped by his place, and the arrival of the bag-and-tag brigade.

The first few minutes of the recording were taken up with random noises that had triggered the voice-activation mechanism. Footsteps—Kolb seemed to be pacing. Muttered words, unintelligible. A banging sound—he might have thrown something.

Then the ringing of the phone. On the second ring Kolb picked up. She expected to hear her own voice on the line. Instead there was a brief interval of silence—no hello from Kolb. Then a man's voice, soft and muffled. "You there?"

Kolb: "I'm here."

"I thought you might be at work, but I don't know your hours—"

"What do you want?"

"We need to have a conversation."

"We're having one."

"In person."

"Can't it wait?"

"No."

"There a problem?"

"Yes."

"What?"

"Aren't you the one who's always telling me not to say too much on the phone? We need to meet. Below, half hour. Can you be there?"

"Yeah, but—"

Click, and a dial tone. The call was over.

There was a sharp bang as Kolb slammed down the phone. Obviously he hadn't liked being ordered around. Still, he would comply. Abby could hear him making preparations to leave—the jingle of keys, the tread of shoes, the slam of the door.

Silence again. The next recording was her call, setting up their date, followed by her arrival at the apartment. She didn't care about that stuff. She found the start of the first phone call again.

The man with the muffled voice had said there was a problem. Could he have alerted Kolb that Abby Hollister wasn't who she claimed to be? Or was there some other hitch in their plans for the evening?

"We need to meet," the man was saying. "Below, half hour."

She played that part once more.

"Below, half hour."

What the hell was that about? Below what?

Somewhere in the drainage system, possibly. But she doubted Kolb or his partner would risk entry in daylight. Was there a location in LA that could be described as "below"? The subway system? Nobody referred to the LA Metro as "below." She'd never heard any place called by that name.

Or had she? There was something faintly familiar about the term.

She would never recall it trying to force the memory. Leaning back in her seat, she relaxed her body and mind, taking herself through a simplified version of this evening's meditation session. She let her thoughts roam free. They came and went like puffballs, and she watched them with interest but without commitment and with no sense of urgency.

She remembered the Kris Barwood case, which had changed her life and, according to Wyatt, had made her grow hard and remote. Maybe he was right. She'd put up barriers to keep people out. But without barriers she would be too vulnerable. Although he was a cop, Wyatt was curiously trusting in some ways. Trust was something Abby couldn't afford. She spent too much of her time in the company of dangerous and unpredictable men, men like Kolb, sharing their sad lives, shadowing them from their seedy apartments to nightspots, strip clubs, bars. She lived deep inside the dark belly of the city, where trust was not an option, where no one made eye contact or risked a smile. There was the LA most people saw, and then there was the secret underworld, lying below the city like the network of storm drains used by the Rain Man and his partner, a different landscape, below the palm trees, below the pavement, below ground. . . .

Her eyes opened. That was it. The name that had eluded her.

A bar she'd visited on one of her cases, years ago. A dimly lit subterranean grotto smelling of sweat and alcohol. Below Ground.

As far as she knew, it was still in business. As a meeting place for two men who didn't care to be noticed, it was ideal.

She backed out of her parking space and headed across town. Another few raindrops spattered her windshield. She whisked them away with the wipers. New drops fell.

Not yet a downpour. But it was coming.

Soon.

39

Michaelson and Tess joined Kolb in the interrogation room. Tess hated to see how pleased Kolb looked.

"I suppose you're wondering," Kolb said with mock gravity, "why I've called you here tonight."

"Can it," Michaelson snapped. "Agent McCallum tells me you've offered to lead a rescue party to the victim."

"She tells you, huh? Like you weren't eavesdropping the whole time?"

"Just answer the question."

"Did you ask one?"

"Are you willing to lead us to the victim?"

"In exchange for a commitment from the DA not to seek the death penalty. A written commitment."

"That's already in the works."

"It needs to be signed, sealed, and delivered before I help you out."

"We require some preliminary information before we can close the deal."

"Like what?"

"The entryway you plan to use. We need to set up a staging area."

Kolb considered this. "Good-faith gesture on my part, is that it?"

"Something like that."

"Okay, what the hell. I trust you, you trust me—right?

The location's not far from here. There's a ravine on the UCLA campus near the athletic field, with a tunnel entrance buried in the side of the creek. Not big enough for a vehicle. We'll have to hike in. Gate is padlocked, but the lock can be picked, no problem. Nice out-of-the-way location. Nobody can see you there. Campus security doesn't patrol the ravine. You can park a car in the brush at the bottom of the trench and leave it with minimal risk of being ticketed or towed."

"And the location of the victim?" Michaelson asked.

Kolb grinned at them both. "Sorry, friends. I'm not *that* trusting. Anyway, I couldn't tell you even if I wanted to. Like I told Tess, I need to see the marks we left on the walls."

"What if I don't believe you?"

"What if we just sit here and debate it while Madeleine drowns?"

Michaelson drew a deep breath. "I'll get you the written commitment you need. Then you'll take a rescue team into the tunnels."

"And who does that team include?"

"I haven't made the assignments yet."

"I've got a suggestion."

"You don't get to choose the personnel."

"I'll be a lot more cooperative if I get what I want."

"And what is it you want?"

Tess knew. She spoke before Kolb could reply. "He wants me as an escort."

Kolb winked at her. "You understand me. I like that in a woman."

"If you think," Michaelson began, "that I'm allowing Agent McCallum to accompany you alone—"

"Not alone. I just want her with me. She wants to be there, too. She loves the spotlight. Always has to be center stage. Don't you, Tess?"

"I'm going," Tess said. "Count on it."

"And," Michaelson added, "she'll be accompanied by at least two other agents. And Mason from DWP." To Tess he said, "You need somebody with you who's got experience in those tunnels."

"We don't need any outside experts." Kolb smiled. "I've acquired plenty of experience, believe me."

Michaelson ignored him. He got up, signaling for Tess to follow. "We'll be back with our agreement in writing ASAP, Mr. Kolb."

"I'll be here," Kolb said placidly.

In the hall, Michaelson summoned Crandall and Larkin from the observation room and told them to get started on the UCLA staging ground.

"Sir," Larkin said, "you mentioned backup in the tunnels. I'd like to volunteer."

Crandall coughed. "So, uh, so would I."

Michaelson nodded. "Fine. Establish a staging area at the ravine. I need to get on the DA's back and expedite the paperwork."

He and Larkin headed down the hall. Tess pulled Crandall aside. "You really want to go into the tunnels?" she asked him, keeping her voice low.

" 'Want to' might be putting it a bit strongly."

"There are other agents who can do this, Crandall. Agents who don't get nervous in enclosed spaces."

"I'll be okay."

"We can't afford to have you slow us down."

"I won't. Don't worry about me. I'll be fine."

Tess wasn't sure she believed him. She had a feeling Crandall was trying to prove something. He'd told her how he'd failed at every business opportunity, how he attributed his placement in the Bureau to nepotism. Maybe this was his chance to be his own man. If so, she couldn't take that chance away from him.

"All right, Rick," she said gently.

"Tess . . ." He hesitated. "I'm sorry I said you weren't a team player."

The apology took her by surprise. "Actually, I think you were right."

"You nailed the Rain Man. That's all that matters."

"No, it's not all that matters. Following procedure matters, too."

Crandall smiled. "I didn't think you were a stickler for the rule book."

"Maybe I'm learning to be."

"In that case, you'd better remember to wear your ID tag. If Michaelson notices you don't have it on, he'll ream you for sure."

He moved away down the hall, and Tess studied the front of her blouse. The tag was gone. Possibly it had fallen off, or . . .

Then she understood. "Oh, *hell*."

40

Below Ground was still where Abby remembered it, near the corner of Vermont and Olympic. She parked her Civic at the curb and opened the glove compartment, taking out an envelope containing some info on Kolb—address, phone number, place of work—and a photo she'd snapped surreptitiously last year. It was the kind of stuff she always carried with her when working a case. Never knew when it might come in handy—like right now.

Her cell phone rang. She recognized the number on the caller ID screen. "Hey, Tess."

"Did you steal my goddamn ID?"

"Your what?" she asked innocently.

On the other end of the line, she heard Tess suck in a quick, angry breath. "What arc you up to, Abby?"

"Me? I'm relaxing at home, soaking my footsies."

"Quit lying and tell me what's going on."

"Lying? That hurts, Tess. Really. Mistrust between friends is an ugly thing."

"Abby, damn it—"

"Don't you have bigger things to worry about than me? Saving Madeleine Grant's life, for instance?"

There was a pause. When she spoke again, Tess sounded different. "So you know about that."

"I have a way of finding things out. Guess you didn't trust me enough to play it straight with me."

"I felt it was better if you weren't involved."

Better for who? Abby wondered. *Madeleine—or you?* But what she said was, "I assume it's the same MO as Paula Weissman and Angela Morris."

"Except for the ransom demand. Kolb's release in exchange for her whereabouts. Now I suppose you're going to say 'I told you so.' "

"Because Kolb has a partner? And because said partner was scoping out Madeleine's house? No, I'm not petty enough to bring that up."

Tess sighed. "What I can't figure out is, why Madeleine? Why not a random victim like the others?"

"Because Kolb hates Madeleine. He and his partner must have discussed it in advance. Kolb wanted to get her, one way or the other."

"When you were in his apartment, did you see any signs of continuing interest in Madeleine?"

"No. But the apartment wasn't where he kept his stash of goodies. Anyway, there could be another reason for their choosing Madeleine. With her, they have more leverage."

"Leverage?"

"You have a relationship with her. A connection. That makes it personal for you."

"They don't know anything about that."

"They might. Somehow."

"If they did"—Tess's voice was hollow—"then it's my fault she was taken."

"It's Kolb's fault," Abby said firmly. "He's calling the shots."

"Well, he certainly is now. We made a deal with him to lead us to Madeleine. In exchange the DA won't push for the death penalty."

Abby gave this idea a moment of hard thought. "I don't buy it. Kolb doesn't want to rot in jail for life. It's not a good outcome for him."

"It's the best he's going to get."

"The guy was a cop. He knows most people on death row

in California die of old age. Capital punishment isn't a credible threat."

"It was credible enough to make him cooperate."

"But not to give up his partner?"

"He claims he doesn't know the partner's name."

"That has to be a lie. He's too paranoid to work with somebody he hadn't checked out."

"We can revisit the subject with him later. Right now Madeleine is the priority."

"He's counting on you to think that way."

"Well, what do you want us to do, Abby? Let her die?"

"Of course not. But you're missing something."

"What?"

"I don't know. Something."

"That's very helpful. I'll make a note of it."

"You're letting him control you, Tess. You're giving him the power."

Tess sighed. "Damn, you're a pain in the ass. I want my ID back."

"Haven't got it," Abby said cheerfully. "Cross my heart and hope to—"

The call was already over. Tess had clicked off.

"—die," Abby finished.

She didn't like what was happening in Westwood, but she couldn't blame the feds for playing Kolb's game. There wasn't much time left. The rain, though still spotty, was coming down harder than before.

Envelope in hand, she went into Below Ground, descending the long stairwell into the gloom.

The bar was as grungy as ever. Whoever ran this dive was doing his part to relieve America's dependence on foreign energy. She'd been in funhouses that were more brightly lit. Didn't matter, though. She was used to getting around in shadowy places.

By now it was after nine o'clock, and Below Ground was doing a brisk business. The booths and corner tables were full, and there were only a handful of empty spots at the bar.

She bellied up to one of them and got the bartender's attention.

"What'll it be?" he asked in a voice that couldn't care less.

She didn't wish to advertise her temporary status as a federal agent too loudly. She crooked a finger at him until he leaned close, then flashed Tess McCallum's ID. "We need to talk," she said quietly.

He gave her a complicated look that managed to convey contempt, resignation, and a smidgen of fear. "There's an office back there, second door on the right. Give me a minute."

She walked down the hallway, past a pay phone and unisex restroom, and found the office. He joined her almost immediately. In the interim he'd decided to play it tough. His arms were thrust out, fists planted on his hips. "What's this about?"

She sat on his desk, swinging her legs, her body language an intentional counterpoint to his. "How long have you been on duty?"

"Since we opened at noon."

"There were two men in here today. I doubt they sat at the bar. Probably in one of the booths, for privacy. One of them was this man. Look familiar?"

She handed him the photo of Kolb. He glanced at it. "No."

He tried to give it back. She wouldn't take it.

"Look a little harder. And if it helps jog your memory any, you might want to keep in mind that lying to a federal agent is a criminal offense." Impersonating a federal agent was an even more serious offense, a fact she chose not to mention.

Reluctantly he studied the photo again. "Okay, I guess I remember this dude."

"He was in here today?"

"Yeah."

"What time?"

"Hell, I don't know."

"Take a stab at it."

"Sometime in the afternoon. Lunch hour. One o'clock, one thirty."

"See? You did know, after all. Who was he with?"

"The guy he's always with. They always sit together."

"You know the name of this other guy?"

"I don't know anybody's name. That's kind of a company policy around here."

"Fair enough. What can you tell me about this second man?"

"Not much. He's not the type who stands out. I mean, we get some folks in here you definitely wouldn't forget. He's not one of them. He's one of the clones."

"Clones?"

"That's what I call them. The business types. They all look the same in their jackets and ties. Can't tell one from the other. I'll bet their own mothers couldn't tell them apart."

"I find that doubtful. So this guy was wearing a business suit?"

"Jacket, button-down shirt—I don't remember if he had a necktie or not."

"He always dresses that way?"

"As far as I recall. Some of them come in on weekends looking totally different. Like they're snakes that just shed their skin. They look so boring, and then they let their hair down and go wild."

She thought of the stalkers she'd studied. "I know what you mean."

"But this guy—if he has a wild side, he hides it. Even the music he listens to isn't exactly balls-to-the-wall."

"How do you know what music he likes?"

"We got a jukebox. He's always pumping in his spare change. Same two songs, over and over, the only ones he likes."

"And they are?"

" 'Summer Wind' and 'All the Way.' "

"Why those two in particular, do you think?"

"No mystery about it. They're the only Sinatra tunes we've got."

So the guy was a Rat Packer. It didn't seem like a piece of information likely to narrow the list of suspects, especially since there was no list of suspects to begin with. The jukebox could be dusted for fingerprints, but the buttons probably picked up hundreds of prints in the course of each day.

She pressed the bartender for description. All she could get from him was that the man was between twenty-five and forty-five, dark hair, average build. "Like I said, a clone."

He was probably telling the truth. She thanked him for his cooperation and told him other agents would be in touch. She left before he could request another look at her ID.

Outside, rain was sprinkling lightly. She thought she heard far-off thunder, but it might have been only the rumble of traffic.

She didn't think the drainage system would be flooded yet, but it wouldn't be long now. And her big lead hadn't amounted to much. Kolb's partner remained a mystery.

All she knew about him for sure was that he was a Sinatra fan.

41

A dozen agents assembled at the ravine on the UCLA campus in a drizzle of rain. Mason, the DWP engineer, checked the gate and found that the padlock was missing. "Somebody got it off somehow."

"Take a look at this." Larkin was aiming a flashlight at the ground a few yards from the drain entrance. "Tire marks."

Michaelson wanted to know if the evidence could be salvaged from the rain. Tess didn't think so. The slow drizzle was obliterating the tread marks even as they watched.

"Well, put a tarp over it or something," Michaelson yelled at no one in particular.

Other agents hastened to comply. Crandall drove a Bureau car close to the drain entry point and turned on the high beams, illuminating the passageway. "It'll help get us started, anyway," he said.

Tess glanced at him. "You're sure you want to do this?"

He gave her a look of peculiar intensity. "I've got a job to do." His voice was tight.

She didn't push it. Someone from the support staff was passing out knee-high rubber boots. Tess and the other members of the rescue party slipped them on over their shoes.

"Put these on, too." Mason handed out heavy vinyl DWP jackets. "I had them sent over. They offer better protection against the cold than those flimsy FBI jackets of yours."

Tess demurred. "It's not that cold out."

"It's colder in there, thirty feet under. The drafty air and cold water can cause hypothermia. Put it on."

"I'll stick to my trench coat."

"Wear this under your coat."

"No, thanks."

Mason shrugged, donning a jacket. "Your funeral."

She supposed she seemed churlish in refusing the extra layer of warmth, but she didn't want to hamper her movements if she had to reach for the service pistol in the reinforced pocket of her coat.

When they were ready, Kolb was hustled out of the Bureau car where he'd been held. "Give him boots," Tess said. "No jacket."

Kolb grinned. "You want me to freeze, Tess?"

"I don't want you wearing a heavy jacket. I want to be able to see your hands."

He held them up, manacled at the wrists. "Get a good look."

Michaelson was on his cell phone, speaking softly and urgently. When he clicked off, he gestured to Tess. She joined him, away from the others.

"Abby Hollister has disappeared," he said. His jaw was working as he ground his teeth.

"I thought we knew that already."

"We knew she left the field office. Now she's disappeared entirely. I sent three agents to her address. They got the landlord to open up. He says she's hardly ever there. The apartment is furnished, but there's no sign of recent occupancy. And there was a break-in, but no obvious theft or damage."

"So?"

"So it doesn't make sense. Then they ran a credit check and found her paper trail goes back only so far. You know what that suggests?"

"Phony ID."

"Phony ID, phony apartment, an unreported B-and-E—

something is not right with this woman. I think she's a ghost, like Kolb said."

"And what do you want me to do about it?"

"Kolb also said she was working with you."

"We're not going over that again, are we?"

"This is your last chance to come clean."

"I've got nothing to come clean about," she said staunchly.

Michaelson glared at her. "When I find Hollister, I'll learn what you've been up to. If it turns out you've been pursuing your own agenda, I'll have your ass."

She forced a smile. "My ass? I don't think so. I'm way out of your league."

"Keep it up, McCallum. I'm on the case. I've caught the scent."

"Well, I guess that's why they call you the Nose."

He went pale. "Who calls me that?"

"Everybody. Didn't you know?" She walked away, hoping Abby was as good at disappearing as she claimed.

Crandall and Larkin, both wearing DWP jackets, met her at the tunnel entrance. "I guess we're ready," Larkin said. "Unless you want to wait for LAPD. They're sending a SWAT team, but it could take another ten minutes."

The rain was picking up. "We don't have another ten minutes," Tess said. "Anyway, more people will only slow us down."

"Then I guess"—Crandall coughed—"I guess we go in."

She gave him a hard look, testing his resolve. He glanced away and said nothing.

"All right," she said with a clap of her hands. "Mason and I lead the way. Kolb's in the middle. Crandall and Larkin take up the rear."

"Will your cell phones work down there?" Michaelson asked Mason.

"Not necessarily. Sometimes yes, sometimes no. You can't count on it."

"How about the radios?" The feds were carrying Bureau-issued Handy-Talkies clipped to their belts.

"Same answer."

"If we need help," Tess said, "we'll find a way to get the message out. Everybody have a flashlight?"

"Not me." That was Kolb.

"You don't get one. You won't be going off on your own."

"Tess, I'm beginning to think you don't like me."

She turned her back on him and spoke to Michaelson. "My cell will be on. If the weather deteriorates rapidly, call and let me know."

"If I can get through," Michaelson said.

"Right." She said a silent prayer that the worst of the rain would hold off a little longer. "Okay—let's go."

42

Abby was a block away from Below Ground when she saw a lighted sign against the starless sky. A storage yard.

She thought of the padlock key. Although Kolb could have rented storage space anywhere in the city, most likely he would choose a familiar neighborhood. The area near his apartment would be too obvious. But who would ever think to look here?

It was a long shot, but what the hell. All she had so far was a generic description of a businessman who liked Ol' Blue Eyes.

She pulled up to the gate, which was locked and could be opened only by entering an access code into a keypad. A sign claimed there was a storage manager on duty twenty-four hours a day.

She honked her horn approximately a million times until the guy showed up, trotting out of the shadows between the sheds. "What's the problem?" he shouted from behind the gate.

Abby lowered her window and showed him the FBI tag. "I'm Special Agent McCallum of the Federal Bureau of Investigation, and I have a few questions for you."

This guy, unlike the cop outside Kolb's apartment and the bartender at Below Ground, actually tried taking a close look at her ID, but since he had to peer through the gate in the dark, he wasn't able to see that the photo failed to match the bearer.

Abby didn't want him looking for long. "You going to open up or what?"

"Okay, okay, give me a minute."

He punched in a code on his side of the fence. The gate rolled open, and Abby pulled into the lot. She thrust Kolb's photo out the window, where it was immediately speckled by raindrops. "Do you rent a storage unit to this man?"

"I don't know every guy who rents here."

"Do you know *this* guy?"

The storage manager took the photo and held it under the cone of illumination from a security light mounted on the fence. "Yeah, I've seen him around."

"You know his name?"

"If you're so interested in him, shouldn't *you* know his name?"

"We have a feeling"—she used the plural to remind him that she represented the greater power of the Bureau—"this individual didn't use his real name."

"I don't know it off the top of my head. Lemme look at the registry. When I see it on the list, I'll remember."

He stepped inside a tollbooth-size hut and spent some time hunched over a computer monitor. When he emerged, the rain was falling harder.

"William Johnson. That's the name he gave. He pays in cash every month—which is unusual, obviously."

"He gives you a name like Johnson and pays in cash, and it doesn't occur to you that something funny is going on?"

"Hey, get off my case, Agent Scully. I just work here."

Abby frowned at him, but secretly she enjoyed the Agent Scully quip. She would have to remember to use that one on Tess. "Just show me his unit," she said in her most authoritative tone.

The storage manager jogged across the storage yard while she followed in her car at three miles an hour. He came to a corner unit and rapped on the metal roll-up door.

"This is it. But I don't have a key. That's our official policy. The customer keeps both keys. The only way we can get this baby open is to call a locksmith."

"Not quite." Abby produced the key she'd cut from the key blank, which she'd been prescient enough to carry in her purse. "I come prepared."

She was one of the few people who actually kept gloves in the glove compartment, and she pulled them on before leaving the car. It seemed like the sort of thing an FBI agent would do. As the storage manager watched, she tried the key in the padlock. The copy wasn't perfect, and she had to jiggle it a little, but she got the lock to open. She raised the door and turned on the overhead light.

Behind her, the storage manager thought of something. "Hey, you got a search warrant?"

"I don't need a search warrant. Exigent circumstances." In police work there really was such a thing as exigent circumstances, but Abby was pretty sure the current situation would not qualify, mainly because she was not, in fact, a law-enforcement officer.

"I thought you people always needed a search warrant," the guy persisted.

"I thought *you* just worked here. Now I'd like to thank you for your cooperation. Leave me alone."

The guy grumbled, considered putting up a fight, reconsidered in light of the fact that he didn't give a shit, and walked away.

Abby explored the locker. The first thing she noticed was the carpet on the floor—cheap, short-nap, burnt orange. Now she knew where the fibers in Angela Morris's car had come from.

There were shelves on the walls. On one of them rested a laptop computer, plugged into an outlet to keep its battery charged. Probably the hard drive contained useful information, but it would take time to defeat whatever security measures Kolb had installed—time she didn't have, with the rain coming down. She needed some solid information, fast.

She looked through a couple of outfits obviously intended

as disguises. Nothing helpful there. Stored near the clothes were false beards and other Halloween getups. She almost ignored them, then noticed a Ziploc plastic bag at the bottom of the pile. She pulled it out and instantly recognized its contents. False paper. Documents purchased on the black market that would allow a person to change his identity. She'd bought a few packets of fake ID herself, though nowadays she preferred to prepare her aliases personally.

She opened the bag and dumped its contents onto the floor, then knelt and rummaged through them. A pair of passport holders caught her eye. She flipped open the first one and saw a photo of an unsmiling William Kolb, identified as William Allen. It was smart of him not to use the William Johnson identity, which might have been tracked down before he could get out of the city. Smart also to keep using the first name William. It was always best to retain your own first name when assuming a new identity. A person had an instinctive response to hearing his name, which was hard to fake. That was why she was always Abby somebody—Abby Hollister, Abby Gallagher, whatever.

But what really interested her was the second passport. She opened it and saw the man who was Kolb's partner. He was identified as Edward Ringer. In his photo he, unlike Kolb, was smiling—a nervous, self-conscious smile.

She'd seen that smile before. She'd seen it in the FBI field office earlier tonight, when this man had been the only person to congratulate Tess on Kolb's capture.

The DWP liaison.

Mason. That was his name.

43

Tess and Mason stepped into the tunnel, followed by Kolb, then Crandall and Larkin. The Bureau sedan's high beams cast the team's elongated shadows down the pipeline. Tess caught a glimmer of movement near her feet and looked down to see small silvery shapes.

"Drain minnows," Mason said. "There's lots of aquatic life in here. Watch out for the eels."

Tess wasn't sure if he was joking. She preferred not to know.

They proceeded down the passage, shining their flashlights into the dark. Gang graffiti and taggers' marks crawled like fungus over the round concrete walls. "I'm surprised the taggers come in here," Tess said.

"They go all over. Not just taggers. Drainers, mostly." Mason answered her questioning glance. "People who explore the drainage system. They have all kinds of names for themselves—drainers, creepers, infiltrators. They like to mark their territory."

"Dangerous hobby."

"Especially if you run into the mole people."

From his tone, she knew this was no joke. "Let me guess—tunnel squatters."

Mason shrugged. "Everybody's gotta live somewhere."

She thought of the vagrant she and Crandall had run into.

Movement distracted her. A scurrying crowd of small reddish spiders, skittering higher on the walls, away from the
flashlights' beams.

The floor was slick with a coat of slime. Tess had to plant
each foot carefully to avoid slipping. She braced herself
against the wall with her free hand.

Behind her, Kolb went down on one knee. "Fuck."

"Stop clowning around," Crandall snapped, his voice
cracking like a boy's.

Kolb climbed awkwardly to his feet. "You try negotiating
this shit in handcuffs."

"Just move."

Two steps later, Kolb fell again.

"This isn't going to work," Tess said. "He can't keep his
balance unless he can grab on to the walls."

"What can we do about that?" Larkin asked.

Tess hesitated. "Uncuff him."

Nobody moved.

"You think that's a good idea?" Mason said slowly.

"We'll never make good time if we have to stop every
thirty seconds to help him up. And if he sprains an ankle, we
may not be able to continue at all."

"And if he makes a run for it?" Larkin asked.

"He can't. Not in this slop." To Crandall she said, "Un-
hook him."

Crandall fished in his trousers for the key. "You're the
boss."

He freed Kolb's hands and pocketed the cuffs.

"He could have hidden a gun in here," Larkin said. "Un-
hooking him might be what he's counting on us to do."

Tess knew it. "That's why you're going to watch him so
closely he can't get a jump on you. Right?"

Reluctantly Larkin nodded.

Kolb massaged his wrists. "Good going, Tess," he said. "I
knew you weren't a total bitch."

"Thanks for the vote of confidence. Let's move. We
haven't got much time."

The water streaming into the tunnel from outside was rising higher and running faster even as she spoke.

For the third consecutive time, Abby got Tess's voice mail.

"Damn." She ended the call and stuck her cell phone back into her purse. Either Tess had turned off her phone or she was already underground, where the signal couldn't reach her. If she was underground, Mason would be with her. He was the tunnel expert, after all.

Their plan was obvious now. They hadn't been stupid enough to think Kolb would be set free. All they'd wanted was to manipulate the feds into taking Kolb into the tunnels, with Mason at his side. Mason would wait until the rescue party was deep inside the drain system, then slip Kolb a gun and stand back as his partner opened fire.

Massacre in the tunnels. By the time anyone found the bodies and figured out what had happened, Mason and Kolb would have collected their passports and vanished.

She let out a moan of frustration. Calling Tess hadn't worked. Calling the Bureau field office would do no good— nobody would believe her, at least not in time. If she could track down Tess and the others in the tunnels . . . But she had no idea where they'd gone in. The drainage system was huge, covering the whole of LA. They could be anywhere.

"Damn," she said again, for emphasis.

Still, there were always options. She was standing in Kolb's private sanctum, surrounded by his secrets. There must be something here she could use.

The laptop probably contained some information, but she didn't have time to hunt through directories and subdirectories in search of it. What else was here? A bunch of furniture left over from Kolb's last apartment. A large scrapbook that looked familiar—she flipped through it and recognized it as the scrapbook on the Mobius case, which Kolb had been keeping before his arrest. She'd seen it in his apartment last year. No new pages had been added. No help there.

She kept looking. Her gaze, circling the locker, settled on something that looked like a portable computer resting on a shelf. But it was too small, and besides, Kolb already had a computer.

She took it off the shelf. It was a slim, lightweight pad, more like a tablet PC than a laptop, with a decent-size LED screen and no keypad. She found the power switch. The device booted up instantly, the screen glowing with a map of city streets. No, not streets—drainage pipelines.

She knew what this was. A GIS database. GIS—geographic information system. Recorder's maps of the drainage network, converted from paper charts to geo-coded images, were digitally stored on the tablet's hard drive. A storm-drain inspector toted the lightweight device around and accessed the maps by entering commands on the touch screen. Mason would have had access to the DWP's inventory of tablets. He'd procured one for Kolb.

She wondered why Kolb hadn't taken the GIS reader when he took the other items needed for tonight's job. She supposed he'd already committed the details to memory—and if he got caught, he didn't want the device found with him. It would have implicated Mason immediately.

Currently displayed was a citywide overview of the entire drainage system. She pressed the screen and opened a drop-down menu, displaying a list of recently viewed files. The file names were odd—each was a number from one to four, except for the fifth, which was named *Backup*.

She clicked on number one and found herself looking at the area where Angela Morris, the first victim, had been kidnapped. On his first outing Kolb apparently hadn't driven Angela very far from the abduction site. Mason had modified the file, digitally drawing a red line from a tunnel system entryway, through a major artery, to a side passage marked with an X, where Angela presumably had been secured.

Abby brought up file number two. As expected, X marked the site where the drowned body of Paula Weissman—

victim number two—had been found, manacled to a handrail.

File number three was a map of the neighborhood near the river—the neighborhood where Kolb had driven her tonight. The access point he'd been planning to use was nearby, again marked in red.

That left file number four and *Backup*. Number four was a map of the Silver Lake district of North Hollywood. Mason and Kolb had planned a minimum of four abductions, and this was to have been the fourth.

Mason could have taken Madeleine Grant to this spot. With the third abduction foiled, he might have skipped ahead to the arrangements for number four.

There was still the file named *Backup*. Probably it was a copy of a map she'd already reviewed, but she looked anyway.

What came up on the screen was a new location, in West LA.

Now she got it. The *Backup* file was Mason and Kolb's backup plan—their emergency plan if Kolb was apprehended.

The red line on this map entered the tunnel system via an access point alongside the Santa Monica Freeway, then wound its way to a red X below the intersection of Olympic and Sepulveda. The X stood either for Madeleine's location or for the site where gunfire would break out—or both.

West LA was halfway across town. Abby could never get there in time to make a difference. Surface streets or freeways—it wouldn't matter. Both would be clogged with traffic even at this hour. But there might be another option.

From the maps, it was obvious the main arteries of the drainage system ran parallel to the city's major thoroughfares. And the main lines must be large enough to accommodate a service vehicle, or DWP crews would never be able to make repairs. Where a DWP truck could go, her Civic could go also.

It was one way to beat the traffic. All she needed was a

way to get inside the system. She returned to the citywide overview, then zoomed in on Vermont and Olympic, the neighborhood of the storage yard. The nearest major artery ran underneath Olympic Boulevard. She looked for an access point large enough to accommodate her car and found one three blocks west.

Tucking the GIS reader under her arm, she jumped back into her car. As she sped out of the storage yard, she had to switch on her windshield wipers. The rain was falling hard now. The tunnels must be starting to flood. She wasn't sure her Honda would be able to navigate the passageways if the water was deep, but she would worry about that little problem when she came to it.

Right now she just wanted to get inside.

44

"Okay," Mason said, "we're coming to a split."

Ahead, the tunnel divided into two pipelines.

"Which way?" Tess asked Kolb.

He studied the walls. Amid a tangle of graffiti and black mold he singled out a small orange arrow pointing to the left. "That one," he said, indicating the left tunnel.

Tess silently admitted she never would have seen the mark.

They took the left passage. The distant glow of the Bureau car's high beams had long since vanished. Only their flashlights lit the gloom. Above their heads, traffic passed over manhole covers, producing a series of echoing thumps, a ragged, metallic pulse. Water drizzled from drain holes in the lids, spritzing the tunnel in a chill mist. More water trickled out of side pipes, splashing down walls darkened with slime.

"It's not coming down too hard yet," Tess said.

Mason didn't seem reassured. "It can change in a hurry. When the clouds open up, this place turns into whitewater rapids. The speed of the current increases with the volume of water."

"It's only up to our ankles now."

"Even a shallow current can knock you down and sweep you away. You can drown in six inches of water—or get banged into a wall—"

"You're just brimming over with positive thinking, aren't you?"

"I've seen enough to know you don't fool around inside this system in a wet weather flow."

"We'll be high and dry before the rain gets heavy," Tess said with more optimism than she felt. She saw a line of metal rungs embedded in the wall, ascending into a shaft. "Where do those go?"

"To a manhole or a catch basin. They're called step irons."

"It's a way out, anyway."

"If the step irons hold. Sometimes they're loose or rusted through. And you can't always open the drain lid from below. The manhole covers are mostly too heavy to lift, even if they're not locked down or rusted in place. The curb-side drain lids are lighter. You can usually push one of those away."

"How much do they weigh?"

"Hundred pounds, maybe."

"I can't lift a hundred pounds."

"Then you'd be up Shit Creek, Agent McCallum," Kolb quipped from behind her.

She didn't acknowledge the remark.

"Don't worry about it," Kolb added. "Drowning's not a bad way to go. They say your whole life flashes before your eyes."

"Be quiet."

"What would be the highlights of your life, Tess? Your first kiss? First tongue up your asshole?"

"Shut the fuck up," Crandall snapped.

"Relax. I'm only having some fun with the lady."

"Just keep your goddamn mouth shut."

Tess was tired of Kolb's voice, tired of the wet concrete smell, the darkness, the water sloshing around her boots. "Focus on the job at hand," she told him. "Which direction?"

They'd come to another split. Kolb pointed out the orange arrow. "To the right."

"We getting close?" Larkin asked.

"Patience is a virtue," Kolb said mildly.

Crandall sneezed, the noise echoing in the dark like a small explosion. "How do we know this butthead isn't jerking our chain?"

"In case you forgot," Kolb said, "my life is contingent on finding this bitch alive. I'd say I have a pretty strong motive to cooperate."

"I don't buy it," Crandall insisted. "You sure you're not just looking for an excuse to turn back?"

Tess had been thinking the same thing. Crandall's claustrophobia might be getting out of control. Well, he would have to tough it out. There was no turning back now.

As if to confirm that thought, Tess's flashlight, probing the tunnel ahead, picked out a woman's shoe, floating toward them in the current.

"Mason, take a look at that."

He fished it out of the stream. "This Madeleine Grant's?"

Tess shook her head. "I don't know."

Mason let go of the shoe. It dropped back into the water and drifted past the rescuers into a side tunnel.

Tess raised her voice. "Madeleine!"

A flurry of echoes was the only reply.

"Don't waste your breath," Kolb said. "Even if she hears you, she won't be able to answer. She'll be gagged like the others. Can't have her yelling up through a drain grate and attracting attention from someone on the surface."

"You guys had it all worked out, didn't you?" Larkin said as they kept walking. "Got it down to a science."

"Everybody needs to make a living."

"You piece of shit," Crandall said, his voice tremulous and too high.

"You're awfully judgmental for a big, bad federal agent. Then again, you aren't so big and bad, are you? You're, what, about twelve years old?"

Crandall said nothing.

"Now, Tess, on the other hand," Kolb went on, "isn't shocked by anything I say. Or by anything I've done. She's got experience in the field. In the bedroom, too. Not that she draws any distinction there. What was the name of that special agent you were humping, the one Mobius iced—"

"God damn it, stop talking to her like that!" Crandall wanted to sound tough, but his thin, shaky voice conveyed only panic.

Kolb laughed. "Chivalry lives on, even at the FBI. Hey, Tess, I think somebody's sweet on you."

Tess ignored him.

"You should tell her how you feel, boy. Don't hold your feelings inside. You know how the song goes. 'If somebody loves you . . .' "

"Shut up," Mason barked. Suddenly he was the one who sounded nervous.

Kolb broke into song. " 'It's no good unless they love you . . .' "

"Isn't there any way to keep him quiet?" Larkin asked.

" 'All the way . . . !' "

Tess turned to face him. "Stop it, Kolb. Now."

He stopped, a wide grin on his face. When she was sure he was going to restrain himself, she started walking again.

Behind her, Kolb began humming the same tune, just loud enough to be audible. Tess decided not to make an issue of it. The man was like a child. He just wanted attention.

She glanced behind her at Larkin and Crandall. "You guys okay back there?" She was interested only in Crandall but didn't want to single him out.

"We'd be doing better," Crandall said, "if we could stop the nocturnal serenades."

Tess saw the pallor of his skin. She didn't think he was fine. To distract him, she tried a little levity as they continued walking. "You shouldn't object, Rick. He's singing your song."

Crandall forced a laugh. "It's Ed's song, really. He's the one who turned me on to Sinatra."

"That true, Mason?" Tess asked. "You're a Rat Packer?"

Mason seemed uncomfortable. "I guess so. Rick and I started talking one day after I started working as a liaison. Got on the subject of music. I tried to wean him off his taste in country-pop."

"It worked," Tess said, remembering her car ride yesterday. "I wouldn't have taken you for a devotee of the golden oldies."

"I used to play a little keyboard in college. Was part of a jazz combo. We did a lot of retro stuff, mainly Sinatra."

"Really?"

"You're surprised?"

"It's just . . . well, I can't quite picture you as a jazzman."

"Why? I'm too uptight?"

"You're too boring," Kolb said. "That's what she means."

Tess frowned. "Pay no attention to him. That isn't what I meant."

Mason looked away. "I guess we all have our hidden talents."

Behind her, Kolb asked, "What's your hidden talent, Tess? Has it got anything to do with blow jobs?"

"I think it has more to do with locking up people like you," Tess said evenly.

"I'm not locked up now."

"Enjoy it while it lasts."

They reached another crossing point. Even Tess could see the orange arrow this time. "To the left—correct?"

Kolb grunted assent. "Very good, Special Agent. You learn fast." She heard the smile in his voice as he added, "But maybe not fast enough."

Tess almost asked him what that was supposed to mean, but stopped herself.

It didn't matter. It was just another one of his games.

45

Abby ran a red light and heard the blare of somebody's horn.

"Hey, I'm fighting crime here," she muttered. "Gimme a break."

It was one hell of a crime, too. She could see how it had come together. After his release from prison, Kolb had met Mason—probably at Below Ground, a place whose diverse clientele included ex-convicts and city employees. They'd started talking, and eventually it had occurred to them that their particular assets would make them a good team. Kolb had the street smarts, the toughness, the willingness to kill. Mason had some money, some knowledge of computers, and most important, expertise in navigating the drainage system.

No doubt they both wanted money, the kind of big tax-free score only a daring crime spree could produce. But people's motives always ran deeper than cash. In Kolb's case, he hated the city that had put him in jail, costing him his livelihood and his future. He wanted to make Los Angeles pay.

Mason's motive was unknown, but Abby guessed it had something to do with his patronage of Below Ground in the first place. He was a bureaucrat looking for a walk on the wild side. Probably he knew he would be chosen as the DWP's liaison to the Bureau. Perhaps he'd even volunteered for the job.

As an insider privy to the investigation, he could keep Kolb apprised of new developments. He would know which entrances to the tunnel system were being watched by law enforcement. Having the keys to the entry points, he could open them up for Kolb before each abduction and resecure them afterward. That way no evidence of a break-in would be found, and no one would know which access points Kolb had used.

With all he'd brought to the table, Mason probably thought of himself as the leader of the team. Abby knew better. Kolb would never accept a secondary position. Whatever Mason had expected, Kolb had ended up calling the shots.

Maybe it was Kolb's idea to use Madeleine in the backup plan. Or maybe Mason had improvised that detail. Either way, Madeleine was a plausible choice. She lived in Bel Air, not far from the intersection of Olympic and Sepulveda chosen as the spot where the victim would be held.

Taking Madeleine into the tunnels posed minimal risk. Law enforcement stakeouts of the tunnel access points would have been withdrawn once Kolb was arrested.

Of course, there was no certainty Mason had actually put Madeleine underground. He might have killed her already. But Abby doubted it. Mason probably didn't think of himself as a killer. She didn't believe he could execute Madeleine in cold blood. She didn't think he was planning to take out the rescue party, either. He would get the gun to Kolb and let Kolb do the job.

She tried to figure out how Mason had handled the abduction. He'd already been in the field office when she and Tess arrived. He'd seen Kolb in custody. He must have ducked out immediately afterward, grabbed Madeleine, then used an untraceable cell phone to call the FBI and play the tape of her voice.

At the next corner she swung onto a side street, her tires kicking up a huge fountain of spray. If the map was right, there ought to be a tunnel entrance around here. She flicked on her high beams but saw only a narrow street that dead-ended at a cyclone fence. The fence bore a sign that warned NO TRESPASSING.

She took the fence at forty miles an hour, plowing it down and hoping the torn metal didn't puncture her tires. Then she was fishtailing through a muddy vacant lot and down a slippery incline to a ravine flowing with rainwater. Unlike the LA River, this channel wasn't lined with concrete. It was basically a ditch, but apparently it served the same flood-control purpose as its more citified cousin. On the far side of the wash, large double doors, secured by a padlock and embedded in a steel frame, were built into the ravine wall.

For a moment she thought about smashing through the doors the way she'd mowed down the fence, but these doors looked more formidable than chicken wire. She pumped the brakes, and the Honda slewed crazily in the mud and spun to a stop. She left the car, drawing her revolver from her purse. With one shot she shattered the padlock's hasp. She pulled it down and started to push the doors open, but it wasn't necessary because the sudden inrush of water did the job for her.

When she looked down, she saw that water was above her ankles. It occurred to her that entering the tunnels under these conditions might be the last thing she would ever do. If her car stalled out, she would be trapped just like Madeleine and the other two victims.

But even as she considered this possibility, she was already sliding into the driver's seat and gunning the engine.

The Civic's tires blew out piles of mud before gaining enough traction to lurch forward. She straightened it out and aimed it at the open doorway.

After that, she had no more control of the car. The water took her in its flow and shot her through the doors like a raft launched into the rapids. There was a dizzy moment when the Civic teetered on the brink of a descent into darkness, then leaned forward, headlights throwing their glare on what seemed like a vertical hill of rushing water, and plunged down.

Objectively, Abby knew the descent wasn't vertical. She was rolling down an access ramp that would take her into the drainage artery that paralleled Olympic Boulevard. The tunnels weren't that deep—maybe thirty feet underground—and the descent couldn't possibly last for more than a few seconds. It only felt like a lifetime.

With a thunderous splash, the car hit bottom, leveling out and flying instantly into a long, high-ceilinged corridor wide enough for vehicular traffic. She just had time to orient herself and swing the steering wheel to the left, and then she was driving west below Olympic. Because the passageway was so broad, the water was shallower here, and because the floor sloped down in the center, her tires were able to find good purchase on the sides of the track. Her high beams provided visibility for about a hundred feet—enough to see that the tunnel proceeded straight and unblocked.

No more obstacles. She hit the gas and tested the Civic's rebuilt engine.

The tunnel raced past, the rounded concrete walls a blur of speed. Water streamed down from manholes evenly spaced overhead. Every ten yards a curtain of rainwater smacked into the roof and windshield. Her wipers flicked, sweeping the glass clean in time for the next dousing.

More water rushed into the corridor from portholes in the walls—side passageways and service tunnels. The noise was thunderous and incessant, a vast monotonous rumble like an earthquake that wouldn't stop.

She wondered how long she could keep going before the rising water disabled her engine and turned the Civic into a raft. Well, not a raft, exactly. A raft would float. The car would sink to the bottom. She could force her way out and be swept away by the current, or she could be trapped inside the car as it filled with water.

"That's not a happy thought," she told herself sternly. "Think happy thoughts."

She fished her cell phone out of her handbag and pressed

redial. Tess's voice mail continued to answer. The call still wasn't getting through.

Or maybe Tess wasn't answering because she was already dead.

"Happy thoughts," she reminded herself.

On the bright side, she was making incredible time. The speedometer needle was pinned at seventy. If she encountered no difficulties along the way, she should reach the intersection of Olympic and Sepulveda in about five minutes. The city had better hope commuters didn't find out about this.

She reached a crossing point between the Olympic artery and a north–south drainage line. Where the two lines met, stormwater eddied and foamed in a surging backwash. The confusion of currents threatened to send the car into a spin. She hung on to the wheel with both fists and fought to keep the tires straight.

Maybe commuters wouldn't like this shortcut, after all.

The GIS reader lay on the passenger seat, its screen glowing in the dark, but she couldn't check the map and maintain control of the car at the same time. She would have to hope she remembered the layout of the tunnels near Olympic and Sepulveda accurately. She didn't exactly have a photographic memory, but a crisis seemed to sharpen her mind considerably. And if barreling through a flooded storm sewer at seventy miles an hour on a rescue mission didn't constitute a crisis, she didn't know what did.

Another tunnel juncture approached. This time she made out the name of the intersecting pipeline stenciled on the concrete wall: FAIRFAX AVE. The Civic careened through the churning whitewater, the tires slipping to the left, the driver's-side door scraping the wall before she steered back to the center of the corridor.

Good thing she was planning to get rid of this car. She had a feeling it wasn't going to be very presentable by the end of this excursion.

She kept redialing. Still nothing. She pressed the button again—

And heard a click as the call was answered. "McCallum."
The connection was shaky, full of static and echo. Abby
had to shout into the phone. "It's Mason, Tess. Mason is
Kolb's partner!"

"What?" Crackle and hiss, Tess's voice fading. "Hello?"

"*It's Mason!*" Abby screamed.

The line went dead. The connection had been lost.

There was no way to know if the message had gotten
through.

46

It's Mason.

Tess had caught those words before the call cut out. For a second she couldn't process the information.

Then there was a mental click like a shifting of tumblers in a lock, and she got it.

Kolb and Mason. Partners.

Her mind seemed to accelerate to a furious velocity. She was making a dozen different connections at once. Mason, her only friend at the field office—of course he wanted to be her friend, so he could get close to her. Mason coming late to the supervisors' meeting—*he'd* searched her workstation in her absence and found her notes on Madeleine. Mason, knowing he would be part of the search team, handing out heavy DWP jackets that would hamper the agents from reaching for their firearms—while concealing a gun of his own.

It wasn't a series of thoughts but a single pattern coming together as a whole. She'd once seen a film of a shattering flowerpot played in reverse, the scattered pieces magically reassembling. This was like that.

In the time it took her to put the cell phone in her pocket she understood everything.

At her side Mason turned to her. "Who called?"

She shouldn't look at him. *Shouldn't look at him.*

Too late.

In the shared glow of their flashlights he saw her face, read her eyes. And he knew.

He lashed out with his flashlight, swatting her across the cheek.

She stumbled, grabbing for her gun as she fell sprawling in the water.

She rolled onto her side. Mason was drawing his gun from beneath the vinyl jacket. Her fingers closed over the SIG Sauer in her coat pocket.

She didn't bother to pull it free. She fired through the pocket, three quick shots, recoil slamming her elbow against the concrete floor.

Mason fell backward, his flashlight dropping with a splash.

Tess shouted something, but with her ears ringing from the echoes of her own gunfire, even she couldn't hear what she said.

Crandall and Larkin were drawing their weapons. Not fast enough. Confusion and the heavy, unfamiliar jackets slowed them down.

Kolb had no jacket. And no confusion.

As Mason toppled backward, Kolb grabbed him, propping the body against his own, then snatched the gun out of Mason's hand.

Tess wanted to fire again, but Mason's body blocked the shot.

Kolb pivoted. Muzzle flashes, new blasts of pistol reports.

Behind him, Larkin and Crandall went down.

Tess knew he would shoot her next. With Mason's body as a shield, he could fire at her with minimal risk of being cut down.

She was still holding the flashlight in her left hand. She switched it off.

Mason's flash had been swept away by the current. Larkin's and Crandall's were dark—either smashed or lost. Kolb had no flashlight. With hers off, there was only darkness. Kolb could see nothing.

She risked scrambling to a new position a yard or two farther down the tunnel. Kolb couldn't hear her—his ears would be ringing like hers.

The two of them were deprived of sight and hearing. She waited. Kolb hadn't run. He would never get out of the tunnels without light. He needed a flash—hers. And he wanted her dead. He'd told her the scrapbook was all about her. His obsession with Mobius, his hatred of women—it all crystallized around her.

He wouldn't leave, not when he was so close to killing her. He would wait for his chance.

And she would give it to him.

With her left hand she extended the flashlight away from her body, holding it toward the middle of the tunnel.

Her right hand steadied the gun.

She clicked the flashlight on.

Instantly, two booming reports, a new cascade of echoes.

Kolb, firing at the light. His gun at the center of purple muzzle flashes expanding into dark.

She fired dead-center into the purple. She wasn't sure how many rounds she expended. Though she'd been taught to keep count, somehow she forgot.

After six, eight, ten shots, she stopped firing. She crouched in the streaming water. Her flash was still on. Kolb would have fired at her if he could.

She swept the beam over the tunnel and saw no one standing there.

Bodies in the current, forming a tangled logjam. Mason and Kolb together.

He could be playing possum. She approached him with caution. The yellow cone of light from her flash picked out his eyes. They were open and unblinking under the water. That was when she knew he was dead.

The current around her boots was pink with blood from the two bodies, and perhaps from Larkin and Crandall.

She beamed the flash deeper down the tunnel and saw the two agents together, huddled against the wall, Larkin pale and shivering and half-conscious, Crandall looking shell-shocked but intact.

"Tess!" Crandall shouted over the din in her ears. "You okay?"

She bypassed the bodies and made her way toward the two agents. "I'm all right," she said. "You?"

"Yeah."

"You're not shot?"

He looked sheepish. "Slipped on this fucking slime when I was trying to unholster my piece. Fell on my ass." He produced his flashlight and snapped it on. "I turned this thing off and played dead. Not very heroic, I guess."

"It was smart, Rick. He had the drop on you. The only reason he didn't nail you was that he thought you were dead."

"When he fired at you . . . I wanted to shoot, but I couldn't see anything. I was afraid I'd hit you instead."

"You did the right thing. Don't worry about it. How's Larkin?"

"Wounded. Gut-shot."

"You hang in there, Peter." She got out her cell. "We're getting help. You hang on."

"You sure you're okay?" Crandall asked. "You're bleeding."

She touched her face and felt something warm oozing down her cheek. Blood from the cut inflicted by Mason's flashlight. "I'm fine."

"What about Madeleine Grant? We still going after her?"

Tess shook her head as she speed-dialed Michaelson. "She was never even down here. It was all a ruse. She's probably already dead."

47

The water was deep now. Abby wasn't sure how much longer she could keep going. But she was nearing her destination. She'd caught the words BEVERLY GLEN on the tunnel wall at a crossing point a mile or so back. Sepulveda wasn't far away.

The Civic sluiced through the rising current, spraying huge fans of water on both sides. The deluge from the manholes overhead was now constant, as if there were no gap between one drain cover and the next. The noise around her was thunderous and deafening. She'd never imagined that water could generate so much sheer sound.

Keeping the car on track required all her strength. The influx of rainwater from tributary pipelines threatened constantly to kick the car sideways. Her hands were white-knuckled on the steering wheel. The muscles of her forearms burned with fatigue.

Ahead, her high beams picked out a cascading trough of water from a side channel—a big channel, big enough to be the north–south trunk line that paralleled Sepulveda. She pumped her brakes, but the car didn't slow. Her momentum and the speed of the current carried her forward. She was going to shoot right past the intersection.

She stomped down hard on the brake pedal. The car fishtailed and slammed against the tunnel wall. The engine coughed, struggled, and died. The headlights stayed on.

She cranked the ignition key, pumped the gas pedal, but the car wouldn't start. This was the end of the line. She hoped like hell she'd stopped at the right intersection, because she sure wasn't going any farther.

She snapped open the glove compartment and rummaged inside for the flashlight she kept there, a better one than the penlight in her purse. This was the big Maglite model powered by six D-cells. It would do almost as good a job of lighting her way as the car's headlights.

Swiveling in her seat, she beamed the flash at the tunnel's far wall and found the word stenciled there—SEPULVEDA. She'd guessed right.

Now she just had to find the rescue party or Madeleine—assuming any of them were in the vicinity.

Before leaving the car, she picked up the GIS reader to recheck the map. The screen glowed in the darkness. The red X marked a square junction room linking two pipelines, one of which entered the Olympic artery immediately west of the Sepulveda line. All she had to do was get into that service tunnel and make her way straight to the junction room. On the map it looked easy—a short hike. It might be a tad more difficult in practice.

She checked her purse. She had her phone, her gun, her penlight flash, and a picklock that would serve as a handcuff key if she found Madeleine. She fastened the clasp and slung the purse over her shoulder.

Time to get wet.

She crawled over to the passenger side of the car, which would put her a little closer to the porthole she intended to enter. Opening the car door was harder than she'd expected. The weight of water running past held the door shut. She thought she might have to break the window and climb out, but with effort she forced the door open just wide enough to make her exit, splashing into the knee-high current.

The force of the flow took her by surprise and almost knocked her down. She grabbed hold of the door handle and hung on until she'd steadied herself against the tide.

Then she directed the flashlight at the porthole and slogged toward it. She needed to travel only a few steps, but with each stride she had to fight to keep her balance. If she fell down, she would be picked up by the water and sent hurtling downriver.

She was out of breath, fighting to find some oxygen in the waterlogged air, when she reached the porthole.

A grinding metallic noise caught her attention. She glanced back in time to see the Civic pull away from the wall and slip past her. The car increased its speed and drifted out of sight.

"'Bye Old Paint," she murmured.

The Civic hadn't owed her anything, and she would've had to get rid of it, anyway, but she was still sorry to see it go.

She turned back to the tunnel and scanned the interior in the Maglite's glow. The tunnel was round and small, less than five feet in diameter. Water was flowing out at a steady clip. To climb in, she would have to boost herself up—ordinarily no problem, but with the water smacking her in the face and with the rim of the tunnel coated in slippery muck, it would pose a considerable challenge.

Worse, the tunnel itself slanted toward her at a slight incline. If the floor was as slippery as the rim, she would never be able to negotiate the passageway. Then she saw a line of handholds set in the tunnel wall on the right-hand side. Unfortunately the nearest one was out of her reach. She would have to get into the tunnel and then grab hold of it—if she could.

She clipped the flashlight to her belt, then tried several times to hoist herself up. Her fingers kept sliding off the rim. She used the heel of her hand to scrape away the worst of the scum, then finally got a grip on the rough concrete and hauled herself inside.

Instantly the rush of water attempted to repel her into the Olympic artery. She wedged a knee against the side of the tunnel and twisted sideways to seize the nearest handrail. The iron rung swiveled in her grasp, one end popping out of the wall, and for a bad moment she was sure she would be propelled into the main pipeline and swept away.

The other end of the rung held. She pulled herself along the pipe, maneuvering from handhold to handhold. Water splashed her in the face, half blinding her, some of it getting into her lungs and sinuses, making it harder to breathe.

The flashlight in her belt was still guiding her. She thought she saw the entrance to the junction room not far ahead.

A surge of current raced down the pipeline, banging her hard against the wall and nearly dislodging the Maglite. She kept one hand on the rail and grabbed hold of the flash with the other. A second wall of water smashed into her, stripping her purse from her shoulder. The strap, reinforced with wire, didn't tear, but with both hands occupied she couldn't snag the purse before it spun away into the foaming water. Gone.

She didn't care about the credit cards, driver's license, and other ID, all of which was in the now-defunct Abby Hollister name, but the gun was a serious loss. She still had the Maglite, though. That was the highest priority. She reattached it to her belt, then climbed the handholds up the rest of the slide and through a porthole into a small flooded chamber.

The junction room.

Here the water was waist-high. She braced herself against a wall, sucking in air, and beamed the flash around the room. On the opposite wall she saw a ladder of iron rungs ascending a narrow shaft.

Handcuffed to the lowest rung was Madeleine Grant.

Her eyes were the widest Abby had ever seen. They stared out from behind a net of sopping hair, eyes that were wild and helpless and terrified. A torrent of water streamed down from what must be a manhole or drainage basin at the top of the shaft, dousing her in a sizzling spray. Her left wrist, shackled, was red and bleeding from her efforts to free herself. She made no sound, at least none Abby could hear. Her mouth was sealed with duct tape.

Abby waded across the room, fighting the current, and reached Madeleine. "It's okay," she was saying, "it's okay, I'm here, it's okay."

With a sharp yank she stripped off the duct tape, and then Madeleine was screaming.

48

Tess got off the phone with Michaelson and briefed Crandall. "SWAT is on the scene. They're coming down. Should take them about five minutes to reach us."

Crandall looked nervous. "Water's rising fast."

"We'd better assist Larkin back toward the entrance. LAPD can meet us halfway. We—" She stopped. "You hear that?"

"Hear what?"

She shushed him. Over the roar of the current rose another sound, high-pitched, keening.

Screams.

"It's Madeleine," Tess said. "She's down here, after all. Not far away."

"We can't leave Larkin."

"*You* can't leave Larkin. Help him to his feet and get him out of here."

"What about you?"

"I'm going after her."

"The goddamn tunnels are flooding, Tess."

"I noticed. Just go."

"LAPD may not be able to reach you."

"Don't worry about me. I'll get out somehow. Go."

She didn't wait for an answer.

*   *   *

"It's okay, it's okay"—Abby had to shout to be heard over the pounding water and Madeleine's screams—"calm down, I'm here, it's okay."

That was a lie. It was not okay. She'd lost her purse and, with it, her picklock. She had no way to unlock the handcuffs. Under other circumstances she would have shot them off. But she'd lost her damn gun, too.

At least Madeleine was buying it. Or maybe she'd just run out of strength. Either way she let her screams die away into hiccoughing sobs.

"Just get me out," Madeleine whimpered, her thin body shaking.

"I will; don't worry."

Another lie. Abby had no certainty she could free Madeleine, and with the water still rising—nearly chest-high now—there was plenty of reason to worry.

Abby could climb up the shaft if she had to. But Madeleine couldn't move, not as long as she was shackled to the lowest rung. She would be submerged soon.

Madeleine had lapsed into quiet weeping. Abby wondered if she even knew where she was anymore. She'd believed she could protect herself. She'd bought a gun and learned to use it. But she'd found there were some things she couldn't defend against. She'd discovered how helpless she really was. The knowledge seemed to have broken her. She'd put up a fight, though—tugging at the handcuffs until her wrist was bloody and torn. . . .

But it wasn't the handcuffs that were the weak point. It was the iron rung embedded in the wall.

Abby had seen how loose those rungs could be. She'd nearly ripped one free of the tunnel wall while maneuvering up the slide.

If she could detach this rung from the wall, Madeleine would be free.

The bottom rung was underwater. Abby took three quick breaths without exhaling, building up oxygen in her bloodstream, and submerged.

Her flashlight, hooked onto her belt, was still working. It was supposed to be waterproof, and it hadn't conked out yet. Its glow cut through the murky water, revealing the bottom rung, a chunk of iron shaped like a staple, its two short ends sunk into the moss-encrusted concrete wall.

She scraped away the moss to expose the rung. It was dark with rust, which could be good or bad—good if the rust had weakened the metal, bad if it meant the rung was rusted in place. She cupped her hand around the nearest end, trying to pry it free. Already she felt a growing need for air. Still, she didn't surface. She could feel the bar weakening. . . .

It popped free in a cloud of rust particles. She broke the surface and gulped air.

The water was higher now. Madeleine was in it up to her neck. She wasn't crying anymore. Her drawn face looked weirdly calm.

"You should go, Abby." Madeleine spoke softly, the words inaudible, but Abby read her lips in the flashlight's bobbing glare. "You need to go."

Abby leaned close and shouted to be heard. "I'm getting you out. Hang on!"

She gulped three more oxygenating breaths and resubmerged. One end of the rung was free, but the other remained in place, solidly anchored in the concrete. Unless she could increase the clearance between the bar and the wall, she couldn't extricate the handcuff.

She grabbed the rung and tried to wrest it away from the wall, hoping it was sufficiently rusted to bend or fracture. No such luck. The rung was solid, not rusted through. There was no chance of separating the rung from the wall without loosening the other end.

This end was harder to reach than the first. Madeleine's hand partly blocked it, and the slow stream of red droplets issuing from her wrist impeded visibility. Abby reached underneath the rung and got hold of the bar, grappling with it, but the damn thing wouldn't budge.

She shifted her position, tried attacking it from a different angle. Still, it refused to loosen. Must be rusted solid, fused with the wall. If she could crack it apart . . .

First she needed air. She surfaced, grabbing quick, shallow breaths. Water was slopping against Madeleine's chin, her mouth. In seconds it would reach her nostrils.

Down again, this time with a new plan. She unhooked the flashlight from her belt and turned it around so the base was extending outward. Using the flashlight as a hammer, she pounded the step iron. Shuddering jolts of pain radiated through her arm. The beam flickered and dimmed. On the fourth strike it winked out.

Darkness, opaque and solid. She'd known the flash couldn't take that kind of punishment, but the loss of light still unnerved her.

In the dark she could only guess at the position of the rung. She kept hammering, hearing loud clangs of impact, feeling new vibrations in her elbow and shoulder.

The metal must have given way by now. But when her other hand, groping, found the step iron and tugged at it, the thing still wouldn't move.

Light penetrated the darkness for a drawn-out moment. She saw the rung stubbornly rooted in the wall. Then a new slam of darkness like the closing of a door. Lightning stroke, she realized. It had illuminated the junction room through the grated drain lid at the top of the shaft.

She surfaced in another lightning flash. Madeleine wasn't there. She was gone. For a wild instant Abby thought she'd broken free. Then she understood that Madeleine was now beneath the water.

Furious desperation seized her. She snatched another breath and plunged down, pawing at the step iron, the handcuffs and chain, anything she could touch, not caring what it was, wanting only to find a way to break the death grip on this woman's wrist while there was still time.

Another lightning stroke. Glimpse of Madeleine dropping

lower in the water. Eyes staring. Bubbles streaming from her parted lips.

Darkness again. Abby hammered at the rung until the flashlight slipped out of her hand and fell away into the gloom. She braced herself against the wall and put both hands on the step iron, fighting to tug it loose.

A new burst of light, stronger than the last. Closer. Not like lightning. More like . . .

A flashlight. Behind her.

She turned. Past the glare she saw Tess, hair writhing around her face in eerie slow motion.

Tess pushed her clear of the ladder, then, as Abby watched, pressed her gun to the handcuff chain and fired.

Abby had time to wonder if the gun would work underwater or if the action would be jammed by grime and debris, and then a muzzle flash erupted in a purple cloud. The bullet severed the chain.

Abby grabbed Madeleine's arm. Tess encircled her waist. Together they lifted her out of the water, hauling her higher up the ladder. Abby averted Madeleine's face from the downrush of rainwater from the grate and felt for a pulse or a breath. None.

She knew CPR, of course. No doubt Tess did, too, but this was Abby's client, her responsibility. She tilted Madeleine's head, pinched her nostrils, and blew into her mouth, giving her two long, slow exhalations. No response. She locked her mouth on Madeleine's and repeated the procedure. Still nothing.

She tried again. She would try all night if she had to. She would breathe life back into this woman no matter what.

Tess hung on to the ladder, beaming her flashlight on Abby, partially shielding her from the downpour. Abby caught a glimpse of her face, haggard and pale.

Then she was expelling air into Madeleine's lungs again, willing to woman to wake up. She couldn't have been out for long. She could still be saved.

Distantly she remembered Wyatt saying the job had made her hard and tough. Wyatt was wrong. If she'd grown hard, uncaring, she wouldn't be here in this flooded storm drain trying to force life back into the limp body of a woman she didn't even particularly like. Whatever kind of mess she'd made of her personal relationships, she always had the job, and she would not fail at it.

Mouth-to-mouth wasn't working. She pressed both hands below Madeleine's breastbone and pumped downward, performing the Heimlich maneuver, trying to force out any water or obstruction in Madeleine's throat. Again, again, again, a dozen times without pause, then two more rescue breaths. Some water had spilled out of Madeleine's mouth, but her vitals were still flatlining. All right, then. Chest compressions. Restart the heart. She worked Madeleine's chest, counting aloud until she reached fifteen. Two more rescue breaths. The Heimlich maneuver again, ten more abdominal thrusts. More water dribbled down Madeleine's chin, but there was no coughing, no vomiting, no sign of life. Rescue breaths. Chest compressions. Rescue breaths. Abdominal thrusts. Rescue breaths—

Tess's hand was on her shoulder, easing her back.

She looked at Tess and saw understanding and resignation.

"She's gone, Abby!" Tess yelled above the roar.

Abby shook her head.

"She's gone!" Tess repeated.

"Not yet." Abby bent to administer another round of CPR. Tess stopped her. Abby tried to shake her off. "I can get her back!"

"You can't!"

Abby looked at Madeleine, lifeless on the iron rungs. Tess was right. It was over.

She released her hold on the body, and Madeleine settled into the murk, dropping slowly, weighted down by the water in her lungs.

As Abby watched in the glow of Tess's flashlight,

Madeleine sank under the surface and was gone. It felt like a betrayal, letting her go like that.

"What do we do now?" she asked blankly. For once in her life she was at a loss for action.

Tess pointed upward, toward the grate. "We climb."

49

Tess didn't wait for Abby to respond. The loss of Madeleine had left her uncharacteristically dazed. What she needed was a push. Tess grabbed her by the collar and thrust her higher up the ladder.

"Climb!" she shouted.

Abby scaled the ladder. Tess followed her up the narrow shaft. The climb was more difficult than she'd expected. The step irons were slippery, coated with black algae, and rain from the drain basin overhead poured down in a furious waterfall. But her flashlight, clipped to her belt, still worked, its beam augmented by bursts of lightning through the grate.

The lightning flashes told her the grate must be exposed to view. Nobody had parked an SUV on it, thank God. But she remembered Mason saying drain lids could be too heavy to lift or could be corroded in place, immovable.

Well, Mason was dead and she was alive, so she figured his opinion didn't count for much.

Halfway up the ladder now. It rose thirty feet, she estimated, with the opening still five yards above her. Abby, nimbler than she was, climbed faster, pulling ahead.

Tess glanced down and saw blackness below her, and a faint swirl of water flecked with white foam.

Madeleine was in that water somewhere. She would remain submerged until the putrefaction of her stomach contents produced gases that expanded her belly. Then she would float to the surface to be recovered in the tunnel network—unless she was washed out of the drain system altogether, into the sea.

Above her, Abby scrambled off the ladder, then extended a hand to Tess, helping her up the rest of the way.

They were in a drop box, the concrete basin beneath the grate that collected street runoff before channeling it into the tunnel system. The basin was narrow and low, offering no room to stand, the floor littered with fast-food containers, newspapers, leaves and twigs, and somebody's shoe. The drain lid was directly overhead, water pouring through the rectangular iron grille.

Abby pushed on the lid, straining to force it upward. That was wrong. Tess had seen one of these things opened at a crime scene during a search for evidence.

"Not that way!" she shouted over the rain's roar. "We have to slide it, *slide it* to the side!" Together they hooked their fingers around the bars and forced the grate sideways until it slid off the groove of its track. "Now push up!"

They heaved the lid up, popping it clear of the slot. Leaves and other debris spilled down on them from above. Coughing, Tess blinked grit out of her eyes.

Abby gestured for Tess to climb the remaining set of rungs to the surface. Using the rungs as handholds and footholds, she raised herself out of the gutter box. It was installed under a curb on a dark, flooded side street, empty of vehicles and pedestrians. She climbed out and felt a rush of light-headedness at the abrupt transition from the tunnels to the outside world. She had trouble processing her environment. Everything seemed suddenly too big and too far away, and her stomach was twisting with a surge of nausea, silvery sparkles glittering across her field of vision—

An arm around her waist. Abby, holding her.

"Let's sit you down," Abby said, no longer shouting, because the rain wasn't so loud up here, in a world without echoes.

Abby assisted her onto the sidewalk and under the canopy of a store closed for the night.

"I'm all right now," Tess said.

"Sit down, anyway. Take a load off."

Tess sank down against the shop front, planting herself on the wet sidewalk. Abby plopped down beside her.

"Hell of a ride," Abby said. "Wanna go again?"

Tess wondered how she could joke about it, but when she looked at Abby, she saw the pain in her eyes. Humor was only her defense mechanism. Tess was surprised she hadn't realized it before.

She watched the sheets of rain streaming off the canopy. The gash on her cheek was starting to sting, but she barely felt it. "I'm going to have a lot of explaining to do," she said.

Abby shrugged. "What's to explain? Mason tried to pull an ambush, but you were too quick for him."

"And the phone call that warned me about it?"

"Does anybody know about that call besides us?"

Tess considered the question. She'd been walking alongside Mason. He knew—but he was dead. Kolb might've noticed. He was dead, too. Crandall and Larkin had been too far behind to see or hear anything. "I guess not."

"Just say you saw Mason going for his gun, and you got him before he got you." Abby ran her fingers through her wet, tangled hair. "That's not the way it was supposed to go down, of course. They were planning to wait till you got to the junction room."

"How do you know that?"

"Mason wouldn't have put Madeleine in the storm sewers if he hadn't needed her as a diversion. He assumed once you found her, you'd let your guard down. He would hand his gun to Kolb, and Kolb would pull off a Valentine's Day Massacre before you knew what was happening."

It made sense. "And I never even saw it coming," Tess said.

"You're not paid to be omniscient."

Tess managed a smile. "Funny. Somebody said something just like that to me earlier today. Said I can only do my best, shouldn't beat myself up if I'm less than perfect." She looked at Abby. "And neither should you."

Abby didn't return her gaze. "I'm not beating myself up. Masochism has never held much appeal for me."

"You believe you should have saved Madeleine." Tess touched her arm. "But you did all you could, Abby."

With a slight repositioning of her body, Abby pulled free of Tess's hand. "That doesn't bring her back."

There had to be some words to say. Tess tried to come up with them. "At least she's the last one who'll drown in the tunnels. The last innocent victim."

Abby was quiet for a long moment. When she spoke, her voice was barely louder than the rain. "Madeleine wasn't so innocent."

"What do you mean?"

"She planted the evidence that put Kolb away."

Tess blinked. At first she couldn't make any sense of what Abby had said. "You . . . you *knew* about that?"

Abby glanced at her and chuckled. "You did, too, huh? Did Madeleine tell you?"

"Yes."

"And you kept it to yourself. Cool."

All gentleness was gone from Tess's voice. "How long have you known?"

"Since I visited Kolb's apartment last year."

"How?"

"When I picked the lock on his door, I noticed that some-body else had been there before me. Somebody who'd left scratch marks on the lock."

"That could have been anyone."

Abby shook her head. "I knew it was Madeleine. I'd already sized her up as a person who'd go to considerable lengths to take care of herself. I hadn't expected her to go quite that far, however. It was my fault, at least partly."

"Your fault?"

"In my preliminary report I gave her Kolb's unlisted address. I indicated I'd be paying a visit to his premises in the near future. Obviously that was all the information she needed. She got there ahead of me. Resourceful woman. You have to admire that." Abby saw Tess's face and added, "Well, maybe *you* don't."

Tess still couldn't put it together. "You never told Madeleine what you'd guessed?"

"Believe it or not, I can be discreet when I need to be. Some things are better left unsaid."

"So when you found the kidnapping gear in Kolb's apartment . . ."

"I knew Madeleine had bought it and stashed it there."

"You knew," Tess said.

"Yes."

"You knew the evidence was a plant. You knew Kolb had been set up."

"Righty-o." Abby sounded tired. "But I also knew Kolb was our guy. His e-mails to Madeleine were stored on his computer. Madeleine couldn't have faked that evidence. Getting into Kolb's apartment was one thing, but there was no way an amateur could've gotten past the security on Kolb's PC."

"The e-mails were harassment. The kidnapping gear was what showed intent to do harm."

"True. Whether or not Kolb would have carried out an abduction, I didn't know. Madeleine clearly wanted me to think he would. Me—and the police."

"And you went along with her plan." Tess's voice was colder than the rain.

"Yup. I put the evidence in plain view and brought the fire department to the scene. Didn't you ever wonder why I resorted to setting a fire when there are easier ways to get attention?"

The question had never occurred to Tess. "No."

"I was hoping the fire brigade would break down the door and smash the lock. Unfortunately, they got the landlord to open up, and the lock stayed intact—which meant the tamper marks were found, the DA's office got suspicious, and Kolb cut a better deal than he deserved."

Tess sat up straight, anger stiffening her spine. "Than he deserved? He was *framed*."

Abby waved off the attack with a listless hand. "He was guilty."

"The evidence was phony."

"Only some of it."

"Some—all—it doesn't *matter*. Don't you understand that? For God's sake, Abby—"

"Would you have wanted me to wait till I had better evidence? Like Madeleine's dead body?"

"You sent Kolb away on planted evidence. And he knew the evidence was planted. He must have assumed the city was trying to frame him."

"No doubt."

"That's what turned him against the city. That's what made him crazy enough to become the Rain Man."

"He was borderline crazy, anyway," Abby said with a shrug.

"And you pushed him over the edge."

"It's possible."

"You *created* the Rain Man."

Abby looked at her, no apology on her face. "Maybe I did. That's why I had to take him out. I clean up my own messes."

Messes, Tess thought. *Messes.* "Angela Morris, Paula Weissman . . ."

"I couldn't foresee that."

"But you were responsible."

"Not necessarily. He might have done it anyway, even without being framed. Prison changes people. Toughens them, radicalizes them."

"He might not have gone to prison at all without the evidence of intent to kidnap. You made him paranoid and violent. You took a stalker and turned him into a killer." .

"Those are the risks of the game," Abby said.

"It's no game, Abby."

"Sure it is. It's a contest between them and us. It's blood sport. I play the percentages. My assessment of Kolb was that he was dangerous. Madeleine's freelancing gave me a way to make sure he was taken off the streets. I took advantage of it. I'm not sorry. Given the same circumstances, I would do it again."

"And create another killer."

"I saved Madeleine's life," Abby snapped.

"Not tonight."

Abby turned away. There was a long silence between them, broken only by the sibilant fall of rain.

Finally Abby said, "Still, you've got to admit, I did save *your* butt."

Tess shut her eyes. Suddenly her anger was gone, replaced by a great weariness. "You did. And I guess I haven't thanked you for it."

"Don't get all mushy on me. That tender moment we shared back at the field office was sappy enough."

"Speaking of which . . ." She pointed to the ID tag, which somehow hadn't been washed away and was still clipped to Abby's shirt.

Abby removed the tag with a smile and handed it back. "Thanks for the loan. Came in handy. By the way, Kolb kept a storage locker near Vermont and Olympic. Lots of neat stuff inside. I left the door open for you."

"Did anyone see you there?"

"Yeah, the storage manager. I also visited this bar called Below Ground in the same neighborhood. The bartender and I had a conversation."

Tess sighed. "That'll come out, you know. Michaelson was already going half-crazy trying to find you. When he learns you were running around town investigating the case, he'll go into overdrive."

"Just wait until my car turns up in the drainage system."

"Your *car*? Oh, my God."

"Don't worry about it."

"When they find your car, Michaelson will *know* you were down there."

"He'll know Abby Hollister was down there. That's the name the car is registered under, just like my fake apartment. He'll figure Hollister was some kind of unlicensed PI hired by Madeleine Grant. He'll question Madeleine's household staff. That's okay. They only know me by my alias."

"He won't stop looking for you," Tess said.

"Of course he will. Don't you get it? Abby Hollister *died* in the tunnels. The car is proof. She drowned, and her body got swept into the ocean through one of the beach outfalls. Nobody spends any time looking for a dead person. So don't sweat it, Tess. Abby Hollister is dead." She got up, stretching. "And Abby Sinclair is dead tired. I'm getting out of here. You can call your playmates at the Bureau and have them pick you up."

Tess stood also. "Where are you going?"

"To catch a cab or a bus, thumb a ride, something. I don't live far from here. Maybe I'll walk home." She nodded at the streaming downpour. "Nice night for a walk, don't you think?"

"Abby . . . I'm sorry for what I said."

"No, you aren't. You meant every word. Maybe you were even right."

"But that's not going to change how you do business, is it?"

"Nope."

Tess needed to say more. "Whatever happened last year,

without you we wouldn't have gotten Kolb. Not this soon. Maybe not ever."

"Well, that'll be our little secret. As far as everyone else is concerned, you identified Kolb and nabbed him. You snuffed the bad guys and ended the Rain Man's reign of terror." Abby smiled, a slow, sad smile, rare for her. "And you did it alone."

Tess watched her walk away until she disappeared behind silvery sheets of rain.

50

"You wanted to see me?" Tess asked, entering the ADIC's office. She deliberately avoided calling him *sir*.

"Shut the door," Michaelson said from behind his desk. He looked oddly small sitting there, although at the news conference earlier today he'd been puffed up to his full height as he explained how the case had been cleared.

Tess, in the hospital getting stitches in her cheek and a full workover from a battery of doctors, hadn't been able to attend. She'd watched the event on TV, amused to see Michaelson spend most of the question period fielding inquiries about her role in the investigation. Maybe that was why he seemed to have shrunk in his chair.

"Sit down, please." Michaelson was being very formal. Tess didn't know what to make of it. She took the chair opposite the desk and waited.

"So." He rapped the desk blotter with his knuckles. "How are you feeling?"

"The ER gave me a clean bill of health."

"That cut on your face—"

"They say it won't leave a scar. I'll be as photogenic as ever in a couple of weeks."

"Well, good. You've been through quite an ordeal. You're entitled to some R-and-R."

"All I want to do is get back to Denver. Crandall picked

me up at the hospital. He's waiting in the parking lot to drive me to LAX for a two-thirty flight."

"That was quick."

"No reason to delay it. I'm ready to go." Tess sighed. "More than ready."

"Homesick?"

She was, but she didn't admit it. "There's a lot of work piling up on my desk. How's the investigation into Ed Mason coming along?"

"We found the bank account numbers at his residence. We ought to be able to recover the two million dollars paid for Paula Weissman."

"Let the taxpayers rejoice. Anything else turn up?"

"An impressive collection of vintage LPs. Two fully packed suitcases in his car—he was planning a quick escape."

"There was nothing holding him to LA, I take it."

"He was unmarried, no close relatives, and apparently no friends. His life consisted of his job, his record collection, and fantasizing about the perfect crime."

"How do you know that?"

"He had another collection besides record albums. True-crime books, hundreds of them. Evidently he liked to imagine himself as another D. B. Cooper, someone who could fleece the system, make a clean getaway, and end up as a legend in his own time. Anyway, that's what the shrinks say. At the very least, he saw himself as something more than a humdrum civil servant."

"Don't we all."

"His fantasy life was probably harmless enough until Kolb started working on him. Mason let himself be talked into their partnership. It was his dream scenario. He would pull off the crime of the century and pocket a few million dollars."

"At a cost of a few lives."

"Until last night, he never had to deal with the victims personally. I suppose that made it easier for him. They were just part of the game he had going in his mind. They were never real."

They'd been real to somebody, Tess thought. She said nothing. Michaelson, too, was silent.

"Was there something more you wanted to discuss?" she asked finally.

"We haven't found her body yet."

"Madeleine Grant?"

"Well, yes. Her, too. But I was referring to Abby Hollister—if that was her real name." Michaelson gave Tess a hard stare. "You, of course, have no idea what she was doing in the storm sewers?"

"No."

"You never saw her down there?"

"Of course not."

"She was some kind of operator, obviously. All her paper was forged. Good-quality stuff. She knew what she was doing."

"Apparently so."

"At least, until she drove into the tunnels during a rainstorm. She must have drowned."

"Must have. If that's all you need to discuss . . ."

She made a motion to rise. Michaelson waved her back to her seat. "We're not through yet, Agent McCallum."

Another silence stretched between them. Tess began to wonder if he'd learned the truth about Abby and was simply prolonging the tension before he made a formal accusation of misconduct.

"Do they really call me that?" he asked at last.

She blinked. "Call you what?"

"The Nose."

"Oh."

"Do they?"

"No," she said. "I made it up. I apologize. It was childish of me."

Michaelson studied her, uncertain whether he could believe her. After a few seconds he looked away, perhaps preferring not to know. "Apology accepted. You've seen Larkin, I'm sure."

"Yes, at the hospital. His prognosis is good."

"Crandall did a fine job getting him out of there. Both agents will receive commendations. Agent Larkin will, however, be sidelined for several months of rehabilitation. I'll be needing a replacement. A new deputy to the assistant director. It's quite a prestigious post, as you know."

She began to see where this was leading, but she couldn't believe it. Michaelson would never—*never*—make her this offer.

"Yes." She watched him with almost impersonal fascination.

"Well, you see . . ." He swallowed hard, as if fighting to suppress a bad taste in his mouth. "FBI HQ thinks it would be a good idea, from a public-relations standpoint . . . that is, considering the success you've enjoyed in Los Angeles on two separate occasions . . . considering the reputation you've made for yourself in this town . . ."

Now it made sense. It hadn't been his idea at all. Washington was forcing him to offer her the post. And he was hating every minute of it.

Tess leaned back in her chair. The meeting had turned out to be fun.

"What I'm saying is, the position is open, and it"—he pronounced the words with visible effort—"it can be yours. If you want it."

She let him dangle for an unconscionably long moment.

"I don't," she said. "Thanks, anyway."

He cocked his head as if he hadn't heard. "You don't?"

"No, Richard. I don't. I like Denver. I like running things. Working in LA as your deputy is not my idea of a good time."

"I assure you, the discomfort entailed by that arrangement would be mutual."

"If you keep on sweet-talking me like that, I might change my mind."

He studied her. "I don't understand you, McCallum. Anyone else would jump at the chance to be assigned to this office—especially at such a high level. I won't be here forever. When I move on, you'd be poised to take over as assistant director."

"Sounds good on paper. But I'm not sure I'm cut out to be an assistant director."

"You'll get no argument from me about that."

She winced, knowing she'd set herself up for that one. "The higher you go in the bureaucracy, the more your job is about politics and not about the work. I want it to be about the work."

"Well, good for you. You keep doing the work, and I'll keep moving up the ladder. Then when I get to be director, I'll have the pleasure of firing you. It will be my first official act. After that, you won't have the work anymore. You won't have anything."

"You're a charmer, Richard. Don't ever change." Tess rose. "Are we done?"

"Thankfully, yes."

She was opening the door when he said, "You didn't seem surprised."

"By the job offer? I have a poker face."

"I meant you weren't surprised to hear that Abby Hollister's body hasn't been found."

"Should I have been?"

Michaelson looked at her across the office. "I know you're holding out on me. And I intend to get to the bottom of things sooner or later. Unless you'd care to unburden yourself right now."

She hesitated. "All right, Richard. I have to admit, I've been lying to you."

He leaned forward, his face drawn taut with anticipation. "Have you?"

"I'm afraid so. Actually, they *do* call you the Nose. Well, I shouldn't say *they*. I should say *we*. As in all of us, everybody, all the time. It's a semiofficial nickname, I guess."

"Get out, Tess."

"Don't take it personally. That particular feature of yours just happens to be the only thing about you that makes a lasting impression."

"Get *out.*"

She left the office. As she rode the elevator, she activated her cell phone, which had somehow survived her underwater adventure, and called Josh Green, the Denver ASAC.

"I'm coming home," she said. "I need an airport pickup at four." She told him the airline and flight number.

"It'll be arranged. Congratulations, Tess. You're all over the news. A media superstar—again."

"I don't want to be a superstar." She got off at the ground floor. "By the way . . . is that dinner invitation still open?"

"You taking me up on it?"

"I am."

"What happened to the unwritten rule against fraternizing with a subordinate?"

"I've decided there are some occasions when it may—just *may*—be permissible to break the rules. I'll see you, Josh."

"We'll leave a light on for you."

She found Crandall in the parking lot by the Bureau sedan she'd commandeered on Monday night. It was his car again. He slid behind the wheel, and she slipped into the passenger seat.

"LAX, here we come," Crandall said, shifting into drive. "How about some music for the trip?"

"I'm not in a Sinatra kind of mood."

"Me neither. After last night, I may never be a Rat Packer again. What do you say we go classic country?"

He switched on the radio. A clear tenor voice filled the speakers. John Denver singing "Rocky Mountain High."

"Appropriate, given your destination," Crandall said.

"The song title? Or his last name?"

"Both, actually. Maybe it's a . . . what's the word . . . synchronicity."

"A sign from above. Could be." Tess smiled. "A little pat on the back, a way of saying, 'Job well done.' "

"You deserve it."

"I think it's meant for both of us."

Crandall pulled onto the San Diego Freeway, heading south. Traffic was light under a cloudless sky. "Hey, you know what? I got a call from my father."

"I'll bet he's proud of you."

"Claims he is. I didn't have the heart tell him all I really did was fall on my ass."

"You survived a firefight in close quarters. You kept your head. You got Larkin to safety. Don't sell yourself short."

He was embarrassed but, she thought, secretly pleased. "At least I've proven I'm not a complete screwup at everything I try."

"There you go. That's the attitude."

"Can't believe it was Mason, though. I mean, he was so friendly to me. Sucked me right in."

"Me, too."

"And all the time he was just trolling for info. And I gave it to him."

"Everybody did. He was the civilian liaison. He sat in on the meetings. He knew everything—which entryways would be watched, which neighborhoods we would concentrate on. He knew it all, courtesy of his friends at the FBI."

"But *you* weren't fooled."

"Sure I was."

"Not in the tunnels. If you had been, he would've gotten the drop on you. And don't tell me it was just luck."

Tess thought of the phone call that had saved her life. "No," she said quietly. "It wasn't luck."

They rode into the midday glare. Crandall flipped down the visor to shield his eyes. "Hear the forecast?" he asked. "No more storms. Sunshine as far as the eye can see."

She looked at him. He was so young. "Don't believe it, Rick. It always rains eventually."

"All the more reason to enjoy the blue skies while they last."

Tess couldn't argue with that. She turned up the radio and let the music take her home.

Author's Note

The Los Angeles storm-drain system is every bit as labyrinthine and treacherous as this story indicates, and has been put to good use in many previous thrillers, among them the film noir classic *He Walked By Night*, the great science-fiction movie *Them!*, and Michael Connelly's outstanding debut novel, *The Black Echo*. Although it's true that some foolhardy adventure seekers enjoy "infiltrating" storm sewers, this pastime is more than perilous—it can be suicidal, even on days without rain. Don't try it. The life you save will be your own.

The two protagonists in *Dangerous Games* have appeared separately in two earlier books of mine. Tess McCallum is featured in *Next Victim*, while Abby Sinclair is the focus of *The Shadow Hunter*.

The fragments of Hegel quoted in the story are generally accurate, though sometimes slightly reworded for easier reading. The poem containing the famous line "I am the master of my fate, I am the captain of my soul" is "Invictus" (1875) by William Ernest Henley. The quotation from the Book of Judges that serves as an epigraph is from the King James version of the Bible.

I'd like to thank all the people who helped me with *Dangerous Games*, especially: Doug Grad, senior editor at New American Library, who first suggested having a couple of my previous characters team up; copy editor Tiffany Yates, who caught a lot of mistakes; my agent, Jane Dystel of Dystel & Goderich Literary Management, who handled the project with her trademark expertise and care; and Miriam Goderich, also of DGLM, who offered helpful comments and counsel.

As always, readers are invited to visit my Web site at www.michaelprescott.net, where you'll find information on my other six books, as well as interviews, essays, deleted material from some of my earlier titles, and an e-mail address if you'd like to contact me.

Michael Prescott began his career as a screenwriter and freelance journalist. In addition to *Dangerous Games*, he has authored six previous suspense thrillers. Currently at work on a new novel, he divides his time between the Arizona desert and the New Jersey shore.

You can contact Michael Prescott at his Web site: www.michaelprescott.net.